Miranda Acland worked in communication. ⌐apital Radio and what is now Bauer for 20 years. A graduate of the Fa ⌐r Academy, she is a student of meditation and has co-edited two books on Buddhist teachings. She has travelled widely but now spends most of her time at home on the Isle of Wight with her family, her spaniels, ducks and chickens. *Far from Home* is her first novel.

For Michael

Miranda Acland

FAR FROM HOME

AUSTIN MACAULEY PUBLISHERS™

LONDON * CAMBRIDGE * NEW YORK * SHARJAH

A CIP catalogue record for this title is available from the British Library.

ISBN 9781528938990 (Paperback)
ISBN 9781398490055 (ePub e-book)

www.austinmacauley.com

First Published 2024
Austin Macauley Publishers Ltd®
1 Canada Square
Canary Wharf
London
E14 5AA

I would like to thank my extremely patient husband, Michael and my daughters, Tara and Susanna, for giving me the courage to keep going with Far From Home through thick and thin. To my friends and book club members who read and were enthused about the book—thank you; that was very important! A particular thank you to Baba Hobart, who willingly gave me her expertise, boundless enthusiasm and refusal to take no for an answer, which got me over the finishing line.

I am also grateful to Sabrina Broadbent and my fellow students at the Faber Academy, where I learned much about how to write a novel and to Austin Macauley who made it possible for it to appear in print.

It has taken a long time for me to achieve my childhood dream of becoming a writer, and there have been a lot of diversions along the way. I owe a debt of gratitude to everyone who has supported me on that journey. Thank you.

Chapter 1
The Crash

It was starting to rain as the motorbike sputtered up the empty road cut into the rock along the side of the valley. The air was thin and cold up here but the boy on the Royal Enfield Bullet was wearing only a jumper and jeans, the wind whipping right through to the bare skin underneath.

His shoulders were tensed under his crash helmet as he braked into each bend and then accelerated out of it, building speed. Every few moments he glanced up towards the head of the valley and the snow-covered Annapurna mountains beyond, deadly white Himalayan peaks and ridges piercing through the thin layer of cloud, glinting in the October sun. Far down below him he could see a silver thread of meltwater tumbling past in the opposite direction.

The cloud came down and the mountains disappeared. The road was little more than a track now, red-brown earth, wet with mud and scattered with scree, as he scrambled the bike towards the next bend.

It happened in a second—the wheels slewing sideways, the bike flattening and skidding out from underneath him, and then he was falling, his body thudding heavily on the edge of the road and then on down the sheer slope all the way to the bottom. His shoulder took the first bounce, then his hip, then his head as flesh and bone smashed against the bare rock. At last, he lay motionless half in, half out of the ice-cold stream below, his body awkward, his face splashed with blood and dirt, loose stones raining down after him, the broken bike way above him, the air heavy with the smell of leaking petrol.

And then silence fell, that mountain silence deepened by millennia of wind, ice and snow; a silence broken only by a dog barking in the distance down towards Pokhara and the flapping of tattered prayer flags strung out like washing from a chorten high up in the mountains above, breathing out the words of the Buddha.

The boy didn't hear the gang of grubby Gurung children shouting as they scrambled down the slope towards him. They came from nowhere, hard-limbed little dots of colour and woolly hats against the cold, apparently flowing out of the folds in the rock itself, following the sound of crunching metal. They crowded around his broken body as the stream leaped and foamed around it, pushing each other out of the way to get a better look and then shrinking back, daring each other to prod him to see if he was dead or alive. Then like a flock of starlings they turned together and scattered, shouting for help to come.

* * *

In one of the Bir Hospital's five operating theatres in Kathmandu, Dr Sharma and his team were already well into the third hour of the operation. Although the Soviet-style block was never going to win any prizes for architecture and the fabric of the building was basic, at least it was well equipped and well lit. Outside in the city streets heavy rush hour traffic might be bumping over the potholes and children might be playing with rubbish in dirty puddles, but inside the theatre Dr Sharma always insisted on surgical standards of cleanliness and an atmosphere of calm, quiet professionalism.

The doctor paused for a moment to take stock. The boy's jumper had been cut open and lay peeled back underneath him. The helmet had been cautiously removed, although the neck brace remained in place. The worst of the mud and blood had been sponged off. Deep cuts on the boy's hands and arms had been stitched with fine nylon thread. Regular beeps from the monitors behind him reassured him that the boy's life was not in immediate danger. A line was feeding anaesthetic into the base of his spine and his shattered leg was being pinned back into place meticulously with screws and a large metal plate. Blood and bone were gradually being restored to order.

Dr Sharma took another look at the X-rays pinned up on the theatre's lightbox and then back at the boy's face, which had by some miracle escaped injury. His vital signs had all stabilised, which was good—his breathing, heart rate, blood pressure, body temperature were all steady. At least he hadn't broken his neck and there were no obvious skull fractures on the X-rays either, although he would need a CT scan to confirm that. And he wasn't unduly worried about the shattered leg, the broken pelvis and ribs, the severe bruising or the many cuts

10

and abrasions on his body. Those would all mend in time, even if he couldn't guarantee the boy wouldn't walk with a limp.

No, what worried him most was the fact that the boy had arrived in a coma and had clearly sustained several severe blows to the head. His helmet had been of doubtful age and quality and looked badly damaged. Any sort of internal bleeding could lead to a dangerous build-up of pressure and the risk of brain damage or even death, although he hoped not. The boy was going to need very careful monitoring over the next hours and days. Especially being a Westerner— because there was no way he, Dr Sharma, was going to be accused of third-world medical care by the boy's nearest and dearest, whoever they turned out to be.

But in the meantime the boy was deeply unconscious, unreachable. It was unlikely he would ever be able to remember the events immediately before and after the crash.

Who was this boy? He had been brought into the hospital with no passport, no papers, no driving licence, no ID of any sort. But then again, after the journey he'd had into the hospital his papers could be anywhere by now, along with the rest of his stuff.

It didn't really add up. There didn't seem to be any other casualties. He must have skidded off the road, perhaps going too fast—but, he shrugged, that wasn't so surprising for a boy his age on roads he wouldn't have known well. The hospital's disaster response unit was used to picking up the pieces from local road accidents in the Himalayas. But this boy was no local. Above the broken body his face was unlined and soft-skinned, eyes firmly shut as if in a deep sleep, like a child. What on earth had this man-child been doing that he had ended up more dead than alive in a stream at the bottom of some valley halfway to Tibet?

He was healthy, or at least he had been before the crash, but thin, a little too thin, and he hadn't had anything to eat or drink for several hours. Early twenties he'd guess, weathered skin, scraggy hair bleached by the sun and a half-hearted beard—probably been travelling for a while. Medium height and build. White, looked European or North American but it was impossible to know for sure. Even English, perhaps! Cheap clothes bought locally—a rough woollen jumper of the sort you could buy from any local market; jeans, ditto.

Just a few rupees in his jeans pocket and a cheap lighter but no cigarettes. He'd been travelling light, by anyone's standards. But he had good teeth, soft hands, neat nails, and that indicated a comfortable upbringing. Somebody's child.

Dr Sharma nodded to his team and they went back to work.

* * *

The boy can hear voices murmuring above him, but he can't make any sense of what they are saying. It sounds like complete gibberish. Although he is in the darkness, he can tell there are people around him, bending over him, looking down at his body. Assuming his body is still there because he can't feel it and he can't move it. Feet, legs, arms—nothing.

Then panic gets him in the pit of his stomach. Shit. He's got to get out of here. He's got to get over those mountains, although the mountains don't seem to be there anymore. Yeah, whatever. So where is he now and is it safe? Who are these people? Are they about to kill him? Perhaps they already have and that's why he can't move. He's shouting but no sound's coming out, no one can hear him. It's as if he isn't here. But if he isn't here, where is he?

Someone starts speaking in English. At last. *Cerebral oedema, intensive care.* He sounds like he knows what he's talking about. A doctor perhaps. God, what have they done to him? Why practically kill him and then start patching him up again? It doesn't make any sense.

He's really got to get a grip on things.

"Excuse me? Hello?—Look, I've got to get going now. Could someone sort these children out for me? They're making a bloody awful racket. They must be in the water with me. I'd do it myself but I really can't stay any longer. I have to get over the mountains and I'm very cold. Can someone give me a hand?"

Nothing happens. The doctor, if he is a doctor, hasn't heard him. He's busy talking to the others.

"I want him on a ventilator and I want him monitored round the clock. I'm not having anything go wrong with this one, so make sure you do it properly. I'll be back to see him this evening and until then I want to know if anything changes, anything."

* * *

Holding up his latex-gloved hands Dr Sharma turned sideways and pushed open the double doors of the operating theatre with a practised swing of his hip and was immediately accosted by two men from the Nepalese traffic police.

Routine procedure in this sort of situation, of course, and you had to give them a chance—they were only doing their job after all, and they must have been hanging around for hours. They'd be home late tonight and they weren't the only ones. But it wasn't every day he had a Westerner like this one on his operating table.

He started updating them on the boy's condition as he pulled off his surgical mask and removed the bloodstained gloves.

"Not good. We've stitched him up as well as we can but he's going to need some luck to pull through. I can't make any promises at this stage. He has some serious injuries and we may still need to operate to relieve the pressure on his brain. His life is still in danger. And I can't tell you what happened to him because I don't know. You'd better come with me."

Back in his office, the doctor sat down behind what passed for his desk.

"We're just going to have to wait until he's conscious. But that's going to take time. He may have suffered extensive brain damage already and that could get worse if we have to operate. His memory may take a while to come back and there's a good chance he won't remember anything about the accident at all."

He eyeballed both policemen one after the other, taking his time.

"Any information you can give us about what happened up there would certainly help with his treatment."

He hoped that hadn't sounded too sarcastic. But if he was prepared to share what he knew, they could damn well do the same. After all, he was one of the hospital's most senior doctors with far more training and experience behind him than they would ever have in a lifetime's traffic policing. And you don't get that kind of experience in Nepal. He had worked with the senior of the two men enough times before for him to know all this perfectly well. His own manner could be brisk at times, admittedly, but it must be obvious that he was concerned about this patient.

After what seemed like an interminable wait, the policeman nodded his agreement.

"Our team picked him up from Pokhara this morning and we flew him straight down here on the internal flight. I understand some of the local villagers found him and got him down to a local tea shop, although we don't have all the details.

"We sent somebody up to look at the crash scene. It looks like he skidded on some mud and gravel as he came round a corner. He went off the road and down a steep drop, ended up in a river. He was freezing cold and wet—I'm surprised he hasn't got hypothermia. By the time he got to us he was unconscious, he wouldn't have known anything about what was happening. Just as well or the journey down would have been terrible for him.

"The motorbike is badly damaged but we have retained the number plates—they're Indian. We can check with the border and see if they know when he came into Nepal. Perhaps he has not been here long."

"So he said nothing on the way here? He wasn't complaining about the pain?"

"No, nothing. As I have said, he was unconscious."

"Thank you. Perhaps you could update me if you receive any further information. I will call you as soon as he regains consciousness."

* * *

The boy can't make sense of what's happening. Nothing's joining up properly. He's in his bedroom at home, there's a big oak tree in the garden outside and he can see the branches through his window. It's definitely his window because his Blues Brothers poster is stuck up beside it with blue tack. Although it's sunny outside his family are all in his bedroom with him which is really weird.

They're standing around his bed and they all seem to be dressed in green scrubs. He can hear their voices but he can't understand what they're saying. They're looking down at him but he can't see their faces because he's above them now, looking down at his own body. He's not in his bed at home, he's on some sort of metal trolley. He's got plastic tubes coming out of him and someone is doing something to his head.

Then he's going higher, not in the room anymore. At last, he's reached the mountains, he's looking down at their knife-edged peaks. The snow is flecked with diamonds. There is a string of prayer flags on a mountain pass, red, green, yellow, blue, white. They are for him. He feels the warmth of the sun, the blue of the sky.

The wind's picking up and he's still rising. He's above the blue now, it's getting whiter. He can see everything he's done, everything he's been in his whole life, and it's all so simple. He realises everything's going to be all right. A ball of pure white energy appears and he's part of it, it's pulling him in and that's what he wants. There's a woman standing in front of him, he knows her but he doesn't know who she is.

She's tall and pale and beautiful with blonde hair and she's skinny—although she's a woman she looks like a child, or a teenager at least. He knows her voice and he loves it when she smiles. She's wearing a woollen shawl, it's got beautiful soft purples and greens in it, with a deep red fringe, he's seen them like that in India, he loves the look of that shawl, the weavy feel of it, he knows exactly how it lifts at the edge when she moves and then falls back into place. It reminds him—but she's shaking her head, she wants him to go back. It's not time yet.

He doesn't want to go back, not now, everything he's ever wanted is right here. But it's not going to happen. He's back on the metal trolley again, here are the nurses in scrubs and just as everything starts to join up again the picture goes dark.

* * *

Dr Sharma arrived at the entrance of the Bir Hospital. It was quite extraordinary how although it was one of the oldest hospitals, right in the centre of Kathmandu, it always managed to look as if it was still under construction. A single telegraph pole supported hundreds of telephone lines as well as street lighting and power cables. No wonder the power supply was erratic, and their backup generator was far from adequate, even after the fight they'd had to get it.

As usual the entrance was crowded with hospital visitors, staff, students and all sorts of other people with no obvious reason for being there, arriving and leaving, on foot, by bicycle, some in a hurry, others just hanging around. He always wore his doctor's coat and a preoccupied air when arriving and leaving, so as to avoid tiresome delays.

Up on the intensive care ward he went straight to the boy. The ward could hardly be considered luxurious by Western standards, he was only too well aware, with its flaking walls, speckled lino floor and rudimentary furniture.

Although the boy, still unconscious, couldn't see that. But he seemed to be recovering well, certainly as well as could be expected at this stage. They'd had to operate on his brain in the end, it had been unavoidable—they simply couldn't risk any further swelling. But it had gone well and he was out of immediate danger, although still critical. His broken body was beginning to heal too. As for who he was or what might be going on inside that head of his, there had been no further clue.

Satisfied, he turned his attention to the nursing staff who, as usual, were not performing nearly as well as he would have liked.

* * *

The boy is dreaming. He keeps dreaming the same dream. He's lying in the dark, listening to people's footsteps and hearing hushed voices, but he can never understand them. And he can hear a beeping noise from some sort of machinery. A factory perhaps? Each time he tries to concentrate as hard as he can, searching for clues, but his mind keeps sliding away again.

* * *

Another dream and he knows where he is this time. He's in his secret den inside the weeping willow tree in the garden at home. The branches come right down to the ground and there's a space inside so you can creep in and no one can see you. It's always nice and dry in there and it's sunny today so it's really warm and snug. He's scrounged the cushions from the window seat in the kitchen to sit on and he's got some strawberry laces in a white paper bag that he bought in the village Post Office, so it is like a little house of his own.

He did all this because his best friend is coming today. She's a girl and she is a year or two older than him, although he's bigger than her. He wants to be as much like her as possible and still be a boy. They've both just broken up from school and they've got the whole summer holidays ahead of them. They'll be together all the time. It has to be the best feeling in the world.

She's shaking him. "Come on, it doesn't hurt much, we've done it loads of times at school. Look, I've done it already, I *swear* it doesn't hurt." He's holding one of his mother's sewing needles in one trembling hand and at last he pushes it hard into his other thumb. A small bead of blood appears on the skin and he peers at it, fascinated.

"Come on, quickly or my blood will all be gone."

"Will you be my real sister then?"

He turns this idea over in his mind. He doesn't have a real sister or a real brother either. But it would be good to pretend.

"Yes because we'll have the same blood—you press your thumb against mine and all the blood mixes and your blood goes into me and my blood goes into you. There. Now we're brother and sister!"

She looks at him triumphantly and he can see that she is just as pleased as he is.

* * *

The beeping noise again. This beeping dream is becoming more real. He senses there are broken people lying in the darkness around him. He can smell the sterilised smell of hospitals and the smell of sickness and suffering too. So he must be in hospital. He must be broken as well. He can't move or talk or see, but at least nothing seems to hurt. There are nurses looking after him.

Sometimes he hears that voice speaking in English. Not an English person, but someone who speaks English well. Definitely a man, but it's not a very deep voice. He never answers questions though, so he's not much help.

Cerebral oedema. What is cerebral oedema? It sounds like something to do with the brain. Is it serious? Is that why he feels so confused all the time? He's getting fed up with this. Oh for fuck's sake, come on, why can't you tell me something I can understand? And the doctor always spends ages looking at one of his legs, too. The doctor seems pleased, though, mostly. So he's probably alive because if he was dead, he wouldn't still be here. But how do you know if you are dead?

There is nothing about this place that is familiar, no one he knows, nothing he understands. Lying on this bed he's helpless, his body is theirs, but inside he closes in. He can almost feel his heart, his liver, his whole abdomen shrinking. Not his lungs, though—he can always hear them breathing.

* * *

Dr Sharma was in his office on the telephone. For a senior consultant at the height of his career, he seemed to spend an awful lot of time on the telephone when he could have been in the operating theatre. But in this case he didn't mind—in fact he had been waiting for this call. It was the policeman who had visited him before about the boy.

"Dr Sharma. I am calling to inform you that we have updated our information on your unidentified patient. The motorbike entered Nepal from India only a few days before the crash, at Sonauli, so we are assuming the boy did also. He is likely to have travelled by road to Kathmandu before continuing to Pokhara."

Well, yes. Presumably he didn't arrive by parachute.

"We are also conducting enquiries with the locals in the area of the crash, but I am not hopeful this will give us any further information. We need to talk to him. We need a name so we can check Kathmandu hotel registers, missing persons—and his nationality would also be helpful."

Dr Sharma sighed, ignoring the sarcasm in the policeman's voice. "I am sorry but that is totally impossible," he said. "He's had a major operation. I have to keep him sedated. I am absolutely not prepared to take any risks with him at this stage. His condition is still critical."

There was a loaded silence on the other end of the line, so the doctor changed the subject.

"What's your view on where could he have been going? There's nothing up there except vultures. Once you get past Pokhara it's a dead end unless you're travelling with crampons and a team of sherpas."

"Agreed. Perhaps he went up on a sightseeing trip."

At least he's got a sense of humour, thought the doctor. Could the boy have been going to meet someone? But if you were planning a trip up a mountain, surely you would wear a jacket of some sort.

Chapter 2
Emma

Emma had already been awake a while when she opened her eyes. Total darkness. A bad sign—the dark should be lifting by now, even though the clocks would be changing soon. It must be earlier than she thought. She turned over in bed to look at her clock radio, moving gently to avoid waking herself up even more. 4:30 AM… still two hours before she had to get up. So if she could get another two hours' sleep maybe she'd be OK. At least it was Thursday today and only one more day to get through until the weekend.

She was under so much pressure at work and being tired all the time just made it harder. She'd been lucky to get her traineeship at Withers & Co. Some of her contemporaries from law school still hadn't got one and there weren't enough jobs to go round. Fortunately, her father had been able to pull a few strings or she would probably have struggled too. He'd chosen Withers and it was a good firm, big enough to give her some solid experience but not so big that she'd get lost.

Now she had to prove herself and they made it perfectly clear that you were only ever as good as the last project you worked on. You were under the microscope all the time; you couldn't afford off days.

She turned over again and again. Although the summer was well and truly over she seemed to be radiating heat. She kicked the bedspread, the cushions and even her much loved teddy bear onto the floor and pushed the duvet down to her waist. She felt the skin on her arms start to chill in the night air flowing over her from the open sash window, but it did nothing to cool the rest of her down.

The Antitrust Department was definitely the most interesting area she'd worked on so far. But you really did have to be on the ball. She didn't envy Margaret Chalmers, the senior partner in the department, with the acquisition they were working on at the moment. The corporate guys had been working on that radio deal for years, and now it had been referred to the Competition Commission everyone was looking at them to get it through. No deal, no fee. It would take months of work and they were up against some of the best legal brains in the business. Obviously she was a long way from being in the hot seat but she still couldn't afford to let anybody down.

4:40 AM. Perhaps her clock had actually stopped? The red LED *was* flickering a bit. No. 4:41 AM. Did it really have to be quite so bright? You could bet that at about 6 AM she'd finally fall into a deep sleep and then the alarm would go off half an hour later. She always got up at 6:30 AM though, as soon as the radio came on with the news, to give her time to get ready. You had to look smart at work, they had guidelines—a skirt suit below the knee or a trouser suit, matching. Clean hair, no open-toed shoes, minimal make-up. You had to make the effort if you wanted to get on.

And anyway, it was easier travelling on the tube before it got too crowded. Less tiring. If she could get a seat at least she could get on with some reading, even if it was only an out-of-date copy of The Lawyer which everyone else had already read. And it was better to get in before the office got too busy, so she could change out of her trainers without feeling everyone was staring at her, and make a comprehensive list of all the things she needed to get done while there was still some peace and quiet. It helped to be on top of things. Make sure she didn't forget anything or mess up.

Like yesterday. There were some good things about yesterday, definitely. She'd done a good job on her analysis of broadcast overlap areas in the West Country—and she'd been thanked for it, too, so it must have been all right. But then like an idiot she'd screwed up on the conference call they'd had with the client at the end of the day, picked up the wrong sheet off her desk and ended up giving the data for completely the wrong area. She felt her face flush again just thinking about it.

She pulled the duvet up around her ears, cold now.

Joe was coming round for supper later on. Hopefully she wouldn't be too tired for that. Oh Lord, what was she going to give him to eat? Why hadn't she thought about that before? She wanted to impress him, in a casual sort of way. The trouble was, food shopping at lunchtime wasn't really on, even though Safeways at the Barbican was just up the road. Bags of leaky shopping taking up all the space in the office fridge and then lugging it all home on the tube in the rush hour. But she could always leave a shopping list on the kitchen unit for

Jessie, she wouldn't mind. Another thing to think about between 6:30 AM and 7:15 AM.

Extraordinary to think that she was Joe's girlfriend now. Could she call herself that? After all the time they spent together as children, messing about in the school holidays down in Somerset. She would have followed him over a cliff in those days—on her bike, probably, just behind his well-preserved green Raleigh. Alex had always been there, of course, but days with all three of them had been the best.

Ever since she was nine years old, when her father had first bought the cottage in Exford, she and Alex had been friends. Alex was a year or two younger than her and she would never have ended up being *his* girlfriend because it wasn't like that. But they had always been really close friends. Now he'd gone away she missed him more than she ever expected. It was as if there was some sort of connection between them that she couldn't put her finger on, even at 4:50 AM. If she had believed in God, she might have said they were soul mates.

* * *

Emma managed to get through the day without disaster and even left work earlier than usual, which meant she was swept back to Moorgate tube at the height of the rush hour and had to buy her Evening Standard from the station kiosk without even slowing down. Honestly. Was she the only person in the City who didn't usually go home at 5:30?

She had the flat all to herself this evening because her father was away in Milan on business. At her age, it was probably high time she moved out, but after all it was only the two of them and they'd always got on well enough. And anyway, why leave a perfectly comfortable flat at the top of a mansion block overlooking Regents Park, with a well-stocked drinks tray, her own en-suite bathroom and Jessie to look after her if she didn't have to?

In the lobby, she picked up their post, took the lift up to the fourth floor and then let herself in through the heavy front door to the flat, already running through in her mind what she needed to get done before Joe arrived. Now she was home the tiredness was hard to ignore. She dropped the letters onto the hall table and went on into the drawing room to sit down, just for five minutes.

It was a relief in a way to be on her own, it gave her some recovery time. Without stopping to take her coat off she collapsed into one of the deep sofas, breathing in the faint lingering floral scent and the stillness of the air. When her father was home, the place positively shook with his presence as he surged from kitchen to study to drawing room and back, looking for things, shouting instructions and creating mess. But that was what she had grown up with; it was home.

She wondered what Joe really thought of it or whether he felt out of place here amongst the luxuries earned by another generation. Through his eyes perhaps the matched cushions arranged neatly on every sofa and chair looked too contrived, the buttoned ottoman groaning with coffee table books about Italian Gardens, Ceramics from Isfahan, Venice in Peril too extravagant, the collection of modern art on the walls too—urban.

She was well aware that most of her friends, including Joe, were sharing chaotic student flats in places like Clapham and Barons Court now, living in cramped unhoovered rooms with unattractive carpets and soft furnishings of dubious provenance. For the first time, she felt a little uncomfortable that she still lived at home, like a child playing at being grown up without having earned it. Being independent was a rite of passage she'd have to face up to sooner or later. Perhaps it would even do her good.

She got up quickly and went into the kitchen to check that Jessie had got everything on her list. Yes, it was all there and what's more, the French beans were neatly trimmed, ready to cook, and there were two places laid at the breakfast bar for them. There was even a note to say she had left a bottle of Sancerre in the fridge along with some crudités, which Emma found neatly arranged on a wooden board with some olives, caperberries and sun-dried tomatoes she must have found in the cupboard.

Emma grinned to herself, imagining what her father would say. It was a family joke that Jessie adored Emma and would do anything for her. She had been with them for as long as Emma could remember, first as a nanny and later as a housekeeper, accomplice, counsellor and confidante. Somewhere along the way her father had bought a one-bedroom flat downstairs where Jessie lived with her knitting, an imitation gas fire and a television set in her bedroom. She was part of the family and always would be.

It was completely understood that she would look after Emma's own children as soon as she could be persuaded to produce some. For this reason Jessie was all in favour of Joe's arrival in Emma's life, particularly since she had known

Joe for almost as long as Emma had. As far as she was concerned it was a step in the right direction.

Emma checked her watch and decided to get ready first and cook later. Perhaps she'd feel better after a hot bath and a change of clothes. Back in her bedroom, about as far away from the kitchen as you could get, she stripped off her prickly skirt suit, white shirt and tights, leaving them in a heap on the floor.

She headed on into her bathroom, turning on the brass taps full blast and pouring a generous shot of Floris bath oil into the water. She tied all her thick, dark hair up out of the way, leaving a heavy fringe to curl down almost into her eyes. As the stephanotis steam filled the bathroom she felt the heat flush her cheeks and curl the wisps of hair that had escaped around her face. At last. She sank into the water and closed her eyes, letting the warmth wrap around her.

She hadn't seen Joe since last Sunday and she had been over that in her mind so many times that she'd pretty much worn out the memory of it. They'd met for brunch first, her favourite—eggs Benedict, fresh orange juice and an endless supply of French coffee. Then she had persuaded him to be taken to the Tate Gallery to admire some of her favourite modern art—a lightening tour of Bacon, Warhol, Hockney, Pollock, even Picasso and Dali—and afterwards he had retaliated by making her walk all the way along the South Bank as far as Blackfriars Bridge and back.

It had seemed so perfect at the time, but had she imagined how much he had seemed to like her? They'd only spoken once since Sunday so he obviously hadn't been spending a lot of time thinking about her. She was starting to wonder whether things between them would have changed this evening.

She had decided to wear her new Miss Selfridge sweater dress with some patterned tights and suede pumps. It was cosy and feminine and she reckoned it suited her shape, which she liked to think of as 'petite', although definitely not 'curvy'. She peered into the steamy mirror above the basin. Her hair was still curling from the bath, giving her an unusually tousled look she rather liked. A bit of blusher and mascara and she was ready.

She'd finally lost touch with Joe when he'd gone off to Bristol to do his degree. By then, he'd seemed so far ahead of her and Alex. It wasn't until last year when Alex had come to London that she'd met Joe again and they had exchanged numbers, promising to meet up. Much to her surprise, Joe had been as good as his word. He'd got in touch and introduced her to some of his friends, who she'd gradually got to know. He'd been kind to her and looked out for her in the rather polite, old-fashioned way she supposed he had been brought up to do.

She soon realised she was attracted to him, although God knows she tried not to be. He was definitely good-looking, much more so than Alex, and it was easy to warm to his laid-back charm, his lazy smile, his way of taking everything with a pinch of salt and yet remaining unquestionably in charge. But she knew she was not the only one who was interested in him. He had some very attractive female friends and she could see Joe appealed to them too—and it was only a matter of time before he ended up with one of them. Whenever they were together she couldn't help checking out where he was and who he was talking to, and whether he was singling anyone out. But he wasn't. Especially her.

Then one hot evening at the end of August they'd all been having drinks on a Friday night after work at their usual Pitcher & Piano in Cornhill. It just happened that everyone else had plans for the rest of the evening so she and Joe had ended up walking back to the tube together. That was when Joe had suggested they went for something to eat.

He seemed pleased when she agreed. In no time, he'd flagged down a taxi and they were heading off to a burger place he knew in Notting Hill Gate. They'd both ordered cheeseburgers, she remembered, with fries and salad with blue cheese dressing, just what you needed after Friday night drinks—and they were clinking their glasses together in a little celebration, she wasn't quite sure what of, when Joe caught her hand and held it. She froze, trying hard not to give herself away and looking hard at the queue of hungry customers that was forming over by the door.

"We're good together, aren't we, Em?" Joe said.

She nodded, wondering what he meant. At that moment, their cheeseburgers arrived and Joe fell on his as if he hadn't eaten for weeks, which had made her laugh, and everything went back to normal. They chatted on about friends, the weekend, films they wanted to see, and by the time their Mississippi Mud Cake arrived with two spoons she seriously thought she might have imagined the whole thing.

Once they were outside, Joe announced that he wanted to go for a stroll.

"Ahh—look. There's Hyde Park, just across the road! We could walk up towards Marble Arch and then we'll get a taxi for you. It's a lovely evening. I could do with some fresh air."

And he'd loped off, clapping an arm around her shoulder as if it didn't belong to him at all. She'd practically had to break into a trot to keep up, but once she'd managed to get him to slow down she realised it had been a good suggestion of his after all. He did seem to really want to put his arm around her and whether he meant anything by it or not she decided to relax and enjoy it while it lasted. It had been a stifling hot day but now the air was cool and the parched leaves of the plane trees above them were just beginning to rustle.

In the distance, they could see the traffic hustling along Lancaster Gate, but inside the park it seemed as if time had been suspended. It was almost like being in a movie and it seemed surprisingly natural when he leaned in and kissed her.

"I've wanted to do that for such a long time," he said and immediately kissed her again, this time with his arms wrapped around her.

Well, what an astonishing turn of events, she thought. She'd spent so long trying to act normal with Joe that she hardly dared react. Perhaps he was drunk? Or joking? She looked up at him and saw that he was neither. She could barely remember how they got to Marble Arch except that they had held hands like a couple of children and then Joe had put her in a taxi as promised, given the driver directions to Regent Mansions and then kissed her goodnight before waving her off.

She'd got home, put her pyjamas on back to front and gone to bed in a state of shock. And she'd hardly finished her cornflakes the next morning when he was on the phone asking when he could see her again. No wonder sometimes it all seemed too good to be true.

Her father had seemed genuinely pleased for her. He could see having Joe around made her happy and he said if anyone was going to have his precious daughter it might as well be Joe, who he had always liked. It turned out that most of their friends had thought they were together anyway. The person with the most to lose from their relationship was Alex.

* * *

"What are we going to do about Alex?" Joe said, peering out of the drawing room windows at the trees in the park opposite. "We're going to have to tell him soon. Do you think he'll be OK about it?"

Although Joe was concerned about his younger brother, he wasn't really expecting their relationship to change much. He'd had to think carefully about

25

his own feelings for Emma to be sure he was doing the right thing, given the circumstances, and that had been quite hard enough without having to think about Alex's as well. He assumed that after a rather awkward conversation Alex would just man up and get over it.

"I'm not sure, Joe. I just don't know. We're very close, you know, we've been spending a lot of time together. I would hate to lose that and I would miss him terribly.

"But I'm not really sure why... we're just friends, after all, although sometimes it seems like more than that. It's a bit weird, it's not like there has ever been anything between us. And obviously it doesn't make any difference to you and me."

"I know that, Em. I was there from the beginning, remember? I would miss him too and I'm not going out with him either."

"I'd hate to think I might lose him. I don't want to lose either of you."

Joe turned away from the window to face her, sliding his hands into the pockets of his jeans, and noticed that her eyes had started to water alarmingly.

"I know. But I'm worried about him too, you know. He *is* my little brother. Although I'm sure he can look after himself. I expect he'll be absolutely fine."

"Yeah. I hope so."

There were now definitely tears rolling down Emma's cheeks. Joe cleared himself a small space amongst the mountain of cushions on the sofa and sank down beside her, putting his arm around her.

"It's all right, Em. Please don't cry. You worry too much."

"People always say that."

"Well, they're right."

He gave her what he hoped was a reassuring hug.

"Now. Did you say there were some beers in the fridge? I'll get them."

He jumped up again and headed into the kitchen but Emma beat him to it, pulling out two bottles of Budweiser and asking whether he'd have preferred a pint of John Smith's. The joke seemed to cheer her up, thank goodness. Then she checked the oven and he caught a tantalising glimpse of homemade pie with one of those curly pastry rose things on the top that reminded him of his mother.

"I hope this pie's going to be all right," Emma said as she put the potatoes on.

"It looks pretty good to me! I bet Jessie made it."

"Well obviously I would have made it if I'd had time—I've made pies before, you know!"

"Don't tell me the girl can cook as *well*!"

Looking pleased, Emma wriggled up onto a stool beside him at the counter, where they drank the beer out of the bottles, picked at the olives and eyed the caperberries with deep suspicion. She told him he absolutely had to go and see Dances with Wolves, the new Kevin Costner film, which she and her friend Annabel had seen earlier in the week. He told her how worried everyone was at work about the economic outlook now inflation was heading for double figures and unemployment was creeping up again. With Labour riding high in the opinion polls, how much longer could Maggie Thatcher really stay in power? Then he saw Emma hiding a yawn and noticed how pale she was.

"Did you say you were going to go and see the doctor this week?"

"Yes, I did. I went yesterday. Dad said I should."

"And what did he say?"

"Oh, nothing much really. Except that he thinks I might need to go and talk to somebody about my mother. A therapist or something."

"What on earth's the point of that? I thought—"

"I know. I can't remember her at all, I was too young. And I hardly know anything about her either except what Dad's told me, which is nothing basically. I mean, I know she died in a car crash and I've seen one or two old photos, but I've got no idea what she was really like. I've given up trying to get Dad to talk about her, he just clams up. He doesn't seem to realise that he's not the only person who lost her. I did, too. There's just one thing I've got to remember her by and that's a dusty old book which isn't even in English. Apparently, it's some sort of Indian religious text."

"Can I see it?"

"Sure."

He watched her trot off down the hall to her bedroom, an almost childlike figure in her woolly dress and little shoes, and reappear a few moments later with a faded brown volume in her hand. She studied the drawing of a chariot drawn by four perfect white horses on the flyleaf and then handed it over.

"I wondered whether—yes. It is! It's the Bhagavad Gita! How amazing—I love this book! You're right, it's part of one of the Hindu scriptures. There's a warrior prince called Arjuna. He's on the battlefield reviewing his army but he's in despair because he doesn't want to kill his enemies. It's his conversation with his charioteer Krishna, who is God in human form. The battlefield is an allegory though, it's really Krishna's teaching about the soul's battle against evil and how to live a holy life. It's in Sanskrit."

Emma looked gratifyingly impressed, even though he *had* done his degree in religion and theology.

"But why on earth would she have had that? Oh, I wish I knew more about her. You don't realise how lucky you are to have had such an amazing mother, Joe. Lorna always made your house such a happy place. Sometimes I used to pretend she was my mother too. Do you mind sharing her with me?"

"Be my guest! It must have been tough, growing up without your mother."

"Yes—although it's hard for me to know what I've missed, really. Dad always tried to make up for it. And we had Jessie—and Aunt Jackie. You wait until you meet Aunt Jackie! She and Dad are like this"—she crossed her fingers and held them up—"and she doesn't have any children of her own so I get the full force."

"But—what's the point of going to talk to somebody about your mother if you can't remember her?"

"Well, exactly. And anyway I don't see what difference it would make now. All I needed was a few sleeping pills."

Thankfully, after that the conversation moved on to firmer ground. Jessie's pie, which turned out to be chicken and leek, was perfectly cooked and delicious, and with her father away he was able to stay the night with her for once. Much as he liked Richard it was sometimes awkward that Emma still lived at home—but that was a bridge he wasn't quite ready to cross yet.

Chapter 3
Bir Hospital

In the Bir Hospital's overcrowded intensive care ward up on the fourth floor, Dr Sharma pulled up a plastic chair by the side of the boy's bed. He rested his head in his hands and watched his patient lying motionless, his breathing regulated by a ventilator. There was no doubt that he was still a very sick young man, but things did seem to be settling down. The nursing staff had had no particular problems to report. All they could do now was wait.

He was satisfied that no further medical intervention was needed at this stage so he supposed this must be a social call—and in fact, he did seem to be chatting to the boy. Or chatting to himself, more like. Well, perhaps a moment for reflection was not such a bad thing in a hectic schedule like his, and even unconscious the boy was no worse a listener than most of the people he worked with around here.

Anyway, it was important to keep tabs on the situation. It wasn't every day you got a Western patient in this sort of state carted into intensive care in a place like Kathmandu, let alone one with no apparent identity. It had caused quite a stir and he certainly wasn't going to have anybody else on the medical staff sticking their nose in.

"I have a feeling you are English. Even if you're not English, you can probably understand English. I'm sorry, please forgive my bad pronunciation. One day I hope to go to England and after that, it will be much better."

A little self-conscious now, he adopted a more formal tone.

"Perhaps I should introduce myself. I am your doctor. My name is Dr Sharma. Please try not to worry, I have many years' experience and you are in good hands.

"I trained here in Kathmandu, but I have worked up in those hills near Pokhara where they found you. Oh my goodness, they need doctors badly up there. Ayurvedic medicine is all very well, but it doesn't cure cancer. Yes, I know the area well. They are poor people, the Gurung, they live hand to mouth, with a tiny plot of land, a few coffee plants, perhaps a goat or two and some chickens if they're lucky. No running water, no sanitation. Disease, malnutrition, infant mortality are commonplace. It's a very hard life. What on earth were you doing there, English boy?"

* * *

The boy can hear a low murmuring voice somewhere near his head, someone who says he's a doctor. At least he's speaking in English, although his pronunciation is frightful. He is talking about Pokhara. What on earth is Pokhara? It sounds like some sort of disease, a bit like cholera. But hang on. Didn't he travel from Kathmandu to Pokhara? When he left Kathmandu, he went to Pokhara. It's not a disease at all, it's a *town*. Although that doesn't explain what the hell he was doing in Nepal in the first place. Or where he is now. It's not hanging together at all. It's bloody exhausting, that's what it is.

Now the doctor has gone, the ward is quiet and he is dreaming again. There are vast mountain peaks in the distance. Ah, it must be the Himalayas! He's washing his face and cooling his feet in a stream by the side of the road. He's turning to check on his bike every few minutes. He's exhausted, his eyes are gritty with dust and he really wants to lie down on the grass right there and sleep. But he's got to keep going, got to push on, so he gets back on the bike and fires up the engine.

The clouds are rolling down to a big lake in the distance, it's like a lurid, badly printed postcard, the ones you see in the tea shops, the green of the trees, then the white mountains, then the deep blue sky reflected in the water. There are even little open boats painted all different colours, yellow, turquoise, red, green, ready to take tourists out for trips. It looks calm, normal, safe. He feels better.

On the road, he starts to pass more signs of habitation—wiry old men carrying crazy amounts of vegetation on their backs, young girls carrying children wrapped in neat papooses. Now there are telegraph poles and advertising posters for Coca Cola, Everest beer, Real fruit juice. He's in the outskirts of the town, there are a lot more motorbikes and trucks on the road. The dust is worse and it's getting really hard to concentrate. It's a lot noisier too—an argument breaks out up ahead and suddenly everyone is joining in, shouting and hooting.

It startles him, he can't handle it. He needs to eat and he stops at a supermarket to buy some sort of sandwich. The supermarket is actually called Buddha. Surely you wouldn't get a supermarket called Jesus back home. He really needs to sleep but stopping in the middle of the day would just be too dangerous, so he presses on. He's starting to shiver in his T-shirt, it's colder up here, the altitude's a lot higher. He stops by the lake and buys a thick yak wool jumper, puts it on and gets back on the bike again.

On the way out of town, there are cows lying across the road. He's got used to this now. They have rights, these cows, and they know it. They're bony like everyone else around here but they're not frightened, they're safe as houses. Unlike him. He knows he has to skirt around them carefully, treat them with respect. They seem to get everywhere—he saw a cow snoozing in a gift shop once. Where was that? The gift shop had once been a temple where the cow had been a regular guest. Now, it just visited the jewellery counter instead.

In his wing mirror, he sees the cows getting up, lurching onto their bony knees. They're starting to lumber after him and they're picking up speed, bunching together in an alarming way. He tries not to panic. They know something, they must be in on it too. He's going faster now but they just keep coming, he can't shake them off. He's lost his bag from the back of his bike.

He looks up at the mountains ahead, looking for a way through. There must be roads and villages up there, perhaps he can get into Tibet. Then he'd be able to get into China from there. He doesn't think they can follow him into Tibet, it will be safer for him there, even if he gets picked up by the Chinese authorities. He's so tired of being on the run.

* * *

The doctor's voice is back. It's closer now and he is almost whispering. What on earth is he talking about?

"I have a son, you know. He's a clever boy, nine years old and already he wants to be a doctor like me! I tell him he will have to work very hard at his school books, but that is the same in England, no? Maybe he can do his medical training here in Nepal. Maybe he will go to India, or to China or the USSR. Or maybe he could even go to England! That would be incredible. Of course, England has all the best medical schools.

"And I have two daughters, Rita and Sonia. You see, they have names that are English as well as Nepalese. One day it might help them to get ahead. We are bringing them up in a modern way. They are receiving a proper education and they will choose their own husbands, like in England. It is important always to look forward, not back. Where is your family, English boy? Surely they are worried about you."

The boy struggles through his confusion. Who are Rita and Sonia? Does he know them? The names don't ring a bell at all. He does remember two girls though, he met them somewhere. They all took a train together. So are they here as well? No, he must have left them behind because he knows he didn't have the chance to say goodbye. So why is this doctor talking about them now? Are they in the hospital too? What happened to them? He just can't remember.

But he does remember Pokhara more clearly now, it's the town by the lake, with the prayer flags and the pagodas. The air is cool and clear and the Annapurna peaks are awesome. He is swimming, the icy water biting into him, clouds rolling down from the mountains and turning to mist on the lake's surface. He is walking past tea shops and stalls groaning with Tibetan singing bowls and prayer wheels, wondering what to buy, and at every street corner there is Annapurna again, steady like an altar above all the telegraph wires and cables.

The road signs here are in Nepali, a script full of curls and hooks hanging from a dead straight rail, with its breath of eastern mystery, of a religion not understood. Now it's dark and he's drinking beer with a ragged gaggle of travellers in a local bar, smoking Camel cigarettes. They're all bragging about where they want to travel next, trying to outdo each other with the most obscure places they can think of. One wants to go to Bodh Gaya, where the Buddha reached enlightenment under the Bodhi tree. Another wants to go on a pilgrimage to Mount Kailash in the Trans Himalaya, at the source of the Ganges, the Brahmaputra and the Indus, home of Lord Shiva and his wife Parvati. He is thinking, what I really want is to go home, I've had enough adventure. But he does not say it out loud.

Now he's back on his motorbike and the road is threading on upwards through clumps of thatched mud huts with juice-green rice terraces and papery banana trees. It's jungle, but how come there is jungle so close to snow-covered mountains? Whenever he stops the bike the sound of insects is as loud as an aeroplane. The road is getting steeper, he's riding past the tops of trees whose roots are far down below him. A pheasant strolls into the road, trailing its long tail feathers behind it. What the hell is a pheasant doing up here? Is this where they come from?

His mind slips a gear and now he's back home, walking up a hedgerow with his spaniel, Captain. The brambles are loaded with blackberries, still wet from the rain, and they taste earthy and sweet. Every now and then he collects a few in the palm of his hand for Captain to snuffle up all at once with his soft muzzle. Then they're both crashing through the wood side by side, hunting up the undergrowth until a pheasant makes a break for the open, clucking and flapping, straining to get its waterlogged body up and away in time.

* * *

He listens whenever he can, whenever he's not too tired. He can't see anything, it's just black behind his eyes. He can tell when the nurses are there because he can hear their feet on the lino and sense their presence. He has learned to recognise them by their voices but he can't tell what they are doing unless they are touching him, checking his pulse and his blood pressure or dressing his legs.

He hears the sound of pain in all its human voices. Heavy things move about, metal rattles, wheels squeak. Sometimes he senses panic, urgency. Other times are calmer and he can hear the steady humming and beeping of machinery or a nurse talking. He listens for the doctor. His voice is familiar now, the only familiar thing he has. When he hears that voice, he wants to call out. With the doctor beside him, he feels a little safer. But he doesn't come today.

He trusts the doctor now, but there are people out there who could be dangerous. He hears their voices, too. Anyone could be out there. He's listening for a sign, a warning, although he's not sure how he will recognise it. If he's going to die, a few seconds' warning would be nice. Or is he dead already? Perhaps the doctor will tell him. Or perhaps he's dead too.

* * *

He must be in Kathmandu. Climbing mountains is what you do in Kathmandu. At least, getting ready to climb mountains. The shops are full of crampons, ice axes and Everest boots and you can stock up on groceries from all

33

over the world to make you feel at home as you climb. You can visit the Rum Doodle Bar as he did and see Edmund Hillary's and Sherpa Tensing's signatures on the wall from their ascent of Everest in the fifties. Here people call the mountains the 'Hymarlia'. To be a traveller with any credibility you have to be going at least to Everest base camp, as a bare minimum.

He keeps reminding himself he is in Kathmandu. It sounds so bohemian, such a long way from home. Where hippies went in the 60s. The Beatles. Hendrix. He is wandering around the hundreds of temples in the Old City, killing time, waiting for something. What is it he's waiting for? He can't remember. Someone tells him that in Durbar Square there is a temple for every day of the year, but they all look exactly the same, an architectural car crash between China and India with ornately carved wooden columns and pagoda roofs so close to each other they almost interlock.

Down at ground level, there are carpets of pigeons lifting and scattering in front of prowling dogs. Loose-robed monks holding alms bowls in their outstretched hands. Trays of flickering butter lamps, flowers and red powdered dye to offer to whichever god or goddess takes your fancy. In a doorway, he can see two magnificent sadhus in orange robes, hair in dreadlocks and skin smeared in ash. They look strangely familiar.

In Freak Street, he finds only ghosts from the 60s. Now it's all antiques and artworks, mandalas and doorknobs, Buddhas and thangkas, although people still ask him in a whisper if he wants hashish. One shop is selling nothing but the Nepali hats he has seen the old men wearing, woven in soft pastel shades and stacked like waves in a winter sea. Another is piled high with cosy hand-stitched blankets and quilts for the cold.

Now he's climbing up hundreds of steps to a Buddhist temple on top of a hill. There are monkeys everywhere, spilling out of the trees into the courtyard, putting on a show of acrobatics, playing up to the audience. Inside the temple, he turns the prayer wheels one by one with his fingers, enjoying the feel of the ritual, and buys some prayer flags to hang in the wind just in case there is someone to hear them. Outside there are some scruffy teenagers with little black and brown birds packed into a wire cage. You can pay to set one free but they just go and catch them again.

* * *

Dr Sharma stared down at the boy, struck again by how incongruous he looked on the sparse iron bed with its absence of Western adornments. It always seemed so quiet in here. Outside in the centre of Kathmandu people were struggling and sweating in the midday heat; in here the struggle was a more primordial one as people fought for recovery, even for life itself, without any conscious effort at all. The sheer strength of that life force and the body's extraordinary ability to heal seemed more miraculous to him with every passing year of his career.

And this body was doing well, Dr Sharma was pleased to note, all things considered, in the sense that it was definitely healing. The leg looked as if it was starting to knit together nicely. The pelvis and ribs would take a while, but barring infection they should mend. He had been most fortunate not to have suffered more serious internal damage. Although looking down at him, fortunate was not necessarily a word you would use to describe someone with injuries of this degree. Thank goodness for morphine. He reviewed the dosage and then wrote up an order for a further set of blood tests to check for any sign of infection. It wouldn't take much for the boy's condition to become unstable.

It was the brain injury that was the hardest to assess. He was confident that he had followed all the right procedures, but the brain was still such a mystery to the medical profession. He would expect there to be some cognitive damage, but assessing the extent of that damage and how well the boy's brain would compensate for it was almost impossible. At this stage, he could not even be sure that he would ever fully regain consciousness. And there was nothing more the doctors could do to help. From here on, this boy's brain would have to do its healing all by itself.

No further sign of who he was or where he had come from. Dr Sharma's instinct was that he was English, but then again he could be German, with that scraggy, almost gingery beard. Not that you could see much of him with all those bandages. Surely somebody, somewhere must be missing him and searching for him. What if they never found him here? He tried to imagine his own son in a hospital far away from home and hoped that if that ever happened, he would be looked after too. He took up his station again on the plastic chair.

"What's your story, boy? Where were you going on that mountain road? There's nothing up there, you know. Nothing at all except mud huts and goats. Were you alone? Somebody must be wondering where you are. But who?"

The boy knows he isn't at home. He knows he's in hospital. But not in England or even Europe. Perhaps he's in some sort of parallel universe. Or a transition between worlds. Does that mean he will never go home? Because actually, that's what he'd really like to do now, go home. Whatever home is. He sifts and dredges through his brain, looking for clues.

He can remember his mother. He can see her stirring a huge bubbling pan of marmalade on the stove. She's got the radio on in the background, some sort of phone-in programme, and every now and then she looks up at it in disbelief, eyes rolling. She's got a shoal of fat Kilner jars standing by all sterilised and ready and she's testing little dots of marmalade in a saucer of cold water to see if it sets. She moves swiftly, expertly, like a scientist in a laboratory, but with an apron instead of a lab coat.

This is the house he grew up in. It's at the top of a hill, you can see for miles, and there's always mud on the road because of the cows going in and out of the farmyard opposite. When it rains, it fills the whole landscape. In the summer, there's lots of lavender. Mum has a kitchen garden full of vegetables, onions, carrots, lettuces, potatoes, she has to wash the earth off before she cooks them. She's usually busy in the kitchen when they get home.

After school, they sit around the kitchen table for tea. They're always hungry. Up one end there's a huge pile of stuff that doesn't seem to live anywhere else— newspapers, letters, sewing, Christmas cards, mysterious nuts and bolts, photographs, bird food, glue—and they sweep it all out of the way so they can do their homework. The dresser's crammed full of stuff, too, plates and jugs and things they made at school years ago. The dog sits under the table and they feed him scraps when no one is looking. They've got a cat too, somewhere.

Home isn't hot like it is here. At home, you go out walking in the rain and come back soaking wet. Then you sprawl on the floor in front of the fire, warming up your damp skin inside a big baggy jumper. There's the smell of hot, singed dog and the luxury of knowing there is nothing to do for the rest of the day except play Monopoly and drink hot chocolate while the wind screams through the trees outside.

* * *

"Can you hear me? They say sometimes people can, even if they are in a coma. It's possible.

"So just in case you can hear me, I'll tell you what I know. You are in the Bir Hospital in Kathmandu. It is a very fine hospital, the oldest and busiest in Nepal.

"You had a road accident. You were on a motorbike. No one else was involved. We think you came to Nepal from India. You were up on a mountain road beyond Pokhara, heading towards the Annapurna Mountain range. We cannot understand why you were there.

"The police brought you from there to this hospital by plane. This is normal. I must tell you that you have been quite badly injured, but please try not to worry, you are doing very well. I hope you are comfortable and not feeling too much pain. We have a problem because we cannot identify you. We don't know who you are or where you have come from. We would like to let someone know you are here, but this has not been possible. One day you will come back to us and then we will know. I look forward to meeting you very much."

Dr Sharma looked closely at the boy's face and hands but there was no response at all, no sign that he had heard anything. He sighed and sat down, lost in thought.

* * *

The boy grabs onto this new information like a drowning man. Is the doctor telling the truth or is this another trick?

"OK, OK. I'll answer your questions," the boy says. "But first, you have to tell me what's really going on here. What have they done to me? Where are they? What's going to happen to me when they come back?"

He waits expectantly in the dark, but the doctor doesn't hear him.

He's in Kathmandu, yes. He's OK with that. He was in Kathmandu before. But could he really have come from India? Surely he would remember. But he is certain he has never been to India.

Hang on! He remembers crossing some sort of border. There's a messy tangle of buses, rickshaws, bicycles and luggage. The noise is unbelievable, horns, music, shouting. He can't understand what the immigration officers are saying to him. He's trying to find out whether he should change his Indian rupees into Nepalese ones. Nobody tells him.

Then he's through, in a herd of charging traffic and people, into no man's land and through the stucco archway on the other side. Welcome to Nepal, say the hand-painted letters above the road. Triangular red national flags and crested insignia are painted on either side, making it look more like the entrance to a yacht club than a country.

Getting into Nepal feels like a huge relief. So the doctor's right, he was in India. But he needs to put India behind him. There's something black and frightening there.

* * *

When Dr Sharma got back to his office, the two policemen were there again, waiting for him. Their question hung silently in the air until the doctor shook his head and shrugged his shoulders, holding his hands out palms upward in a gesture of helplessness.

"Nothing, I'm afraid. Not a flicker. It's still too early to tell when it will be. But as I said, you will be the first to know. You?"

The older policeman spoke, "Nothing on the boy, no match to anyone reported missing. Nothing at all."

Chapter 4
Richard's Dinner

"Where's the star anise, Em? Em*ma*? Do we have any star anise in this blasted kitchen?"

Emma's father Richard crashed through the double doors of the drawing room sporting a diminutive apron, with shirt sleeves rolled up above bony elbows and demanding his daughter's attention. It was all very well she and Jackie lounging around chatting while he got on with all the hard work in the kitchen—which he really didn't mind doing—but there wasn't a moment to lose if the duck wasn't going to be ruined.

Emma's response was very gratifying. She jumped up immediately and followed him back to the kitchen, murmuring morale-boosting encouragement all the way. She found the star anise, of course, right at the back of the cupboard, and then calmly put away the sugar, cocoa, balsamic vinegar and all the other things that he had turfed out in the commotion.

As for Jackie, she had stayed firmly where she was with the latest issue of House and Garden, having quite clearly never even heard of star anise. But then she always was much more at home in drawing rooms than kitchens, bless her, at her best on a well-designed sofa with a glass of chilled champagne in her hand. Her experience of kitchens was strictly limited to designing them and they were usually so minimalistic that you'd be lucky to make a piece of toast in them.

But Richard was always happy to cook for his sister, his daughter and anyone else who he could persuade to drop round. In fact, he thoroughly enjoyed it. It was relaxing after a rigorous day at work and it seemed to meet some deep, primordial need to provide for his family as well. He refused to be constrained by recipes or even basic cookery techniques, which he considered not only completely unnecessary but a positive threat to his natural creativity. People were always very kind about the results so he must be doing something right, although it was true the kitchen usually needed spring cleaning at the end of it.

Besides, he would do anything for Jackie because he was heavily in her debt. Sometimes he wondered how he would have ever managed without her. Years ago, when he lost Frances, Jackie had helped him find the flat overlooking the park and turn it into a home for him and Emma. He wouldn't have had the first clue how to do that. Ever since then she had taken full responsibility for its elegance and maintenance. The two of them had always been close and although Jackie would have loved to have had children of her own, it hadn't happened— Emma was the only offspring either of them had managed to produce.

It had been pretty tough bringing Emma up as a single parent, especially when she was small and he was working as a junior lawyer, in the office all hours and sometimes through the night when there was a deal on. He'd hired Jessie by then to take care of the housekeeping. But as Emma grew up it dawned on him that there was a bit more to raising children than cooking and making beds, and he had turned to Jackie to fill the gap.

It had worked. Jackie had played the role of mother-but-not-mother with enthusiasm and skill, especially through Emma's teenage years which they had navigated with remarkably little angst. He liked to think that it made up in some small way for Jackie's childlessness, too. He was pleased and relieved that the two of them had emerged from it with such a close relationship and it always gave him great pleasure seeing them laughing together.

Jackie had always looked after him, too. He hadn't wanted to settle down with anyone else after Frances. Having made such a disastrous mistake with her he wasn't sure he could trust his judgement on women anymore. It had been so much easier to concentrate on his work, where people were generally much easier to deal with.

Anyway, he couldn't face that awful business of taking girls out to dinner, trying to work out whether he liked them and whether they liked him or just the dinner. Probably the latter in his case, as he didn't believe in eating in mediocre restaurants. And the one thing he wanted to avoid at all costs was aspiring stepmothers trying out their parenting skills on Emma during her formative years. There had been liaisons, yes, but nothing serious and even then strictly on the basis that his home life was out of bounds. He never spoke about them to Emma.

Fortunately, he loved his job. He had been made Senior Partner of his law firm a couple of years ago, an accolade which had been the cause of much celebration at Regent Mansions. Dealing with the firm's corporate clients was his forte and it had certainly helped him to get to the top. He had always understood that turning on the charm and telling the right jokes in the boardroom was just as important as any professional advice he might be there to dispense. But he liked to think it was also down to his sense of fair play and his determination to do what was right, even if it wasn't always in the firm's best interests.

There had been plenty of occasions when he had been put to the test on that one, but he had always stood firm and won through in the end. As a result, his clients and his colleagues trusted him and knew that he would not let them down. He had dealt with the issue of business entertaining by asking Jackie to accompany him. She was an absolute natural and it neatly solved the problem of either turning up on his own or with someone he hardly knew.

Fortunately, Jackie's long-suffering husband Robert took all this in his stride. Robert was an accountant at KPMG and it was obvious from the start that although he was perfectly competent he was never going to set the world on fire.

When he married Jackie Richard had thought his sister could have done better, although he kept this to himself. But as time went by he realised Jackie had more than enough fire for both of them and what she actually needed was Robert's steadiness. What he had seen as a weakness had turned out to be a strength and he had grown to like Robert and respect him for the support he gave Jackie. After all, they had a relationship that had stood the test of time, something that he was only too well aware he had failed to achieve himself.

Humming under his breath he turned the duck breasts over in the pan and looked at them approvingly as they simmered away in their raspberry and star anise sauce. Then he clamped the whole thing down with a tight-fitting lid and checked on the red cabbage and roast potatoes. Raymond Blanc it wasn't, sadly—Galloping Gourmet more like, he grinned to himself, as he hung up his apron and bounded off to join Jackie and Emma in the other room.

"And what are you two cooking up in here?" he teased them, seeing Emma exchanging glances with Jackie and clearly enjoying some little conspiracy.

It amused him to see them sitting side by side on the sofa sipping champagne, with opposite knees elegantly crossed towards each other, toes tipping up and down in time. The same diminutive figures, the same thick, bouncy hair falling into their eyes, the same habit of looking intently at one outstretched foot, the same infectious laugh which almost seemed to take them by surprise, throwing their heads back at the same angle. If it hadn't been for a generation's difference in fashion, they could have been sisters.

"Supper smells good, Dad! Look, Jackie's got something to show us."

"Oh, yes? So what have you got for us, my love?" he said, pouring himself a large glass of whisky and sinking into the sofa beside them with a contented sigh. How nice to have a bit of time to spend with his two favourite girls before the others arrived for dinner. He eyed up the picture frame Jackie had propped up back to front against the wall opposite and then chuckled at the expectant look on their faces.

"I do hope you'll like it, Richard—I think it's really rather interesting."

Jackie walked over to the picture and turned it round with a flourish.

"It's by a young, up-and-coming artist I've just come across, Fiona Rae. She was at Goldsmiths College with Damien Hirst. She's one of his Young British Artists."

Richard got up and scrutinised the painting with Emma, hardly noticing that Jackie had stopped speaking. It was an abstract, a chaotic assembly of coloured circles that looked like pastel bullseyes, with snatches of black and white paint dragged into curves and puffs, here a pale pink zig-zag, there a yellow bolt of lightning, all on a soft mauve background.

Richard immediately liked the bursts of energy coming from the picture. It had a busy, getting-on-with-it look which he could relate to, with its sharp contrasts and clear shapes. It was also undeniably modern, young and exciting, and the soft colours cut with the black and white made it attractive to look at. The problem was that the longer he looked at it, the more uncomfortable he felt. Something about it was fragmented, dislocated, unresolved. It seemed almost manic, as if the artist hadn't quite been able to keep up with the energy and ideas that she wanted to express. It was disturbing.

His Galloping Gourmet mood evaporating he looked across at Emma, who was still totally absorbed in the picture, and wondered what she would make of it. Over the years he had encouraged her to share his interest in modern art and he was very proud of how knowledgeable she had become. They usually agreed on what they liked and didn't like, more or less—it was something they both took seriously and discussed often, building up their own shared paradigm which

42

they applied to new pieces. This disordered jaggedness, exciting though it was, wasn't their usual style and he assumed she wouldn't like it.

But whatever it was about the picture that made him recoil from it seemed to have the opposite effect on Emma.

"It's fascinating. You know, it reminds me of something, I can't quite put my finger on what. There's something here that's familiar. I think it's rather good. Yes, I like it!"

As Jackie chatted on about the artist, explaining that the Saatchi Gallery were keen on her and that she had already been nominated for the Turner Prize, Richard tried hard not to dampen Emma's enthusiasm. But as he smiled and nodded he was wondering why she had identified with the picture so much when he had been repelled by it. He had a feeling he already knew—and that was what worried him.

* * *

An hour later, Richard sat at the head of the polished dining table and surveyed the scene, his mood restored to its usual buoyant authority. He had invited Mark Holden, a fellow lawyer and friend of many years' standing, to join them for dinner. Mark was deep in conversation with Jackie about Salman Rushdie's latest book The Satanic Verses and Ayatollah Khomeini's subsequent *fatwa*. Although somewhat outside the scope of Jackie's day-to-day repartee with fabric designers in Fulham Road she was holding her own as the argument turned this way and that.

Jackie's husband Robert, who had come straight from work and as a result had a rather unhealthy grey tinge to him, was talking to Emma.

"And what has my favourite niece been up to lately?" he asked. "Where's that young man of yours got to? I hope he's behaving himself or he'll have me to answer to."

"AND Dad—" Emma wriggled in her chair and examined her cheese knife as she began to talk about Joe. "He's fine, everything's fine. He'd be here only he's gone to a work dinner—one of those black tie things at Grosvenor House." She looked up and smiled to show it was true, everything really was OK. "Actually, he's doing really well. He's on Fidelity's graduate trainee programme and he's already passed his first lot of exams—and he's only been there a year.

He's working as an analyst at the moment, but one day he'll become a fund manager if all goes well."

Robert looked suitably impressed.

"Is he enjoying it?"

"Oh, yes, I think so—I think he could really get somewhere if he works hard. He's ambitious, especially considering his father's been plodding along out in the wilds of Somerset all his life. Joe isn't like that at all. And he really has to use his brain in this job, too. He likes mental challenges. He got a First at Bristol, you know—in Religion and Theology."

Robert looked surprised.

"I know! There's a lot more to Joe than meets the eye—you'll have to get to know him a bit better. Yes, he wrote his dissertation about the religions of ancient India. You don't want to get into an argument with him about religion unless you're prepared to stay up all night…"

Emma tucked a lock of hair behind her ear as she laughed with Robert, then immediately untucked it again.

"What about you, Uncle Bob? What have you been up to?"

Robert had taken his tie off and was rolling it into a neat ball. "Oh, same old same old, you know. Someone's got to keep the show on the road—Jackie's the one who has all the excitement in our family. Now. Don't tell a soul, but I'm taking her to a lovely little hotel I've found in Cornwall for our anniversary— it's a surprise. But you have to help me. How am I going to get her packed and into the car without an interrogation worthy of MI5?"

The duck 'a la framboise', or Regent Duck as it had now been christened, had all been consumed with great gusto and now a ripe Reblochon was going round, followed by a basketful of seeded crackers. Richard didn't approve of puddings. After a few glasses of Richard's very drinkable claret, Mark's voice was getting noticeably louder and more emphatic.

"The objection to The Satanic Verses has been very disappointing. This country has an enshrined right to freedom of expression. I believe that is absolutely fundamental."

"Well, I don't see why Rushdie has to be so—inflammatory. Does he have to go around deliberately upsetting people? It's all very well defending our right to freedom of speech, I'm all for that. But he's putting other people's lives in danger, quite unnecessarily. And who gets to pay the bill for his 24-hour police protection? WE do, Mark, and it must cost a fortune! Is that really fair?" Jackie could not have sounded more affronted if she was personally writing the cheque.

"It's not just about Rushdie, it's the principle of the thing. We have to stand up for our values or we are in grave danger of losing them."

Emma exchanged grins with her father as she pulled her chair further under the table and leaned her elbows on the thick leather of her placemat.

"I hope it's not too boring for you, darling, hanging around with a bunch of old farts like us."

"Dad! Firstly, you're hardly an old fart and neither's Jackie. And secondly, this is my family, remember? You, Jackie, Robert—you're all I've got! You know I always love it when everyone's here. Oh and thirdly, how would you ever get the use out of your brand new, unbelievably expensive, family-size frying pan otherwise? I didn't spend the entire morning in Divertimenti with you last Saturday for nothing!"

"Fair point, darling. Fair point."

Richard noticed Jackie trying to catch Robert's eye. He gave Mark a meaningful glance and then turned to his sister.

"Robert looks tired, Jackie—his conference in Athens seems to have knocked the stuffing out of him a bit. I hope it didn't wear him out too much, all that high finance?"

"Oh, *Richard*! No, actually it's me that needs to go home now because I'm off to Geneva at the crack of dawn. I've got an American client out there with a new chalet in Villars to do up. Oh yes, darling, underground pool and gym, home cinema, everything coated in lashings of fur—such fun! Robert and I are looking forward to our skiing invitation already!"

"Sounds like you're busy then!"

"Why, do you need something for the flat? I'm sure I can squeeze it in somewhere."

"I need you to go home and get your beauty sleep before I have to throw you out of here."

* * *

Emma cleared the table with her father and piled up the plates in the kitchen for Jessie to deal with the next morning, along with a fleet of glasses, the Divertimenti frying pan, assorted casseroles and roasting tins, a very congested sieve, the Magimix and a pinkish gravy-spattered hob. Then they both repaired to the relative order of the drawing room for a breather before they went to bed.

"Your duck was a huge success, Dad."

"Yes, I do believe it was. Did you have a good evening, darling? It was rather fun, wasn't it? Mark's always good value and he was on cracking form tonight."

They sat in companionable silence for a while. Emma knew Mark fairly well and she was always pleased to see Jackie and Robert. She laughed to herself as she remembered her conversation with her uncle—he always managed to make her feel special somehow. Maybe that was why she was so fond of him. She wondered whether her father went through his old conversations in his mind like that too, but it seemed unlikely. At the moment, it didn't look like there could possibly be anything going on behind those tortoiseshell glasses at all.

Then something seemed to galvanise him and he sprang up out of the sofa to take a closer look at the picture Jackie had brought.

"You know I'm surprised you like it so much, Em. Tell me what you like about it," he said, turning to look at her.

"Why—don't you like it?"

She could hear the hesitancy in her voice. Perhaps it had been a mistake to say what she thought about the picture until she had gauged her father's reaction. It always made her uncomfortable when he disagreed with her, and having to defend her position under interrogation was even worse—for some reason, her mind would go completely blank and she would no longer be capable of stringing even a simple sentence together.

But thankfully her father had decided to be a bit more tactful on this occasion.

"It's not that I don't like it exactly, but I'm not sure I could live with it, you know? You don't know quite where you are with it. There's no focal point— every time you manage to latch on to something, something else seems to drag you away. You want to look at it but it keeps—getting away."

"Yes—but I suppose that's what I find fascinating. It makes you want to go on to the next thing and the next, and you feel that there's no end to it, that—that there's no limit to where you could go with it if you wanted to."

Richard looked at her in alarm.

"What's the matter, Dad? Have I said something wrong?"

"Not at all, darling, no. Sorry. You reminded me of—something."

"Something? What do you mean?"

"Nothing."

"What did I remind you of, Dad? It was something about my mother, wasn't it."

"I said, it was *nothing*."

She knew there was no point in going on—the subject was closed. It was always the same. She wondered why she bothered at all when every time she tried to talk about her mother it just caused a horrible row. But at least this time her father seemed keen to make up for his moment of bad temper. He came and sat down next to her, patting her on the knee in what she took to be a conciliatory fashion. She relented and smiled back.

"Anyway, how are things? How are you getting on?"

"Yes, fine. Joe's sorry he couldn't come this evening. Did I tell you he's taking me to Paris for my birthday? Yes, I know! Very exciting. And work's fine—today was pretty boring. Honestly—didn't you ever get fed up with all the photocopying and stuff when you were doing your training? I keep wondering if this was what I spent three years at university and then a year at law school for."

"Welcome to the real world, darling! Don't worry, it'll get better. We all have to start somewhere. Oh yes, I remember it well."

He put his arm around her shoulders and gave her a sympathetic squeeze.

"Any thoughts about what you want to go for when you've finished your training?"

"Well—" She hesitated, hoping that now they had managed to get the conversation back on an even keel her father would not disapprove of what she was about to say or that she would not be too downcast if he did.

"I was thinking that maybe I'd quite like to work in-house, on the client side, once I've got some experience. I need to find out a bit more about it—I'm not really sure yet."

But Richard smiled and gave her another hug. "Good idea, darling! You'll be one of my clients one day! Wouldn't that be fun!"

"Do you think I really could, Dad?"

"Of course! You could do anything you wanted. I'm so proud of you, Em."

It was Richard who had encouraged her to do her degree in law, and he had been thrilled when she had followed his advice. She had chosen a London university, too, after he had been utterly scathing about universities in almost all other parts of the country. It had certainly been a lot more comfortable to carry on living at Regent Mansions, but anyway he regarded the notion of some grotty suburban flat with a bunch of unwashed students for flatmates as completely ridiculous when she already had a perfectly good home in London.

After Law School (chosen by him), he had helped her find articles with a small London law firm he knew. He always claimed that he was merely acting in her best interests, but she liked to think that it was also because he wanted her to carry on keeping him company. The truth was that it suited them both.

Her confidence boosted again, Emma changed the subject.

"Actually, there *is* one thing I'm a bit worried about—well, it's Alex. I haven't heard from him for quite a while and neither has Joe. We're not sure where he is. We've had the odd postcard but they haven't made much sense—he sounds completely out of it. And they've been from the oddest of places. We're worried something might have gone wrong—you know what he's like. But how would we know? How long do you wait before you decide someone's gone missing? And what are you supposed to do about it?"

"Woah! Hang on! I'm sure he's absolutely fine, Em. He's *definitely* not a missing person. You've always worried too much about him. He's better off out of the way at the moment. After all, he went travelling to give you and Joe a bit of breathing space. Perhaps he's just being tactful. Kinder to give him a bit of breathing space too. He's actually done the right thing for once. Just let him be, Em."

Emma knew her father wasn't a big fan of Alex's. He didn't seem to understand what she saw in him, dismissing him as 'a bit of a drifter' and 'a bad influence'. He'd failed to hide his relief when Alex left and probably thought (and hoped) that was the last they'd see of him. So she couldn't really expect him to understand why she was worried now, just because he hadn't been in touch. And it didn't make much sense to her either. She just had an uneasy feeling she would never see him again.

"You're probably right, Dad."

At least he approved of Joe, thank goodness.

Chapter 5
Lorna's Funeral

In the Bir Hospital in Kathmandu, the boy's memory stirs.

* * *

The little car park half way up the hill is already full of cars and everyone is walking in single file through the gate and up the steep path through the graveyard. They are high up, behind them you can see for miles across Exmoor. Behind them there are new-born lambs still close to their mothers, daffodils in the hedgerows, blossom on bare twigs, cold blue sky, new life. In front of them is the whitewashed church, stark against the dark woods behind.

They are arriving at a funeral. It is his mother's.

He's feeling numb. The last few days have been weird. His mother's dead body has been removed from the house and put away somewhere, no one wants to ask where. The depth of his father's misery is unfathomable. So many things to do, people to call, decisions to make. The dining room has become an ops room, the table covered in papers, letters, hymns and to-do lists. Do they make it that way so you don't have to think about it? But it doesn't go away, does it, it's there all the time, just beneath the surface, so real it isn't real. Like being in a tunnel.

They walk to the front of the church, he and his brother, holding their father between them. He can feel sympathy rising from the congregation like heat off the tarmac on a hot day. It helps, even if all that emotion makes him less steady. Then he sees her coffin already there in the nave of the church and it's like being hit in the solar plexus. Pale wood. Florist flowers. Is she really in there? Her dead body hadn't looked like her. Peaceful, but vacant. Lips too plump, skin too smooth, expression too bland. Her earthly remains. It had been quite clear that she herself was long gone.

They slide into the polished pew, two boys with their father hunched between them, and he wonders how hard it will be to stop his father from breaking down in racking, embarrassing sobs. She'd have got them through this. Without her it's like travelling in a foreign country.

His numbness wears off during the first hymn and he starts to take in what's going on. The church is small but it's full of half-familiar faces, respectful black clothes. She died before her time. People are not ready—he can feel them thinking, she was no age. It could have been me. Then he realises that she's right here, she's in the church right now. Not in the coffin, but all around them. Above the altar, reflecting in the stained glass windows, weaving through the congregation. There's no doubt about it, it's almost like a physical presence. He breathes deeply to make room in his chest for another wave of sadness and the smell of lilies almost knocks him out.

The hymn ends, the congregation sits down, people rustle and shuffle in the pews, check the order of service. His brother gets up and walks to the lectern, his heels clicking in the respectful silence that has fallen. His dark hair is neat above the collar of his dark wool suit. When did he get so self-assured? He clears his throat, takes his time. Everyone holds their breath.

"For those of you who don't know, my mother—Lorna—was diagnosed with breast cancer in February of last year. It was already at an advanced stage and I think she had known about it for some time. But you know, she wasn't afraid.

"They told her she needed extensive surgery followed by reconstruction and chemotherapy, but she refused to have the treatment. We all begged her to change her mind, but she still refused. She knew how ill she was and she had already faced up to the fact that she was going to die, but in the meantime, she wanted to go on living. As usual, she showed us how to accept the situation with grace and the most remarkable courage.

"And you know, as usual, she was absolutely right. With no surgery or chemo to cope with, we were able to look after her at home and we could keep on talking until we had said everything, we needed to say. Christmas was a very special time for us, knowing it was probably her last, but it was a happy time and one that we will treasure. She died peacefully last Saturday, at home, and we were all with her right up to the end. I can tell you that she was not in pain, she was not afraid—she was ready. She was extraordinary."

He pauses and takes a long look at his notes, composing himself for the next bit. The congregation collectively breathes out.

"With Dad's help, Mum created a happy home and a strong, loving family for my brother and I to grow up in and I would like to thank her now, publicly, for that. I am starting to understand how important that has been in making me who I am.

"Everyone here today will know a different Lorna. You might have played bridge with her or sang in the choir with her. She did the night shift once a month for the Samaritans in Taunton, just being there on the end of a telephone for anyone who needed her. Although I know she wasn't an easy person to get to know, those who knew her found her to be a loyal friend.

"She loved her home, her garden, her decorating, sewing, reading—she loved her life. And she had an extraordinarily powerful influence on everyone around her, not just her family. People say it was that quiet certainty she had, that calmness, that groundedness about her which just reassured you. She had it sorted. I like to think that she died because she had done everything she came here to do. She's gone on ahead while we all stumble about in the dark trying to figure it out.

"She wanted her funeral to be here. We had plenty of time to talk about it. She loved going for walks through the woods behind here up to Selworthy Beacon and she always came into the church before she went home. She said she found it peaceful. She wasn't a religious person in the traditional sense—she didn't go to Sunday services because she said they were far too noisy. I know what she means, actually. But she was one of the most spiritual people I know.

"She chose her own readings for today and I'm going to read you this one, *Footprints in the Sand.*"

And off he goes. He stumbles over the last couple of words of the poem, grabs at his notes and sweeps back to the pew, head bowed. The vicar sits in thoughtful silence for a moment, allowing people time to compose themselves, and then rises purposefully, launching the organist and congregation into *Be Still My Soul*.

The front row is not singing, a growl being the most that they can collectively manage at the best of times. Music has always been Lorna's department. His brother puts an arm around their father, who has tears rolling silently down his cheeks. He's impressed by how much his brother seems to have grown up suddenly. There's no way on earth he can compete with that.

The church has disappeared. He is barefoot, wearing some sort of loose white cotton pyjamas, and he is sitting cross-legged on the floor in a little round temple full of other cross-legged people. It's deeply peaceful. There's a smoky smell of incense in the air which reminds him of something if he could only remember what. The sun is just coming up, lifting the darkness in the temple, but it is already hot.

He is talking to himself. *Tune in to the stillness. Observe your breath. Bring your attention to the breath as it crosses the skin below your nose.*

He is at an ashram which must be somewhere in India. He is learning to meditate. He is sleepy because he has just got out of bed and it is very early in the morning. He is also hungry. But he is really trying to get this right and it's difficult. He brings his attention back to his breath again and concentrates on the movement of his ribs, squeezing the air in and out of his lungs. *Let your mind come to stillness. Observe the thoughts drifting through your mind and then just—let them go.* So simple, really.

Sometimes he feels a sense of contentment, a feeling that everything is going to be all right. Other times he just falls asleep or finds himself wondering what is for lunch. Or breakfast. Bread and jam. Parathas, pickle, curd, scrambled eggs. Probably some sort of lentil curry. And a large cup of milky coffee—yeah right. Bugger. Lost it again.

He opens his eyes and crosses his legs the other way, looking around the room to see if he is disturbing anyone. But no, they are all sitting absolutely still, eyelids gently closed, apparently getting the hang of it perfectly well. Lucky bastards. He watches the smoke from the incense stick rising and twisting upwards in the still air. The pain in his hips and knees is getting worse, he's not at all sure he is designed for sitting cross-legged.

He can't sit on his 'sit bones' anymore because they're hurting too. But other than that it feels all right, being here. Home seems a distant memory and that's good. He doesn't want to think about home. They keep telling you here just to leave everything as it is and that suits him fine.

The person sitting next to him is someone he knows. It's his friend Scott. He met Scott somewhere along the way, he can't remember exactly where. He likes Scott and it's good to have a friend here with him. He's pleased that Scott seems to be getting it—he's sitting there like all the others, eyes closed, absorbed. Although Scott is tall and lean, built like a sportsman, they both know that he is fragile inside.

The boy nods, content. Then he closes his eyes again and breathes in, trying to sense the air moving in and out of his nose.

* * *

He is back at the funeral and it's his turn to walk up the steps to the lectern. He makes it without falling down. He starts to speak in a low voice, which falters and then gathers strength.

"I am Lorna's and James's adopted son. My name is Alex."

"They say if you are adopted you're special because your parents chose you. I think that's a load of rubbish actually—but I do know I was lucky to have James and Lorna as my adoptive parents. They're the only parents I've ever wanted.

"My brother Joe spoke beautifully about our mother just now and it's not easy to add to that. I'm not like Joe—I wasn't clever at school and I always seemed to get into trouble. Still do, in fact. So you see, I needed a lot of help. Lorna saved me. I hope I never disappoint her."

He looked intently at the cobalt blue glass in one of the aisle windows and waited for the lump in his throat to go down.

"I know she is here with us now, today. I'm trying to think of this as her leaving party. All her friends are here to see her off. We all have our own stories and memories of her. She's done brilliantly here but it's time for her to move on. Perhaps she's got another life to go to somewhere else, who knows? And although we'll miss her, we know it's the right thing for her. We'll see her again, but not here. We'll all keep in touch with her in our own way. She knows we wish her well and we have to be happy for her, we have to let her go. Because if we are sad it will only make it harder for her to leave."

From the front pew, his father gives him a watery smile for the first time in days.

* * *

Another dream and the boy—Alex—wonders where he is. In this dream, he has just woken up and all his bones are aching like hell. His iron bed is narrow and lumpy, with a mattress he doesn't want to think too much about. He is wearing most of his clothes because he is covered only by a thin grey blanket and it's freezing. There are urns of jaunty flowers painted on the whitewashed walls beside him, but it doesn't disguise the fact that the room is primitive. Cold air is seeping through the cracks around the wooden beams and timbers and the weak morning light is flowing unimpeded through the bare windows.

He has been woken by the sound of muezzin wailing into their microphones from the tops of minarets across town, calling people to prayer. He is both thrilled and alienated by the sound.

He knows that outside, beyond the building's wooden balustrade, there's a sandstone landscape dotted with sea green minarets, sculpted sandcastles, colonnades and fortresses. He knows there are hidden treasures down there because he has seen them—a tiled turquoise bird of paradise surrounded by whorls of Arabic script, a carved wooden door and of course, carpets, always the best quality.

If you're not careful you accept a glass of mint tea—no obligation, of course—and before you know it, a bevy of gap-toothed Uzbeks has herded you into a darkened room piled high with carpets and every single one is being unfurled with a flap and a flourish. Come on, guys. Do I look like someone in the market for a carpet?

Already he can smell the fatty smoke of meat being cooked on open fires in the street below. It gets in your clothes, like the sand and the dust, and he's been travelling for a while now. People have been moving across these Asian miles for centuries, that's what the caravanserais are for. He is travelling by bus but otherwise, it is much the same. He has forgotten where he came from and where he is going, so he just keeps moving on.

* * *

The funeral is over and the cars are streaming up the gravel drive to the house, past the front door and into the field, which the farmer's boys from across the road have turned into a car park with sacking and straw to cover up the worst of the mud. Now they're coaxing the cars into imaginary bays, just as if they were cows in the milking parlour back at the farm. Dad and Joe have gone to the cemetery, the business end of the funeral. He and Emma are in charge of the tea.

The blue sky is long gone and it has started to rain. People are arriving with coats and umbrellas, bringing the cold in with them through the thick oak front door. Somehow Emma has found a couple of fan heaters to plug in and she's pressganged a relay of teenagers to hang coats on the hooks further down the hall too. The umbrellas are dripping away into the log basket; so presumably, there must be a pile of logs turfed out on the floor somewhere.

Now she has stationed herself behind the dining room table, which she has covered with a white linen cloth, pouring out cups of tea. How does she know how to do all this stuff? Her face is pale, with dark rings under her eyes. She looks over at him, catches his eye and smiles, to keep him going.

Lorna's presence in the house grabs you round the throat and it reminds you of the ridiculousness of her death. Over the past few days he has got used to this, but now he sees it again on every face. Without Dad and Joe here he has become the lightning rod for this tide of emotion. Family friends and relatives are coming up to him one after another and unburdening themselves of their shock, their sadness, even their anger at the unjustness of it all. There's almost a queue.

It's the first time he has really understood that adults are people too, people who have messy emotions they can't always deal with. They seem to be looking to him of all people for comfort, God knows why. He supposes this is a ritual that has to be gone through and they are trying to be kind, with their gentle voices, a hand on the elbow or an arm around the shoulder. He knows he has to play his part too, with just the right mixture of sadness and acceptance, although he's mostly messing it up. He even knows that they will all feel better about it afterwards, even him. But my God, it's hard. It's sucking the life out of him.

He makes an excuse and bolts into the kitchen where Emma is filling the kettle again. Joe stamps in through the back door, shaking out his umbrella. He asks where Dad is and Joe says he is outside getting a breath of air in the garden. In the pouring rain. They all look at each other, unable to deal with this level of loss. Then the two boys follow Emma and the teapot back out to the coal face.

* * *

Whoever you may be, come. He's reading poetry by Rumi, a Sufi mystic from the thirteenth century. It's quite good. He's in Konya and it's pretty intense— seriously religious, full of half-crazed mystics. The men are mostly heavily bearded, like Fidel Castro replicas, and the women wear headscarves that swamp the whole top half of their bodies.

They call Rumi Mevlana here. He's been to Mevlana's tomb, that's where he got the poetry. Mevlana believed in love. More fool him. But he did get made a saint, so he must have got something right. They have whirling dervishes here, they actually exist. They wear swirly white skirts and brown felt hats and they whirl round and round until they're in some sort of sacred trance. Or just bewildered, presumably, which is how he feels most of the time, without any whirling at all.

He arrived in Konya on a bus from Istanbul and now he's on another bus, in Cappadocia. He has just woken up, but he's still tired. They pass mile upon mile of pointy little mountains, worn away like stumps of rotten teeth. They're riddled with caves and sometimes they stop and visit houses, churches, whole villages burrowed out of the rock by troglodytes thousands of years ago. Who are troglodytes anyway? Weren't they in Lord of the Rings?

They stop to drink Turkish coffee and watch an old Turkish woman baking flatbread over a wood fire. They all eat some. This encourages a wave of camaraderie from his fellow travellers, but he doesn't respond. He doesn't want to have to explain what he's doing here. He's not sure himself.

* * *

The cars have swept away, most of them, and there's a hard core of family left lingering in the hall. A couple of cousins from Yorkshire. No one's quite sure where they fit in but they're very friendly, very sympathetic. Funny how funerals bring people out of the woodwork. A rather formal aunt and uncle, she in a hat, who can't seem to work up the momentum to leave.

A couple with a baby, more cousins. These ones he did know. Rachel and Steve, who'd come down from Reading. They had got married late and immediately embarked on reproducing, which they took very seriously. Now they were rarely separated from their children, even though you had to wonder whether a funeral was really the right place for them.

Steve's mother had been Lorna's godmother, back in the day, and Steve had taken it upon himself to maintain the connection. Good of them to come, really. God knows what the baby was called. Emma in stockinged feet, down on the floor trying to entertain the baby's older brother, also nameless, as far as he was concerned anyway. She hadn't wanted to ask her own father to the funeral; he wondered why.

It all seemed to have gone well if you could ever describe a funeral as having gone well. It had been well attended, which is all you could hope for really. No one had broken down and sobbed uncontrollably. There had been enough tea.

People's sadness had been assuaged. His mother's body had been dealt with. So what happens now? Are they all supposed to just get on with their lives as if nothing had happened?

His father obviously thinks so. Already back in his cords and a matted old jumper, he shuffles past the various cousins and announces he's off to take the dog for a walk, apparently unaware that it's dark outside and still pouring. People smile and then exchange worried glances as soon as he's gone.

"Let him go," Joe says. "Poor dad. He's got to deal with it in his own way."

Haven't we all, thought Alex.

* * *

He's clutching his knees to his chest on the largest, flattest boulder he can find, staring out to sea. It's supposed to be good for swimming here but there's not much sand, just rocks. If you half close your eyes you can pretend you're in Cornwall, almost.

South Cornwall though—there are no cliffs, so surging, sucking Atlantic surf. It even rained less than an hour ago. It seems an unlikely place for a palace but there is one and also the remains of luxurious private houses with ornamental gardens all along the beachfront, dotted with palm trees. It looks a bit like the cover of Hotel California, just a tattered memory of exotic summers idled away by the Shah and his crowd in the days when Iran was still Persia.

Now it's all the Ayatollah's and the feeling here is less than thrilled. It's all hijabs and chadors, mullahs and fatwas and all the usual fear and suspicion that goes with an oppressive regime or perhaps he's imagining it. Perhaps it's just his own sombre mood which makes it seem such a dump. The Caspian Sea should be romantic, exciting, mythical. Shouldn't it? But it turns out that one sea is pretty much like another in the end. Grey, deep.

He's swimming now. He's left his clothes in a heap beside his rucksack on the boulder. Swimming naked is undoubtedly verboten but he doesn't care and the beach is deserted anyway.

He's picked his way across the rocks and paddled out beyond the waves. He's picked up a rhythm, a steady kick with his arms slicing cleanly through the water. His sports master at the West Somerset Community College would have been cheered to see it. A slight roll, probably not strictly necessary on style grounds, but it's keeping the water out of his eyes. Not that it's that salty, anyway. The light is starting to fade. Back in the town, the prayer mats will be coming out but he won't be there to see them tonight.

And then that's all there is—left, right, left, right. That's all he has to think about. No past, no future. Just this, now, these arms pulling him forward one by one, this water sliding past his skin, this empty horizon. If he keeps swimming, perhaps he'll swim out of this world completely, leaving hardly a ripple behind him. He keeps going.

Chapter 6
Saturday in London

"So do you think I should talk to Jackie then?" Emma asked Joe, frowning at her egg and bacon sandwich and picking the fatty bits of bacon out of it. "She must know *something* about my mother. And no, it's no good asking Dad. He just won't talk about it and it only causes a row. And I can't stand that."

Emma had become so preoccupied with finding out once and for all what her mother had been like that she had asked Joe to meet her for an emergency lunch on the steps of St Paul's Cathedral, which happened to be roughly half way between Fidelity and Withers & Co. She knew Joe had a bit of a thing about St Paul's and would happily turn up there on the flimsiest of pretexts. In fact, it was a miracle she had not yet been subjected to the full Joe Russell trademark tour, but she had made it quite clear on the phone that that was not the purpose of today's visit.

But the steps were as good a place as any to sit and talk and she and Joe were perched side by side in the autumn sunshine, dwarfed by the massive classical portico behind them. They both had white paper sandwich bags balanced on their knees and they were doing their best to keep the mayonnaise away from their work suits, which they were still self-conscious about wearing.

Emma looked up at Joe's familiar face, hair springing up from his otherwise neat head after a heavy morning's analysing, and smiled with relief. Being able to meet up like this, having a running dialogue, being part of each other's lives, was a lot better than wondering what he had been doing for the last four days and why he hadn't called her.

"Joe? I think I should, don't you? Talk to Jackie. About my mother."

"Yeah, sure. Why not?" he shrugged, as if they were back in the sandwich shop discussing whether to buy a Kit Kat.

"But Em, are you sure you can handle whatever might come out of it? Maybe there's a reason why you don't know much about her. Maybe it's better that way."

Emma considered this and then dismissed it. How could you not want to know about your own mother? Of course she could handle it. Anyway, she'd cross that bridge when she came to it.

"And," Joe added, "if Jackie does come up with the goods, surely she'll have to tell your father? She wouldn't do it behind his back, would she?"

"I know, that's the thing. It's bound to upset him and I don't want to ruin things between us. He's the only parent I've got, after all."

"Exactly."

"Joe! You don't want me to do this, do you?"

"Em, I want you to be happy. If you think it will make you happy, then go ahead and do it. I'm just worried that you might get more than you bargained for, that's all. I don't want you to be upset."

He put an arm around her shoulders and she leaned against him, oblivious to the patchwork of lunchtime secretaries and tourists picnicking all around them. Joe made her feel safe and right now she couldn't see how knowing more about her mother could be anything but a good thing.

"I always thought it was odd that Alex never wanted to know about his birth parents."

"I don't think he thought about it that much, he just accepted it. He always knew he was adopted, it was never a secret. He was only a baby. He always considered Mum and Dad to be his parents. I don't remember him ever mentioning his birth parents, I don't think it was a big deal for him. But then he knew absolutely nothing about them anyway so there wouldn't have been much point in him wondering. Perhaps that made it easier in a way."

"I've never understood that. Surely they must have had to sign adoption papers or something? They must have known who his mother was at least. How can you adopt someone without knowing who their parents are?"

"It wasn't like that. Mum and Dad had already had me and they weren't planning to adopt a child at all. I think they were asked if they would have Alex because he'd been abandoned. I'm not sure exactly how it all happened but they were thinking of having another child and I don't think Mum wanted to turn him away. You know what Mum could be like—she thought it was fate that brought Alex to us, that it was meant to be. I do know he had nothing except the shawl he was wrapped in when he arrived and we never knew exactly where he came from. That's the way she always talked to Alex about it and he just accepted it."

"Mmm. Yes, I think he did."

She flapped away the pigeons scrapping over the bacon fat around her feet, brushed the crumbs from the front of her jacket and screwed up the paper bag into a ball.

"Have you got any plans for this weekend?"

"Dad's coming up—Southampton are playing away at Chelsea."

"I think I might go to Kensington Market then if you're going to be watching football." Emma rolled her eyes. "And there's a party with Shula's lot on Saturday evening—d'you want to come?"

For once, Joe looked uncomfortable. "Do you mind if I don't, Em? They're Alex's crowd really and anyway I'll have Dad. Look, why don't we take Dad out for something to eat and then you can go on to the party afterwards and I'll take him home. That should keep everyone happy."

"Brilliant idea!" She kissed him goodbye and headed back to the office. As usual, talking to Joe had made it all seem much simpler. She would ask Jackie about her mother and then she would know.

* * *

It was Saturday afternoon by the time Emma got to Kensington market and by then it was pretty busy. Although the day was half gone she had had a good lie-in, which she had badly needed. She and her father had had a proper cooked breakfast for once, plus croissants, marmalade and all the newspapers. She'd even gone back to bed for a bit and listened to some music, then spent a happy hour reorganising her entire music collection before eventually changing out of her pyjamas into something she could actually travel on the tube in.

With Joe at the football all afternoon, she was looking forward to going shopping and her hard-earned cash was burning a hole in her pocket. A perfect Saturday. Or it would be if only she could stop worrying about Alex.

She was drawn to several jewellery stalls as she wandered into the market and she was inspecting some moonstone earrings—their milky whiteness had something mysterious about it which appealed to her—when she was hit by a wave of nostalgia. It was something to do with that sweet, earthy smell—what was it? It reminded her of something, something so familiar, but then it slipped away again. She breathed it in deeply. She loved that smell. Patchouli, wasn't it?

Forgetting everything else she tracked the heady scent down to its source, which turned out to be a new-age shop thick with the smoke of incense and haunting native American music. Standing guard by the door was an amethyst crystal in a sleeve of rock almost as big as she was, like purple seeds inside a massive pod.

When her eyes adjusted to the semi-darkness inside, she could see Indian headdresses and a quiver of arrows on the walls, hand-woven rugs and blankets, tables loaded with runes and polished crystals, drawers spilling open with scarves and shawls pouring onto the bare floorboards below. She leaned down to peer at something she couldn't quite make out in the darkness and then recoiled when she realised it was the bleached skeleton of a huge bear paw.

"Have you come to have your cards done, dear?" A soothing, disembodied voice came out of the darkness. Emma looked over her shoulder, wondering if it was addressing her or someone else. But no, it was just her.

"You're here to have your Tarot cards done, I think?"

She could see the owner of the voice now, a rather brittle, dry woman. There was a curtain half-drawn across an alcove at the back of the shop and she could just see a table and two chairs behind it. Of course, she knew what Tarot cards were, but then, what did they look like? She had never seen any.

She had a feeling it could be dangerous to have your cards read, like going to a seance. You could be tempting evil spirits or something. Wasn't there a death card that you weren't meant to get? But the woman didn't seem to be waiting for an answer and anyway it would be a bit of an adventure to tell Joe and the others about later. Emma obediently followed her behind the curtain and sat down.

"We'll do your palm first, my love."

Emma found her familiarity comforting. She watched as the woman switched on a desk lamp on the table between them and got out a huge magnifying glass. She looked surprisingly ordinary, not witch-like at all, although her skin was a little pale and papery and her black hair was thin and broken at the ends. She was dressed simply in a pale grey polo neck and a clear crystal pendant with a filigree setting in a pretty leaf pattern, not unlike the moonstone earrings she'd been looking at. Then Emma noticed that in spite of the semi-darkness, the pupils of her eyes were tiny as if she was looking into a bright light.

"Ahhh—yes. You've got a nice steady lifeline. That's good—although your early years look a little unsettled. There's some confusion—did you lose your mother?" she looked up abruptly.

Emma nodded, surprised.

"But yes—I think you're on the right path. And here I can see a strong relationship and it will last—a good man, my dear. Yes, he will bring you happiness."

She switched off the lamp and reached for a fat pack of cards, which she shuffled thoughtfully for a moment or two and then handed to Emma.

"Take the cards and give them a good shuffle, that's it—now think hard about what you want the cards to tell you."

Emma felt a bit silly now. How ridiculous, asking the cards a question! Presumably it would have to be something simple, with a yes or no answer. The woman had already told her about Joe. So she thought about what was uppermost in her mind—is Alex all right? Is Alex all right? The cards were battered and dog-eared and there seemed to be a lot more than 52 of them, but they felt surprisingly light as she shuffled.

"All right, dear, that's enough. Now divide them into three piles, just roughly. And put them back together again in any order you like. Now once more. That's it."

She took the pack from Emma and started to deal the cards out onto the rich velvet tablecloth in the shape of a cross and then added another four cards in a column up the right-hand side until there were ten cards on the table. They both leaned in expectantly. The cards were beautiful, a sea of soft colours and pictures. The illustrations were almost childlike in their simplicity.

The Death card wasn't there—perhaps there wasn't one after all. She could see a girl with long blonde hair weeping on her bed, a boy with a golden cup, a huge heart pierced by three arrows, The World, The Sun. Right in the middle was The Fool. Oh dear, was that her?

The woman, who had gone into some sort of momentary trance, suddenly started talking fast.

"You're still very young and you have been well protected. But it's time for you to come out of the shadows now, my dear, and find out who you really are. Don't let others live your life for you. You must start making your own decisions from now on.

"This card in the centre will tell us what lies behind your question. This is where we will find the heart of the matter. Ah, The Tower—The Tower is always a sign of upheaval and awakening. It has already begun and there is no going back. There are things that will be revealed to you and they will change your life. But something is troubling you and you are right to be concerned, my dear. Someone close to this matter is in mortal danger and you sense this."

Emma felt something clutch at her stomach. Alex. I *knew* something was wrong.

The woman carried on talking, but Emma was only half listening. "Emotional loss—pay attention to coming events—news which will make things clearer—some difficult choices—searching for someone who you will find in an unexpected place—future happiness—" the woman looked up. "Is there a problem, dear?"

"Um, yes. Well, yes, there is actually. You said someone was in danger. What do you mean? How much danger? Where is he? What's happened?"

"We'll need to start again."

She picked up the cards and started to shuffle them. She didn't seem very surprised, but then, Emma supposed, if you spent your time reading the future, nothing should surprise you very much.

This time she laid out just three cards in a row. "It's a boy, a young man. This is a critical point in his life. He is not in a safe place and there are dangerous people around him. I can't see his future clearly." She looked up. "I can see needles, dressings, drips. I think he may end up in hospital, my dear. That's all I can tell you." And she stood up abruptly—the reading was over.

* * *

Emma stumbled out of the shop. If it even was a shop because the woman had disappeared and there was no one else about. No customers, either. It was almost as if she had imagined the whole thing, like visiting another dimension. Back on planet Earth, she walked on through the market, going through the motions of picking over sweatshirts and beaded tops, but she hardly saw them.

All she could think about was what the woman had said. What on earth had Alex gone and done? Where was he—and how were they supposed to find him? It was all very well muttering about drips and hospitals but a bit more detail would have been helpful. In fact, all the woman had done was frighten the life out of her without giving her any way of actually doing anything to help.

It had all been a bit close to the bone about her, too. What on earth had she meant—find out who you really are? She knew perfectly well who she was. She was a trainee lawyer, for goodness sake, and doing very well. But then again, she was quite different when she was with Alex. He seemed to bring out another side in her which her father wouldn't recognise and doubtless wouldn't approve of. So which one was the real her?

The woman had seemed quite shaken herself, too. By the time they'd finished, she'd looked as though she had seen a ghost. And now Emma came to think about it, she had been in such a hurry to get rid of her that she hadn't even asked for any payment. Which made it so much harder to dismiss the whole thing as a load of old nonsense.

* * *

Joe had managed to get a table in a relatively quiet corner of the Kings Head and he and his father were deep in conversation over a couple of pints of Boddingtons when Emma arrived. The pub was already crowded and voices were rising in the warm, steamy atmosphere. Joe caught sight of Emma standing up on tiptoe as she fought her way through and waved and grinned at her until she slid onto the leather seat beside him, shoving the hallowed red and white Southampton scarves out of the way and giving him a kiss on the cheek.

Amused at her properness in front of his father, he gave her hand a quick squeeze out of sight under the table.

"How was the match? Did you win?"

"Drew. But we've had a grand afternoon, haven't we, Joe?"

Joe nodded and smiled affectionately at his father. He could see Emma was a little awkward about breaking up their afternoon of father-and-son camaraderie, but soon he had her laughing and chatting, her cheeks glowing with the after-effects of a couple of glasses of house red and a decent plate of shepherd's pie. It made him happy to bring them both together like this, two of the most important people in his life. As the meal came to an end and their thoughts turned towards leaving, he noticed his father had gone quiet.

"How are things at home, Dad?"

"Well, I think I've mastered the washing machine and I can do pretty good scrambled eggs and ham and baked potatoes—and Mrs Jeffreys does more in the house now, with the beds and the ironing—"

Joe tried to picture his father cooking supper on his own in the kitchen at home and failed. He had absolutely no idea how he coped with the loneliness or what on earth anyone could do to help. Joe still felt the loss of his mother and thought about her most days, but he knew that for his father it was more than that—her presence was still there in the house, her photos, her memories, even her clothes and books. It was hard to accept that her flesh and blood had gone. Gone where? Sometimes his father even seemed angry that she had left him like that, as if she had done it on purpose. It was very upsetting.

"I've got her ashes upstairs. I don't know what to do with them, Joe."

The bravado had gone and his father looked utterly defeated. He even looks smaller, Joe thought. He's lost substance somehow, his shoulders bent over, the spring in his step gone. The father he had always looked up to, the head of the family, now needed his help and protection—their roles had flipped. Another step-change. They were coming thick and fast at the moment. But if was up to him to take care of his father, his own sadness would have to take second place.

"Perhaps we could plant a tree in the garden for her? Something unusual— like a rowan perhaps. We could scatter her ashes there and then you could go and talk to her whenever you felt like it. We all could."

"Mmm, that's an idea. Let me think about it, Joe."

James went through the motions of considering the possibility, nodding and scratching his chin, but they both knew perfectly well that Joe would just go ahead and organise it.

* * *

The music from the party was throbbing right across St George's Square by the time Emma slipped unnoticed through the smart black front door of number 32, overheating in her puffa after the brisk walk from the tube station.

Although the hall was full of vaguely familiar people shouting, laughing and pushing past each other there was no one she actually knew, so she started to edge her way in and out of the rooms on either side. It was best to look as if she was looking for someone, even if it did mean squeezing past so many people.

And anyway she genuinely wanted to know whether her usual crowd—hers and Alex's, she remembered with a lurch—were here.

Arriving without Alex was making her nervous. With him living up in London, they had got used to going to parties together. They were so comfortable with each other that it was as if they were a couple without actually being one. It was a perfect arrangement, having someone who was so popular with everybody on hand to look after her, and she had obviously relied on him more than she thought. Now she wondered if she would be as welcome here on her own. Perhaps this wasn't her crowd after all, just Alex's.

Once she had traded her bottle of wine for a glass of someone else's she flicked her hair back and went upstairs towards the music. What would normally have been an elegant townhouse drawing room had been stripped out for a live band. Someone must have some good connections. The atmosphere immediately sucked her in—the swagger of the band, the barely veiled aggression, the bass that was going right through her, the cigarette smoke, the energy of a mass of people dancing and shouting to make themselves heard above the noise. She recognised one of the guitarists and felt a buzz of excitement. Yes, she did belong here, this was absolutely a part of who she was.

She paused for a moment to watch the lead singer, a girl not much older than she was with an immaculate figure. She was strutting up and down in hot pants, black suede cowboy boots and, strangely, black gloves, her bleached hair and huge diamanté earrings escaping out of a sweat band. She could sing, too, dammit. She was so cool it almost took your breath away. Emma could feel the approval coming from the musicians behind her and practically every other male in the room. How was anyone supposed to compete with that?

Dispirited, she turned away and then at last spotted some people she knew. She shouldered her way through the crowd until she reached them, holding her glass up out of the way. They seemed gratifyingly pleased to see her, hugs and kisses and 'where have you beens' all round, exaggerated smiles and nods to make up for the fact that any sort of conversation was completely out of the question.

Someone offered her a Marlboro and she bent over the lighter, nodding her head and raising her cigarette in thanks. Then one of the girls pointed towards the door and a few minutes later they were in the garden, sprawled over a set of elegant wrought iron garden furniture. Who on earth lived here? Someone rolled a joint and passed it around. Emma breathed in the familiar musky smell as it floated through the warm autumn air. No, it didn't quite fit in with Withers & Co or her father or even with Joe come to that, but there was no doubt a part of her felt perfectly at home here.

"I had no idea Johnny even *played* guitar!"

"Aren't they great?"

"Did you *see* what Louise was wearing?"

"Oh my God."

"How's your show coming on, Chris? Can we all come?"

"Has anyone seen Dead Poets Society yet? It's supposed to be *brilliant*—"

"Let's all go and see it next week!"

"What's Alex up to at the moment, Em?"

Oh no. For a few blissful minutes, Emma had actually forgotten about Alex, but now the Tarot reading came flooding back. She hadn't told Joe about it yet, mostly because his father had been there and they were busy talking about other things. But she wondered if he would take it seriously or just dismiss it as some silly nonsense. Which maybe it was, but there was something unnerving about it too. The woman had been too spot on about her mother just to ignore completely. She wasn't sure he would understand that.

"The thing is, I'm really worried about him. His postcards have been weird, and now I haven't heard from him for weeks. And I think I would have, even though—even though—well he *promised* me he would keep in touch."

Tears had started rolling down her cheeks and now they had started they kept on coming as several days' worth of anxiety rose to the surface. She looked up, wondering whether she was fooling herself. Why would he keep in touch with her when it was because of her that he'd left? Is that what they thought? Did they think it was all her fault?

Tamsin, a well-built girl with blonde spiky hair and a rather motherly voice who had always been kind to Emma, got up and put her arms around her.

"Of *course* you would, Em. Of course you would," she breathed. She buried Emma's face in her large bosom and massaged her back, exchanging concerned glances with the others.

"I'm sure there's a perfectly sensible explanation, Em. Could there be some reason why he hasn't been in touch? Did he tell you where he was going next?" Chris, one of Alex's fellow art students, went for a safer, more business-like tone.

Here goes, thought Emma and coming up from Tamsin's bosom for air, she told them about the Tarot reading.

"She said he was in danger, that he might end up in hospital—she was muttering about drips and needles and things. She even said his future was hanging in the balance! The thing is, I've had a feeling that something awful has happened."

She looked around, searching people's faces, and was relieved to see that they were all concerned and no one was treating it as a joke.

"So I *am* worried, yes. I can't help it. I did hear from him a few weeks ago, from somewhere in Central Asia I've never heard of. It just doesn't sound very safe. He said he was heading towards Pakistan. And now nothing."

"But what can we do?"

"I know."

"We don't even know what country he's in."

"But—he really could be fine, you know. Perhaps he's just somewhere you can't buy postcards—or perhaps he's actually having a good time? No news is good news and all that."

"And your Tarot reader might not even have been talking about Alex at all!"

"You're bound to be worried, Em, but we could be massively jumping to conclusions here."

The thought that Alex might actually be fine after all cheered Emma up. What a fuss she had made, probably over nothing. They were right—it could easily be a good sign that he wasn't writing home every five minutes. After all, there was no reason to think that anything was wrong. To her relief, the conversation started to move on. Then someone shouted down from the balcony above them and they all went back inside.

Chapter 7
The Golden Temple

In the Bir Hospital, Alex's memories are starting to link up with each other. He knows he was living in London and he knows why he left. The places he has travelled through are settling like stepping stones across a stream. If he goes back to the beginning, maybe he can pick his way across to where he is now. Then everything will make sense. So he stands on the far bank and steps out.

* * *

When it happened, when Joe and Emma got together, at first he didn't realise it would mean starting his life all over again.

Things had been starting to work out a lot better. London was great—big enough to melt away into, to disappear off the radar whenever you felt like it. At art college, he found other people like him—people who didn't care about salaries and careers, but who could talk all night about principles, social justice and of course, art.

He took his foundation course in painting, sculpture, drawing and photography, although he already knew he would specialise in painting. College was an exciting place to work with its well-equipped studios and inspiring materials, and he was spurred on by the enthusiasm of his teachers and fellow students. For the first time, people admired what he was doing. For the first time, he was really good at something that mattered.

He quickly became part of the crowd, asked to every party and every get-together. There were always plenty of pretty girls around and he enjoyed flirting with them, having a laugh, but there was no one special. It was the same with the boys—he had lots of mates, at football banter level, but no best mates. He didn't want to let anyone get too close.

But Emma was different; she was like family. She'd always lived in London and fortunately for him, she had decided to stay and do her degree at UCL. She turned up on the doorstep the minute he arrived in London and immediately took charge of him. Since then, they'd talked on the telephone most days and seen each other all the time. They were such close friends that she was part of his life, almost part of him, and it made him feel at home. He couldn't imagine that with anyone else.

He couldn't wait for Joe to leave Bristol and come up to London the following year. For once, he was ahead of his older brother and could give him the lowdown. Although in the event Joe had found his own way, hanging out with friends from work and uni rather than Alex's art school crowd, they still saw each other a lot. It was inevitable that Joe and Emma, who had gone on to law school by then, would see each other too. He knew he would share her with his brother—after all, he always had. And whenever they all got together it was just like old times.

That day, the day everything changed, Emma had asked him to meet her after college for a drink. When he arrived, it had seemed slightly odd that Joe was there too. He hid his surprise as he hugged them both and went to get a beer, rapidly rethinking what sort of drink this was going to be with all three of them there. As soon as he sat down he knew something was wrong. Joe glanced at Emma and then launched into what was obviously a prepared speech.

"Alex. There's something we need to tell you. It's not a big deal really, but— well, obviously we wanted to tell you first. Ahh—Emma and I—"

Alex looked from one to the other, wondering why Joe was starting to sound just like their father and what on earth was coming next.

"Emma and I are—together. We've got together. We're going out together."

Alex had never seen his brother look so uncomfortable. Perhaps he was joking. But why joke about something like this? He looked at Emma, expecting her to start laughing, but she just stared into her drink.

"I don't understand. What do you mean?" Alex said stupidly, waiting for his brain to catch up.

"Well, obviously we knew each other in Somerset, but we were children then. Then I went to Bristol and when I came to London and we met up again, things were different. She'd grown up—we've all grown up, haven't we? I waited a while to make sure that I hadn't got it wrong because it was a bit of an unusual situation. I knew there would be no going back. And I wasn't sure how Emma felt about me, either."

He looked up and tried to catch Emma's eye, but she looked away.

Alex tried to imagine Joe and Emma together, talking about their relationship. When was this? How come he didn't know? How long had they kept this secret from him? Obviously they hadn't slept together, that would be unthinkable. Had they? Oh, God.

"But I am sure. And fortunately, so is she."

Now they were both looking at him, waiting for him to say something. The awkwardness was unbearable.

"Wow! That's amazing—great! I'm really happy for you." He did his best to smile and Joe and Emma both visibly relaxed.

"I knew you'd be OK with it!" Emma said, on the edge of her seat now. "It won't make any difference, I promise. We'll still be friends, Alex. That's never going to change."

"Of course not! Anyway, we won't let it!"

Of course nothing would change, Alex thought. *After all, it wasn't as if Emma had ever been his girlfriend.*

They were all relieved as they swiftly moved the conversation on, three friends laughing and chatting together in the pub and managing to behave as if nothing had happened.

* * *

But as Emma and Joe's relationship settled down, it dawned on him that he had lost her. She and Joe had their own lives together, their own conversations, their own secrets, and he felt ignored by both of them. Emma was no longer available to be his best and oldest friend. His brother Joe was busy being in love.

It became impossible for him to actually be with them. If they were all together, it was Joe and Emma plus Alex, the gooseberry now. Joe and Alex was just about OK, although they had to pretend Emma didn't exist. But Alex and Emma was out of the question. How could he go out for the evening with his brother's girlfriend?

He tried to tell himself it didn't matter. Joe would always be his brother, after all. Blood was thicker than water—even if they had no shared blood, as such. But surely nothing could take away the childhood they had spent together. If anyone was going to have Emma, wasn't it better it was Joe than anyone else? He couldn't contemplate Emma going off with some loser who nobody liked. But then, why did Emma have to go off with anyone at all—?

Somehow, he had thought she'd just always be there. Had he overlooked the possibility he might be in love with her himself? Perhaps he had completely fucked up by letting Joe get there first. But no, that didn't feel right either. She was special, but it had never been like that. She was special in some special way he couldn't for the life of him fathom out.

But the fact remained that by getting together they had closed him out, even if unintentionally. Without them his life gradually lost purpose and nothing mattered much anymore. He couldn't paint, all his enthusiasm for his work evaporated. Parties bored him, so he stayed at home and drank alone. He couldn't sleep, but getting up seemed pointless.

Thinking of Joe and Emma together in the same city as him drove him mad. He wanted to know where they were and what they were doing and when he did know, that drove him mad too. When he was with them, it was getting harder and harder to pretend everything was fine. And worst of all, he couldn't understand what was happening to him. Why did it matter so much? Why did he feel so useless, so rejected and so alone?

Things got so bad that there just didn't seem any point in hanging around. But he could hardly go home. A problem child who was supposed to have grown up was the last thing his father needed and anyway, what on earth would he do with himself in Somerset? He wondered whether he should go abroad, go travelling. Why not? He'd started at art college without taking a gap year, but there was nothing to keep him in London now. Maybe it would distract him, help him move on. Maybe he could even start a whole new life somewhere.

The next day he went to Trailfinders in Kensington High Street, the best place for cheap air tickets, before he could change his mind.

"Where are you thinking of going? Any ideas?" The weather-beaten Aussie at the desk who would clearly rather be surfing tried hard to be helpful.

"Somewhere far away. Somewhere that's not like here."

"Sounds like you'll be needing a round-the-world ticket."

"I don't know if I'm coming back."

He looked up and saw the four slim minarets of the Hagia Sophia on a poster behind the Aussie's desk.

"Istanbul. How about Istanbul? That would do fine. I could start there."

He bought himself a backpack, a sleeping bag, some walking boots and as an afterthought, some sun cream. He said goodbye to all his student friends, who assumed he was going on holiday and told him how jealous they were. Yeah, right. Then there was an awkward last evening with Joe and Emma at Joe's flat in Clapham.

"Are you sure you're doing the right thing, Alex? Dropping out of college and going off like this—I wish you wouldn't. I'm going to miss you so much." *And I'll miss you too, Em*, Alex thought, but the difference is that you've already gone.

"You'll be fine, Em. You've got Joe, haven't you—"

"But where are you going? How long are you going to be away?"

"A while. I don't know yet."

Alex noticed Joe passing Emma the large, not-quite-clean white handkerchief he always had somewhere about his person. Even that degree of silent collusion was enough to make him feel uncomfortable.

"Look after yourself, Alex. Take care. I'll miss you too, old chap."

"Alex, promise me you'll keep in touch. Let us know where you are. And don't be away too long—" Emma broke off to sob into the handkerchief and Alex looked away quickly.

"Don't worry about me. I'll be fine." He managed to look Joe straight in the eye. "I'll be fine."

"'Course you will."

* * *

At Heathrow, it finally got the better of him. As he left behind everything and everyone he had ever known, his mind closed down. Airports, buses and hotels passed by without impacting on his consciousness at all. Istanbul caught him in its currents and washed him backwards and forwards between continents. He grazed on grilled fish in the bars under the Galata Bridge and drifted round the harem at the Topkapi Palace, daydreaming of sultans and eunuchs.

Istanbul passed him on to Ephesus which baked his body in the heat and on to Pammukale which soothed him in its hot springs flowing over travertine

74

terraces. He catnapped in cafés thick with the acrid smell of Turkish tobacco and the clacking of endless games of backgammon. At night he lay awake, dogged by unknown fears and aching from fatigue. He drifted on through Cappadocia, drinking raki to ease his unfathomable pain. He shuffled through palaces and mosques in Tehran and Mashhad, Bokhara and Candahar, his vision blurred while his mind turned inwards, trying to find the edge of normality.

He travelled by train, bus, lorry, bus again, to Kabul, Peshawar and Islamabad, disinterested in the dangers of roaming through such hostile regions. His skin burned and his feet hardened. He sent postcards to Joe, Emma, Emma-and-Joe, Joe-and-Emma. As he crossed over into Pakistan his mind began to clear at last and he realised the place he had been heading for all along was India.

* * *

He arrived at the border at Wagah on a sweaty bus from Lahore and walked the last 200 yards to the Pakistan immigration office. He suffered through the usual baffling interrogations, pointless requests for information and filleting of his bags as permission to cross was denied and given, denied and given again.

Eventually, he was released into the custody of a handful of Pakistani border guards, who were trussed up in heavy black uniforms, goose stepping backwards and forwards in front of a huge pair of gates. Although he assumed this display of aggression was only for show and their cockatoo hats looked like a massive piss-take, he felt so conspicuous in his shorts and flip-flops that he half expected to be shot at any moment.

But as the gates slid back and he walked past the Pakistani crescent and star for the last time, out of Islam and into India, his spirits lifted. Pakistan's alienness had suited his mood, but now he stepped into a country deeply stained by its British legacy. He immediately felt much more at home with the Indian guards in their khaki uniforms, direct descendants of those of the British Army during the days of the Raj, and even after a predictable tussle with the Indian Immigration Office, he felt more upbeat than he had done for some time.

This tenseness at the India-Pakistan border reminded him with a start that they were once one country until Gandhi and partition. He must actually be standing on the Radcliffe Line, created by the British to divide Muslims and Hindus. He felt the hairs on his neck rise at the thought of those millions of

Indians moving across the land with everything they possessed, caught on the wrong side of the new border.

India had been ripped apart like Siamese twins separated without anaesthetic and it had been his own countrymen who had decided who should have the heart, who the liver; the British Empire which had presided over this carnage. Recognising the familiar pain of separation, he shuddered, half expecting to be dragged to his feet and beaten up for the sins of his forefathers.

He had hardly arrived and already he could see that the British were an indelible part of India's history. After all, they had ruled India for nearly a hundred years. Whole generations of well-meaning members of the British middle classes had tried to organise India their way, treating the natives as little more than an inconvenience, like cholera or typhoid, while keeping themselves amused with their pig sticking, tiger hunting and consorting with Maharajahs and Nawabs.

What on earth did they think they were doing? It was downright embarrassing. But then, he supposed, empires have been rising and falling all through history, it wasn't just the British. Easy to criticise with the benefit of hindsight, but when you are caught up in the rising empire it must all make perfect sense.

* * *

Buoyed by the change in his mood he set off down the Grand Trunk Road, named by the British presumably, towards the nearest railway station at Atari. There he squeezed onto a train to Amritsar along with what seemed like most of the local population. By the time they pulled into Amritsar station and poured out onto the platform forty minutes later, the excitement had reached boiling point. The station itself was full to overflowing and the noise was unbelievable.

He watched as a group of elderly women swathed in saris manhandled heavy suitcases while their Sikh husbands looked on impassively in their perfectly pleated turbans. Whole tribes of people were sitting around on the ground or lying crashed out under lumpy blankets, with no apparent plans for catching trains at all. There was an overpowering smell of animal dung. Outside in the street there was even more chaos, with animals, rickshaws, lorries, taxis and cars, some with astonishingly heavy loads, all travelling in different directions and all demanding right of way.

Once he had got used to the horns, whistles and competing bhangra music he explained to the rickshaw driver who had been hopping around in front of him that he needed somewhere to stay. This seemed to cause great delight. As soon as formal introductions had been completed he was escorted to Sudip's luxury rickshaw and they shot out into the thick of the traffic. Powered by Sudip's wiry body they bumped and jolted through the centre of town, hot and dusty, past tantalising glimpses of markets, shops and alleyways to be explored later until the traffic thinned out and they pulled up abruptly outside an ugly modern building.

Sudip leapt out, somehow managing to hop, nod and shake his head at Alex all at the same time. Then he started running backwards and forwards between the rickshaw and the building, entreating Alex to make his way along an imaginary red carpet to the entrance of what turned out to be a youth hostel. At the last moment, he had a change of heart and insisted on an immediate excursion to the Golden Temple (by rickshaw), which he explained with the help of the hostel receptionist was the number one highlight of not only Amritsar but, in fact, the whole of Punjab and the entire Sikh religion.

By the time Alex had worked out what Sudip was on about, it all seemed to have been arranged. Sudip and the rickshaw settled down to wait indefinitely while he made his arrangements with the hostel and dropped his backpack off in a violently orange but apparently clean bedroom and off they went again.

* * *

The Golden Temple turned out to be quite something. By the time Alex had handed in his shoes, covered his head with a standard issue orange bandana and paddled through the shallow pool of water at the entrance, he was one step away from being a pilgrim himself. He could hear the sound of singing and chanting in the air, almost like a heavenly choir.

The temple was coated in gold and floated on a marble island in the middle of a huge rectangular lake, which reflected its white icing parapets, dipped in more gold, against the blue afternoon sky. It was certainly an incredible tourist attraction but it was more than that—it had the most profound sense of peace which immediately calmed and soothed him after his hot and dusty journey.

As he padded barefoot around the marble colonnades he watched the faithful immerse themselves in the sacred water, sit loose-limbed in prayer or lie weak in the shade, some of them obviously sick or even dying. He sat for some time on the spotless marble floor, moved at the simplicity of the devotion around him. He could see that here people's spiritual life was inseparable from their daily life and it made him wonder for the first time why the British denied this part of their lives back home, pretending that it did not exist at all or at least only in church on Sunday mornings.

After a while, he tagged on to a caravan of bobbing turbans and bandanas moving along a causeway across the Pool of Nectar, as the lake had turned out to be called, towards the golden shrine itself. This was where the religious fervour became hysterical. There were priests reciting prayers from the Guru Granth Sahib and singing hymns, which he realised was what he could hear being relayed through speakers outside. Heaps of rupee notes were being raked up off the floor amongst the marigold flowers and some sort of sticky brown devotional pudding was going around in little bowls made out of fresh leaves.

He sat down in a quiet corner inside the shrine and closed his eyes, absorbing the devotion of the pilgrims passing through. Perhaps they would take him with them. Perhaps he could live without Emma after all.

He was exploring one or two small shrines around the edge of the Pool of Nectar when he came upon a sign 'Free kitchen remains open for 24 hours to all the classes of people,' which reminded him that he had not eaten since breakfast that morning in Lahore. A soup kitchen for the poor, he assumed, but maybe they would have something for hungry visitors to buy.

He heard the langar long before he saw it. There was a deafening clatter of plates—40,000 metal ones, as it turned out—and as he walked under the archway inscribed with prayers he could see a huge dining room where several hundred people were sitting cross-legged in long lines on the floor, eating from standard issue metal plates and drinking from metal cups. Keeping this huge multinational lunch party going was an army of volunteers chopping onions, stirring vast vats of lentil dhal with wooden paddles big enough to propel a canoe with, rolling out chapattis, swabbing floors and washing up all those thousands of plates.

Alex watched as one sitting ended and the next one began. Intrigued, he filed in and took his place on one of the long canvas mats running down the length of the room, embarrassed at the stiffness of his hips, and found himself sitting next to what looked like another Westerner.

"Hi, I'm Scott," his dining companion volunteered in a flat Canadian drawl and offered his hand to shake. "It's pretty awesome, huh?"

"Alex." He offered a polite hand but left Scott's question to hang in the air. He watched as his plate was filled with ladlefuls of dhal from a galvanised metal bucket, followed shortly afterwards by a dollop of soupy spinach, mounds of rice and as many chapatis as he could eat.

"They're great believers in hospitality, aren't they, the Sikhs? Thousands and thousands of people a day they feed here, all day long, totally free. And you don't have to be poor or a pilgrim—everyone's welcome. All funded by donations, plus food that's given to them for nothing and volunteers to help cook it. Incredible. It must be the biggest free kitchen in the world, huh?"

Scott scooped up a handful of dhal and rice in his fingers and gestured to Alex to follow suit. He's just trying to be friendly, Alex thought, tearing into a chapatti. He's probably harmless. Besides, the food actually tasted good—and he realised he was ravenously hungry for the first time since he left home.

Scott didn't seem put off in the slightest by Alex's reluctance to engage in conversation and over the next five minutes he rattled through an impressive synopsis of his entire life story. He had grown up in Vancouver, where he had been on track to become a professional field hockey player. He had already made the senior squad when a bad knee injury meant he'd needed an operation on an anterior cruciate ligament. After six months out of the game, they'd finally told him he wasn't going to make it back to the team.

He'd been devastated and with no idea what else to do with his life he'd set off with a backpack hoping that things would become clearer along the way. A few months in India had changed everything, even though he was still working on a Plan B.

Scott's candidness was hard to resist and in response, Alex tried to sum up what had brought him to India.

"Yeah, I'm in the middle of a bit of a rethink, too. I was at art college in London but things got a bit—I came here overland from Istanbul but I've only just arrived in India today, really."

"From Istanbul—wow! You sure must have seen some stuff."

Then Scott started talking about his experience of India.

"You know, I'm beginning to think there are some things that make a lot of sense here. I mean, it's chaos most of the time and you never get a straight answer to anything and there's poverty and sickness and the smell is appalling. I know all that. But there's something childlike about people here that's so incredibly smart. They don't complicate their lives, they're good at just living. They totally understand what it's all about. Perhaps it's because their religion is so strong that it influences everything they do. It's the most important thing in their lives. It's completely natural, like breathing. I like that."

Alex nodded, his interest sparked, and at last he turned to face Scott.

"It's funny you should say that. I was thinking pretty much the same thing today—perhaps I should spend some time here too."

"You know what I'm going to do?" Scott said. "After this, I'm going to go to an ashram up in Rishikesh. The whole place is nuts about yoga and meditation and there are lots of ashrams there but I've heard good things about this one. Rishikesh isn't all that far from here; in fact, it's just as you start to go up into the Himalayas. Who knows what it'll be like but I figure it's one way to get under the skin of the place. Get off the tourist trail for a bit, have some time to think. Thought I'd give it a try, anyway. Why not, huh?"

Alex had vaguely heard of ashrams because a friend of a friend had once gone to one to learn to be a yoga teacher, but they had always sounded quite bohemian, even by his standards. He looked at Scott with new respect.

"But don't you have to be into spiritual stuff or at least yoga? You can't just turn up, can you?"

At this point, the meal ended. Hundreds of people stood up, picked up their plates and cups and started to shuffle out of the dining room. The clatter made it impossible for Scott to answer so he signalled to Alex to follow him outside. They sat in the shade of the colonnade, leaning their backs against the wall and unfolding their aching legs out in front of them with relief. As they gazed through one of the sculpted white arches at the evening sun shining on the enchanted pool, Scott picked up seamlessly where he had left off.

"I'm pretty sure you don't have to be, no. But I don't think there would be much point in going to an ashram if you weren't looking for a deeper experience. Some small step towards enlightenment, perhaps. And finding the right guru is important—they all have their own. This ashram has a woman who's meant to be pretty good."

"And you can just go and stay there for as long as you want?"

"Apparently. Everyone helps out and I'm sure the living arrangements can be pretty primitive, but then I guess we're all used to that, huh? Yoga, meditation, vegetarian food, no cigarettes or alcohol or anything like that—pretty clean living. Hey, why don't you come over? Look, I'll write it down for you in case you feel like giving it a try. It'd be good to see you there."

Scott's enthusiasm was persuasive and Alex found himself promising to think about it. As they said goodbye he folded the piece of paper up carefully and put it in his jeans pocket.

"Thanks. I might just do that."

* * *

Back in his orange hostel room Alex took his few possessions out of his backpack and put them on the table. He had got used to travelling light and letting plans take shape by themselves. Joe would no doubt call it drifting and wouldn't approve. Emma—well, Emma would probably worry about the state he had got himself into, drinking too much and eating too little. It wasn't just carelessness on his part—it had actually felt right to give his body a hard time, an expression of his pain.

Looking in the mirror now he was shocked at his drawn face and scraggy body. Perhaps meeting Scott at the Golden Temple was meant to happen and an enforced period of clean living was what he needed. The alternative was to set off on his own, taking trains, visiting palaces and drinking beer, but there was nothing to stop him doing that afterwards. Scott had been a little overwhelming to start with, but he meant well and he was perfectly good company. It might do him good. At the very least, it would be an experience. As Scott said—why not?

By the time he woke up the next morning, he was ready to make plans to leave. He established from the hostel receptionist that he needed to catch another train, the fabulously named Shatabdi Express to Delhi, and get off at Ambala Junction. From there, he should be able to taxi or hitch up to the ashram.

He packed up his backpack and after a quick stop to grab some bread and jam and a cup of coffee he was on his way back to the station. He wondered whether Scott would actually be at the ashram when he got there or not, but in a way it didn't matter that much. It was the ashram itself that interested him.

Chapter 8
Paris

Emma was in her bedroom getting her things together for the weekend in Paris when the phone rang at the other end of the flat. It was Joe.

"Joe, I can't talk to you now—I've only just got back from the office and I'm never going to make it to the airport by seven o'clock at this rate! Have you packed?"

"Of course. How long can it take to pack a clean shirt and a washbag? I don't understand why girls always need so much stuff just to go away for the weekend—"

"Girls? What do you mean, girls? How many other girls have you taken away for the weekend then?" Although Emma was joking and she assumed Joe was too, she hated the thought of him going anywhere with anyone else.

"OK, tell me what to pack then—how smart do I need to be for dinner? I just can't find the right clothes at all—I've only got a T-shirt on at the moment."

"Em, you will look lovely, you always do. In fact the fewer clothes, the better... Now, I've got the plane tickets and I'm meeting you at the Air France check-in desk at Terminal 2. Got that? Don't forget your passport!"

Oh God, what if she'd forgotten her passport! What an idiot. She went straight back to her bedroom to get it. It usually lived in the top drawer of the pine chest beside her bed, but today it wasn't there. Perhaps she'd moved it to her desk?

A family of teddy bears in various stages of disintegration looked on impassively from their chair as she rummaged, throwing things out onto the floor. A handful of pencils and pens, some old cheque book stubs, a postcard of a swimming pool from a David Hockney exhibition she'd been to with Alex last year, a carved wooden keyring, a broken string of blue beads, the inevitable paper clips and rubber bands—but definitely no passport.

Oh, for goodness sake. Why wasn't it there? And why did it have to disappear just when she needed it in a hurry? But hang on. Hang on. Hadn't her father taken it to the office a couple of months ago?

Yes, that's right. His PA Caroline had asked for it so that she could take a copy. A few months earlier she and her father had been staying with some friends in the Florida Keys when it was hit by Hurricane Andrew. There had been a mad scramble for flights home and Caroline had been caught out because she hadn't had Emma's passport details. They'd ended up stuck in the Ritz-Carlton in Miami for days with Richard in an absolute fury. There was no way Caroline was going to let that *that* happen again.

I hope to God she sent it home again, Emma thought as she raced into her father's study. What if it was still in the office? There would be no weekend in Paris, Joe would be left waiting with the tickets at the airport, she'd feel such a fool. "Oh, please let it be here somewhere," she muttered to herself as she sat down in her father's leather swivel chair and started picking through the endless piles of stuff heaped up in front of her.

She didn't often come into his study. It was definitely her father's territory, a cave full of dark wood, leather and antiques created by Jackie in a manly forest green. She hardly ever even caught a glimpse inside because the door was usually firmly closed, and now she felt like an intruder. She was taken aback by the chaos that she found in there. How did he manage to get anything done in this mess? She had always thought he was so on top of everything.

She opened up a couple of folders. It looked like Caroline had a system of sending a folder home every day—each folder was neatly labelled with a date and had a random collection of stuff inside. Her passport could be tucked inside any one of them, so she was going to have to go through everything. It could take ages. This can't be happening, she thought as she started opening folders, trying to be calm and methodical instead of getting into a stupid panic. She really couldn't afford to waste any time.

But it wasn't there, that precious little blue/black passport with the gold lion and unicorn that she could see so clearly in her mind's eye. Not in the folders, not on the desk, nowhere in sight. She breathed in the inky, leathery air and breathed out slowly, her breath shaking. She could always ring him, but he was bound to be in a meeting and she didn't have time for that. Perhaps he had put it away in one of the desk drawers to keep it safe. Yes, of course! That would make sense.

She started turning out each drawer of the big partner's desk, making herself check each one thoroughly before going on to the next to be sure that wherever it was, she couldn't possibly miss it.

She'd got down to the bottom drawer when she found the battered little oblong tin box. It was exactly the sort of place you would put a passport for safe keeping and relief started to flood over her. This was where it would be. She pulled the box out onto her lap, turned the key in the lock and opened it up. Inside was a wad of photographs of her mother which she had never seen before.

All thoughts of her passport evaporated as her shaking fingers pulled out the photographs and undid the elastic band. Here was Frances in a burnt orange crochet shift dress and yellow plastic sunglasses, bathed in sunshine, a daisy chain round her neck. She appeared to be dancing barefoot in a field; her arms were waving above her head and she looked totally absorbed, apparently unaware of whoever had taken the photograph.

In the next one, she had picked up a tambourine. Another was a close-up of her face, her pale skin already showing a few fine lines, her blue eyes rimmed with kohl, holding a cigarette close to her mouth. Emma smiled at the next one— her parents standing side by side, her father in a lumpy elephant cord jacket with long hair curling over his collar, a thick moustache and deep sideburns and a protective arm around her mother, whose skinny body was swamped in a purple, blue and lemon kaftan with matching bandana. She was taller than Emma had imagined, almost the same height as her father.

Emma was proud to see that she was beautiful and very cool too, although there was disappointingly little resemblance to herself. She had been a genuine 60's hippy, even if there was something about her angular body and the way she was standing that made her look more like a self-conscious teenager than a pioneer of free love.

Her father had sat on this lot all these years, right under her nose. How *could* he? *Why*? Oh God, I really don't have time for this now, Emma thought as she remembered her missing passport with a stab. She flicked through the rest of the photos quickly—Frances on the beach in a bikini, a portable radio by her head, hip bones visible through her skin. Pushing a pram, startled by the camera. Was the baby in the pram her? Presumably. Standing in front of a huge canvas, paint on her clothes and in her hair, laughing. This collection was a treasure trove compared to the one dog-eared photo she kept inside the cover of the Bhagavad

Gita, up until now her only piece of hard evidence that her mother had ever existed.

At the bottom of the box, there was a small cream envelope with 'Richard' handwritten on the front. There was a letter inside. Could this be from her mother too? She hesitated, aware that now she was just snooping. But she couldn't resist. And anyway, didn't she have a right to know what was in that letter? It must be important for her father to have kept it all these years. Perhaps here at last was the sort of information she was looking for. If he wasn't going to tell her, she would just have to find out for herself.

She opened it up. It covered just one sheet and it was written in watery blue ink. At the bottom it read 'With all my love, Frances.' Yes, it was from her mother! It was dated, too—3 March 1969.

'Darling Richard,' she had written in such loopy handwriting that it was hard to make out clearly. 'By the time you read this I will be dead—' Oh my God, it looked like a suicide note. But her mother presumably hadn't known she was going to be killed in a car crash, so how come she'd written this letter? Had it been just a suicide threat, a cry for help perhaps? Or had her father managed to stop her? Perhaps it was just some sort of game or a joke. This was no help at all! it just made things a whole load more complicated.

Her eyes blurred as she stared at the page, bewildered. Well, it was her own fault for digging around in things that didn't belong to her. What was she thinking? And what about the passport and the packing and Joe? She folded the letter, put it back in its envelope and stashed it away in her jeans pocket, even though she felt like a thief doing it. She locked the photographs back into the tin and put them away again, artfully returning everything else to its previous state of chaos, and then raced back to her room.

Joe was right, she was making this packing far too complicated, she didn't need to take much at all. Better put the letter somewhere safe first. She picked up her handbag and unzipped the inner pocket—where her passport was tucked in all ready for its trip to Paris. Surely she'd looked there? Honestly! Hugely relieved, she slipped the letter in beside it and checked her watch. Nearly time to go—she could read it properly later.

* * *

It was such a struggle getting to Heathrow on the Piccadilly Line in the rush hour that she hardly had a chance to even think about the letter. You could always feel the hostility towards a suitcase, even a small one, taking up space on a crowded tube that could have been occupied by a person just trying to get home from the office. But a taxi would have been far too expensive and anyway, heaven knows how long it would have taken at this time of day. There was nothing worse than being stuck in the back of a cab watching the minutes and pounds tick by. At least you knew where you were with a tube.

At the Air France desk there was Joe, tall and distinguished in his dark grey overcoat with the collar turned up at the back. She still felt a little thrill every time she saw him from a distance and realised that it was her he was waiting for.

He leaned down to give her a kiss and she saw that as promised he was travelling light, with just a small pack which he was determined to hold on to as hand luggage even though her wheelie suitcase had to go in the hold. Their passports sat on the counter side by side as the lipsticked Air France woman issued luggage tags and boarding passes, unaware that this was something new for them—their first journey abroad together.

"Let's have a look at your passport photo then—ouch! Is that really you?"

Emma snatched at the passport, which Joe was holding up in the air, laughing.

"Joe! Give it back!"

But Joe hadn't finished with it yet and he held it well out of her reach.

"Emerald Venus Fry—" he read. "Wow! You kept quiet about that one!"

Emma was uncomfortable now. "Well, wouldn't you? Emerald is bad enough, but Venus—I've always hated it. Don't laugh, Joe! That's really mean."

"OK, OK! Calm down! I was only teasing. D'you want to know what mine is? Joseph David Russell. I'm not mad about Joseph either. But Emerald Venus—" Joe was shaking his head and laughing again.

"Shut up!" But now Emma was laughing too.

By this time, they were at Passport Control so they had to be serious again. Then there was all the hassle of getting through security, queuing up for two lots of French francs, checking out the Duty-Free, buying magazines for the journey, realising they were late and running to the gate, boarding the plane, finding an empty locker to stow Joe's pack, sitting down, standing up again and taking their coats off, stowing them away and then sitting down with their seat belts fastened ready for take-off.

By this time, Emma could hardly wait to tell Joe about the letter, although she was wary of choosing the wrong moment and annoying him. Anyway, he was chatting away about the weekend to come, the highlights of which seemed to revolve around plenty of steak frites and vin ordinaire, although he did promise to take her to the Musée d'Orsay to see the Boudins and the Cézannes too. Once he'd pulled out his copy of NME, she decided it was time to take the plunge.

"Joe, I found something! I found a letter from my mother!"

"What?" Joe looked at her as if she had completely lost her mind.

"Because when you said on the phone don't forget your passport, I thought I'd lost it so I was looking for it in Dad's desk because he took it in for Caroline to copy for her file after all that hoo-ha in Florida and I found this letter!"

At that moment, the plane lifted into the air and they both had to look out of the window until they were sure they were not going to crash land on top of Hounslow. Then Emma unzipped the inner pocket of her handbag and pulled out the letter.

"You're going to have to start again, Em. What is this letter and where did it come from?"

Emma explained about the missing passport, the tin box and the photos. Surely it wasn't that complicated—why did he keep asking her irrelevant questions? Obviously, she'd found her passport—the only thing that was important now was to read the letter, but she couldn't do that until he had caught up.

"So have you read it then? What does it say?"

"I had a quick look at it but I didn't have time to read it properly."

"Well, are you going to read it?" Joe sounded nervous.

"Of course I'm going to read it, Joe. I've never even seen her writing before!"

She could hardly breathe as she unfolded the letter and read it through slowly from start to finish, then silently handed it to Joe.

Darling Richard,

By the time you read this, I will be dead and out of your life and Emma's for ever. I can hardly bear to leave her, but it's better this way. I don't think we can get through any more of this, I'm sure you will agree with that. Don't worry, I've got it all worked out and you won't ever know the details.

I know how much I have hurt you and you didn't deserve it. I wish things had been different, that I had managed things better or that even now I could stay.

But I don't think I'll ever be able to make you happy or anyone happy for that matter. I'm so sorry, Richard. It would have been so much better for you if we had never met.

As for Emma, I shouldn't have taken her away from you. Sometimes, I am so tired and confused that I can't even look after myself, let alone a child. She will be so much better off with you. Take good care of her—I know you will. Tell her how much I loved her and that I did my best. Goodbye, Richard.

With all my love, Frances

As soon as Joe finished reading he looked up at Emma. "Wow."

But Emma was looking confused. "It looks pretty much like a suicide note, doesn't it? But obviously she did come back, although it can't have been for long because this was only just before she died."

"Unless—"

Emma stared blankly at Joe.

"Unless she didn't die in a car crash—"

"But she did."

"How? Was she driving? Where were you? Were you hurt? Was anyone else involved? Was it her fault? Did she die instantly or was she taken to hospital? Where was she buried? Have you EVER heard or seen anything in detail about what happened?"

"No—no. But that's not surprising, is it? I don't know much about her life, so why would I know about her death? Dad hasn't told me anything, so why would he tell me about the accident?"

"Isn't that a bit odd in itself? As you say, she *is* your mother. Look, I don't know. It's nothing to do with me. I expect she did die in a car crash. But I do think that it's just possible she may not have done after all."

"If she didn't die in a car crash," Emma said slowly, her mind only capable of taking things one step at a time, "then she might not even be dead. So where is she?"

"Let's not get carried away, Em. There's no reason to think she's alive. Surely any mother would want to see her daughter at some time or other. If she was alive, you would know. She would have come back or at least been in touch. There would have been something."

"Then there's all that stuff about her taking me away. If only I could remember—there was a bundle of photos of her too, some of them with Dad.

You know, Joe, she was never real before. Now, I know she *was* real. She and Dad—" Then her chin wobbled and to her horror, she started to cry, really cry with puffy eyes and her mouth all twisted out of shape.

She pulled her scarf up around her face, not wanting Joe to see her like that and then she was tucked into his chest and he was stroking her hair until gradually the sobs subsided and she felt calm enough to surface again.

"I think I'm going to talk to Jackie as soon as we get back."

"Are you OK, Em? Yes, I think you should do that. But can we just agree on one thing? Let's try not to talk about it again until we get home. I'm so looking forward to this weekend and we don't want to spoil it by tormenting ourselves about your mother the whole time. It won't solve anything anyway."

"No, you're right," Emma said as she rearranged the combs that pinned her hair back on either side and picked up the gin and tonic which Joe had managed to procure while she was buried in his chest. Proper, fizzy tonic in tins. And he *was* right, as usual. She was determined not to mention it again, even if she couldn't guarantee to put it out of her mind completely. She even managed a smile as they touched their plastic glasses together and drank to a happy weekend ahead.

* * *

They stayed in a little hotel near the Panthéon and found the name of the nearest Metro station, Les Gobelins, hilariously funny. The hotel had at some point been invaded by spidery indoor plants, some of which had perished in the dark hallway; the lucky survivors had congregated *en masse* on a gruesome outdoor patio with once white plastic chairs and sea green uplighters illuminating the puddles and autumn leaves. Joe joked that only the goblins were missing.

The furniture in their room was vintage flat-pack and the bath took an age to fill up, but it didn't bother them. In the morning, they wandered out onto the Boulevard Saint-Marcel and ordered massive cups of café au lait and croissants for breakfast in the brasserie on the corner, where a friendly waiter took a biro to their plan touristique and muddled them up with instructions to take the M7 and change at Châtelet or Pyramides or Opéra.

They went to the Musée d'Orsay, they ate steak frites and drank vin rouge and they strolled along the Seine. They admired the artistic displays of vegetables, meats and cheeses at the Place Monge market and wandered up the Champs-Elysées to the Arc de Triomphe. On Sunday, they went to Notre Dame.

"Do you believe in God?" Emma whispered to Joe as they sat close together in one of the polished wood pews.

They had queued for nearly an hour to get in to the cathedral, climbed the 387 steps to the top, squeezed past the gargoyles and admired, with slightly shaky knees on Emma's part, the stunning view of Paris in all directions. Now they were gazing up at the magnificent Gothic arches and high vaulted ceilings of the cathedral itself, glowing in the light of hundreds of chandeliers.

"I mean, look at all those people lighting candles and saying prayers. What good do they think it's going to do? I think it's almost criminal, deceiving people like that and taking money from them too. People are so gullible. It shouldn't be allowed."

"Well, it's true, religion does have a track record of taking advantage of people. There's a lot of nonsense that goes on in most religions, especially when they fall into the wrong hands. But underneath all that I think there *is* something there and you know, if you boil it down enough, it's pretty much the same whatever religion you look at. It's nearly always about love and looking after each other—compassion. I believe in that."

"But look at that." Emma nodded towards the statue of Jesus on the cross at the centre of the ornate gothic altar. "How could Jesus be the actual, biological son of God? If you don't believe in Jesus, does that mean you can't go to heaven? What if you happen to be born in Japan or the Congo or—you might never have even heard of Jesus. Are you doomed to eternal hellfire just because of geography? It seems such nonsense. No. I believe that this is all there is and we just have to get on with it by ourselves. There's no one up there to help us."

"When I go into a church, especially a cathedral like this, I do feel something. I don't know what it is, but there's a mystery about it. It would be the same in a temple I think or a mosque. Don't you feel it? It's enough to make me think that maybe we don't know everything there is to know, that there's something important out there you can't see or touch."

Joe shrugged his shoulders and smiled, which effectively stopped the conversation from developing into an argument.

"Come on. Are you feeling strong enough for the Boulevard St Germain? Perhaps we should stop for a drink at the Deux Magots. You would probably have got on well with Jean-Paul Sartre."

It wasn't until Emma was sitting on the plane back to London, nursing her sore feet and clutching a box of Ladurée macaroons to prove to her father that they had made the pilgrimage to the Rue Bonaparte he had insisted on, that she allowed herself to think about her mother's letter. Joe was plugged into his Walkman beside her with his eyes closed. She turned towards him and laughed to see his head nodding in time to the beat, a goofy expression on his face. Not the time to bring it up again with him again, then.

Her mother had loved her! But why had she taken her away from her father and where had they gone? How long for? Days, months, years? This was not just her mother's story, it was hers as well. Had her parents been happy together? It didn't sound like it. But it couldn't have been that bad because they got married, after all. Or at least, she had always assumed they had. Was she at all like her mother, because she didn't look much like her, and if so, in what way? If she was still alive what would it be like to meet her after all this time? She tried to imagine her mother turning up at Regent Mansions in that orange crochet dress and it freaked her out.

Would her father have been very different with her mother around? She was so used to seeing him on his own or with Jackie or with work colleagues. She'd always assumed he was too old to get married again, but seeing him in that photo made her realise that he probably hadn't been much older than she was now when her mother died. Or didn't die. He could easily have married again, but he'd never even had a girlfriend.

The idea of having a stepmother was too dreadful to contemplate. But why *hadn't* he ever found someone else? Didn't he feel lonely sometimes? What was going to happen when she moved out and left him on his own? Would she be responsible for him for the rest of her life? And why, *why*, couldn't he just tell her what happened?

Chapter 9
Rishikesh

As his train pulled out of Amritsar station Alex stared out of the window, hardly registering the squalor of the suburbs as it faded into open fields dotted with stooped figures labouring in the heat. First he had asked four different people where to catch the Shatabdi Express and had received four different answers. Then when he finally arrived at platform 2 an argument between two men standing beside him had escalated into a fight, which soon included several more people who had tried to break it up but had ended up joining in.

Goodness knows what it had all been about but one of the original men, who had clearly lost the argument, had got a brutal kicking from the mob until he lay unconscious on the ground. It had been uncomfortable to watch and it had revealed an undercurrent of violence unimaginable at the Golden Temple the day before.

The hordes of people and the racket inside the carriage did nothing to soothe his nerves, either. The train hooted constantly to clear the line of fruit sellers, cars, dogs, cows and children. In fact, the railway seemed to be an essential place to do business, rather than private property to be defended from trespassers as it was back home. It was pretty hectic inside the carriage too, with at least half a dozen conversations taking place at the same time, probably in half a dozen dialects for all he knew, and a pervasive smell of sweat and curry which were both getting stronger in the rising heat.

His fellow passengers rummaged in luggage racks for bags and snacks, adjusted seating arrangements, rearranged saris, passed round infants and hung out of windows. It all seemed a long way away from the London train to Tiverton Parkway, where you would never dream of even making eye contact with anyone.

It was also hard to resist. Sitting quietly, looking out of the window or reading his book for the next few hours just wasn't going to happen. Soon he had lots of new friends who wanted to know who he was and where he came from, and as he smiled, chatted, admired babies and shared samosas, the hours passed and his anxiety was forgotten.

* * *

Several hours later the train clanked into Ambala Cantonment, where Alex extricated himself from his newly acquired extended family and got off. He had been expecting some remote little place miles from anywhere but Ambala Cantonment was hardly that. It had once been an important British army base, occupying a key position on the Grand Trunk Road at the crossroads between Shimla to the North, a sanctuary for delicate British skins during the grilling summer heat of the plains, Delhi to the south, Uttar Pradesh to the East and Lahore to the west. Now it was a key station for the Indian Air Force.

Alex wandered along the tree-lined avenues, past colonial bungalows with their comfortable verandas and ornamental gardens, so at odds with the heat and dust of the Indian city. He imagined what it must have been like to live here then—gin and tonics on the veranda, dinners at the Club and barouches home, the Memsahibs visiting each other, criticising each other's domestic arrangements and marrying each other off while the Sahibs in their topis got on with building the railways and establishing the rule of law.

He met their ghosts drifting amongst the headstones in the overgrown British Christian Cemetery and tried to see things from their point of view. They told him how hard they had worked to build the very infrastructure that India now rested on—its judiciary, transport, education, local government and military training. Not to mention the Indian people's high degree of literacy and ability to speak English.

Without those foundations would India have even survived after independence, let alone taken up such a prominent position on the world stage? Not such a one-way street for the British after all—especially when you added in the heat, the deaths from cholera and typhoid and the children left behind to grow up in vicarages all over England.

* * *

But, Alex thought, perhaps his own ancestors had been here too. How would he know? He had come from nowhere, he had no history. No family likeness to anyone he'd ever known or was ever likely to know. No family talent to look out for, no predictor of body size, shape, character or medical vulnerability. He might as well have arrived from another planet. His adoptive family had been the one thing that connected him to this world, but now Lorna was dead, James was paralysed by grief and Joe and Emma weren't there for him, he wasn't connected at all. Perhaps it was not so surprising that he had fallen apart.

He walked into Ambala city and checked into the Sunrise Hotel, which was not nearly as exotic as its name implied, then set off to explore. Modern Ambala was an industrial town peppered with a few grimy temples, but nothing which could hold a candle to the Golden Temple at Amritsar. It was definitely not on the tourist trail but it would give him a chance to acclimatise for a day or two and immerse himself in the real India, whatever that was. Apart from anything else he needed to get hold of something to wear on the ashram since Scott had made it clear that his jeans and T shirt would not do.

He plunged into the semi-darkness of the Ambala Cloth Market and was soon seated on the carpet of a showroom packed to the rafters with shelves of glittering saris, slices of red, yellow, green, blue and every other colour with gorgeous glimpses of beadwork and embroidery. After a compulsory cup of tea, he managed to convince the crestfallen tailor/proprietor that he really did only want a plain white suit, and an hour later he emerged the proud owner a of white cotton Punjabi outfit with loose drawstring trousers and a tunic top that came down to his knees. It was so comfortable that he couldn't wait to start wearing it.

The Golden Temple had awakened Alex's curiosity about the Sikhs and in Ambala, he had plenty of opportunity to learn more about them. He had assumed their turbans came ready-made but now he discovered they were expertly hand-wrapped around waist-length black hair which was never cut. He found himself inspecting every turban he saw and evaluating the skill involved in its creation, marvelling at their perfect swoops and folds. But there was something simmering beneath the surface here too and the vicious-looking daggers he spotted tucked into some of those Sikh waistbands unnerved him. Every covert conversation or angry exchange amongst the locals set him on edge.

So he kept himself to himself as he walked, shopped, admired motorbikes, ate at Mr Singh's Fast Food Cafe and drank the local Kingfisher beer. When he was ready to move on he packed up his backpack, walked to the trunk road and waited in the 40-degree heat until he got a ride up to Rishikesh.

* * *

Unlike Ambala, Rishikesh was beautiful and very much on the tourist trail. It featured the usual heaps of stones and sand along every roadside—Indian towns seemed to be permanently under construction—but at its heart it turned out to be a delightful hill station nestled along the banks of the Ganges in the tree-covered foothills of the Himalayas.

Here the air was cool and clear and there was that holiness in the air again—Hindu temples silent in prayer high above the river, bathing ghats for pilgrims and saddhus in orange robes who seemed to look right into your soul, guttering candles, bells and incense. And it was apparently the yoga capital of the world, thick with ashrams.

This was what he had come here for and he wasn't going to spend another two days wandering around the town. Instead he quickly secured a rickshaw and handed the driver the now crumpled piece of paper Scott had given him. The ashram was apparently a little out of town, not on the Ganges at all, which unleashed a stream of suggestions from his driver of many other superior ashrams that would definitely please him more. But this time Alex managed to impose his will on the excitable man behind the handlebars and a short time later he reached the end of his journey.

Well, at least it exists, Alex thought as he arranged his few possessions around the sparse dormitory he had been allocated by what passed as the management. That's one up for Scott's credibility. In Ambala, he had begun to wonder whether he had dreamed the whole thing. After all, he had come all the way here as a result of a casual conversation with a stranger in a temple. It could have turned out to be a wild goose chase. But it wasn't as if he had anything better to do and here he was, armed with his comfortable white trousers and ready for an indefinite period of clean living. Something in that conversation with Scott must have struck a chord.

And here was Scott in the doorway, smiling broadly and blocking out the light, looking extraordinarily at home.

"Alex! Hey, buddy! You made it! What do you think? Come on, let me show you around."

Scott's unbridled enthusiasm made Alex acutely conscious of his British reserve, but he managed to return the clap on the back without too much awkwardness. It looked like he was going to end up getting to know Scott pretty well and he hoped he could cope with all the bonhomie. But he seemed nice enough and it would be good to have a friendly face around. God knows he needed one.

"Glad you got here! Though I kinda thought you would—you looked the type."

The type. What on earth did that mean? Was there a type? It was true he didn't look too good at the moment with his hollow cheeks and skinny legs, but that wouldn't take long to sort out. So what had marked him out as someone who needed an ashram? Was it that obvious?

Scott laughed at Alex's expression. "Look, it's none of my business. It's just that I could see you looked lost—as though you were searching for something, trying to make sense of things. I don't know. Troubled. I mean, you're travelling alone and you don't seem to have much of a plan. Hey, I'm probably way off. But you *are* here."

Alex nodded as casually as he could manage. Scott was absolutely right, he was a bit lost, rather more so than he had realised in fact. But how had Scott worked that out so quickly when he'd hardly worked it out himself? He had absolutely no idea what was going on inside Scott's mind or what to make of him. But then, they hadn't really talked about it. They were hardly more than strangers, after all. Perhaps he would be able to pick up something of Scott's easy manner and ability to read people. Perhaps Scott could even help him.

They walked round the ashram together, Scott in his white pyjamas and Alex still in dusty jeans and T-shirt, while Scott talked him through how things worked. He already seemed to know everyone and everything, even though he could only have been here a couple of days. How the hell did he do that? He made it all look so easy.

"You get up early, when it's still dark, for two hours of meditation before breakfast. It's hard getting out of bed but there's something magical about being up at that time of the morning. And once you get going it's wonderful, so peaceful—you're going to love it. It's done me so much good already."

They were standing in front of a little open-air temple supported by carved wooden columns decorated with Indian gods and goddesses engaged in surprisingly un-temple-like activities. It was almost completely hidden behind a large tree laden with some sort of green fruit. Scott was proffering an arm as if it was his personal domain.

"That's where we do the morning meditation and yesterday we had some monks chanting too. After breakfast there's Satsang, which is a sort of pep talk, although we haven't seen the guru yet."

Alex was listening carefully. Scott seemed so genuine that he wanted to trust him.

"The food's all vegetarian, but it's fine. And you're in bed by about 9 o'clock, but you'll be absolutely exhausted by then."

"Did they give you a dormitory? This is mine here. There's three of us—me, a guy from Wales called Aidan and a New Yorker, an ex-banker, poor sod—but we've got one spare. Why don't you get yourself moved in here? Let's go and talk to the office about it."

And without waiting for an answer he loped off across the lawn towards the main building. Alex hung back, wondering if Scott was going to turn out to be a hyperactive maniac with verbal diarrhoea or possibly worse, but then Scott stopped suddenly and turned to Alex.

"I love the stillness here. There's no hurry, is there? Let's just sit here in the garden for a while."

He threw himself onto the grass and gazed up at the sky, shielding his eyes against the sun. Relieved, Alex followed suit and felt himself relax into companionable silence. Yes, perhaps this had been a good move after all, he thought, as they laughed at a family of monkeys crashing through the branches above them. Perhaps everything was going to be all right.

* * *

To begin with, Alex found meditating almost impossible. It sounded perfectly simple, but although he would sit quite still in a sort of cross-legged tailor's pose—the full lotus position being completely out of the question—for what felt like hours but usually turned out to be only a few minutes, watching for the *ma—om*—vibration on each in and out breath, his mind just would not stop jumping about.

However hard he tried to hold his attention still, after a moment or two he would suddenly realise with a start that he'd drifted off again. It was quite extraordinary the things he found himself thinking about and it took all his willpower not to become absorbed in them but to let them go and come back to his breath again. Whenever he sneaked a look at Scott and the others they all seemed to be getting on fine, so why couldn't he do it? Perhaps he just wasn't made for meditation and he would never get the hang of it. Maybe it just wasn't for him. What was the point of thinking about nothing anyway? Surely being alive was about engaging with life, not checking out and pretending you weren't really there.

But gradually he learned that being patient and sticking at it were lessons in themselves. Things that were worth having didn't always come to you instantly, you had to put in the effort. He came to believe that once you did start to find that stillness, you would gradually develop the wisdom to sort out your problems and ease your suffering without even realising you were doing it. If you were lucky you might even find something divine in there too. Surely that was worth waiting for.

* * *

As Alex and Scott settled into the ashram routine of meditation, morning Satsangs, vegetarian brunches and yoga—and carrying out their communal duties, Scott in the kitchens, Alex in the vegetable garden—they became firm friends.

Scott was different from anyone Alex had ever known before, with his confident manner and ability to talk about absolutely anything, but, as Alex discovered, underneath he was prone to all the same feelings of pain and self-doubt as anyone else. Although he had the knack of making life look easy, he had already had his fair share of troubles. He told Alex about growing up in the suburbs of Vancouver, the eldest of three brothers. His father worked in town in commercial real estate and his mother stayed home to look after the kids. Life was comfortable and as children they had wanted for nothing.

Scott had had an easy time at school too—he was not especially bright but he got on well with the other kids and he was good at sport. His childhood had been one of order, achievement and healthy competition and as he grew into a teenager he developed a real talent for field hockey. He was picked up by the national squad at 16 and was all set for a career as a professional field hockey player. Life could hardly have been better, although he admitted he had taken it all pretty much for granted at the time.

"Then I had the injury. It was such a stupid fall—early in the season and I was trying to impress the coach I suppose—but I went for an awkward tackle, it got messy and I twisted my leg badly as I went down. Had to be carried off the pitch, couldn't put my foot to the ground. They told me I'd torn the cruciate ligament in my knee and I'd need reconstructive surgery—six months out, minimum.

"Well, we went for a second opinion and a third, but the picture just got worse and worse. I think I knew then that I would never play hockey for the national team again. You can't imagine how that felt, Alex. It's all I'd ever wanted to do.

"So I had the operation. It went OK. I had to do a lot of exercises and physio to get my knee moving properly again. I was on crutches for a while and the pain was pretty bad. And I was gutted about not being able to play. I suppose it must have been pretty tough on Mum, me being such a miserable sod and totally dependent on her. I was just so wrapped up in my own problems. But I honestly don't remember her being down—I'm sure I would have noticed. I'm sure I would.

"Apparently, she'd been ill for a while and she was on antidepressants—I had no idea. First thing we knew, when it happened, was that the police rang Dad to say they'd found our car on the Lion's Gate Bridge. They found her body in the water a few hours later."

For a moment, Alex didn't understand.

"Did she have an accident or something?"

"No. She jumped off."

Alex couldn't hide his shock. He tried to imagine how he would have felt if Lorna had committed suicide. And it sounded as though Scott felt he was partly to blame. What a nightmare.

Scott saw Alex's expression and nodded.

"It was dreadful. I don't know how much Dad knew about what was going on, but us kids had no idea at all. I still don't understand why she did it. Dad says to think of it like an illness, not something that was caused by anything that was happening in her life. But surely there must have been signs. I just didn't notice.

"The others were too young but she did so much for me, she supported me all through school and field hockey, drove me to endless practices and matches. And I only realised how important she was to me after she'd gone. I never even thought about whether she was OK. I took her for granted. I should have been there for her and I wasn't."

"But you were a child, Scott! Surely if anyone could have helped her, it would have been your Dad?"

"I know. That's what I tell myself. I think it was even worse for him. It was all he could do to keep his head above water and look after the other two after she died. I couldn't expect him to help me with my problems."

"So you decided to leave?"

"Not straight away, I couldn't have done. I was in such a state, what with Mum and my life in such a mess. You see, up until then, all I'd had to worry about was whether I passed a test or got picked for a team. Everything else stayed the same. But then I lost my future and my mother."

"Yes. I think I know how that feels."

"But there was one person who did really help me—my physio. She knew I was struggling and she arranged for me to see a psychotherapist. I wasn't that happy about it to start with, I can tell you. But then I thought, well, it can't make things any worse. And it did help after a while. Gradually I started to make a bit more sense of things. Ironic really, that if it hadn't been for my knee injury, I probably wouldn't be here now."

"So in one way I'm glad it happened. Not glad that I got injured and had to stop playing hockey or that my mother died, because they were both awful. But glad that I had to wake up and start thinking a bit differently. Sometimes you need something to wake you up. It's taught me so much that I wouldn't have learned otherwise and it's made me more grateful for what I have—I wasn't before when I had so much. I think I'm starting to have a better idea what I'm here for now and it's not just about playing hockey."

Alex couldn't help but be impressed. Scott's was a terrible story and yet he had managed to come out of it in better shape. Was it possible he could do the same?

"So that's my story. What's yours, Alex?"

Alex's own problems suddenly seemed rather trivial compared to Scott's. And yet here he was, wandering aimlessly around Asia, with no plan for the future at all. Scott had spotted it straight off. And now Scott had told his story so honestly, Alex felt he had no choice but to do the same.

"My mother died too, of cancer. A couple of years ago. Dad was pretty cut up, still is. But she'd been ill for a while so it wasn't a shock when it happened.

"Although in fact she wasn't my natural mother—I'm adopted. I loved her like a real mother and I love my father and my brother Joe too. I've always thought of them as my real family. I was lucky I guess—things could have been a hell of a lot worse."

"Have you ever tried to contact your birth mother?"

"No. I couldn't even if I wanted to, there's no way of tracing her. She gave me up when I was a baby. Dumped on a doorstep, pretty much, like you read in the papers. But I try not to think about her—and I would never want my family to think I was ungrateful or that they weren't enough for me. Actually, it's never bothered me. It's better this way."

But it hadn't been a great start in life really now he came to think about it and at some level he must have always known that. Out here he was starting to see things differently. His mother had abandoned him, hadn't she, so she obviously hadn't wanted him. That's why he'd always done his best to keep his head down, in case it happened again. He always knew he didn't have the right to the same sort of happiness as Joe.

"So you're adopted. I guess that's pretty tough. What else?"

Damn Scott's perceptiveness.

"Well—it's nothing really. But there's someone who was a good friend of mine, her name's Emma. I've always been closer to her than anyone else, pretty much ever since I can remember. Then a couple of months ago she started going out with my brother Joe. It meant I sort of lost her. Both of them, in fact, I lost both of them at the same time."

"It sounds stupid, doesn't it? I mean, I had lots of other friends, but no one I was close to like them. I felt like they had abandoned me. I suppose that was what I was always most afraid of, you know, after being given up as a baby and everything and then it went and happened again."

Yes, that was it. He might as well have been back on the doorstep, wrapped in an old shawl.

"Was she your girlfriend then, this Emma?"

"No. No. She was just a friend."

Just a friend or someone he loved or someone he wished was his girlfriend and not Joe's? Was it losing her that had caused him so much pain or was there more to it than that? Well, he was certainly in the right place to try and figure it out. He needed to start all over again. Work out who on earth he was and what he wanted to do with his life, even if that had to be without Joe and Em. Anyway, it wasn't as if they had died or anything. And as Scott said, it could be a good thing in a way when something like this happened and you had to wake up.

* * *

The ex-banker from New York didn't last long, but Alex and Scott soon made friends with Aiden, the fourth member of their dormitory. Aiden had been brought up on a farm in the Brecon Beacons where everyone farmed. But Aiden hadn't turned out to be much of a farmer, so he left the mud and the rain for a better life.

He had already spent several years rattling around South East Asia and had an air of casual worldliness that the boys couldn't help admiring. He kept them entertained with his endless travellers' tales, usually involving him narrowly escaping with his life, but he was a good storyteller and they enjoyed his intelligence, quick wit and pearls of wisdom.

His arrival at the ashram had been the result of his most recent scrape. He had been up in the Kashmir valley close to the Pakistani border, 'minding his own business', when he had apparently been taken for a mujahideen and kidnapped by a gang of Pandits with AK-47s. Despite this unfortunate case of mistaken identity, or perhaps because of it, he had ended up fleeing south with them from Islamic persecution until they had eventually reached sanctuary at Dharamsala. History didn't relate exactly how he had limped from there to the ashram, but since then he seemed to have made a remarkable recovery.

"Yeah. It was a bit shit, man. But I can handle it, I've seen stuff like that before. And hey, here I am! Although I have to tell you, guys. This ashram's not the best I've ever come across."

Alex could see that Scott was taken in by Aiden, but then Scott trusted people easily, as he himself had experienced. Alex wasn't so convinced about Aiden's stories or about the ashram itself, come to that.

"Well, it's a beautiful place and meditation's a really good thing—I get all that. But what's the point in coming to an ashram with a famous guru if she's not bloody well here? Apparently, she's been away for months. In America, supposedly. I'm starting to wonder if she even exists. No one seems to know when she's coming back. And the rest of them could be trying to brainwash us for all we know. I wouldn't put it past them."

"Oh come on, Alex, you can't believe that!" Scott looked genuinely shocked at the idea, but Aiden nodded.

"Alex's right, Scott. What you've got here is a relatively small set-up, a starter ashram if you like. It's great for finding your feet, learning how to get started. It's very peaceful, not too demanding. But if you're serious about what you're doing, you need a guru who you can really learn from. It's not as comfortable, sure—more challenging. But if life is a school and we come here to learn, there's no point in spending all of it in primary."

Put like that, both Alex and Scott had to agree. It was true that life in this ashram was comfortable and they had both felt that they had made a good start. But now the thought of moving on had been planted it grew and flourished, leaving their satisfaction with the ashram wilting in the shade. By the time the three of them discussed it again they were more than ready to move on, with Aiden their self-appointed leader.

Chapter 10
The Caprice

"Em, darling. I've been expecting this phone call for a long time now." Jackie's voice on the phone had been reassuring. "Of course you want to know about your mother, I completely understand. I'll tell you whatever I can, although I don't know the whole story. I've always respected your father's decision not to talk to you about Frances, but you're not a child anymore and it's time you knew the truth. Now, we'll need something to eat and I think a decent bottle of wine would help as well, don't you? Meet me at the Caprice tomorrow at 1 o'clock, I've got a table there."

Emma had been relieved the call had gone so well. Her aunt had not been angry and she had not refused to help. In fact, although it had taken her several days to actually pick up the phone and dial the number, in the end it had been so easy that she wondered why she hadn't thought of asking before, as Jackie had obviously expected her to. Perhaps it was true that at the ripe old age of 23 she was only just starting to grow up.

Now here she was, tucked away at a discreet table at the Caprice, trying to look as though she came here all the time and waiting for Jackie to arrive. Could she really be about to find out all about her mother or was she just going to get the bollocking from her aunt that she probably deserved? She had declined the waiter's offer of a drink, which might have seemed presumptuous and anyway she would probably have chosen the wrong thing.

Instead she was going through the motions of studying the menu, but her eyes were just looking right through it to an unseen point under the table somewhere. In fact, she seemed to have frozen into some kind of trance, wanting to know how this potentially pivotal moment in her life was going to turn out and not wanting to know at the same time. Perhaps it would change everything. But as the Tarot woman had said, there was no going back now.

There was a flurry over by the revolving door as her aunt arrived, looking as neat and beautifully tailored as ever, and she watched, intrigued, as both the maître d'hôtel and the barman paid their respects. Of course—Jackie must be a regular here, lunching with clients must be an important part of her business. Emma rapidly updated the impression of her she had automatically copied from her father, who tended to treat her as a glorified housekeeper with a bit of a knack for fabrics and cushions—in the nicest possible way.

Jackie was escorted to the table by a relay of ingratiating waiters, who seated and napkinned her as a team. She settled in her chair and much to Emma's relief came straight to the point.

"Now, I'm going to tell you everything I know, darling. But I must tell you straight away that I have never seen or heard from your mother since she left that day, the day Richard got the letter you found."

"So she's not dead?" Emma could hardly breathe.

"Well, I don't know for sure. All we have to go on is that letter you found. It's a long story, which I will tell you in a minute, but we knew after that she would never come back. I always hoped against hope that she would at least make contact or that perhaps I would come across something she had painted, but there's been absolutely nothing. Nothing at all. So my guess is that she did take her life, just as she said she would. Poor Frances.

"Your father decided it would be better to tell you she was dead rather than have you spend your whole childhood wondering whether she was about to come back. He was trying to protect you, darling. He didn't want you to know that Frances had walked out on you until you were old enough to understand why. It could have affected you very badly, you know. You might have even thought it was your fault in some way, which of course it wasn't at all."

"So there was no car crash? Oh my God, Joe was right! I can't believe it. All these years Dad's been lying to me. How could he do that? How could he let me believe something so awful? And what else has he lied about? How am I supposed to trust him about anything now?" Emma couldn't keep the anger out of her voice, even though she knew she shouldn't be taking it out on Jackie.

"I'm afraid he did, yes. I know. Yes, he did lie to you, I can't tell you he didn't. But you must try and understand why he did it. It was a ghastly situation and he did what he thought was best for you. He almost convinced himself it was true. And actually, I think it did work out for the best, although of course there was always going to be this moment to deal with. I can tell you, I've never known him lie about anything else and I should know. There are no other secrets. And I've said I'll tell you whatever you want to know."

"Well, I need to know all about her. I've got a lot of catching up to do— What was she like? Am I like her? How did Dad meet her? Do you think she could still be alive, Jackie?"

"OK. I'll tell you the whole story, but let's order first. Have you decided what you want to eat?"

Emma shook her head.

"Why don't we have the Dover sole then? It's very good here."

At the slightest turn of her head, a waiter appeared by her side.

"We'll both have the crispy duck salad and then Dover sole with green beans and spinach. And a bottle of the Sancerre, please. Is that all right for you, darling?"

Relieved, Emma nodded and handed the menu back to the waiter. "It sounds quite delicious," she said automatically and then added, "Jackie, I'm sorry. I didn't mean to snap at you. It's just a bit of a shock."

"Quite all right, darling. Of course it is." She reached out her hand towards Emma's over the table.

"But why didn't you tell me before?"

"I decided long ago that I would when you asked. I wasn't prepared to lie to your face and your father knows that. You asked and here we are."

Jackie picked up her glass to taste the wine as the waiter stood to attention and presented the bottle, label uppermost. She nodded her approval and he poured some into Emma's glass, then hers.

"Come on. Have some of this and I'll tell you all about her."

Jackie held her glass out to Emma's and clinked it, almost in celebration— of belated adulthood perhaps, Emma thought, but nevertheless, it made her feel better. She could hardly have asked for a more helpful response from her aunt, after all.

"So. They met at university. Richard was in his final year at Exeter doing his law degree and they met at a party. Frances had only just arrived, to do an Art Foundation Course there. She had so much talent. Anyway, they met at a party and Richard was immediately attracted to her. Strange really because she wasn't like his other friends at all. She was a real live wire, a bit crazy. Well, you've seen pictures of her."

Emma raised her eyebrows.

"I have now, yes."

"I must say she was very attractive, with that lovely blonde hair and being so tall and slim. Really striking, the sort of girl everyone notices when she walks into a room. And anyway, you couldn't fail to notice her because she had so much energy, she was so full of life. She seemed to be everywhere, talking and laughing with everybody all the time. And you couldn't help liking her because she was such fun to be with.

"She was always in a hurry, Frances was. Sometimes she couldn't seem to speak fast enough to keep up with all the crazy things coming out of her brain. She threw herself headlong into everything she did and I know that sometimes she didn't sleep for days. She was painting a lot, but it didn't stop there—there were all sorts of other things going on too. She started buying music, The Who, Jimi Hendrix, Simon and Garfunkel, anything and everything, she had a huge collection and sometimes she'd stay up and dance all night—and she was never short of dance partners.

"Richard got fed up with all that, but he had to accept it was part of who she was. Then she'd drag everyone up onto the roof for breakfast. And then she'd move on to poetry. That's why I wondered whether she was dropping acid—LSD—but Richard insisted she wasn't. Her enthusiasm was electrifying, I suppose she was what everybody wanted to be at that time. People were in awe of her.

"To start with, I thought she and Richard were good for each other. He was definitely a steadying influence on her and she brought out the lighter side in him. He had been working so hard for his degree and it was good to see him lighten up a bit. He fell totally in love with her and he wanted to take care of her."

The crispy duck salad arrived and Jackie stopped talking while she ate a couple of chunks, chewing absent-mindedly.

"Frances had some pretty wild friends, but she could keep up with them. Richard found that difficult sometimes—he wasn't like them. They were preoccupied with different things. They questioned everything, pushed the boundaries all the time. If that included taking drugs, going on rallies and whipping up anarchy, then so much the better.

"They cared deeply about things like poverty, injustice and inequality and they thought they could change the world. They took Vietnam very personally. There was to be no more war, just peace and love. Richard wasn't comfortable with that, he had more respect for the status quo I suppose. I'm afraid he thought they were rather irresponsible."

Jackie looked thoughtful as she speared a cherry tomato.

"Did you like her?"

"Yes. I did. We were about the same age, after all. She was good company and she was kind, too—there was never any edge to her. She was always very kind to me and there was no reason for her to be. We always got on well. But I don't think I ever really knew her and I'm not sure that even Richard did. There was something unreachable about her, you just didn't quite know what was really going on inside. And of course, I hated it when she upset Richard.

"You see, it wasn't all parties and fun. There was a darker side to her too, I don't know where it came from, but at times she was very hard to be with. She could be really negative, destructive even and say dreadful things that were hard to understand and forgive. It was her depression coming to the surface, I suppose, although we didn't really understand that then."

Jackie looked down at her plate as she went on.

"That summer she took an overdose of sleeping pills. Yes, she'd already tried to kill herself once before. Richard was working hard for his finals so he wasn't spending a lot of time with her. One evening, he got a call from a friend of hers. She was hysterical, said that she'd been worried about Frances so she'd gone round to see her, but she was asleep and she couldn't wake her. It turned out that she'd had swallowed a whole bottle of temazepam, goodness knows how she'd got hold of them."

Jackie hesitated and looked up at Emma.

"This must be awful for you, darling."

"It's OK, Jackie. I need to know this. I need you to tell me everything."

Although Emma was finding it hard to take it all in, she wasn't about to stop her aunt now.

"OK. Well, Richard called an ambulance and they rushed her to A&E. They had to pump her stomach and she only survived because they got to her in time. By the next morning, it would have been a different story. It was more than just a cry for help—she was serious.

"Richard didn't want to let her out of his sight after that, he was so terrified of losing her. She absolutely refused to get help, he was the only person she trusted. He was endlessly patient with her. I suppose you feel more responsible for somebody after something like that—he saved her life, after all.

"Anyway, he got his law degree and they went away for the summer, driving through France and Italy in his beaten up old Morris Minor. It did her the world of good. When they came back, she seemed much better. She'd put on a bit of weight and when I saw her laughing again, I thought thank goodness, the old Frances is back. They seemed so happy and relaxed together."

"Richard was starting at Law School in London that September and he asked Frances to come and live with him. They rented a little flat in Maida Vale and she started to paint again. She enrolled in a course at Chelsea College of Art to help get her portfolio together—she decided she wanted to do an art degree the following year."

Jackie paused as they were presented with two whole Dover sole to admire before they were whisked away and expertly filleted. Emma stared at the tidy fillets on her plate, grateful that she was not going to be expected to wrestle with anything as tiresome as a fish on the bone. A plateful of half lemons, each individually wrapped in muslin to catch the pips, glided onto the table between them.

"I thought then that everything would be all right. I knew Richard had decided he wanted to marry her, but felt he should wait until he had finished Law School and had a job. Frances seemed a lot more settled and I thought she might be able to make a decent living as an artist. She was a bit subdued, but then she'd grown up a lot since she and Richard first met and her suicide attempt had been a pretty shocking episode for her. For both of them. But it seemed to have brought them closer together.

"The trouble was, as Frances' energy came back she started to go off the rails again. She'd made a new crowd of friends at art school and of course she wanted to go out with them in the evening sometimes—which Richard accepted, although he didn't like it very much. But then she started not coming home. I think we all realised that there were other men on the scene, although they never lasted very long—I'm afraid she had quite a reputation for that. She was spending a lot of money, too. Not only on going out, but on clothes, books, jewellery—sometimes she didn't even take the stuff out of the bags.

"Richard was pretty busy with his Law School work but he's not a fool, he knew what was going on. He was angry and upset with her and he couldn't cope with the way she was behaving. I think he must have felt she'd let him down after everything he'd done for her. So when she decided she wanted to go back to Exeter and live with some of her old student friends, it seemed to be for the best.

"Of course, Richard missed her. There was no question that he still loved her, but his life was an awful lot easier without her around. He threw himself into his studying, passed his exams and got his first job at Chambers."

"But that can't have been the end of it." Emma was confused—Jackie hadn't said anything about a baby. Where did she fit in? And what about the suicide note?

"No. It wasn't. It wasn't the end of it at all."

Jackie paused as she thought about how to tell the next part of the story.

"I was at Exeter myself by then, so I saw her from time to time. She always asked me about Richard. I could see things weren't going well—she had scars on her arms where she had cut them. I was worried about her, but I wasn't sure what I could do to help. I'm sorry, Em, this must be so hard for you. But it's part of who she is and I'm trying to be honest with you. She wasn't well and her lifestyle at Exeter was making her worse.

"Then I bumped into her in the street one rainy afternoon. She was soaked to the skin and she seemed very upset, so I persuaded her to come and have a cup of tea with me in my digs. While we dried her things on the radiator, she told me she had made a terrible mistake leaving Richard and she would give anything to have her life with him back again. She kept asking me over and over again about him and whether there was any sign that he still cared about her.

"Well, I just wasn't sure what to do. I didn't want them to get back together if it was just going to be a disaster all over again and why would it be any different this time? But then, they clearly did love each other and they had been happy before—perhaps it had just been an unfortunate phase. She certainly didn't seem to be capable of anything like that now.

"In the end I thought, well, Richard's going to have to make up his own mind about this. So I agreed with Frances that I would tell him about our conversation and leave it up to him to get in touch with her if he wanted to. She agreed that if she didn't hear from him, she would leave him alone. And off she went.

"I've often wondered whether I did the right thing keeping my side of that bargain. It would certainly have saved a lot of heartache if I hadn't. But I didn't feel it was up to me to decide for them and in any case, they would probably have got back together anyway in the end, with or without me sticking my oar in.

"So Frances came back to Maida Vale and for a while all went well. Frances seemed to be reasonably settled—no dramas. I suppose I wasn't particularly surprised when they told me that she was pregnant—it seemed the right thing to do, somehow. I didn't see them much at that time, although I know the pregnancy affected her mood quite badly. But she really wanted to make a go of it and I admired her for that. Richard doted on her and he was so excited about the new arrival. It was a happy time for them.

"But it was a difficult labour and it was exhausting for her. I remember going to see you both at St Mary's—you were such a lovely baby, darling, but Frances seemed very fragile. I don't think Richard had any idea how hard it was for her to cope afterwards. He was putting all his efforts into his career now that he had a family to provide for and I don't think he was around as much as he should have been. He certainly wasn't a hands-on father.

"Frances was on her own at home with you a lot and I think she had post-natal depression. You know, she always was a great mother, a real natural and wonderful with you. But she was beginning to realise just how hard it was going to be for her to bring up a child when her own head was all over the place."

Jackie paused while their plates were whisked away and then carried on in a low voice. Emma was totally absorbed. What on earth was coming next?

"Well, she left again. And she took you with her."

"But where did she go? Where did *we* go?"

"I never found out exactly where she went. I know she didn't go home—her family life was very difficult. Her father died when she was about ten, shut himself in the garage with the car engine running. Her mother had to go out to work and Frances was the mother of the family. She practically brought up her younger brothers. She left as soon as she could for Exeter and she never went back. So I knew she wouldn't go there.

"She told me later that she joined some sort of commune in an old B&B in Exeter. She said she felt relaxed there. The commune had connections with an organisation in India and they did yoga and meditation, which helped her a lot. It was all very back-to-nature, anti-establishment, peace and love, which of course she felt very much at home with. And she liked having people around her all the time—for the company and also to help look after you. I think they had a lot of fun, actually. I suppose it was a free and easy life.

"But the problem was that soon you weren't a baby anymore and she started worrying that it wasn't the right place for a toddler to grow up. Well, it wasn't, really. And she felt guilty about taking you away from Richard when he was the one person who could give you some stability. She missed him dreadfully and she seemed to be doing OK. So she decided it would be better for both of you to come back to London. She tried so hard to do the right thing, bless her.

"I don't think Richard would have had her back if it hadn't been for you, but it was more complicated now. And I suppose he still hoped she would eventually grow out of her problems and things would work out for them. He certainly still loved her—he always did. But this time he had one condition—that they get married. It had to be all or nothing as far as he was concerned and he wanted that commitment from her.

"Well, she agreed and back you both came to Maida Vale. Richard asked me to keep an eye on her and I did what I could. But I think it was just too much, moving back and getting engaged all at the same time, and it tipped her right over the edge again. It was soon after that that she left for the last time. She never discussed it with Richard, she just left him the letter you found. She couldn't stay, I think we all realised that by then. She'd had such a difficult time and I suppose she just couldn't take any more. And—well, you know the rest of the story."

"So did they ever actually get married or not?"

"No, they didn't, darling. No."

"And you have no idea what happened to her?"

Jackie shook her head.

"We had no way of knowing. It may sound awful to you, but we had to let her go. Richard was the last person who could help her.

"There—you know as much as I do now."

Emma wasn't sure what she had been expecting, but it certainly wasn't this. She had wanted to know what her mother was like, to satisfy her curiosity more than anything, but this untidy, unfinished story only raised more questions. Could her father possibly have been right not to tell her about it before? It was a lot to think about.

"But she could easily still be alive, Jackie. All this time I thought she was dead—and she could be living in the next door street! I'm sorry but I just can't leave it like that."

Emma half rose in her chair as if she was off to scour the neighbourhood right away.

"No. I thought you would say that and I can't say I'm surprised. I think I'd feel much the same. But if she *was* around, you would know. She would have *had* to see you. She loved you very much, you know. And supposing you did find her—what then? You may not like what you find. What if she has another family? Other children? You never know with Frances. You get hurt over and over again and in the end you have to walk away, like Richard did. It's dangerous, Em."

Emma stirred her coffee for some time, weighing this up.

"No. I don't care what she's like, Jackie—she's my mother. I have to know what happened to her. But where on earth do I start?"

Jackie rummaged in her bag until she found her cigarettes and lit one. Emma eyed them enviously, but she never smoked at home.

"I'm still in touch with some of my friends from Exeter days. Maybe somebody might know somebody who lived on this commune. You never know—someone may have known her there. I could make a few calls. I might be able to find out something."

"Would you do that? Soon? This evening even?"

Jackie nodded slowly.

"All right. But I'm also going to call Richard and let him know we've had this conversation. I don't think he will be surprised, but it's only fair to tell him."

Oh, God. She couldn't imagine how he was going to react. Would he be furious with her? Perhaps she'd messed everything up between them. She had wanted him to talk about her mother for so long, but now the prospect was terrifying.

"Well, thank you, Jackie. And thank you for telling me all this. Just one more question—what were her paintings like?"

"They were exciting. Abstract, full of energy and colour, as though the canvas was never quite big enough for them. Oh, yes, she was good. That Fiona Rae I brought round the other day? It reminded me of her. And my God, she could churn stuff out—she always had canvases stacked up against every wall. But Richard got rid of everything when she left, every last tube of paint. He just couldn't bear it."

Chapter 11
Swamiji

"Now we're actually leaving, I'm a bit sad to go," Alex admitted to the others as they packed three similar selections of grubby T-shirts, jeans and primitive washing equipment into three almost identical grunge-grey backpacks. He could have added that now he had got the measure of their peaceful life here the thought of tackling the outside world and then having to start over in a new and more challenging set-up was not an entirely attractive one.

He was enjoying the simple routine, getting up in the dark when the rest of the world was asleep and padding in his bare feet to the temple to sit cross-legged alongside Scott. The silent presence of people meditating, the flicker of the candles reflecting in the glass vase of yellow roses and the wriggle of smoke rising up from the incense sticks on the shrine in front of them created a powerful space which held him, distancing him from his past.

And he felt he was making some sort of progress. Although his mind was far from still, it was slowing down from its usual high-speed clatter. Living on a diet of wholesome vegetarian food had not been nearly as hard as he thought—in fact, he was rather enjoying it. He was starting to look and feel better, the clear air up here was invigorating and the slow pace of life was bringing him moments of real peace. He was even enjoying tending to the cucumbers and yams in the vegetable garden now that he was actually paying a bit more attention to what he was doing. God knows what his friends back home would make of it, but it seemed to be working.

"So where exactly is this ashram, Aiden? What's it going to be like?"

"It'll be what it'll be, you know? I can't tell you *exactly* where it is, but I know how to get there. I guess it'll be a lot bigger than here and more—more full-on. You know, people who are really into it. Other than that, your guess is as good as mine, mate."

"But I guess you've been to a ton of ashrams like this before," Scott said.

"Nope. This is my first ashram, just like you." Aiden smiled benignly, swinging his backpack onto his shoulder.

Alex caught Scott's eye and could see that Scott, like him, was confused.

"For fuck's sake, Aiden. We're only doing this because of you. *You're* the one who's supposed to know what you're doing. 'Cause you've been to loads of ashrams, haven't you? HAVEN'T YOU?"

Alex was shaking. For God's sake. It had been obvious all along that Aiden was flaky, so why on earth had they trusted him? The stories he had told them were obviously just that—stories. What a load of bollocks.

"Hey. Calm down, mate. What's eating you?"

Alex looked away, anger boiling up inside him. He knew if he looked at Aiden now, he'd probably hit him.

"OK. It's OK, Alex." Scott rested a reassuring hand on Alex's arm, but Alex just shrugged it off, then sank onto his bed and put his head in his hands.

What was wrong with everybody? Why couldn't anyone be straight with him? It wasn't just Aiden, Aiden didn't matter. But Joe—he was angry with Joe. Really angry. And he was angry with his mother too, his real mother, whoever she was. Why did people always have to let you down? What on earth had he done to deserve all this?

Gradually, his surroundings came into focus again and he realised that the other two were watching him in stunned silence. Embarrassed, he looked up and tried to sound as normal as possible.

"So how do you know about this place we're going to, Aiden?"

"Heard about it on the grapevine, mate. Just about everyone's heard of it, on account of the guru there being a bit of a legend. You're not worried, are you?"

"Nah. No way!" Scott laughed.

"What are we waiting for?" Alex attempted a smile.

They were laughing and joking again by the time they strode out across the garden, almost as if nothing had happened. If Alex did feel a little sobered by his momentary loss of control, he held Aiden responsible for it. But it had proved he was right not to trust anybody and to keep his feelings well out of sight. He resolved to be more careful in future.

* * *

This time Alex hardly noticed the journey. Aiden had managed to recover some of his credibility, at least in terms of getting them from A to B, and they simply followed him from ashram to bus to train to bus to ashram with very little need to engage with their surroundings at all. The usual mass of humanity on the move, the traffic, the noise, the heat and the dust left them unmoved, so intent were they on the inner journey they hoped to embark on.

"You'd better tell us what you've heard about this guru, Aiden."

"Uh—well, I know his name is Swamiji. That's what everyone calls him anyway. And he's very well respected—he's descended from a long line of gurus going back hundreds of years. Lineage matters if you're a guru. People say he has an aura about him, that just being near him can awaken something in you. And another good thing, he has a large following here in India so he's based here all the time—we're not going to get there and find he has moved to California."

"Well, that'll be a plus." Alex couldn't resist twisting the knife.

"And what about the ashram? You must know *something* about it."

"Look, guys. You'll just have to take it as you find it—I've told you, I don't have all the gen. All I know is that it's called Ramana Ashram and it's somewhere near Bilphor. That's where we're heading now. And I think we have to be vetted by Swamiji, so presumably when we arrive we'll have to have some sort of interview."

Alex and Scott looked at each other in alarm.

"How do you pass an interview with a guru, for heaven's sake?" Alex burst out.

* * *

As it turned out, a few hours later they were indeed required to present themselves before Swamiji.

They had got off the bus in Bilphor and asked around for Ramana Ashram, which was well-known in the area—they were obviously not the first scruffy ashram-seekers to turn up on Bilphor's doorstep. They walked the last leg out of town to the ashram, which was, as promised, impossible to miss—you could see the entrance from miles away, flanked on both sides by an immaculate row of crimson hibiscus bushes.

It looked so much more like a resort hotel than an ashram that they felt they should be arriving with a full set of luggage each or at the very least in a taxi.

116

But they weren't going to turn back now, so they swaggered as best they could under an imposing pagoda roof with 'Ramana International' picked out on the side in brass letters and they were in.

They followed the signs through an impressive garden to the ashram's reception block, where they were adorned with marigold garlands, checked in by a well-groomed receptionist and told to settle in for a lengthy wait. It seemed that they could not be allocated a dormitory until they had seen Swamiji—in fact, they weren't allowed a step further until the interview had taken place. Although they were hot, tired and dusty from their journey, Swamiji wanted to greet them precisely in this condition; and Swamiji was otherwise occupied.

Alex watched the white plastic blades of the fan on the ceiling go round and round, trying to untangle each individual blade from the hypnotic blur of movement as it flew past. If you studied the thing for long enough it looked as though it might be slowing down, exhausted from the endless effort of rotating, but then when you looked away you realised that the pace hadn't changed at all. Like everything else in India, it was merely pacing itself for the long haul.

Once the other two had thrashed out the chances of the Lions winning the Grey Cup for once they had fallen silent as well, wrapped up in their own thoughts. The long wait had somewhat dampened the excitement of their arrival, but they had been given some perfectly acceptable sandwiches to eat, they were out of the worst of the heat and they could hardly quibble about being kept waiting for an earthly hour or two when eternity awaited.

Alex had got over his rage at Aiden—after all, he had delivered them to Ashram Ramana as promised, even if he did talk a lot of bollocks sometimes. Looking across at him now, watching him examining his fingernails as if he had never seen them before, Alex couldn't see any evidence of subterfuge or trickery. Although that didn't mean he had to like the guy.

Despite the fan, all three of them were gradually sinking into some sort of heat-induced trance. How they were going to make any impression on Swamiji in this state, God only knew. In any case, if the life-sized portrait of the guru hanging on the wall opposite them was anything to go by, Alex was quite happy to postpone their meeting with him indefinitely.

Swamiji certainly seemed to have all the hallmarks of serious gurudom. He was seated in the portrait, presumably cross-legged, although the layers of orange robes draped about his person made him appear to have no legs at all—he was simply floating on a sea of marigold petals. He was unlike anyone Alex had ever seen before.

In fact, he hardly looked human at all—more like a giant troll. His grey hair was long and greasy, with a side parting which did not entirely conceal his receding hairline. A series of dark grey moustaches flowed over a beard that was almost white and then the whole lot flowed on down to his belly. But what really got you most were the eyes. Even in a portrait they were mesmerising, fixed on a spiritual horizon invisible to mere mortals, but, one assumed, the source of immense and ineffable wisdom.

Alex had gone along with the whole idea of learning to meditate on the basis that it was a form of mental discipline, a sort of secular relaxation technique which might help him to get his head straightened out. So far, however, he had not taken the spiritual aspect of it terribly seriously, even though he'd had to put up with Aiden banging on the whole time about being on a spiritual journey. Now, he came face to face with a spirituality that was so powerful, even in a picture, that he was forced to accept he was going to have to change his attitude. He wasn't at all sure he was ready for that.

At last, they were granted their interview and looking up at Swamiji Alex felt his nervousness fall away. The guru in orange layers was seated on a raised dais which might as well have been a throne from which his powerful presence radiated. But in spite of his obvious authority he had a cheeky smile which he used often and he spoke in a nasal, surprisingly high pitched, sing-song voice.

He seemed to have completely forgotten the red carnation in one hand as he waved his arms to and fro to emphasise every point. It was enchanting. In front of Swamiji Alex felt stripped bare, as if this man—this being—could see right through him.

"You come here looking for something, heh. Yes, it is here, what you are searching for, waiting to be discovered—within yourself. Maybe you will find it, maybe not. If you do not open your hearts, you will find nothing, no. Nothing.

"Many people like you have come here before. Some find, yes. What you are doing it is very hard, huh. India is not like the West. You will have to be patient. Resistance will be felt, doubts will come. You think you are special, no, no, you are not. You, me, the Queen of England, the Dalit, we are all the same. Oh, yes. We are all one. Listen. Feel. Open your heart. Trust the universe, let life express itself through you. When you try to control everything, you control nothing.

"In the end, it is your choice. All are welcome here. But I insist on one thing only. You come here with your Western baggage, your views, your thinking, all those things you are certain of. You judge, you complain, you criticise. Perhaps you think you have it all worked out. In this, you will find you are incorrect. So you will please leave all your Western baggage at the door. It is not wanted here. You understand me, heh."

Alex was having trouble keeping up. Swamiji was talking so fast that most of the vowels had disappeared, but what he was saying was definitely profound. Yes! This was so right. He wanted to learn to see whatever it was that Swamiji could see and he was trying to remember everything Swamiji had said. Open his heart. Trust the universe. Leave behind the Western baggage. But what did all that actually mean?

He needed some simple instructions, a step-by-step guide he could just follow that would guarantee success. But the interview was over. The energy had left the room. Swamiji was gone.

* * *

"Wow," Aiden said as he flung himself down on the narrow bed next to the window which he had bagged as soon as they walked in. "Wow."

"I guess we passed, guys," said Scott.

Alex didn't trust himself to speak just yet. He hung his marigold garland over the end of his bed, trying not to flatten the damp clumps of petals, and busied himself with sorting and resorting his few possessions. Then, again sensing the other two waiting for him to come back to them, he turned and smiled.

"Well, let's get going! We should go and have a look around before it gets dark. Better get the old pyjamas on again!"

The others looked relieved as they all stripped off their dusty jeans and T-shirts and slipped into their kurta pyjamas as if they were a second skin.

* * *

The ashram was certainly impressive and a lot more organised than the last one. They wandered down white stone paths carved into the dense, jungly vegetation that grew naturally here—giant ferns, bougainvillea, tall trees dripping with waxy starfruit and whole groves of bamboo held up by fat, scarred canes. They crossed a stream which splashed over a selection of artfully arranged rocks and then gathered itself into a glossy pool. Set into the pool's edge was an enormous flat stone worn smooth over millions of years, an open invitation for someone to come and meditate there.

At every crossroads, there were rustic signposts directing you to the langbar, the meditation centre, the office block. It could almost have been a new garden city laid out by well-funded town planners in a science fiction novel. Alex wondered where all the money came from and then remembered about leaving your Western baggage at the door.

It wasn't until the next morning's Satsang that Alex realised quite how big the ashram was. As instructed, he, Scott and Aiden had presented themselves at 6am in the vast white meditation hall which must have held over a thousand people, and it was full. They claimed a little piece of territory as close to the front as they could get, bunching up together for solidarity, and then furtively started to check out their fellow yogis, who were apparently of every age and from every corner of the globe.

Here, sitting in silence and dressed in almost identical white outfits, were the citizens of this science fiction city. It made Alex wonder whether they were all just guinea pigs in some sort of sinister scientific experiment in mind control.

Yesterday Swamiji had made him feel important, loved even, and that his spiritual journey was of special interest. Today Alex understood that he was no more or less important to Swamiji than anyone else here. In awe, he watched Swamiji sit on his throne, namaste, smile his radiant smile, x-ray every section of the room with his eyes—a process which lasted several minutes—and then embark on a long and at times rambling discourse about consciousness, happiness and love.

He realised that nobody was going to give him the step-by-step guide he had wanted to ask for yesterday. There weren't going to be any easy answers and he wasn't going to get a clear view of the path in front of him. The only thing he could do was follow Swamiji's words as best he could, even if sometimes they made no sense at all, bash on with the meditation and trust that eventually he would make some progress. He would just have to be patient and hope for the best.

Alex and Scott quickly got used to the new ashram. Fitting in was not difficult—beards were de rigeur fortunately and they hardly had to worry about what to wear since everyone else was wearing kurta pyjamas too except the staff or the babassu elders, who all wore dark maroon robes. The two of them remained good friends and thanks to Scott's easy-going charm they were soon on namaste terms with some of their new ashram-mates, who drew them into a loose crowd of like-minded Westerners.

Aiden, on the other hand, gravitated towards a rabble of scruffy deadbeats who just wanted to drop out and smoke beedies together at every opportunity, which did nothing to diminish Alex's irritation with him. It was a relief when he packed up his rucksack and moved rooms.

"No hard feelings, eh guys? Time to move on—see you around, I guess."

Scott accepted Aiden's departure without any fuss and the two of them got along just fine without him around. While Scott was definitely better at talking about the emotional stuff, Alex made up for it by looking out for both of them. As they became more familiar with each other's stories, they each felt they almost knew the other's cast of characters personally. They discussed and agreed what was important in life and how committed they were to the path they were on.

They felt supported by the energy that they felt growing stronger the closer they were to Swamiji. They learned how to make the deep bow and chant of *om shanti shanti shanti* to Swamiji at the end of each Satsang. Now that he had become such a distant, exalted figure Alex could hardly believe they had been so casual about their initial private darshan with him and kept going over and over it in his mind.

Alex was determined to make some real progress with his meditation practice now, too. Although his mind still wandered infuriatingly, he could stay concentrated for longer periods of time and the meditation sessions didn't seem such an eternity anymore. He started to experience a deep feeling of peace when his mind did eventually drop into stillness—and he could almost feel it drop, sometimes.

When that happened, he only realised how much time had passed when the tingsha bells sounded for the end of the session, pulling him back to the material world and the dazed yogis all around him sighing, rubbing their eyes and stretching out their cramped bodies. Although he still felt the sharp pain of loneliness and rejection in his life, he was starting to see that the way he had reacted to them was part of the problem. If he could only change the way he felt about his difficulties, then one day perhaps they wouldn't be difficulties anymore.

"How old do you think Swamiji is?"

Alex was sitting with Scott and a few others in the cool night air on the terrace after supper one evening. He knew it wasn't really the right question—Swamiji didn't seem human enough to have an age—but he hoped it would start a conversation about the guru, who intrigued him.

"God knows," answered one of the group, a German boy with aryan blue eyes, who shrugged and then laughed when he realised what he had said. Swamiji was after all in constant communication with the Hindu equivalent of God and was the reincarnation of a long line of spiritual gurus, so God presumably *would* know.

"Anyway, Swamiji isn't his actual name. You can call any swami Swamiji, it's a sort of affectionate name. Like Gandhiji or Papaji. And swami is just a Hindu name for a spiritual teacher."

"Swami or not, he's not averse to a bit of entertaining every now and then, if you know what I mean—"

"Dirty old devil!"

"Plenty of adoring students to choose from, after all. He probably tells them it's part of their spiritual growth."

"Are you *sure*?"

"I don't believe it. That's just gossip, it must be."

"No, no. It's a well-known fact."

There was a stunned silence while the group digested this information. Swamiji commanded most people's respect, but Alex had to admit he had an aura of power about him that could be quite threatening. He always surrounded himself with the same group of ardent followers who looked up at him with devotion but never questioned him. There was an open session for questions at the end of every morning *Satsang*, but you had to be brave—or foolish—to ask one. Alex had seen too many people snubbed and cut down to size to be tempted. Swamiji definitely did not like being challenged.

"He knows he can do what he likes. No one can touch him. He's a powerful man in India, you know. Wealthy, too. And he's not the only one—a lot of these gurus aren't quite what they seem, you know. And it's not just young girls, either. Drugs, fraud, organised crime—"

"But where does all this power and money actually come from? And how could anyone like Swamiji get that to stack up with being a guru?"

"He controls people. A lot of people. And he's very charismatic, after all, we know that. There are plenty of people here who would follow him over a cliff, aren't there? That's where his power comes from. He really would have to be a saint not to be corrupted by it at all."

Alex was furious with himself. In a matter of a week or two, he had allowed Swamiji to get under his skin, but now he realised how trusting he had been. He had made it so easy for Swamiji to betray that trust and the trust of all those around him. He really needed to be a lot more careful.

As he and Scott walked back to their dormitory, Alex brought the subject up again.

"You know where Swamiji lives, don't you?"

Scott shrugged, clearly reluctant to think of Swamiji as a human being in need of any sort of house at all.

"If you follow the path past the meditation hall and the library, there's a load of big trees up there on the right, you know? It's behind that. If you go on up the hill and then look back, you can just see a massive great house with a huge terrace, garden all beautifully laid out, flowers everywhere. I hadn't really thought about it, but that must be his house. He's even got a swimming pool up there, for Chrissakes."

"You've been checking him out, Alex!" Scott was only half joking.

"Hardly—I didn't even put two and two together till just now. Don't you think it's a bit weird, though? Having a lavish place like that? Not really what you'd expect, is it?"

"I don't know—perhaps that's what gurus do, you know? They've got to live somewhere—I guess the guy can't live in a mud hut with no running water when he's got an ashram to look after. I can live with that."

"I don't like it, Scott. I think we need to keep our eyes open."

"Look, Alex, it's really none of our business how he lives. We know he's a great guru, don't we, someone who can help us sort ourselves out. Isn't that what counts? You were cool with him until five minutes ago and now suddenly he's public enemy number one. You're overreacting, Alex."

"Maybe. Maybe not."

"Anyway, it's nine-thirty and I'm heading off to bed now. Back home in Van I wouldn't even have hit the town yet! How life has changed."

"Yeah. Me too." But Alex couldn't sleep, thinking about Swamiji and how his spell had been broken.

Chapter 12
Cards on the Table

Outside the Caprice Emma kissed her aunt goodbye and waved as cheerfully as she could from the back of the taxi that bore her off towards Piccadilly. Then she realised with a jolt where she was. It seemed like weeks since she had taken the tube from work to Green Park, walked past the Ritz and then down Arlington Street to the Caprice, almost a lifetime ago.

Now, doing the journey in reverse, different things jumped out at her—the pink cyclamen in the Ritz window boxes were more vivid, the American accents louder, the breeze as she rounded the corner into Piccadilly more biting.

She had been quite right to take the afternoon off work, she thought as she stumbled out of the taxi and tried to work out how much to tip the driver. It would have been most unwise for her to turn up at Withers & Co in this sort of state— God knows what might have happened. As it was, it seemed to take a superhuman effort to survive the ride back to Regent mansions, get herself up the front steps and then on past the stairs to the lift. Even pressing the lift button was almost more than she could manage.

Once inside she shook her coat off, considered a cup of tea and then collapsed onto the sofa instead. Of course what Jackie had told her had been a shock, but at the same time, hearing someone actually talk about her mother at last had been a huge relief. She had half expected Jackie to back out somehow, to fob her off or tell her nothing. But Jackie hadn't done that at all. She had acknowledged her right to know and had been refreshingly open and honest.

At last, she was being treated like a grown up, a normal human being, and about time too. The problem was that now there was a heaviness in her chest that had not been there before. She had always thought of her mother as someone so special, so perfect. To find out that the reality was very different made things so much more complicated.

She pulled at a loose thread on one of the tapestry cushions and wondered how she would have coped with knowing that as a child. Although she was reluctant to admit it, perhaps her father had been right not to tell her the truth after all. The lie had made life a lot simpler for her and at least she hadn't grown up with some awful sort of complex about being abandoned. There had been so many times when she had desperately missed having a mother, when she had just longed to be like everyone else. But then again, she was closer to her father than a lot of her friends were to both their parents put together.

Jessie had always been there to look after her, picking her up from school, making her tea, dropping her off at swimming parties. Having Jackie around had been great during her teens because she had tried so hard to understand and she had, mostly. And Joe's mother Lorna had been important in a way too, showing her what it was to be the heart and soul of the family. So perhaps she had been lucky, considering. But how could it be lucky to lose your mother and then have your father lie to you about something so important?

She had promised Joe she would ring him as soon as she got in and tell him how it went. With so much stuff swimming around inside her head, she wasn't sure what to tell him, but she picked up the phone on the table beside her and dialled the number.

"How did it go? What happened? Are you all right?"

"Yeah." It was reassuring to hear Joe's voice. She knew her low-key reply would worry him, but she suddenly felt too exhausted to care. Anyway, she shouldn't have to pretend with Joe.

"Em, what happened?"

"I don't know where to start, Joe. Turns out you were right, she didn't die in a car crash at all. But it's much more complicated than that. They were never even married. It's a long story. She left Dad quite soon after I was born and she took me with her, to live on a commune apparently.

"To think I would have known all that if only I could remember—I went with her, Joe! Then she brought me back and left again, that's when she left the note. She'd tried to commit suicide before, Jackie said, when they were both students at Exeter. That's where they met. She sounds—she was—I don't know. A bit crazy I suppose. She was an artist. Jackie reckoned she was very talented."

She thought she would have remembered every single word Jackie had said, but now she couldn't seem to get any of it to make sense. And it wasn't just that, either. She wasn't sure what to think about her mother yet. It wasn't going to be easy to explain everything that Jackie had told her without people thinking badly of her and she wasn't ready for that. She needed to get her head straight first.

"Let's talk about it later."

"Em? Are you sure you're all right?" Joe suddenly sounded old fashioned, almost stuffy, and it irritated her. No, she wasn't all right. How could she possibly be all right? But Joe had warned her that she might find this difficult, which made her want to prove to him that she had done the right thing.

"Look, I can't go through it all on the phone. Let's talk about it later. I'm fine."

"OK. I'll leave you to it then." Emma could tell from his clipped, formal voice that he hadn't liked being pushed away.

"Joe, I didn't mean it like that! I'm exhausted though and I just need a bit of time, that's all. I'll tell you everything later, OK?"

Relieved to be friends again, she and Joe agreed to talk later that evening. The last thing she needed right now was to annoy him and after all, he was only trying to help. This was already getting messy and she hadn't even talked to her father yet. As she put down the phone Emma remembered with a start that she had a mother who could be alive, not dead, and it immediately consumed her again.

Should she try to track her down or was Jackie right that it was a really bad idea? Was it possible now just to go back to the way things were before, knowing her mother could be out there somewhere? But what if she didn't want to be found? What if she was unfriendly, hostile even? And why hadn't her mother ever come looking for *her*? She put her head in her hands and wondered how she was going to cope with all this.

If only she could talk to Alex. Alex would know how she felt, he would know what she should do. She closed her eyes and tried to imagine he was there with her. His familiar face, with its blondish hair and stubbled chin, materialised beside her and he flung himself back against the arm of the sofa in disbelief.

"There's no *way* you can walk away from this, Em. What are you going to do? Say your mother left you when you were a baby *and you don't know where she is?* Come on! Isn't it better to know? For God's sake, Em. Anyway, she sounds really interesting. What are you waiting for?"

She opened her eyes, half expecting to see him there instead of the empty sofa. Oh, Alex, this is ridiculous. Did you really have to take off like that? Where are you? If you're OK, why on earth can't you let me know? I can't cope with worrying about you on top of all this. And why can't you be here when I need you? But she already knew what he would have said and he was right. From thousands of miles away, he had given her the endorsement she needed. Of course she had to try and find her mother, she really had no choice. As for the rest, she would just have to be like Alex and cross that bridge when she came to it.

Satisfied, she slipped off her shoes and swung her stockinged feet up onto the sofa beside her. So much to think about and yet all she could do was stare into space. She tucked herself up into the corner of the sofa with a nice big squashy cushion under her head. She was feeling very drowsy, either because of the Sancerre at lunch or because of the significance of what she had discovered. Both, probably. Soon she felt her eyes closing and she just about managed to pull her coat up over her shoulders before she fell asleep.

* * *

The light was fading when she heard her father's key in the door and shook herself awake. Oh God, she must have been asleep for a couple of hours at least and now she had a heavy head, a dry throat and no idea how she was going to handle this. She felt his presence as much as saw him as he came into the room. She didn't want to look at him anyway, not yet. She had no idea what she was going to find.

"I had a call from Jackie this afternoon."

"Yes."

"So now you know." He sank into an armchair next to her and she watched him deflate, apparently exhausted.

"Well, I expect you're angry with me. I always knew this moment would come and now it has. I had to do it that way, Em. I'd do exactly the same thing again. It was for the best."

There was a hard, defensive edge in his voice. Emma was not ready to give in and admit he was right just yet, so she stayed silent.

"And yes, I probably should have told you before now. But there never seemed to be a right time. I suppose I just couldn't face it. I knew it would open up a can of worms. You don't realise what that woman is capable of."

"It's a lot to take in, Dad."

It was only now, hearing her father admit the story was true, that she could really start to understand how devastating it was. She was alarmed to see all her father's normal joie de vivre had drained away, leaving him looking uncertain and withdrawn. It was obvious that she couldn't afford the luxury of sulking— they were in this together. Before she had time to decide whether she was brave enough or not, the words were out.

"Dad, will you tell me about her?"

A long pause while she waited for her father to weigh up whether he had it in him after all this time. And then he nodded.

"Yes. OK darling, yes of course I will. I'll do my best to, anyway. But Em, you have to do your best to listen and understand, too. I had good reasons for doing what I did, you know. The truth would have been a hell of a lot worse for you. And I need a cup of tea first."

* * *

Emma and her father sat side by side on the sofa and watched the milky bubbles in their tea swirl round and round. It was a huge relief that her father was still talking to her after this and Emma felt a bit guilty now about causing him so much pain. She felt like telling him to forget it, that it didn't matter after all. But it did matter.

Little had been said in the kitchen, but at least it had given them both a bit of time to think. Emma had set the scene by drawing the thick curtains, switching on the table lamps and getting the fire going. At least it looked cosy even if it didn't feel it. Now, she was watching her father warily as his eyes travelled from the bookshelves laden with expensively illustrated modern art books, to the vase of lilies on the coffee table, to the bronze statue of Pan piping away on the mantlepiece and finally, when the moment could be delayed no further, to Emma.

"So what do you want to know?"

Not a brilliant start, Emma thought. She looked straight back at him, fighting to overcome her awkwardness and behave like a grown up.

"Jackie told me a bit about her but I really want to hear the story from you, Dad."

So Richard started to talk to her about her mother at last. It was a little stilted to start with, a little abrupt, but as he talked he gradually came alive. How he had met Frances at university and fallen for her. How they had got together in spite

128

of their obvious differences, his single-mindedness, her wildness and excitability. How he had saved her life after her overdose, taken care of her and brought her to London with him. How she had repaid him by leaving him, not once but three times.

What a failure he had felt that he could never be enough for her. How bitter he still felt, even now, over twenty years later, that she had treated him so badly. That he had been such an idiot as to let her. The anger came boiling out and Emma began to see what her mother had done to him and how he had suffered because of her. But then again, perhaps it wasn't that simple. There were always two sides to every story. What would her mother have said about it all?

"Even after all that I would still have taken her back, you know. I would have looked after her. I must have been completely mad. But despite everything I wanted us all to be together as a family. When she left, I thought she should have stayed. I thought she was very irresponsible to leave you. But looking back on it, it would never have worked out. She just couldn't function as a normal human being, let alone a mother. She just wasn't capable of it. God knows what would have happened if she had stayed. I'd have probably ended up killing her.

"When she left that last time I wanted to forget she'd ever existed. You'd already been carted half way round the country and back and you really needed some stability. I couldn't ever let you think she had walked out on you because you would have spent your whole childhood thinking she was about to come back, waiting for her to walk through the door. Can you imagine what that would have been like? Unbearable. So I decided to tell you she was dead. As far as I was concerned, it was the truth, anyway. And I'm sure it *is* the truth, Em."

"Oh God. Poor dad."

Richard shrugged dismissively as if he had merely run out of petrol rather than saved a life, had his heart broken several times over and then been left as a single parent. But there was so much pain in his eyes that Emma put her arms round his neck and hugged him, her own heartache forgotten for a moment.

"Tell me what she was like."

"Well, she was certainly beautiful." Richard nodded as he remembered. "There was something about her—so full of life and so fragile at the same time. You couldn't not notice her. Once I had seen her, I couldn't forget her. And I suppose we did have a lot of good times together, although sometimes it's hard to remember that."

Emma smiled, picturing the blonde, willowy woman in the kaftan she had seen in the photo, pleased to have a mother who was beautiful and wanting in spite of everything to be proud of her.

"But my God, she could be so infuriating. She wasn't stupid, but she certainly seemed it sometimes. You couldn't talk sense into her. It's not that I don't admire a bit of enthusiasm, you know that, but she was delusional.

"Absolutely convinced she could learn to play the piano in a week. Buying sacks of semi-precious stones to start some sort of new age jewellery business. Picking flowers in the park and selling them from a stall outside the livestock market. Painting for days and nights straight without any sleep. I could go on— Then she'd get cross with me for not 'getting it'. She didn't like it when I tried to pin her down, she wanted to be 'free'. Honestly, Em, in the end I just had to let her get on with it. There were always plenty of other people who would go along with her for the ride."

"How come you stayed together then?"

"Frances needed me. She was like a child in a way. She always told me I wasn't like all the others, that I was the one she really cared about. I suppose I believed her. But—oh, I don't know. What does it matter now anyway? I thought that she would eventually calm down, get it all out of her system, grow up a bit. And she did, at times. I thought it would be worth the wait."

"What do you think happened to her, Dad? Surely you must wonder."

"I don't know. I've no idea."

Emma watched her father's expression go blank. But she hadn't heard enough yet, so she quickly changed tack.

"Am I like her?"

"No, not at all—thank goodness. You're more like me. Like Jackie most of all, actually—sometimes you look *exactly* like her. I don't see any of Frances' restlessness in you. I mean, you're going into law, after all, like me. You know what you want and where you're going and I'm very proud of you. If you'd shown any inclination towards art I would have supported you and so would Jackie, but I think it's fair to say it was never your forté. Apart from a few memorable homemade Easter cards… Jackie was very fond of her, you know."

"She does sound quite fun."

Richard nodded slowly. "Oh yes, she was. There was nothing like being with her when she was on good form. Everybody loved her then. But she wasn't always like that. The rest of the time, I was either looking after her or being driven mad by her.

"Her suicide attempt really shook her up. Once she had recovered from that, I thought she would be all right. People told me I was a fool to stand by her and let her treat me like she did. And then in the end it was *her* who gave up on *me*. I must have been a complete idiot."

Her father looked totally beaten.

"I was thinking today. You must have been only about—24? When she left. That's almost the same age that I am now! Surely you could still have got married to someone else?"

"I suppose so—I suppose I could have done, yes. It was the last thing on my mind to start with. Now, I think it's better like this. Don't you?"

Emma didn't answer. She tried to imagine what sort of person her father might have married and what that would have been like. Someone else taking up Dad's attention and interfering in her life. A stepmother. Oh God. And even having babies! Little half-brothers and sisters. How ghastly. But had he really never even had a girlfriend in the last 20 years? And why had she never thought about it before? She'd always assumed he was too old, but that was obviously nonsense.

Her father had painted a rather more negative picture of her mother than Jackie had, but that was hardly surprising. It was impossible to tell what she was really like. Supposing she actually got the chance meet her one day? Somehow she knew they would get along fine. In fact, the whole situation was completely ridiculous.

"Dad, do you have *any idea* what it's like growing up without a mother? Did you ever think about that? And as if that wasn't enough, you lied to me as well!"

Richard leaned away from her, clearly offended. "It wasn't me who abandoned you! Don't you forget that. She did that all by herself. I did everything I could to get her to stay, even after all that had happened. You can blame me for not telling you the truth, but that's all I'll take the blame for. And even that I did entirely for your benefit."

"But how did you know she wouldn't come back? That would have been a bit awkward, wouldn't it?"

"I was sure she wouldn't. And I was right, wasn't I? There was something final about the way she left. And I knew she was suicidal. Things had gone way past that stage. Actually, I didn't see it at the time, but you could say it was quite brave of her to make that decision. More than I managed to do."

Richard got up and walked over to the window. He stooped slightly as he pulled one of the fringed curtains aside and studied the scratchy shapes of the branches outside.

"I've done everything I could for you, Em. I've tried to be a father and a mother to you, and Jackie has done her best too. But perhaps that wasn't enough."

"I know you have, Dad. I'm sorry. It's not your fault."

She felt she had aged five years in the last half an hour, stepping on eggshells, trying to respect her father's feelings and not letting rip with her own. For a fleeting moment, she wanted the old, invincible, buoyant Dad back, but then—she wasn't a child anymore. Strange to think that her father had been her age once—*was* about her age when all this had happened.

"I want to find her, Dad. I'm sorry if it's going to upset you, but it's something I have to do."

"I was expecting you to say that. I'm really not sure it's wise, though." Richard ran his fingers through his hair, pulling his head down for a moment, then looked back up at her with an attempt at a smile.

"Dad, she's my mother. I have to look for her. Where do you think she would have gone? Do you think I'll be able to find her?"

"I'm sorry, Em, you can't ask me that. And anyway, I haven't a clue where she went. Jackie probably knows more than me. She could have gone anywhere. I doubt if you'll find her, anyway."

"Jackie said she went to a commune."

"She may have done." Richard was looking exhausted.

"Poor Dad. Please don't be upset! Let me get you a drink. You just sit back and relax, I'll make some supper. Is it all right if Joe comes over later?"

Emma could hardly remember a time now when she hadn't known about her mother. It all seemed perfectly normal. And what's more, she hadn't fallen out with her father over it. She was more determined than ever to find her mother now or at least to find out what had happened to her. Time to look forward, not back. She would just have to deal with the emotional fallout as best she could. Surely, it couldn't be any harder than what she had been through already.

* * *

Jackie rang the next morning. She had managed to track somebody down who had been living in a commune in Exeter at roughly the same time as Frances all those years ago.

"She's a friend of a friend, darling. I haven't actually spoken to her, I thought it would be better for you to pick it up from here. I don't know whether she'll be able to help—I don't even know if it's the same commune, but how many communes could there have been in Exeter at that time? Sally says she may well have known her. Her name is Elizabeth Duncan. She's married with three children and lives in Bath. Here's her number—over to you, darling. Good luck and take care—I'm here if you need me."

Chapter 13
Detective Work

"What a terrific morning! You know Aiden did us a favour bringing us here, Alex, even if he may have gone a bit flaky on us. It's doing me the world of good. How about you, huh?"

Alex was sitting with Scott at one end of a long breakfast table on the terrace outside Ramana Ashram's langar. This was one of the rare occasions when chairs were provided, giving their twisted hips and knees an hour off, and they were doing their best to lounge in them. On the table were the messy remains of an unconventional breakfast of lentil pancakes with gravy, chickpeas and fried bread, fruit salad, yogurt and some unspeakable milkshake made out of rose syrup and tapioca. But breakfast was something they both looked forward to every day despite the often impenetrable menu and they usually ate their way through the whole lot.

Although they were not exactly burning through huge amounts of energy they were both young, fit and healthy and a 6 o'clock kick-off with an aarti ceremony and a couple of hours' meditation followed by Satsang with Swamiji meant that by mid-morning they could eat a horse, or at least its vegetarian equivalent.

The air was still and heavy with scent from the jasmine scrambling up the wall of the langar behind them, and the sun had not got up to scorching point yet. Alex had been quiet for a while, watching a powder-green bird as it darted in and out of the crimson flowers of the Gulmohar tree opposite and wondering to himself what kind of bird it was. Then, noticing his Western habit of wanting to identify, classify and take possession of it, he accepted that it was simply a lovely green bird which did not need a name. He looked up at Scott, pushed his fingers through his hair and smiled.

"Good, thanks. Yeah. Good."

"Oh, come on, buddy. You can do better than that."

"Yeah, OK. Well—you know what? I've been thinking about things a lot and it really hurts, Scott. It hurts that I was just given away like that. When I was a baby, I mean. I've always tried to be positive but you can't get away from it. My mother just—gave me up. And I don't think I ever quite fitted in after that. It totally screwed everything up. I'm beginning to understand that now—although it doesn't make it any easier."

"No. I can see that."

"How could she do that, Scott? How could anyone do that?"

"She must have had her reasons, I guess."

"It physically hurts. I never noticed a feeling hurt like this before."

Alex was bent over the table as if he had a violent stomach ache. Scott watched him, concerned.

"But you know, nothing's changed, Alex. It's the same as it's always been. Why should it be such a big deal now when it's never bothered you before?"

Good point, thought Alex, staring at Scott as if he had never seen him before. That is exactly the point, isn't it? Scott had obviously learned something from all that therapy. And although he had been working towards the same question himself, the answer was suddenly crystal clear.

"It's because of all that stuff with Joe and Emma."

Scott said nothing and waited.

"It's the same feeling. Sort of abandoned and unwanted. I suppose it must have brought all the crap about being given up as a baby to the surface."

They both sat in silence for a while. Alex knew that Scott's amateur therapy had done its job; one piece of the puzzle had just fallen into place.

At last, Alex broke the silence. "Well, we'd better get back to the old meditation, hadn't we?"

"You betcha!"

It was a relief to get the conversation back onto a more mundane level and he was thankful Scott hadn't pushed things any further. Instead they decided to go for a stroll around the gardens before the next session began. Alex wondered whether he would ever really get the hang of talking about how he felt. It made him feel so awkward. Was it because of being British or was he just an emotional retard?

Scott had set off at speed with his long, loose-limbed stride, turning every few steps to see if Alex was still listening to him. This ability to talk non-stop usually amused Alex, but today he was too preoccupied to take much notice. After a few minutes, he made his excuses and left, agreeing to meet up again later.

* * *

By lunchtime, Alex's anxious mood had intensified. Far from feeling peaceful after the morning's meditation he just hadn't been able to leave his thoughts behind. He kept going back over the same things again and again like a dog scraping away at a bone and it had made him realise just how much time his mind spent living in the past.

Growing up with Joe. Joe had always seemed so confident, so clever, so grown up. He had started out trying to be like that too but he could never pull it off—it was a race he could never win. So then the only thing to do was to be the opposite to Joe, to take himself out of the race completely. That had affected everything—not trying at school, dropping out, avoiding success of any kind.

Could things have been different if he hadn't done that? Would he have been different? Perhaps underneath he wasn't who he thought he was. So what was he really like then? What was he good at? What were the real reasons why he had ended up doing the things he had done and how valid were they? Could he have made other choices? Could he still make them now? And how was he supposed to know the answers to all these questions?

In despair, his mind had moved on to Swamiji. Was it really true that he was a powerful man in India and, by the sound of it, was abusing that power? After the conversation a few nights ago he had started to take more notice of what was going on at the ashram. It was becoming increasingly obvious to him that there was some sort of cover-up going on. Something was not quite right and it concerned him that Scott continued to be totally unaware of it. When they met up again for lunch he decided to tackle it head on.

"Have you noticed something, Scott? You know the people who lead the ashram, the babassus? I've been watching them. Some of them just don't look the part, you know? They can be really intimidating. Almost like they were heavies or bodyguards of some sort. You'd think they would be really into the whole ashram peacefulness vibe, but they're not. They're really not. And the other thing is, there are so many of them. You'd expect to get to know them all after a bit, wouldn't you? But I keep seeing new ones, more and more of them.

Why are there so many? Where do they go when they're not here? What are they up to? It's like they're Swamiji's private army."

"What the heck're you on about, buddy?"

"And there's another thing, Scott. You know there's a back entrance to the ashram? Not the one by the kitchens but another one, which comes in behind the office building. D'you know where I mean?"

Scott had stopped eating his vegetable curry and was looking at Alex nervously.

"Well, I guess it's mostly for the office staff and for deliveries and things like that. But I've noticed there are a lot of cars going in and out too—big cars, Mercedes, black tinted windows. What the fuck are they doing here? Most people here are living on the ashram, they don't come in and out all the time and anyway, they wouldn't have cars like that. They're not delivery vans and I can't believe the staff are arriving by Mercedes either. It doesn't make any sense."

"Does it really matter? I wouldn't worry too much about it, Alex. Maybe it's something to do with the management, maybe they have another ashram somewhere, I don't know. But I don't think it's any of our business, is it?"

"Maybe. I just think there's something odd going on. Remember what that guy was saying the other night, about ashrams being the perfect cover for organised crime? I think maybe that's what's going on here. That's why there are so many babassus and that's why all these cars are going in and out all the time. I wonder what they're up to."

"Please, Alex. Don't do this—you're imagining it. It's not going to help, you know."

Alex leaned over his curry, too furious to look up. He really didn't want to lose his temper with Scott, but if they couldn't trust Swamiji they might both be in danger here—they might even need to get out. Why the bloody hell couldn't Scott wake up and take some responsibility?

* * *

Over the next few days Alex monitored deliveries through the back entrance whenever he could, while Scott tried to cajole him into forgetting the whole thing.

"I wish you'd just let this go, Alex. I mean, it's not really what we're here for, is it? We don't need to get involved in ashram politics as long as it's working for us. And neither of us is exactly Hercule Poirot either—more like Inspector Clouseau, quite honestly."

"Scott, why the hell can't you take this seriously? No. I'm going to find out what's going on. I'm on to something—it's important."

He was talking more and more quickly now. "What we need to do is keep watch overnight. If there's any real undercover action, that's when it will be. Then at least we'll know one way or another, won't we? You wouldn't expect there to be any deliveries at night, so it should be quiet. If nothing happens, I'll drop it. But I'm going to go tonight. So are you coming with me? There's plenty of cover down there, I've checked."

"Are you *kidding*?"

"Of course not. Oh, all right, just forget it. I'll bloody well go on my own."

Alex stared furiously at the green marble statue of the god Ganesh lurking in the undergrowth by the stone bench where they were sitting. Why on earth did Ganesh have an elephant's head? How *ridiculous*.

"OK, OK! Calm down! If you insist on going, I'll come with you. OK? Can't let you creep around in the dark taking on the Indian mafia on your own, can I? Although there's sure to be a perfectly reasonable explanation."

"We'll see. But thanks, Scott. I appreciate it."

"You're sure you really want to do this???"

Alex nodded. "Absolutely."

* * *

So there they were, later that night, sitting in a clump of scratchy rhododendron bushes with a ringside seat of the ashram's back entrance. Away from the main buildings it was very dark and there was enough of a breeze to cool the bare skin of their forearms.

It was funny how you started worrying about things in the dark, Alex thought, that would never occur to you in the daytime. He had seen lizards around the ashram—did they have snakes? Were they poisonous? Even a poisonous spider could be really dangerous. And what about tigers and leopards? No, that was silly. Anyway, there were high walls all around the perimeter of the ashram and it was hardly as if there was a shortage of guards.

He had just tapped Scott on the arm to suggest a tactical retreat when they heard shouting up by the office building. They could pick out several different voices and although they were a good hundred yards away and speaking in a language neither of them understood, there was no mistaking the tension in the air.

Holding their breath they watched as a convoy of cars swept in through the gate and up the drive. For a moment, their headlights blinded the boys and then plunged them into deeper darkness as they were switched off.

Alex felt his jaw drop and the adrenalin start to move around his body. His blood was up. He nodded at Scott and they crawled through the rhododendrons, working their way over the dry ground until they were almost level with the office block. By the time they got there, sweating now, the convoy had arrived.

In the shaft of light that was coming from the building, Alex could see that a handful of men had spilled out of the cars. There was more shouting as they issued orders to the men on the ground which gave Alex and Scott a chance to get themselves into a good position to see what was going on.

They immediately recognised some of the men as babassus, even though they were now in jeans and T-shirts instead of their normal maroon robes. The way they were moving quickly, working closely together, communicating simply by nodding at each other, made it obvious that they had carried out the same procedure many times before.

Alex and Scott watched as the men unloaded suitcase after suitcase from the cars. It was starting to look almost like a group tour arriving for a week in Tenerife except that the large zip-up black airline cases were all absolutely identical. And they didn't look heavy, judging by the speed at which they were being bundled inside the building. It seemed the ashram was taking delivery of several car bootfuls of outsize luggage.

Within just a few minutes, the convoy was moving again down the drive and sweeping out of the back entrance, headlights coming on in unison as they reached the main road. The crashing inside the office block had subsided and it was again in darkness. The men had melted away and an almost unnatural stillness had descended. It was as if it had never happened.

Scott and Alex breathed out.

"What do you think was in those cases?" Scott whispered.

"Well, I don't think it was the ashram's weekly order of lentils." Alex mentally ran through any other possibilities he could think of. "It's obvious they're running some sort of crime racket here. Don't you think? The only question is, is Swamiji in on it too?"

"I don't know. They were just suitcases, Alex. They could have anything in them."

"But those guys were totally stressed out."

"Yeah—but there could still be a perfectly innocent explanation."

"Like what, Scott? Like WHAT?"

* * *

They regrouped the next morning. Alex wanted to try and get a closer look at the suitcases in the office block before they got moved on—if they hadn't been already. But Scott was reluctant and instead suggested watching the babassus, especially the ones they had seen the previous night, to see if they could work out who was in on it and who wasn't. Again, Alex had to talk him into coming with him. He just couldn't understand why Scott was being so awkward about this. Surely it was obvious by now what was going on.

But Alex managed to prevail over Scott again and after breakfast they set out together for a leisurely walk down a path which just happened to take them to the office block. At the front of the building, facing towards the gardens, was the ashram's main help desk. As planned Scott wandered as casually as he could up the steps and into the shade of the building, where Alex could just about make out the ashram's 'customer services' assistant sitting beneath another life-sized picture of Swamiji in his saffron robes, chuckling like an orange version of Father Christmas.

He watched as Scott leaned against the desk and began to chat up the assistant, something he clearly excelled at. Once he was happy that Scott had her full attention Alex dodged round the side of the building, trying the doors and windows as he went.

He had almost reached the back entrance when he heard footsteps approaching and shrank back into the undergrowth. Someone inside was obviously expecting a visitor—who had just arrived. The back door opened and he heard the two men start to talk in hushed tones as the door closed behind them. As soon as he heard the voices dying away inside the building he pushed open the door and slipped in.

He stood still for a moment as his eyes adjusted to the dim light, trying to get his bearings. He could hear Scott at the front desk earnestly quizzing the assistant on what sort of experience was required before he would be able to become a babassu. He could also hear the voices of the two men in one of the back offices, muffled behind a closed door. He crept slowly along the dusty corridor towards the voices and tiptoed into the office next door. As he started to pick up the gist of what they were saying, he realised to his surprise that they were speaking in English.

"—delivery Tuesday night—further instructions—contract doesn't complete until next week—" then he heard the door open abruptly and he shrank back into the shadows, alarmed. But the two babassus, their business apparently concluded, walked straight past him and out of the building, locking the back door behind them. He heard their footsteps fade away as they headed off in opposite directions.

At least now, Alex knew he had the place to himself. There were several more offices at the back of the building and he started to work methodically through them, looking for the suitcases. Surely, they would be pretty difficult to hide—or perhaps they had been moved on already. Bugger. But no, here they were, at least ten of them, piled up behind an old desk in a dark, otherwise empty room with heavily scratched lino on the floor. The room was obviously used regularly for storage—but the door hadn't even been locked. Not too worried about security then, he thought to himself.

But the cases were all locked individually. Of course. So he was right, they must be hiding something. He tried every single case just to be sure, picking them up, looking them over to see if he could get any hint of what was inside. Not that heavy—all pretty much the same weight, in fact. What would you put inside a whole load of identical locked suitcases that would need a cavalcade of cars and a bunch of guards at dead of night?

Cash. It had to be cash, surely. A payment of some kind perhaps—they'd mentioned a contract. So if this was the payment, what and where were the goods? What on earth were they up to? Those babassus hadn't been messing around last night—the tension had been unmistakeable. There obviously *was* some sort of organised crime going on here and with this much cash lying around, the perpetrators were likely to be dangerous. And he was effectively locked inside the office block with no plausible story as to why he was there.

Keeping as calm as he could he forced open one of the windows to the rear of the building, heaved himself through it and crashed heavily onto the ground below, buckling onto his knees in the dirt as his ankles gave way. As soon as he had picked himself up and dusted himself down, he slunk round to the front under cover of the bushes, then walked quickly away across the garden. But he couldn't help looking back and to his horror he saw Scott and the assistant standing on the front steps watching him.

He hurried back to his room and paced up and down between the narrow beds, impatient for Scott to arrive. Now that the immediate danger was over the panic was rising in his chest and he was struggling to breathe. As soon as he heard Scott's footsteps outside he was at the door to meet him.

"Scott. These guys are running some kind of a money-laundering operation. I heard them talking about a delivery on Tuesday and a contract. Maybe drugs. Heroin. From Afghanistan, probably. But it's not the heroin they've got in those suitcases, it's the cash.

"They pick up the money they get for selling on the heroin and bring it here. It's safer here than anywhere else. Then some of it gets reinvested in the next lot of heroin trades and the rest gets laundered here at the ashram. Through property deals, money orders—I bet they use some of it to run the ashram, pay the salaries, buy the supplies. It's a good cover for them. They're the bank—and instead of cheques, they use convoys manned by babassu guards. That's why they come and go. *That's* why there are so many of them."

Scott grabbed Alex by the wrists and shook him.

"Alex, this has to stop. What's happening to you? Come on, calm down, take some deep breaths. You're scaring me, Alex. You're talking nonsense! Afghanistan, heroin, money laundering—what the hell are you on about? Did you actually see what was inside the cases? Thought not. Did you actually hear them talking about money laundering or drugs? You didn't, did you? I agree the deliveries in the middle of the night are a bit weird, but how would we know what's out of line and what's not here?

"We're outsiders, Alex! Tourists! It's not our country, it's not our gig. And more to the point, it's none of our business. Maybe we just have to go with the fact that there are some things round here we'll never understand, but that it doesn't matter. Let it go."

"Scott, why can't you see what's right in front of your eyes? What's wrong with you?"

"No, it's you, Alex. You're on an ashram in India, for God's sake, not in The Godfather. Have you gone crazy? Just back off, buddy."

"No, Scott! I'm not backing off! Why are you being so fucking stupid about this? If you're not going to back me up, then just—get out of my way."

At that Scott shook his head, turned and walked out.

* * *

That was the last time Alex saw Scott. By the time he realised Scott was missing, there was no trace of him ever having been at the ashram. His backpack was gone and a new soul-searcher had been allocated his bed. Alex was horrified. He wondered how many people had 'disappeared' like this before. Scott had obviously been removed because of his part in the raid on the office building that morning. The receptionist must have realised they were onto them and tipped off the babassus—so she must be in on it too. And they'd put someone else in his room straight away so no one would notice he'd gone.

After all, who would ever know? People moved on all the time here and most of them had only tipped up on the ashram by chance in the first place. They were drop-outs mostly, running away from something, just like him and Scott, not in regular contact with family or friends. Even if anyone had suspicions they would be impossible to prove. He wondered what they'd done with the body. Scott's family—his father and his brothers—they'd never know what had happened. They wouldn't even know where to start looking for him.

But that applied to him too, didn't it? And if they knew Scott was on to them, they would certainly know he knew about it too. That meant they'd have to kill him as well. He briefly considered going to Swamiji and telling him everything. He still couldn't quite believe someone so spiritual, so—ethereal, could really be a criminal mastermind too. But that was far too risky. He was just going to have to run.

He chucked his things into his rucksack and looked around the spartan little dormitory for the last time. He hadn't expected his stay here to end like this. Whatever the babassus were up to there had been something genuine and good here too. He hoped he could hold on to that.

He strolled through the gardens with his backpack as if it was the most natural thing in the world for him to be doing, managed to wave confidently to the guard on duty and then he was through the resort hotel-style entrance, past the hibiscus bushes and out into the hustle and bustle of northern India.

Trying not to look back this time he concentrated on the beautifully normal people on the road, wearing normal clothes, and normal traffic going about its normal, chaotic business. Had he got away with it? He wouldn't know for sure until he had got right away from the ashram, which he needed to do—fast. Walking was no good and he was determined not to give in to the temptation to run. Perhaps he could hitch a lift—?

Less than ten minutes later, after a rapid change of clothes in the undergrowth, he was gratefully swinging his backpack up into the cab of a roasting hot truck whose driver had screeched to a stop and practically begged him to come aboard, nodding his turbaned head and grinning fit to burst.

With every mile that clocked up between him and the ashram he breathed a little more easily, despite the deafening soundtrack of rattling metal, constant horn blowing and raga music. It was only then he realised that yet again he had lost the person who, for the last few weeks at least, he had been closest to.

Chapter 14
Bath

And so Emma found herself, almost exactly one week later, sitting opposite Elizabeth Duncan in the Regency Tea Rooms in Bath.

It had been an exciting moment when Jackie had given her the number, quickly followed by terror at the prospect of ringing a total stranger who may not even have known her mother anyway and even if she had, probably wouldn't much want to help after all this time. Why would she? It seemed too much to hope for that she would be anything but hostile and Emma prepared herself for the worst. At least, it made a change from worrying about Alex. But to her surprise Elizabeth immediately said yes, she had known Frances—in fact, she had even known Emma herself when she was a baby! She would very much like to meet her and tell her what she knew.

Once they had got all the awkward hellos out of the way and ordered some tea Emma looked across at this woman who had unbelievably lived in a commune with her mother all those years ago. Elizabeth Duncan was not what she had expected at all. Obviously, a middle-aged housewife and mother wasn't likely to be wearing orange robes, have dreadlocked hair and smell of incense, but she could at least have been wearing a batik tie-dye skirt or carrying a tote bag. Emma had not expected Elizabeth's respectable middle class tweed, pressed cotton and leather.

And here they were sitting in some sort of antique tea room with an elderly waitress in a lace apron serving them tea for two as if they were a couple of pensioners. It all seemed a long way from how she had imagined commune life to be. But then, perhaps her mother was a perfectly normal housewife and mother somewhere too.

Elizabeth asked about Emma's train journey from London. Emma asked about Elizabeth's children—the eldest, not surprisingly, only a couple of years younger than her. The tea arrived and Elizabeth poured it out. Emma tried to sit up straight but not too straight, wishing she didn't feel so awkward. She knew they had to pretend this was a normal social occasion, to start with anyway. But it was almost as if her mother was at the table too, impatiently waiting for them to get down to business, and Emma was relieved when Elizabeth started to talk about her.

"Your mother—Frances—came to the commune after me. It all sounds very '60s now, I expect, but we were young and pretty determined about what we were doing. When you're that age you think you can change the world, don't you? Things are either black or white, good or bad—you don't want to compromise. We wanted to defy the system and create our own, new way of living."

Emma wondered whether she would ever want to change the world. She hadn't even managed to leave home yet. But she forced herself to concentrate on what Elizabeth was saying.

"We called it a commune because that's what it was—we all lived there as one big family. It had links with a big organisation in India and I suppose they must have owned it, but we despised anything that smacked of capitalism and we weren't at all interested in where the money came from. At least, I suppose somebody must have sorted it all out, but it was never discussed. It had been a bed and breakfast place before the first lot moved in so there was plenty of room and although it was pretty shabby we didn't care—it suited us that way.

"When Frances first arrived she had a baby with her—well, you, of course! She had heard about the commune from a friend of hers and she asked if she could come and live with us for a while. We had no idea what it would be like to have a baby around the place but it was obvious that she needed help and we thought, how hard can it be? I suppose we wanted to do our bit for the sisterhood." Elizabeth gave Emma a wry smile.

"Frances was in bad shape then, just skin and bone. Her mind was all over the place and some days she could honestly hardly string a sentence together. Goodness knows how she'd managed in London. We were worried about her and we did what we could to help. We tried to get her to look after herself a bit better, eat properly, sleep as much as she could—after all there was never any shortage of childcare. She did some yoga and meditation with us and she seemed to find that helpful.

"Gradually, she started to get better and we got to know her. You and she became part of our little community. She told us about how she had met your father at Exeter and how they were living together in London when you were born. I'm not exactly sure why she left him. It's odd because it sounded as though they had been happy together.

"She always said how much she loved him and she obviously missed him. I think it was more to do with what was going on inside her head. Having a baby had completely messed her up and she thought she had to deal with it on her own. I think she was ashamed of not being able to cope and she didn't want to drag your father into it."

"Did Dad know she was there? Did you know him?" Emma brightened at the thought.

"I don't think he did at the time and no, I never met him."

"Oh."

Emma took her elbows off the table and leaned forward to try and encourage Elizabeth to keep talking.

"Could you tell me a bit more about her?"

"We all liked Frances—she was great fun. After a bit, we realised she'd been suffering from depression when she first arrived, but as she recovered her energy came back—she had this wonderful enthusiasm that just swept you along. She was very clever, very creative. She had been at art school in London and painting was part of her life—big, dramatic, abstract canvasses with thick slabs of paint. They really were stunning. She had so much talent, although she didn't seem to realise it.

"Sometimes, she would paint for days and nights straight. There was such an urgency to it, it was almost scary. We encouraged her—we were proud of having an artist in our midst. Every now and then, she would manage to sell one or two pictures and then she would go out and buy more paint and canvasses—she loved all that—and off she would go again. We ended up letting her use the dining room as a studio and we all ate in the kitchen instead. I think in a way she was trying to make sense of life through her painting, although I'm not sure she ever did.

"I think the spiritual side of the commune was important to her as well. She got quite into it. We used to get newsletters and video talks from a guru from the organisation in India and she decided she wanted to follow him. It was all about casting off your old life and committing yourself to following a path to enlightenment, a kind of rebirth. That really appealed to her. You got a new name, you could even have saffron robes to wear—the new dawn, you see—and you became a sort of disciple. Some people on the commune had already signed up for the first stage, although I never did."

So I wasn't totally wrong about the orange robes then, thought Emma, allowing herself to sag slightly into her chair.

"But that's what we wanted to do, turn our back on the material world and search inside ourselves instead. It all sounds a bit ridiculous now I suppose. The whole organisation was part of a worldwide movement at that time. If you were serious about it, you put your spiritual life ahead of everything else. Partners, marriage, children—of course, you were free to make that choice but you couldn't do both. You can't really be free with a brood of children in tow and I can tell you, that's absolutely true. There were no children on these communes, even though most people were in their 20s and 30s."

Elizabeth paused for a moment, clearly struck by how much her own life had changed.

"That was partly why Frances decided to go back to Richard. It was one thing looking after a babe in arms, but a toddler was rather different. It became obvious to all of us that the commune wasn't the right place to bring up a child. Frances could see that. She wanted a proper home for you and she decided you needed your father. Her health was so much better and she was convinced she would be able to settle down in London again. We weren't so sure but it really wasn't up to us and in any case when she decided to do something there was no stopping her. So off she went.

"I think it probably did go all right to start with. We didn't hear from her and we assumed no news was good news. We missed her, of course, and you as well—although we did get our dining room back! But things at the commune were changing too. She wasn't the only one moving on and we had some new arrivals, which always changed the atmosphere. Even so, I don't think we were particularly surprised when she turned up again out of the blue a few months later. But this time she was on her own—she'd left you behind with your father."

"That must have been after she wrote that suicide note to Dad! So she didn't go through with it after all! What happened to her? Where is she now?"

"We'll get to that but I think you need to hear the whole story. You'll see why."

148

"So she just left me behind like—like a piece of luggage! How on earth did she explain that?"

Elizabeth leaned forward and looked hard at her.

"She loved you, Emma. There was absolutely no doubt about that. She left you with your father because she knew it was best for you. She did it *because* she loved you. It was one of the most unselfish things she ever did. It broke her heart and I don't think she ever recovered."

Emma inspected the remains of her tea. Yes, that was pretty much what she'd said in the letter. That she'd done her best. She just hadn't been able to be the mother Emma had always wanted. She could see that. But it was so unfair that it had made *her* suffer too. It certainly hadn't been *her* fault. She looked up at Elizabeth, conscious that tears were rolling down both cheeks now and she was struggling to keep her mouth in the right place.

"Oh, dear. This is an awful lot for you to take in. Are you all right? Shall we go outside and get some air?"

Emma nodded, unable to speak.

"Have you seen the Royal Crescent? It's beautiful—one of the best examples of Georgian architecture in the country. We could walk there. Shall we go and have a look?" said Elizabeth kindly, taking charge.

Emma picked up the motherly tone in her voice and treasured it. This woman knew my mother, she thought. She even knew me. I've never met her before and yet she is bringing my mother alive. Even if I never see her again, I will always remember this day.

By the time they were walking through the narrow streets of the old town, Emma had managed to get a grip. She was determined not to waste this opportunity by feeling sorry for herself—that could wait till later. She asked Elizabeth to carry on with the story.

"Well, soon after Frances came back she got together with a guy called Rob, who'd arrived at the commune while she was away. I don't think it was particularly serious, but Frances seemed to like having him around. That was one of the things about Frances—there was usually some man in the background, even when she was with your father. It was quite awkward sometimes, but it was just part of who she was. She certainly had a knack of picking up admirers.

"Rob was perfectly harmless. He was good looking in a hippyish sort of way, good company, easy to live with, played the guitar—we all liked him well enough. He had done a lot of travelling, mainly in the Far East. He was kind of cool I suppose, not over-troubled by the demands of everyday life, didn't believe in putting down roots. If things got too complicated, he just walked away.

"Well it wasn't long before Frances was pregnant. Rob took it very calmly, he just accepted it, although I don't think he ever really took responsibility for it. Neither of them thought much about what would happen in the future. They both had the same attitude, they just concentrated on today and tomorrow and maybe next week if you were lucky. It was one of the reasons they got along so well.

"Frances seemed happy during that time. Her health was more or less stable. But she was absolutely determined not to go the doctor or the baby clinic or anything like that. She didn't want anyone else involved—this time she wanted to stay outside the system. Maybe that was part of her not really facing up to what was happening—she didn't want her pregnancy to become official. She didn't want to drag us into the system either. Or maybe she didn't want Richard to find out what she was up to. She decided she would have a natural birth at the commune, with us helping her. It was her second child, after all, and it wasn't unusual to have a home birth in those days.

"So we asked a friend of ours who had done a bit of midwifery training to come and help. It all went remarkably smoothly and Frances had a little boy. We all decided on the name for him together—we called him Asha. It means 'hope' in Sanskrit and it seemed right for Frances at the time."

Emma stopped walking and turned to face Elizabeth.

"So my mother actually had this baby? You mean I've got a brother?"

"A half-brother. Yes."

"But—is he alive then? Is he still with her? Where are they now?"

Elizabeth looked away.

"I'm sorry. I'm so sorry to have to tell you this, Emma. I'm afraid your mother is dead. She took her own life when Asha was about 6 months old. She took an overdose when she went to bed one evening and she never woke up. She was dead when we found her."

Of course. It had been too good to be true. It was obvious; she had never once got in touch, after all. Emma had always believed she was dead and she was. Nothing had changed. Emma realised that she had not expected to find her, not really.

"What happened?"

They started to walk again.

"Well, Rob wasn't very impressed with fatherhood—he wasn't interested in babies and he hadn't been getting much of Frances' attention either. So after a while he packed his bags and moved on. He went off to join a commune in East Anglia somewhere I think. Frances just let him go. In fact, she hardly seemed to notice.

"But then she started to go downhill again. She had suffered from post-natal depression when she had you and it was happening again. We realised things weren't great with her but we had no idea at the time how bad it was. Perhaps she missed Rob more than we thought or perhaps the responsibility of being a single mother was too much for her. And then it happened."

Emma tried to imagine Elizabeth finding her mother dead in her bed. "How awful."

"Yes. I wish we could have done more to help. I've gone over it so many times in my head. We should have realised. But I think she had just had enough. She couldn't see how she was going to cope with life, with herself, with Asha. But mainly the depression took over. When you have that sort of illness, you're not rational. I didn't understand that then. Poor Frances, she had such a difficult life. It was all so—tragic."

"It sounds as if you did everything you could."

"Well, I'll always wonder. Anyway, Frances' death changed everything. We were all shocked and very upset. And of course we had to deal with the hospital, the police, the coroner, the funeral, all the endless things that have to be done when someone dies, especially like that. We all had to grow up rather quickly and think about what we were doing with our own lives. I left the commune a few months after that. I moved up to London, got a job and met my husband."

They had arrived at the Royal Crescent. Emma looked at the perfect symmetry and sheer scale of the Georgian façade, its row of ionic columns lined up like the fat pipes of a church organ. Such elegance, such beauty.

Elizabeth was silent for a moment or two as she watched Emma.

"It's funny. When I first saw you earlier, I didn't think you were like Frances at all. But now I can see her in you. She used to love coming here."

Emma shrugged, thinking about her mother. "Dad always says I'm more like him. But then I don't even know what she was like. I don't remember her at all. I always wanted to be like her though. What is it you can see?"

"It's just something about your manner, I suppose. We were good friends, your mother and I. I was very fond of her."

"What happened to Asha? Is he dead too?"

"I've often wondered that myself. Not whether he's dead—there's no reason why he should be. But what happened to him.

"When Frances died, we had to decide what to do about Asha. We had no idea how to get in touch with Rob and he had never wanted any responsibility for Asha anyway. To start with we all looked after him between us—we felt that in a way he was the commune's child and it kept Frances' memory alive for us too. But as time went on it was obvious we couldn't bring him up like that. He needed a proper mother, a proper home. People left the commune and other people who had never even known Frances arrived and we couldn't expect them put up with having him around.

"So we had to find another home for him, but it was tricky because he didn't officially exist. Frances had managed to get through the whole process without ever checking in with the authorities and she certainly hadn't registered his birth. We didn't know where to start unravelling all that. So we had to find someone who would take Asha in unofficially, under the radar.

"Frances had once taken me to a little village called Exford, right in the middle of Exmoor. She and Richard used to love going there for weekends—they used to stay in a B&B next door to the Post Office. It was a pretty little place with an old fashioned village green, right on the river Exe. I thought Frances would have liked her son to grow up there and at least it had some connection with her."

"But I know Exford well! Our cottage is just up the road from there!"

"But I thought you lived in London! You have a cottage in Exford?"

"Not actually in Exford, but pretty near. I used to spend my school holidays there as a child. Do you think that's why Dad bought the cottage—because he used to go there with my mother—?"

They both fell silent while they absorbed this information. Then Elizabeth continued.

"Well, I thought maybe if we went to see the Vicar there he would know what to do. At least, I thought we could trust him not to get us all into trouble and it was better than turning up to a church in the middle of Bath. We told him the whole story. Looking back on it, we really had no idea what we were asking of him. It was a hell of a risk. But amazingly in the end he agreed to help on condition that we handed Asha over to him with no questions asked.

"He said it was better for us not to know anything about Asha's future, there had to be no connection. We had to accept that. That's why I don't know what happened to him. It was dreadful handing him over like that but it seemed the best answer at the time. And I still think it was, in the circumstances."

Emma pictured the village church at Exford with its square tower and overgrown graveyard and shivered. She had never been inside it and even walking past it had always given her the creeps. Strange to think it had been home to her brother all those years ago. She had certainly never come across the Vicar and didn't have the first clue how to get in touch with him.

"Do you think I could find Asha? I suppose he'd be almost grown up by now. After all, he can't be that much younger than me—"

"Well I can tell you who the Vicar was back then. You'd have to check and see if he's still there—unlikely, I should think. But if you *could* find him, if he's even still alive, he might help you. You are Asha's half-sister, after all, and probably his only living blood relative."

Well, what an afternoon this was turning out to be. As they walked back through Royal Victoria Park in the fading light, collars turned up against the early autumn chill, Emma knew she had already got more information out of Elizabeth Duncan than she had dared to hope for. But then again, she wanted every last crumb she could get. After all, she had so few.

"Is there anything else you can tell me about my mother? *Anything*?"

Elizabeth thought as she scuffed her feet through the drifts of autumn leaves at the side of the path.

"She just did things that other people wouldn't do. She pushed the boundaries and it shocked you a bit, but you couldn't help admiring her for it. And she was absolutely hopeless with money. She never did have much of it, but she was generous to a fault. She never really thought things through, she just acted on instinct.

"I remember once—she'd gone into town shopping and she saw a homeless guy outside Tesco's, sitting on the pavement with his dog, begging for some money for a cup of tea. Most people would have walked past—but Frances goes into Tesco's, buys a bottle of vodka and ends up spending the rest of the afternoon sitting on a park bench with him. Then, she brings him back to the commune, dog and all, smelling like a distillery.

"She sat him in the kitchen and we all had to be introduced to him. He'd had a tough time—lived in care up north for most of his childhood until he ran away.

Slept rough after that, making some sort of a living from poaching, the odd bit of manual labour. He'd ended up in borstal and then in prison. He'd never really had much of a chance, poor bloke. But the thing was that Frances wanted us to take him in and help him get back on his feet.

"She was like that, always so concerned for other people, but she had no sense of where to draw the line. She didn't see him as a homeless drunk, just another person with problems a bit like hers."

"What did you do?"

"Well, we all felt sorry for him but we really couldn't take him in. He'd been on the streets for years and was clearly an alcoholic. He could have been violent for all we knew, we could all have been murdered in our beds. Anyway, he needed specialist help. Then there was the dog as well. And whether his story was true, goodness knows. Probably not. So we managed to distract Frances somehow and then I'm afraid we bribed him to go on his way."

"I see what you mean. You can't help admiring her, in a way."

"Oh yes, I know. Frances was always doing things like that."

They both sat and thought for a minute, smiling together as they thought about this story.

"I would love to have known her," Emma said wistfully.

"Yes, she was very special. There aren't many like her."

Chapter 15
Two Girls

In the sweltering heat of the truck, Alex concentrated on some of his newly-learned deep breathing and tried to get his terror under control, superficially at least. He guessed from the turban that the truck driver was probably a Sikh which was encouraging. He thought back to the langar at the Golden Temple at Amritsar and the Sikh tradition of hospitality he had experienced there and hoped it was a general Sikh thing.

The driver's name was Manjit, as he had immediately volunteered, and he seemed friendly enough.

"Where you want to go?" said Manjit, bobbing his head in every direction as if it were only loosely attached to his neck and apparently offering to drive him anywhere on earth he might desire. "In India, a guest is a God and you are my guest!"

Alex smiled, trying to look grateful despite the dart of anger that was flaring up inside him. Kindness and hospitality was all very well but in the end it just made things a whole load more complicated. How was he supposed to know where he was going or where Manjit was going, for that matter? Now, he was going to have to coax the Sikh and his truck back onto whatever route they were on before they picked him up while pretending to be perfectly clear about his own plans and how well it was all going to hang together. Perhaps there was something to be said for straight talking after all.

He did know they were travelling south towards the plains so Alex reckoned Manjit must have come from the mountains where the roads were presumably pretty lethal. The smear of red paste on Manjit's forehead from a recent blessing and the many talismans and deities he had dotted around his cab seemed to bear this out. He started to sound out Manjit to see if his theory was right.

Manjit's head started bobbing again. "I went up there for a delivery of cement, yes. Oh, you need good karma up there—if you meet a truck coming the other way you can be hanging over a cliff. There are falling rocks, snow and sheep also."

He began to look slightly surprised to be alive at all, instead of in pieces thousands of feet below the road in a river bed.

Alex half-listened as Manjit chattered on about hairpin bends and low roofed rock tunnels and noticed the tension on the driver's face ease as he relived his recent near-death experiences. You too, then, he thought. I know how that feels. Once Manjit's joie-de-vivre had returned Alex asked him casually where his cement was going, which unleashed a long and somewhat circular explanation involving a place he'd never heard of just to the north of Delhi.

Delhi—? No, not a good idea. Big, complicated. Perhaps a bit bloody obvious, too. But he had to make a quick decision. Mountains to the north, he'd come from the west—in a split second he decided he was travelling east and passed on this happy news to Manjit. Could he perhaps be dropped off at a railway station somewhere?

This sent Manjit into such a fever of excitement that he took both hands off the wheel. In merely a few hours, he would be passing close to a place called Moradabad, which would be the most ideal spot in the whole of India for Alex to catch a train—all the way to Calcutta if he wanted to. The matter was settled.

Alex had little choice but to trust the Sikh. He seemed genuine enough, if a little volatile, and the long discourse he now embarked on about the magnificence of Indian Railways gave Alex a bit of breathing space. He hadn't heard of Moradabad but that was hardly surprising; anyway, any decent railway station would do. In fact, the more obscure, the better. It was quite possible that Moradabad was not on Manjit's route at all, but Alex's geography and powers of persuasion were not up to the task of establishing this for certain, let alone coming up with an alternative.

As Manjit helpfully explained, to drive in India you need a good horn, good brakes and good luck. The driving conditions were so dreadful that after the first half-dozen potentially fatal near-misses Alex started to find the whole thing hysterically funny. They were basically driving on the left like at home but here this was apparently not at all compulsory, so Manjit was having to weave past tuk-tuks, bullock carts, cars, trucks and even coaches coming at them head on down the left-hand carriageway.

Anyone with a horn was using it pretty much all the time to defend themselves against the constant threat of collision. There was apparently no fast or slow lane either since both lanes were clogged with slow-moving farm vehicles, people stopping to have a pee, animals tethered to the central reservation and overturned trucks with their loads of building materials spilled over the road. Every mile they covered increased Alex's respect for Manjit's driving skills.

"You go to Calcutta?" Manjit asked, apparently determined to entertain his guest with light conversation at the same time as avoiding one disastrous crash after another.

"Er—I think so, yes. Is it far?"

Why on earth hadn't he at least looked at a map of Northern India back in Amritsar before chucking everything in to go to Scott's ashram? (Fuck. Better not think about Scott now.) But even though planning had never been his strong point and certainly hadn't played a big part in his travels so far, a bit of basic geography would have been sensible. What an idiot. He was pretty sure Calcutta was on the east coast of India, but what lay between was a complete blank.

"Very far, very far. But train is very very good. Overnight train, then day— 24 hours, then you reach Calcutta."

OK, thought Alex, well maybe I won't be going quite that far. We'll see.

He picked up some sort of silver medallion on a black leather strap from the dashboard and studied it, wondering whether he would ever feel safe again.

"That's a khanda," Manjit said, nodding approvingly. "It is our Sikh symbol of the divinity and creative power of God. You see the crossed daggers and the wheel in the middle—they are representing the four pillars of the Sikh faith. It has a very special meaning for all Sikhs, like your cross."

It's not *my* cross. That jarred, Alex thought, surprised at how uncomfortable he felt about the inadequacy of his own religion and the apathy of its followers. Funny how a simple truck driver had managed to put the whole lot of them to shame.

In between bouts of conversation with Manjit, Alex was starting to feel very shaken. Was he responsible for Scott's demise? He was the one who had wanted to get involved and he had pushed Scott into coming with him. It was Scott who had warned him off and it was Scott who had ended up dead. By rights, it should have been the other way round.

What on earth had he thought he was doing, sticking his nose in like that? Scott had been right, it was none of their business. He should have just backed off. But like an idiot he had pretended he was in some sort of boys' own adventure and risked both their lives. None of this need have happened at all. But then again, it wasn't him that had killed Scott and anyway Scott had seriously misjudged the situation too. He must have got a shock when he found out how wrong he was.

Alex didn't want to think about what had actually happened to Scott. He just hoped it had been quick. He wondered how many other naive backpackers had met the same fate.

It was strange how unemotional he felt right now about losing his friend, almost matter-of-fact about it. It was as if he was looking at it from a long way away. There must be something really wrong with him. Sitting in Manjit's cab now he started to question whether it had happened at all. Could he have been mistaken? It all suddenly seemed rather far-fetched. After all, was it really such a big deal to find a few suitcases stashed away in an ashram office block?

Yes. Of course it was, or he and Scott would still be back at the ashram meditating and doing yoga, wouldn't they? But there was no doubt that Scott had completely disappeared. Perhaps he should go to the police. How do you do that in India? Can you trust them? It might only make things worse.

As Scott had pointed out, this wasn't their gig. They didn't have a clue how things really worked in India—they were outsiders. What you see on the surface, the assumptions you make, what they want you to think, might have nothing to do with what things were really like. Better to try and put the whole thing as far as possible behind him. At least then, he wouldn't have to put his trust in anyone other than himself.

At last, they drove into Moradabad and juddered to a halt at the railway station in a cloud of cement dust. Alex said a grateful goodbye to Manjit, who had after all rescued him from the ashram and then saved his life several times over with his impressive driving skills. He wished he had something to give him to show his gratitude, but instead it was Manjit who pressed a bag of bananas and the little Sikh khanda on him, refusing to take no for an answer.

As he watched the truck drive away he found himself asking Manjit's Sikh god to keep the driver safe. Then he put the khanda round his neck, hoping it had some divine power that would protect him too.

It was getting dark as he walked into Moradabad's surprisingly modern railway station. After a few moments' study of the departures board, he chose something called the Link Express, which was due within the next hour—that sounds suitably fast and important, he thought as he scanned down the list of stops. The first few towns meant nothing to him, but at 5 AM it was due to arrive in Kanpur, which was in capital letters and sounded vaguely familiar. He decided he would get off there.

You can get further quicker on a train, he thought as he watched the outlines of Uttar Pradesh roll past in the darkness. At least now, he was two legs away from the ashram and he was pretty sure he hadn't been followed in Moradabad. He shuddered as he wondered what was going on at the ashram now and if any of the others had missed him and Scott.

After an hour or so, he wrapped himself up in an Indian Railways sheet and several scratchy blankets against the ferocious air conditioning that Indian trains seemed to specialise in and tried to find a comfortable position to curl up in. The sound of snoring Indians all around him was strangely reassuring.

* * *

Kanpur Central at 5am the next morning felt like a good choice. Even at that hour of the morning he could see it was a big enough and busy enough place to disappear into. Ignoring the usual hopping collection of taxi drivers around him he set off from the station on foot and had soon found and secured a room at the Lake View Hostel, which seemed perfectly sanguine about his unusual arrival time. But perhaps it wasn't unusual in this part of the world to arrive at a hostel in the early hours of the morning. Perhaps in the circumstances he should be careful not to assume anything.

The hostel was hardly glamorous, but it was perfectly adequate and the sight of a comfortable bed with clean sheets made him realise how tired he was after two nights on the trot with little sleep. He crawled into bed gratefully, deciding to allow himself a few hours' rest before trying to pick up where he had left off when he met Scott on that fateful day at the Golden Temple in Amritsar.

It was early afternoon by the time he was awake enough to think about getting up and going out to explore. He had passed out straight away and slept heavily and the sleep had done him good. The memory of his escape from the ashram was starting to fade and he even felt a thrill of excitement at the thought of resuming his travels again. He was also ravenously hungry. In the mirror above the basin, his eyes were a little swollen and his face creased from lying motionless on the pillow for so long. Yup, he really had been tired, but he was fine now. He splashed some cold water onto his face and he was ready to go.

Out in the town he admired the buildings, the people, even the traffic. He thought back to the last time he had done this, in Amritsar, but everything was different now. The experiences of the last few weeks had left him older and wiser. Then he started to wonder what on earth he was doing here, wandering around an Indian town he'd barely heard of thousands of miles away from home. Had it really been necessary to run away like that? But at least now he understood why he had overreacted when Joe and Emma had got together.

Although he was still pretty confused about his feelings for Emma. Why did he feel so angry with Joe for stealing her away from him when he had never even thought of getting together with her himself? He thought back to the time they had spent in London, trying to remember how he had felt about her then. They had almost been a couple, without actually being one. Had he been happy with that? Or had he just been too hopeless to do anything about it?

But surely things weren't so bad that he couldn't go home one day. Perhaps, in view of what had happened at the ashram, the sooner the better. No longer a refugee in search of a new life he could be a traveller now, a tourist even, here to see and experience as much as he could while he had the chance. And there might even be a whole new life waiting to be discovered at home. Why not? It all seemed so simple that he couldn't understand why on earth he had struggled so much with it. He wandered down the Mall Road feeling positively light-headed.

Kanpur, then. It seemed to be even more of a relic of the British Raj than anything in India so far. Of course—Cawnpore. That's why it had sounded vaguely familiar to him. The All Souls' Cathedral he visited had been built by the British to commemorate all those (British) who died in the Indian Mutiny in 1857, complete with memorial garden and cemetery. At least, the British had always called it the Indian Mutiny; here it was known as the First War of Independence. What a neat way to sum up the different perspectives of the two sides.

The British Empire had always been a rather hazy idea to him, consisting of jokes about how much of the world map was coloured pink and the legacy of the British Commonwealth which no one really understood except that it was possibly something to do with the Queen's Christmas Broadcast. It wasn't until you got here that you realised its true significance. Like it or not, generations of British families had lived and died here. The days of the Raj were as much a part of Britain's history as India's.

Kanpur had something else which had deep significance in India too—the Ganges. His first encounter in Rishikesh had been fleeting and seemed like a distant memory now. Here this most sacred of rivers, mother of India, a goddess in its own right, giver of life, healer and undertaker to the dead, brought him right back to thinking about how much religion was part of day-to-day life in India. Spirituality washed through people's daily lives like saffron dye and it was accepted without fuss, without embarrassment. The material world was treated almost with indifference, a temporary affliction of minor importance compared with the eternal. India's spirituality was embracing him, something he hadn't expected, and he realised he was no longer uncomfortable with it at all but comforted by it instead.

He wondered how the dogged Christian faith of India's British rulers had fared in the face of this almost suffocating spiritual embrace. The missionaries who followed in their wake had tackled the job of converting the natives to Christianity with relish, determined to save their souls. But the Goliath of Hinduism in its ancient wisdom had been able to simply embrace Christianity, digest it and move on. He remembered Mrs Moore in A Passage to India and wondered how many others like her had come out here and lost their faith, confused by the strength and ubiquity of Eastern spirituality, and gone home empty. Now, it was that very same spirituality that attracted so many of their descendants.

The next hour was spent totally awed by the beautiful Jain Glass Temple, a riot of intricately decorated murals, stained glass, enamel, mirror and marble depicting the Jain scriptures. He had been just about to embark on the figurines of Lord Mahavira and the 23 Jain Tirthankaras when he looked up and saw two English girls giggling at him in an attempt to engage his attention.

The girls had apparently spent the whole afternoon at the temple and it seemed to have gone to their heads. Alex soon found himself giggling back. After spending 24 hours with little but his own thoughts, he was glad to have someone to talk to and they quickly agreed to retreat to a local bar for a drink.

The girls, whose names were Anna and Nicky, turned out to be good company. They had an easy manner with each other that came of being together so much; they both had the same stories to tell, their speech was peppered with the same words and expressions and they even looked alike with their long, tangled brown hair and clutch of friendship bracelets, all heavy with unspoken significance. They almost finished each other's sentences.

Alex had noticed pairs of girls like these two travelling together before. Despite their attempts to blend in with the locals with their baggy cotton trousers, layered scarves, battered Indian cloth bags and unkempt appearance, you could always spot them a mile off. It was a style of dress all of its own—they didn't seem to notice that Indian women would never dream of going out looking such a fright.

These two came from Guildford where they had been friends since secondary school. They were in their gap year before college—Anna to study medicine at Manchester, Nicky social sciences at Oxford Brooks. Obviously not stupid then, Alex thought, especially Anna.

Their chatter about friends, nights out in London and summer music festivals was a nostalgic blast from home, so familiar and yet so distant. They had both acquired a slightly world-weary, unwashed but contented look and they talked about the ups and downs of travelling on a shoestring with justifiable pride. He warmed to their light-hearted chat, their laughter, their shared sense of humour, and he was soon laughing too as they all weighed each other up and engaged in a little light-hearted flirting over another round of local beers.

The girls were going on to Varanasi next and as they told him about this sacred city, perhaps as old as Indian civilisation itself, a plan began to form between the three of them. There seemed little point in hanging around. Rather than spend another night in Kanpur they would all go together on the overnight train to Varanasi which Alex now wanted to see as much as they did. Buoyed up by their new plans they finished their drinks and hurried off in different directions to pick up their bags, agreeing to meet up again at the station later that evening.

Alex was in high spirits as he arrived back at the Lake View Hostel. He had enjoyed his afternoon's sightseeing and making the decision to go home one day had been something of a breakthrough. He was looking forward to travelling with the two girls and Varanasi sounded amazing. Most of all, he felt his travels were back on track—this was all normal, safe stuff. No drama. So his thoughts were elsewhere as he hurried through the hostel reception, so much so that he barely registered that the two men talking to the receptionist in low voices were policemen.

He bounded up the stairs but the door to his room seemed to be open—he was sure he had locked it earlier. Perhaps he had got the wrong room or the wrong floor? Then with a sinking heart he saw that the flimsy furniture had been upended, bedding strewn on the floor, his few possessions scattered. The police downstairs—is that why they were here? Had the hostel been burgled? But as he inspected the damage he realised this was no ordinary burglary.

No, there was violence and aggression here too. It had been personal and he had been the target. Thank God he hadn't been here at the time or he probably wouldn't have lived to tell the tale. Maybe even now they were watching the hostel. How had they found him here? Could the police downstairs be involved too? At least he had had plans to leave anyway. Perhaps that gave him a head start. Except that he was a drop-out art student up against an organised crime ring—and if they'd found him here, it wasn't going to take them long to catch up with him again.

But perhaps he had just been unlucky. It could have been a simple robbery, perhaps an inside job even, covered up to look like a break-in. And at least he had had his passport and wallet with him at the Temple. He could see most of his things scattered across the floor—if they had been looking for something, it didn't look like they had found it. Shaking, he scooped up whatever he could find and shoved it into his backpack. If they were out there somewhere, there was no sense in walking out of the front door, straight into the trap. He was going to have to find another way out.

He crept along the empty landing and down an unlocked fire escape at the end of the corridor, half expecting a blow or a shot with every step and wondering whether death would be instant or how much it would hurt. Once outside he crouched down behind a pile of rubble and timber and waited to see what would happen next, sweat pouring off him, hardly daring to breathe. Nothing. Perhaps he was overreacting after all.

The urge to move was overpowering and after a few minutes he set off again, working his way back across town towards the railway station, down back alleys, through rubbish tips, taking unexpected twists and turns, sliding inconspicuously in and out of shops and blending in with the crowds wherever he could. He took no chances. Whoever they were, these guys weren't messing around.

Chapter 16
The Vicar of Exford

On the train from Bath back to London, Emma unfolded the scrap of paper Elizabeth had dug out of her handbag. So much hung on that one name she had scribbled on it—Reverend Michael Drake. The nearest thing she had to a piece of evidence that she actually had a brother. She wasn't an only child after all. And yet she wasn't surprised, somehow. It was as if she had always known. She tucked it into her purse for safe keeping.

Reverend Michael Drake had been Vicar of Exford all those years ago. Reverend Michael Drake had taken her brother in when he was a baby. If she could find him, if he was even still alive, perhaps just possibly she might even get to meet Asha. But surely the chances were that the Vicar would have retired and she would never find him, or he would have died by now and without him the trail would go cold.

The chances were that it would turn out like her search for her mother—too late. Much too late. What a pity she hadn't known about all this years ago. Had her father known? No, he couldn't have done, Frances had been long gone by the time Asha was born. And anyway, surely even he wouldn't have kept the existence of a half-brother from her.

She tried to imagine what Asha might look like now. He would be about 21 or 22. About the same age as Alex, in fact, she thought with the usual stab of anxiety. Perhaps Asha would be more like their mother than she was. She wondered how life had turned out for him. At least she had had one of her birth parents.

Perhaps he had had a perfectly happy childhood growing up in a perfectly nice vicarage somewhere with roses growing round the front door and a tribe of lovely brothers and sisters. Tennis on the lawn, sponge cake for tea. Church bells on Sundays. The last thing he would want was a grown-up half-sister coming out of the woodwork talking about his birth mother and stirring things up.

Or perhaps he hadn't been so lucky. He could have had a traumatic childhood with abusive parents who hadn't loved him or cared for him. He could have even grown up in the care system. Goodness knows where he could have ended up. He could be a drug addict or a criminal by now for all she knew. Or perhaps he was at university or maybe working. Or abroad. Or in prison! He could be living with a girlfriend, even have a child. Would he know anything about his birth parents?

There wasn't much to know about his father by the sound of it. But he could have grown up knowing more about their mother than she had. Or perhaps he wouldn't have wanted to know about them at all. Perhaps he wouldn't want to have anything to do with her. Her brother, her own flesh and blood, might want to stay a stranger to her.

There must be a way to find a vicar. The Church must have records of things like that and if she explained everything then hopefully they'd be sympathetic and try to help. That was the point of religion wasn't it, helping people, being compassionate, all that stuff? But could she explain everything when she knew so little? There might not be any official records. People might get into trouble. It might not be such a good idea to go round asking questions. But it wouldn't do any harm to try and find the Vicar. First thing tomorrow morning she would get onto it.

* * *

Emma had promised to ring Joe when she got back, but she just couldn't do it. She felt like a different person to the Emma who had left the house this morning and she needed a bit of space, a bit of time to adjust. So much to think about, so much to hope for. It was all too vague at the moment, too uncertain. She didn't want to make it real by saying it out loud only for Joe to be all practical and dash her hopes. She wasn't even sure what her hopes were yet. And anyway, she had her father to deal with first.

She had left a note to say she would be late back, but she hadn't told him where she was going. She hadn't even told him about Elizabeth Duncan yet. Now she had information about her mother that he didn't have and she wasn't at all sure whether he would even want to know. Let alone about Asha.

In a way, Asha would be his stepson—his daughter's half-brother—almost part of the family. But there was no blood connection between them at all. Frances' son, born after she had left him. Nothing to do with him. No reason for him to be remotely interested except that it would remind him of Frances and the pain he had suffered because of her. Perhaps it was better not to tell him about Asha at all—but she could hardly not tell him. Although she couldn't exactly expect him to be sympathetic. She was going have to manage this one on her own.

She heard him crashing around in the kitchen and headed straight in to face the music. No point in putting it off any longer.

"Hi, darling! You OK?"

Richard looked up from the spitting frying pan, his face flushed, as he reached out for a handful of meticulously sliced mushrooms from the chopping board beside him. He would never ask her straight out where she had been, in acknowledgement of the fact that she was now grown up and entitled to lead her own life, but nevertheless the question was there.

"Fine, Dad."

But she knew her voice didn't sound fine. She took off her coat and sank onto a kitchen stool, the weight of all this new information on her shoulders making her sag. Richard swung round to look at her again, concerned, then pulled the pan off the heat and sat down beside her.

"How about a glass of wine? Here, there's one right here. Coming up."

It was almost as if he already knew, although he couldn't have done. He was just being her normal, kind, great dad, taking care of her as he always had—and she was about to ruin it. For a moment, she wondered whether it was all really worth it, putting her relationship with him at risk like this for the sake of a bit of history. But no, she had needed to know about her mother and in the process she had found out about Asha. They were important too.

"I went to Bath today."

Richard said nothing but his expression encouraged her to go on.

"I went to meet a woman called Elizabeth Duncan. She knew my mother, she lived at that commune in Exeter with her. Jackie got her name from somewhere."

"Ahh."

"This woman Elizabeth knew all about her. My mother, I mean. She told me a lot of things. It's true that she's dead. She died ages ago, although not quite as long ago as you thought. But you know what? Before she died she had another child, a boy. I may have a half-brother."

Emma started to sob, overwhelmed. Saying it out loud had made it seem real. She could hardly believe it when Richard leaped off his stool and wrapped a fatherly arm around her, giving her a comforting squeeze without apparently even registering the impact of this news on himself.

"Oh, darling. This is all much too much for you. I *knew* something like this would happen. That woman always did have the knack of causing complete havoc, and this is an absolute classic. Hang on, let me just turn this lot off and you can tell me all about it."

Emma looked at him thankfully and did her best to pull herself together while he dealt with the frying pan. Then he plumped her down on the sofa amongst the cushions and she told him everything she could remember that Elizabeth had said.

"So she did go back to the commune."

"Yes, she did. You didn't know that, did you? Did you know anything about Asha, Dad?"

"No, no. I told you, I never had any contact with her again after she left that day. That's why I always assumed she was dead. If I had known about Asha—I don't know. That would have been a very difficult one. But I didn't."

She believed him. Thank goodness he hadn't lied to her about that.

"But surely you must have wondered what happened to her?"

"Of course I did. But I had to cut her out of our lives, it was the only way we were ever going to manage. It was so much easier to think of her as being dead. That way I knew we'd have a better chance of getting over it, of putting it behind us. You can't imagine how difficult the whole thing was. And it seemed pretty likely, anyway. She had some serious problems and she'd already tried once, after all. By then, it was not so much a question of if but when. There was nothing I could do to help her, Em. God knows I tried, but I couldn't help her."

"It doesn't sound as if anyone could. Elizabeth said pretty much the same thing."

"But another child—I certainly never considered that. Perhaps I should have done. A boy, she said? Quite a strange name, Asha."

"It means hope, apparently. In Sanskrit."

"I see." Richard's wry smile managed to convey his entire view of communes, Sanskrit names and surprise children in one brief moment. Emma did her best not to let this put her off too much.

"Well, when Frances died they took him to the Vicar at Exford."

"Why on earth—who did?"

Emma explained about how Elizabeth and her friends had looked after him on the commune to start with and then tried to find a home for him and about his lack of birth certificate or indeed any official existence at all.

"But why Exford? I don't understand."

"Because they knew Frances had loved it there. Because you both used to like going there together and she thought it would be a good place for him to grow up. They thought that was what Frances would have wanted."

"Good Lord."

"So if I can find the Vicar I might be able to find out what happened to Asha. I might even be able to meet up with him. Do you think that's possible after all this time, Dad?"

But Richard was so thoroughly shaken himself now that he didn't reply.

* * *

After such a dramatic turn of events, it seemed strange for Emma and her father to sit and have supper together as if nothing had happened, but they managed it somehow. Richard finished off his mushroom creation, which turned out to be fried steak in disguise, and produced an above-average bottle of red to go with it. It was a considerably cosier evening than she was expecting and she was surprised to find that she felt closer to her father than she could remember ever feeling before.

It wasn't just that they were both having to deal with similar experiences of pain and confusion; it was also, Emma realised, that all those years of secrecy about her mother had created a bit of distance between them. That had all been stripped away now and what they were left with was perhaps less perfect but a lot more real. Risking his disapproval had been a big step, but now she had done it once, she could do it again. They would work it out.

They spent the evening going through their favourite memories— Christmases with Robert and Jackie, rabbits and hamsters that had to go back and forth between London and Exmoor on the back seat of the car, swimming in the sea and picnics on the beach, racing down the up escalator at the Tate Gallery when they'd had enough of the pictures, watching Bedknobs and Broomsticks so many times they knew every word, going to A&E with a sore wrist and coming home in a plaster cast.

"We didn't do that badly though, did we?" Richard asked, several glasses of wine later.

"I think we did beautifully, Dad."

"We'll find Asha, don't you worry. I'll get Caroline onto it in the morning. If your Vicar is still on this earth, she'll find him."

* * *

By the following Saturday Emma was another train, this time with her father's blessing, to Tiverton Parkway. Caroline had indeed made short work of establishing that Reverend Michael Drake was, unbelievably, still the Vicar of Exford twenty years on. By 10 AM the morning after her trip to Bath, the marvellous woman had fully briefed and equipped her with the telephone number at the Rectory. Fortunately, it seemed that vicars didn't usually retire until they were 70. Perhaps that's why they always look so old, Emma thought.

She had caught up with Joe the next evening and told him the whole story. It was so much easier to tell now that it had all had time to settle. In fact, it was good to be able to talk about her mother and her half-brother to someone other than her father. It made them seem more matter-of-fact.

Joe had been pleased for her of course and excited, but she could tell he was hiding something and it irritated her after the new Glasnost with her father at home.

"What's the matter, Joe?"

"Nothing. Nothing at all."

"It doesn't seem like nothing. Don't you think it's exciting?"

Joe paused for a second, then said a little too quickly: "Of course, of course, it's really exciting. I expect you'll be all busy with this now."

Emma stared at him.

"I mean, what's going to happen if you do find him, Em? I can see that you want to find out what happened to him and yes, of course it's exciting, all this cloak and dagger detective work. But the chances are that he's spent the vast majority of his life in another world to you, with another family, quite happily minding his own business. Then you turn up on his doorstep. What happens then?

"He may be your brother—half-brother—but you won't know him. You might not even like him. But he's still there, still your brother. Once you've made contact with him you can't undo that, you can't pretend he isn't there. Do you keep in touch? Get together for family gatherings? Or do you just walk away once you've satisfied your curiosity? I'm not sure whether you've thought this through."

Emma studied her thumbnail as she digested all this. Although she knew Joe had a point, he wasn't being at all helpful. What she needed from him right now was support, not a whole load of dire warnings about how naive she was being.

"Do you really think I haven't thought about all that? Why do you always have to be so bloody sensible? I just think it will be all right when we get there."

Joe said nothing.

"You're not seriously suggesting I just let it go, are you? Come on! It's all right for you, you've got a brother! It was always just me and Dad. Now it turns out that all the time I had a brother too—and you're saying just leave it? Is that what you would do? I suppose you'd rather I just stayed here all weekend with you instead."

As soon as the words were out of her mouth she regretted them, but he had managed to really wind her up. She knew there was an element of truth in what she had said, too. Joe didn't like it when something else came along to take up her attention and now it looked like he was going to sulk. She was going to have to be a bit smarter at handling him than this.

"I'm sorry, Joe. I didn't mean to sound like that. But can't you see I have to do this?"

"Yes, of course I can. All I'm saying is that it might not work out as well as you think. Be careful, Em. Would you like me to come with you?"

He's just trying to help after all, Emma thought. I haven't lost him.

"No it's all right. I think it's better if I go on my own. But thank you, Joe. On Sunday I'm all yours, I promise."

So here she was, staring at the blue geometric squares in the upholstery of the train seat beside her, wondering what the Vicar of Exford could possibly be about to tell her. He must have something to say if he had agreed to her coming all the way down from London to see him.

She had no idea how to talk to a vicar. Surely, it was their job to be helpful and nice to people. What should she call him? Would he realise she wasn't a regular churchgoer? Would it make a difference that she didn't believe in God? Perhaps she'd better pretend she did. The train was ripping through the wet Somerset countryside at well over 100 mph but inside the carriage time had stopped. Or at least the past and the present were there all right, but the future had ceased to exist.

* * *

How beautiful it is here, Emma thought as the taxi left Tiverton Parkway behind and started to wind its way up onto Exmoor. It looked different today—as if she'd never seen it properly before. How weird that Asha should have been brought here of all places when she had spent every summer holiday almost as long as she could remember just up the road. She could have even walked past him without knowing. But then it was hardly a coincidence. Her parents had come back to this place time and time again, one way or another. She herself had grown up loving it too and as they drove into Exford, past the village green and the post office, that nostalgic sense of long holidays and sunshine washed over her, reminding her of her childhood.

But here they were at the Rectory, sweeping up the gravel drive, past withering herbaceous borders thick with weeds, and it was time to be grown up about this. The moment of truth. And here was the Vicar himself, throwing open the front door and welcoming her in in a practised, friendly but slightly distant way that he must have perfected over the years with his flock.

He looked almost like a normal person. Old, obviously, but wearing normal clothes. Dog collar, of course, but that was the only giveaway. His children would probably all be grown up by now. She saw no evidence of them as she was ushered into his study, not a single photograph. Only a well-fed ginger and white cat which brought up the rear.

"Do take a seat. This is where I usually put my wedding couples," the Vicar said, pointing at two hard wooden chairs floating side by side in the middle of the room. They must feel like they've been summoned to see the headmaster, she thought, sitting down on one of them and trying to ignore the empty space beside her. What an intriguing glimpse of what vicars spend their time doing when they're not in church. No wonder the borders needed weeding.

The Vicar sat down at his desk with his hands steepled together and waited for her to speak. They exchanged encouraging smiles and listened to the ticking of the antique grandfather clock which dominated everything else in the room. Then Emma launched into the explanation she had rehearsed on the train, trying to sound as down-to-earth and natural as she could. That her mother had lived on a commune in Exeter 20 years ago and had given birth to a son who Emma believed had been brought here. That this child was therefore her brother and she was hoping he might be able to help her trace him.

"And what makes you think he was brought here?" the Vicar asked, giving the cat an affectionate tug round one ear. "Perhaps you'd better tell me all about it."

This outbreak of paternal benevolence had the unfortunate effect of shattering her composure and turning her right back into a child again. She hadn't expected that. But it didn't seem to matter. She ended up telling him far more than she had ever intended; but he was a good listener and encouraged her to keep going, not appearing to mind in the slightest when her feelings got the better of her, merely nodding in sympathy. She was surprised at how much better she felt when she had finished.

"I see. And now you would like to find your brother. The question is—is that the right thing to do after all this time? It's something you must think about very carefully, my dear. I will pray for you."

"So you know where he is?"

The Vicar nodded. "Well, you are right. Someone did bring a boy here and it was probably about 20 years ago. I had forgotten her name, but as soon as you mentioned Elizabeth Duncan I knew it was her. The baby had no identity and no birth certificate, so I never knew exactly who he was or where he came from. But from what you say, it does seem likely that he was your half-brother."

Emma held her breath.

"If you decide you do want to contact him, I will need to talk to him first. He knows nothing of his birth parents and he may not want to know. That has to be up to him."

"Would you do that? Please? I would be so grateful."

"This is a very tricky situation, you know. It was a tricky moral dilemma for me at the time. Of course, I should have taken him straight to the authorities, but I knew he would be so much better off if I could find him a home myself. A good deed if you like. So I kept quiet about where he came from and where he went to. I managed to find him a good family and his adoptive parents knew nothing about his background. He didn't end up in the care system and everyone was happy. I suppose you could say I got away with it. Then you come along!"

Although the Vicar was joking, Emma realised what a risk he had taken and how much trouble her arrival could cause him after all these years.

"Look, don't worry, I'm not about to tell anybody. Anyway, it sounds as though we should be very grateful to you. But I definitely do want to find Asha, I want that more than anything. I can tell you that right now."

"Very well. So be it. It's only fair to both of you. You've persuaded me that it's the right thing to do. I will just have to take the consequences, whatever they may be. Give me a few days and I will let you know how I get on."

The Vicar was standing up now, ready to show her out. Reluctantly, she stood too and allowed herself to be shooed into the hall.

"Can you tell me anything about him? Do you know where he is? Is he near here? Does he look like me?"

The Vicar held up his hand. "I'm sorry, my dear, but you must be patient. I will speak to you again as soon as I can." And with that, the front door closed behind her and the meeting was over.

* * *

Back on the train Emma got out her book but the words wouldn't come into focus. She went over and over what the Vicar had said. It had definitely sounded as though he knew where Asha was. Or had she imagined it? And what a lovely man. At least they were in good hands. She was just going to have to hold her nerve—nothing more she could do for the time being. But she had a good feeling about this now. It was all going to work out, she knew it was. Even if Joe didn't seem to think so.

Chapter 17
Varanasi

By the time Alex arrived at the station to meet the two girls, he had managed to regain at least some semblance of normality. There was absolutely no sign that he'd been followed and now he had calmed down it was easier to think of the break-in at the hostel as simply that—a random break-in by a petty thief. But he didn't mention it to them and he certainly didn't tell them about what had happened at the ashram. They probably wouldn't have believed him, and in any case it was safer for them to know nothing.

Another night on a train in odd-smelling Indian Railways sheets and although the three of them remained fully dressed, sleeping in a bunk alongside the girls brought a feeling of closeness that was uncomfortably out of tune with the short time they had known each other. But it amused him to watch them pulling faces over the on-board biryanis and postponing their visits to the loo until they couldn't be postponed any longer, and he happily joined in with their inconsequential chatter. It was a world which felt safe and familiar to him and made the idea that he was being pursued by a bunch of babassus seem reassuringly absurd.

Varanasi station was the usual scene of total chaos, but with more rubble. Alex noticed a baboon loping along the remains of a wall to the rear of the platform, eying up the passengers like a pickpocket as they got off the train. A group of Hindus with partially shaved heads and skinny pony tails sat in an earnest circle around some sort of barbecue arrangement right in the path of a shoal of zealous taxi drivers heading for the train. An Indian woman was hanging out her washing on the platform opposite, supervised by a gang of tattered children. These people have no concept of personal space, Alex thought. Tourists are allowed their own identity, but Indians are not—they know they don't matter much.

Outside, in what passed for the station car park, they discovered that in true Indian style Varanasi station was 13 kilometres away from Varanasi itself, which explained the superfluity of taxi drivers. Alex manfully took charge and bundled the girls into one of the few vehicles that looked as though it could actually cover 13 kilometres. Then in high spirits they all headed off on roads so badly potholed they might as well have been farm tracks, as befitted the oldest living city in the world.

Their taxi driver delivered them to a guesthouse right on the Ganges above Asi Ghat on the southernmost boundary of the city. It was perfect. Set behind an unprepossessing entrance decorated with beggars was an old-style mansion fit for a Brahmin, with comfortable verandas, traditional Indian furniture and shelves loaded with books in a variety of languages, positively cluttered throughout with exotic candles and bowls of roses.

They could hardly believe their luck as they looked out over the river, broad and still enough here to reflect the burning glow of the morning sun as it rose in the sky, and watched the bathers on the ghat directly below. Apparently, they had arrived in the middle of a prodigious festival dedicated to ancestors, which involved the performing of all kinds of special rituals and prayers by the faithful as they bathed. With characteristic Indian lack of urgency, it was due to last at least ten days.

The steps along the river bank below them were packed with dark-skinned men of every shape and size sitting shoulder to shoulder, preparing to submerge themselves completely in the thick brown water. There were more of them standing up to their waists in the river, arms outstretched in what could have been either supplication or desperation, in strangely neat formation as they balanced on the hidden steps beneath the surface. It reminded Alex of Brighton beach on a hot day when the tide has come in, bunching everyone up along the waterline. But he knew that was hardly a fair comparison; many of these pilgrims would have travelled for hundreds if not thousands of miles to be here, yet the journey would have been of little consequence. This was the crowning moment of their lives.

By nightfall, the activity had become frantic. Aarti ceremonies were being performed all along the river bank to thank the goddess Ganga for another day. Young Brahmin priests were chanting, singing and sweeping fiery ghee burners through the air like synchronised swimmers. To help them along there were bells, drums, cymbals and a small orchestra of other mysterious instruments providing a musical backdrop which did not conform to any recognisable musical rhythm or structure.

The surface of the water itself was strewn with flower garlands and oil lamps which bobbed along in the darkness amongst the marigold petals and bowls filled with rice and other offerings to Mother Ganga. And Asi Ghat with its Kashi Vishwanath Temple seemed to be right at the epicentre of it all.

As they discovered during the course of the next day or two, Varanasi was a city of superlatives. Not just the mighty Ganges, but the temples—a thousand! There was certainly one to stumble over every few yards, some of them tiny, almost like little coal cellars behind bars at the sides of the narrow streets. The Gods!—There are more Gods in India than people and nearly all of them live in Varanasi.

And death. Those lucky enough to die in Varanasi could be cremated and committed to the Ganges. The open air crematorium on the river bank was clearly visible beneath clouds of smoke and ashes, barges loaded with dark logs moored alongside ready to fuel the everlasting bonfire. Processions of mourners shouldered the bodies of dead relatives through the streets towards the river, wrapped only in simple shrouds, ready to be committed to the flames, and stood guard as their corpses were incinerated.

Yes, Alex thought, determined not to be rattled by this—here death is commonplace and dead bodies matter less when you have many lives before and after this one. Here it is the soul that counts and the soul belongs to the Ganges.

As if all this wasn't enough, the Buddha had lived in Varanasi too, 2,500 years ago, relatively recently in Hindu terms, and relics of his bones were said to be buried in the enormous stupa they visited at Sarnath, just outside the city. Although the Buddha had spent the night of his enlightenment at Bodh Gaya, near the border with Nepal, it was in the deer park at Sarnath that he had given his first teaching, enabling his first five disciples to reach enlightenment too, turning the wheel of Dharma and founding a new world religion in the process. This put Sarnath well and truly on the Buddhist map as one of the holiest places on earth to visit. They were almost swept away by busloads of Buddhist monks robed in pink and saffron and garnet and chestnut brown from all over Asia performing their own special rituals to mark one of the most important days of their lives.

This could have been overwhelming but somehow it wasn't. Alex was getting used to this new level of religious intensity—it was really starting to feel quite natural. The girls, however, were a different story. They giggled at the bare chests of the bathers, grew bored by the Brahmins and their interminable ceremonies and dawdled over the goats grazing on the plentiful supply of sacrificial food and flowers regurgitated by the Ganges. They struggled with the death, and he found himself comforting them and in the process comforting himself as well.

"I couldn't bear to watch someone I knew being burned on a bonfire like that, could you?" Nicky asked Alex that evening, looking across at Anna for backup. "That cemetery totally freaked me out. Those huge piles of logs, just there to burn people up. Imagine watching your granny lying there in the flames, Anna—then the whole lot goes in the river, half-burned bits of body and all. And right next door people are actually drinking the stuff as if it was some sort of holy water! Can't they see it must be seriously toxic?"

"I know what you mean," said Alex. "But for them it's the soul that matters, not the bodies being burned. Once you die you don't need your body anymore. For them this world is just temporary, a passing moment. The Ganges is their gateway to another world."

He wondered where that had come from and whether it was what he really believed. It felt very poignant—the devotion of the monks, the saddhus dispensing wisdom from home-made thrones along the river bank, the temples, the Brahmins, even the cows. He rather hoped that some of it would rub off on him and that his soul would benefit too, even if he was not prepared to risk a dip in the Ganges to seal the deal.

It amused him to try and work out which of the girls he liked best, of course. But he rather enjoyed having the attention of both of them and he certainly didn't want to cause any upset between them. It was Nicky who grabbed your attention first because she was so full of life. She said whatever was on her mind—or in her heart—without giving it a moment's thought, which often made them all laugh, and if it sometimes made her look stupid she didn't care. It was easy to find all that life and energy attractive and she was great company—laughing with her raised Alex's spirits.

Anna was quieter than Nicky and more serious, more—grounded. She seemed happy enough to let Nicky take the stage, but whenever the conversation took a more serious turn it was Anna who grew in confidence and Nicky who fell silent. She was not as obviously pretty as Nicky but there was an air of intensity and mystery about her that made her ultimately more interesting.

Alex liked talking to her and he gradually realised that for all Nicky's banter it was actually Anna who was the heart and soul of the friendship. Her thoughtfulness, her intelligence and her loyalty meant that she was probably much more like Emma than Nicky was. He wondered if he was going to end up comparing every girl he ever met with Emma. He knew he would never find anyone who could possibly match her.

The girls were on a four-month trip round India, which they had planned in microscopic detail before they left home. They had started in Delhi and gone straight to Agra to see the Taj Mahal ("awesome—so romantic!"). Then round Rajasthan's palaces and harems, with a blow-out stay at the Lake Palace Hotel as a bit of light relief before taking the train up to Shimla. Now, they were working their way across Northern India towards Calcutta. From there, they were to fly down to the South for some tigers and tea plantations, Kerala and of course the beach at Goa to top up their tans before going home.

"So what do you make of India so far?" Alex asked Nicky.

"Hmmm—interesting—Everyone tells you it's a culture shock, don't they? But it's even more of a culture shock than I was expecting. I'm glad we came, of course. But I don't understand why it gets under people's skin the way it does. The place is gritty with dust, it stinks to high heaven, it's swelteringly hot, people get too close to you all the time, there are beggars and lepers everywhere and the food makes you sick. I don't really get what makes people want to come back here again and again as if it was some sort of Utopia…" Nicky paused, uncertain. "Some of the things we've seen have been amazing, though, haven't they, Anna?"

"Oh yes," Anna agreed, smiling, but not giving away whether or not she herself 'got' India.

So then it was Alex's turn.

"What about you? What are your plans?" Anna asked casually, looking at him closely to see what he would say. She's really not stupid at all, Alex thought.

"I'm not sure. I left England looking for a new life. I was running away really. I didn't think I would ever go back. Well, I didn't know. But bumping into you two and hearing you talk about home has made me think again. And now, yes, I think I do want to go home one day. Not yet, but maybe in a month or two. Yes, I think I do."

"To uni? Or have you done that already?" Anna said, careful not to ask too much, not to intrude.

But Alex found that now he had actually been asked the question, he already knew the answer. Varanasi had brought back to him something that he hadn't realised he had lost until now. It was an artists' paradise, the colours, the intensity, the challenge of capturing the essence of it on paper. That morning he had watched someone working at a series of charcoal drawings of the Ganges, spread out over the black and white tiles on the veranda. He had seen the absorption on the man's face, the excitement as the drawings took shape on the paper. He had looked out across the river and he had wanted to be that man, down on the floor, drawing it, recreating it. It had reminded him how much a part of his life art had always been to him, how much poorer his life had been without it.

So now, when Anna asked that question, he found himself calmly answering it.

"I'm going to paint. I'm an artist."

It was what he'd always wanted to do, after all. How could he have forgotten? And surely he must have some talent. They'd always said so at school and he'd made it to a decent art college where he had easily held his own. He had even sold a few paintings. It would never make him rich, obviously; artists usually struggled to make ends meet. But he didn't need much to live on. He had never had expensive tastes, it wasn't what mattered to him.

He could see now that he didn't have to be like Joe and his friends, have a normal career, lead a normal, comfortable, safe life. He wasn't like them and that was perfectly OK. Obvious, really. He knew that he would always remember this moment when everything dropped into place and that one day he would come back to Varanasi just to paint. At last, he could see his life stretching out in front of him again.

"I was at art college before I came out here." He couldn't seem to get the words out fast enough. "It's what I've always loved doing most. Actually, it's the only thing that really matters to me. I expect I'll be a poverty stricken artist and I'll live in a garret somewhere, waiting for you to come and bring me a few scraps of bread. I won't even get hungry, I'll just paint all day and all night. And then, when I'm wasting away and just about to die of starvation, I'll be discovered—" He laughed as the story dissolved into a fantasy.

"Yes! Yes!" Nicky was bouncing up and down, clapping her hands with excitement. "And we'll organise lots of exhibitions for you and sell your pictures for huge amounts of money and you'll be incredibly famous!"

They all started laughing and once they started they couldn't stop and they grew wide-eyed at what life might have in store for them.

"By then, of course, Anna will be a famous doctor, a specialist in—what in, Anna? Paediatrics, yes! Anna will be in charge of Great Ormond Street. Goodness knows what I'll be—I don't know, the Marketing Director of British Airways! That would be pretty cool, wouldn't it? And I'll have a massive office and lots of secretaries and I'll sweep in and out in an Armani suit and have business lunches every day at The Ivy—"

And their laughter rang out across the still waters of the Ganges, shining under the light of an almost full moon, just another night in a sequence of thousands and millions of nights.

The next morning Alex woke up early, wondering why he felt so full of happiness, and then remembered the new life he had settled on the night before. Surely, something that made him feel this good must be right. And what a place to paint! The boats, the temples all the way along the river bank, the pilgrims, the colours—it would be any artist's dream. He just couldn't wait to get started, even if it was only a few drawings. He had hardly eaten his toast before he was off to see what artists' supplies he could get hold of.

Over the next couple of days, while the girls chatted endlessly and wrote their postcards, Alex spent every spare moment on his drawings and colourwashes. Everything inspired him and he delighted in the creativity which was pouring out of him. The girls were keen to encourage, admire and reassure, but although it was nice of them to be interested he didn't need their encouragement. He had a momentum all of his own.

They walked for miles through the city's crumbling streets, home to as many cows and dogs as humans, visiting temples and markets along the way. They hired a boat and drifted down the Ganges past palaces built by kings and princes determined to die here. They watched young boys flying kites from the roofs of their houses in the fading light of early evening. They made friends with the caretaker at the Kashi Vishwanath Temple next door to the hotel and had their photo taken with the beggar and his monkey outside.

They read random books left behind by other travellers before them and learned which god was Vishnu and which was Shiva. They struck up friendships with some of the other guests and formed a little group that would seem random anywhere else; here the sharing of their experiences, views and beliefs kept them chatting late into the night, buoyed up by the clarity with which their travels enabled them to see life unfolding.

* * *

One morning a couple of days later Alex had got up early to watch the sun rise over the Ganges, an incredible moment not only for him but for all the Hindus on the ghats below him busy making their offerings to the new day. He was attacking his breakfast with gusto in the dining room, his only companion a life-size portrait of Rajiv Gandhi on the wall opposite him, when he heard people arriving at the reception desk outside.

Here come the next lot, he thought, wondering what they would be like and whether they would be friendly. But the last lot can hardly have left yet, he thought—he knew the Guest House was full and there was no way their room would be ready. Would they make a fuss? He leaned back in his chair to have a quick look.

He froze. The group crammed into the tiny reception area definitely did not look like travellers. For a start, there were too many of them and they were all men. At first glance, you might have thought they were plain-clothes policemen or perhaps hotel inspectors if there were such things in India. One of them was interrogating the poor receptionist about whether the guesthouse was full and demanding details of everyone staying there. The others were starting to prowl around the ground floor like hyenas scenting blood. And he could tell straight away that they were babassus.

Any minute now one of them was going to come into the dining room. He had absolutely no time to think, no time to say goodbye to the girls, going back to his room was completely out of the question. Trying not to panic he picked up the bag he had with him from his early morning walk, walked as casually as he could towards the kitchens, smiled genially at the cooks preparing breakfast and strolled out of the back entrance.

As the rancid smell of kitchen rubbish hit him outside he gave in to despair. Here he was, on the run again, just when things were starting to get so much better. Perhaps he was destined to die here after all. This brief, happy interval in Varanasi, the girls, his plans, his painting—it had all been an illusion. It wasn't going to happen. But how were they doing it? Had the girls been set up to spy on him? No, surely not. Other guests at the hotel? But they were all clearly travellers. Or perhaps the police themselves were at the bottom of all this.

He remembered Manjit, the truck driver who had picked him up outside the ashram, complaining about corruption in India, how the police are dogs, how they can be bought by the rich and powerful at the expense of everyone else. Perhaps there was some sort of police spy network attached to the gang. That would explain how they could track him across northern India without actually following him. And if they had found him in Varanasi they would find him anywhere.

As he wheeled round in all directions, terrified, he saw the temple caretaker next door reaching out to him. What was she trying to say? The woman was nodding encouragement as if to say she saw and understood everything. Well, if he ran now they'd soon catch up with him. Perhaps a temple was as good a place to hide as anywhere and for some reason he knew he could trust this woman. There was something other-worldly about her.

The woman hid him in the temple for the rest of the day, even bringing him some scraps to eat at lunchtime. She spoke no English but she reassured him with smiles and nods. Gradually, it dawned on him from the filthy blankets and cooking pots stacked up in one corner that she actually lived in the temple. The woman's only possessions were right here. Her face was lined with age and she had few teeth left. How tough life must have been for her and yet her eyes shone with love and compassion for him. This was spirituality in spades.

Thanks to her he had plenty of time to think. He really needed to get out of India and away from the reach of the Indian police as fast as possible. But flying wasn't an option—he was hardly in a position to stroll into a travel agent, find a flight and book a ticket, and anyway there would be far too much hanging around at the airport with nowhere to hide. If Varanasi even had an airport.

No, he would have to go overland, head north and cross the border into Nepal. A train? Too obvious and anyway would it take him across the border? Probably not. And they would be bound to be watching the station. Travelling by train was exactly what they would expect him to do.

That left a bus. He waited for the early evening crowds and then, vigorously nodding namastes, goodbyes and thank yous to the temple woman, he set off towards the bus station, snaking across town in what he hoped was an unpredictable fashion. He was desperate to look over his shoulder to check if he was being followed but he knew that would attract far too much attention. He wasn't going to risk speaking to anyone at the bus station just yet either, but instead hung around the ticket office as inconspicuously as he could and listened to the stream of travellers queuing up to buy tickets.

This way he worked out that, as he had suspected, the best time to catch a bus to Nepal would be later that night. Lucky English was such a universal language, he thought as he prepared to disappear for a few hours. In a place like this that wasn't too difficult as long as you weren't squeamish about dirt, shit, stinking puddles, dead bodies and rats.

Later that night, hiding in the shadows until the last minute, his face partly concealed behind the folds of a black and white chequered keffiyeh bought from a street trader, Alex slipped onto a bus to Kathmandu.

Chapter 18
The Bank

Emma was examining the patterns on the Indian silk rug in the living room at Regent Mansions. She had been in the office all morning with two back-to-back client meetings but she'd managed to come home early so she could work on a long and complicated report without any distractions. There hadn't been much of a chance yet to mull over what was going on in her private life, thank goodness. Her relationship with her father, for example.

Was it really all OK? He seemed to have taken everything surprisingly well so far but she had definitely gone against his wishes, something she didn't normally do. She didn't like the uncomfortable feeling that gave her in the pit of her stomach. And then there was a new half-brother to think about. She had already invented at least 10 different incarnations of him, which didn't seem at all healthy. Surely the Vicar must have asked him by now and got an answer. How on earth could it take so long? Perhaps Asha had said no and the Vicar just didn't want to tell her. If so, that would be the end of that. Game over.

But at this precise moment the reason why the carpet was receiving such microscopic examination was not her father or Asha. It was Alex.

She was beside herself with worry. There was still no word from him and she'd run out of possible reasons why that might be. She was sure he would never deliberately break off contact with her. They had a bond which she had always believed was indestructible. And anyway, if he was going to do that he would have done it as soon as he'd left London. Why send all those postcards and then suddenly stop? Something had to be wrong.

Perhaps he was in hospital, just as the Tarot cards had said. What if that turned out to be true and she had done nothing? But if anyone should be doing anything, it should be Joe—their father had long since got past the point of worrying about his children. Joe didn't seem that bothered and maybe he was right. Why would Alex think about sending her postcards when he was half way round the world, probably having the time of his life? It wasn't as if there was anything other than a childhood friendship between them, after all.

She pulled a thick file of papers out of her briefcase and sorted them into piles on the dining room table. She just couldn't believe Alex would turn his back on her completely. She picked up an information memorandum from the pile nearest to her and started to read. What if he had got into some kind of trouble? Perhaps she should make some notes to get her points in order before doing any actual drafting.

She wrote the date neatly at the top of the A4 lined pad in front of her and underlined it, then stared at the blank page. The key arguments had been quite clear in her head before she left the office but now the information was just swimming about in front of her. Perhaps a cup of tea might help. No. If no one else was going to do anything about Alex, she would just have to do it herself and it was no good trying to get any work done until she did.

She got up and searched through the dining room cupboards until she found the London business telephone directory. If you were abroad you would go to the British Embassy, but you wouldn't have a British Embassy in London. You do have the Foreign Office, though. Moments later she was dialling the number for the UK Foreign and Commonwealth Office, Consular Division and trying to work out what on earth she was going to say while she waited for an answer.

"Hello, can I help you?"

"I hope so—I want to try and find a missing person."

"I see. I'll need to take some details from you first. What is the full name of the person you wish to trace?"

"Alex Russell. Alex William Russell." Lucky she knew his middle name, she thought. But then, she always had.

"Date and place of birth?"

She knew when his birthday was, of course. He was eighteen months younger than her, so that would make the year 1969. She would have to guess the place of birth. Hopefully it wouldn't matter too much if she got it wrong.

"23.5.69, Exeter."

"When and where did you last hear from him and where would you expect him to be now?"

"I got a postcard from him about—oh—three weeks ago. He was in Pakistan then. He seemed to be travelling east."

"I see. Do you have a hotel name in Pakistan where he was staying?"

"No."

"Itinerary?"

"No."

"What relation are you to the missing person?"

"I'm not actually related to him."

Emma felt her cheeks flush. She sounded like some silly girl who had been dumped by her boyfriend. Obviously, they were going to need to know at least what country he was likely to be in. How were they supposed to find him otherwise? And, of course, it would have to be a relative. Joe was the only one who could deal with this.

"I suppose there's not much you can do, is there?"

"Not really, madam."

"Is there *anything* you can suggest I could do? I'm very worried about him."

The consular official relented.

"The best thing you can do is get in touch with his bank. It'll have to be his next of kin, of course. Ask to look at his credit card transactions. That should give you a better fix on where he is, at least. People don't usually get very far without money."

* * *

By 10 o'clock that evening, Emma and Joe were sitting round James's kitchen table in Somerset with some plastic ham sandwiches and three mugs of Nescafé. As soon as Emma had put down the phone to the Foreign Office she had rung Joe and bullied him into action. Joe had rung his father, his father had rung the bank in Minehead and they had an appointment arranged for 9:00 AM the following morning, the minute the bank opened.

Although Joe had agreed to the plan, he was far from convinced that this mad dash to Somerset was really necessary. As for James, he was somewhat bewildered by the whole thing.

"You know Alex," Emma appealed to them, looking from one to the other. "He wouldn't lose contact like that. None of us have heard from him. That's just not like him. He might need help, you know. But anyway, we'll know the answer once we've been to the bank tomorrow."

Father and son looked at each other. Neither were prone to dramatic behaviour, preferring to adopt an understated reaction to life's ups and downs. Emma wanted to shake them.

"You'd never forgive yourself if something was really wrong and you didn't do anything until it was too late."

They both shifted uncomfortably in their kitchen chairs, still dappled blue in a legacy from Lorna's sponge painting phase. God, father and son were like peas in a pod sometimes. Not really, underneath, but this solidness, this stoicism, this determination not to react, was infuriating. But Joe could be just like Lorna too, sometimes—you could see both his parents in him. Neither she nor Alex could see exactly what they had inherited from theirs. She was missing half the picture and Alex had absolutely no idea.

"Oh, for goodness sake!"

"All right, all *right*, Em! We're here, aren't we? What more do you expect us to do right now? We've done what you wanted and we're going to the bank tomorrow morning. In the meantime, I don't see what more we can do. In fact, I think we should all go to bed."

Joe agreed a timetable for getting up and having breakfast in the morning with Emma and then explained it to James, who nodded obediently. If he did have a view on the latest turn of events he didn't share it.

* * *

The next morning, they were all up bright and early. Emma had not slept well in the spare bedroom and had been upset by several vivid dreams. In one, Joe's body had been trapped in the wreckage of a car crash and her father had walked away down the hard shoulder without turning back. She had been left alone with Joe, who was badly injured, but she couldn't reach him.

In another, she had been wrapped in an Indian shawl with a deep fringe, which smelled of patchouli and reminded her of the Tarot woman. She could sense other people around her, in the shadows, but she couldn't see them. The dreams had been very vivid and remained with her as she boiled eggs and toasted James' sliced Co-op bread.

After breakfast, James drove them into Minehead in his old Volvo and they sat in tense silence while he circled around the one-way system looking for somewhere to park. It was a couple of minutes after 9 o'clock by the time they walked in to the small white stucco building in Wellington Square that passed as the local branch of the Midland Bank. James was old friends with the bank manager and they were ushered straight through the security door and into his office, followed by a clerk carrying two extra chairs—James having obviously failed to mention that there would be three of them.

"Good to see you, James! This must be Joe, by the look of it! And—?"

Muttering apologies, James introduced everybody and they all sat down.

"Now, let me make sure I've got this right. I understood from our conversation yesterday that you want to see recent credit card transactions for your younger son, Alex. Do you think there's something wrong, James?"

Seeing his father was unsure how to respond, Joe cut in.

"No, we don't think there's any cause for alarm. But we haven't heard from him for a while and we're a little concerned."

"Quite so. Well, of course you will understand that it is not normal procedure to discuss these with anyone other than the account holder. But I think in the circumstances it makes sense to share the information with you."

He passed a photocopy across the desk to James, who immediately passed it on to Joe.

"We've gone back six months, which more than covers the time he has been out of the country. As you can see, there are a number of transactions in the UK, then they move abroad."

He took his glasses off and looked directly at James, ignoring the fact that it was Joe who was now in possession of the photocopy.

"It's as clear as day, James—it might as well be a map. Istanbul. Tehran. Ashgabat. Samarkand. Kabul. Lahore. Amritsar. Delhi. Rishikesh. Kanpur. Varanasi. Then he pops up in Kathmandu and buys a plane ticket home. But nothing since then—nothing at all. But I would be worried if I was you, James, especially with the plane ticket. It doesn't look right to me."

"Does it tell us where he was staying in Kathmandu?" asked Emma, thinking back to her conversation with the Foreign Office official the day before.

The manager looked at her briefly, then back at James. "No, I'm afraid not. It's just a cash withdrawal."

* * *

188

James drove them back home in silence. Emma sat in the back and watched the texture of the moor change as they passed. The overpowering smell of dog hair coming from the nest of old blankets beside her had started to annoy her and she got no pleasure from the fact that she had been proved right—in fact, she was just as surprised as the others. Despite her worries, she had still thought that the whole thing would be cleared up in a few minutes and she and Joe would be on their way back to London by lunchtime. Instead it had turned out to be even worse than she thought.

Back round the kitchen table, Joe took charge.

"There's no need to be too worried. There are other gaps. It's possible he has gone up to Everest Base Camp or something."

"He bought a plane ticket home, Joe."

"We don't know when, though. But perhaps we could find out." He peered at the photocopy. "Yes, it tells us here who he bought it from. There can't be that many routes out of Kathmandu. We could probably check."

He hunted through the strata of papers and junk piled up at the other end of the kitchen table until he found an old envelope and a pencil.

"Let's make a list. One. Check out flight home. OK. Two. Could we go back to the Foreign Office for help, Em?"

"We could try, but we haven't got much to go on. And it would have to be you—I can't do it because I'm not a relative."

"OK—Two. Speak to the Foreign Office." Joe put down the pencil. "Do you think I should get on a plane and go out there?"

James looked up, startled, but Emma immediately nodded.

"I think you should, Joe. It'll be much easier to find out what's going on if you're actually there. Otherwise, we're just relying on other people—it's not the same."

"You could be right, Em. Three. Get plane ticket to Kathmandu." He laughed nervously.

Emma nodded. "And I think I should talk to Dad. You never know, he might be able to help. He knows a lot of people."

"Yep, good idea. Four. Talk to Richard. That's probably enough to be going on with. Can you sort out one and four then Em and I'll do two and three?"

Emma nodded her agreement.

"Don't worry. We'll find him, I promise."

"I know we will, Joe. Thank you." Emma breathed a sigh of relief as Joe put his arms round her and kissed her on the cheek.

* * *

By lunchtime, Joe had managed to get himself onto a flight to Kathmandu leaving that night, with a stopover for a few hours in Delhi. He reckoned that if he really had to go half way round the world looking for his brother he might as well get on with it. Emma and he would head back to London that afternoon so Joe could pick up a bag and his passport. Joe had also spoken to the Foreign Office but there hadn't been much they could do. Trekking in Nepal for up to three weeks was not unusual, they said, but they would list him as a missing person with the authorities.

Emma had had less success with Alex's flight home. The travel agent named on the credit card bill had turned out to be obscure and hard to trace—distinctly dodgy, in fact. Finding any contact details for them had proved impossible and anyway they were hardly likely to give details of a visa transaction from three weeks ago to someone calling out of the blue from the UK. She had, however, spoken to her father in the office and the conversation had not gone well.

"Why the hell can't James sort this out? He's James' son, for God's sake. He's nothing to do with me. Quite honestly, Em, I've never understood what you see in that boy. It doesn't surprise me in the slightest that he's drifting about somewhere in Nepal—it sounds like just the sort of thing he *would* do—OK, well look, I'm just rushing out to a meeting. We'll talk about it later."

Where had that come from? She had no idea her father felt like that about Alex. Alex had always been so popular with everybody, people rarely had a bad word to say about him. Now suddenly he seemed to have turned into public enemy number one as far as her father was concerned. Something about Alex had obviously got under his skin. And 'drifting about'—that was unfair. Alex could sometimes be hard to pin down, it was true—she could think of several potential girlfriends who might agree with that—but it was only because he didn't like anyone to get too close. Except her, but that didn't really count.

She'd flinched at the irritation in his voice, too. With everything else that had been going on, she didn't want to upset him any more than necessary. She was obviously going to have to tread carefully where Alex was concerned. At least he seemed to like Joe, thank goodness, but perhaps she'd got that wrong too. The ground rules had changed between them—more honest, maybe, but more uncomfortable. She only had herself to blame for that.

James's job had been number five on the list—making everyone coffee. He had even managed to arrange his entire supply of plastic ham and iceberg lettuce onto three plates, which they ate with more Co-op toast and the end of a bottle of salad cream for lunch.

* * *

As Joe and Emma headed back to London the day took on a surreal atmosphere. Joe had spent his gap year Interrailing round Europe and grape-picking in France; Greece was about the most controversial place he had ever been to. And in a few hours he was off to Kathmandu, a place that neither of them would have been entirely convinced even existed until today.

"What are you going to do when you get there, Joe?"

"I don't know yet. Talk to the police. Go to the Embassy. Ask at hostels."

"You should take some photos of him with you."

"I thought of that." Joe grinned as he pulled a handful of pictures out of his holdall—not that recent and mostly just holiday snaps, but better than nothing. She'd forgotten Alex ever looked that boyish and for the first time she noticed an awkwardness about him, almost as if he knew he didn't really fit in. Perhaps her father had picked up on something after all.

"Do you think Alex is irresponsible, Joe? You know him better than anyone. Do you think he's a drifter?"

Joe looked at her, surprised.

"It's just something Dad said on the phone." She shrugged to show she hadn't taken it too seriously.

"That Alex was a drifter?"

"Kind of, yes."

"He sometimes struggles with things, he always has. It's probably fair to say he hasn't quite worked out who he is yet. Possibly because he doesn't have as much to go on as most people. He knows he's not like us, but he doesn't know who he *is* like. But no, I don't think he's irresponsible, do you?"

"No." Emma gazed out of the window and tried to focus on the hedges and trees flying by, then the fields beyond, then the horizon. "No, I don't."

191

At least I've got one parent, Emma thought. And I'm finding out about the other one at last. Not that I've got very far yet, but at least I know who she was. Dad's the one who knows most about her—I'll get it all out of him sooner or later. But Alex's mother could have been anyone, absolutely anyone.

At Paddington, Joe bought an Evening Standard on the way down to the tube. The platform was crowded and Emma tucked in beside him while they waited for the train. Suddenly, she felt him stiffen.

"God, how awful."

She looked up at him, knowing he would read it out.

"Listen to this. 15 dead in hostel fire in Calcutta. Flames ripped through a hostel popular with backpackers in Calcutta last night, destroying it completely. The fire started at about 1am in the downstairs recreation room, but most of the dead were on the second floor—blah blah—Among the dead are two British girls. Names are being withheld until next of kin have been informed. The cause of the fire has not been identified. There's a picture, look."

"You don't think Alex could have been there, do you?"

"No, no. Of course not. But it makes you think, doesn't it?"

The train rumbled into the station and they pushed their way into the crowded carriage in silence. She had had just about all she could cope with for one day and her eyes were brimming with tears. Those girls could have been her. They could have been Alex. Then it was Joe's stop and in the crush he didn't notice how upset she was and he was saying goodbye in a hurry so he could get to the door in time to get off. "Call you later!" he said and then he was gone.

* * *

By the time Emma surfaced from the tube at Regents Park, she had dried her eyes with a tissue and done her best to cheer up a bit. They had all warned her she wouldn't be able to cope so she couldn't fall to pieces now. As she walked back to Regent Mansions she gave herself a good talking to. When she got there, she was surprised to find Richard was already home.

"Em darling!" his face lit up as she walked through the door. "How are you doing, my poor little thing! What a drama. Sorry about earlier. You caught me at a bad moment."

"Oh Dad!" She sighed with relief as he gave her a perfectly normal hug. One look at her face and he swung into action, coat off, kettle on, sofa plumped up,

192

rug at the ready. She should have known better than to think she could ever fool him. Neither of them mentioned his earlier remarks about Alex—now was definitely not the time.

"Now, I've been making some phone calls this afternoon. Friend of mine in the diplomatic service. Said he could get round all the usual bureaucratic nonsense and go direct to our chaps out in Kathmandu. Anyway, to cut a long story short, he got onto the number two out there and they've agreed to move heaven and earth to find the boy.

"Have you got Joe's flight details? They'll meet him when he arrives. He's doing exactly the right thing, by the way. In the meantime, they're going to check with all the authorities out there. They'll need his full name, date of birth and so on as well. I said we'd call him later this evening."

"Oh Dad—*thank* you. Thank you!"

"Now. How's Joe going to get to the airport? I'll book a car for him. No, I insist. It'll be much easier. Luckily we've always had good relations with Nepal—he can get an entry visa on arrival, he just needs to take a couple of passport photos with him."

He really is quite remarkable, Emma thought as she allowed herself to be bossed and organised. Give him a crisis to deal with and he really is at his best. No wonder he's so good at his job.

She sank back into the cushions. She had done everything she could. She had finally managed to galvanise everyone and there was little more she could do except wait. It was all down to Joe now. What a thing for him to have to do! She hoped he was up to it. What if he went all the way to Kathmandu just to discover Alex had gone trekking, as the Foreign Office had suggested? She almost hoped that Alex *would* turn out to be in trouble now so that she wouldn't have made all this fuss about nothing.

But the bank manager had agreed with her that they were right to be worried. And Alex had been on his way home, too—he'd booked a flight. So either way, he'd be home soon. Surely they could put the nonsense between the three of them behind them now, after all this. If it was Alex who had a girlfriend she wouldn't be jealous. The thing was, nobody believed that she and Alex were really just good friends, that there was nothing more between them. It made people nervous. But it was absolutely true. She had always thought of Alex more like her little brother.

She was dimly aware of her father's voice rising and falling on the phone while she made supper and then cleared up—talking to Joe, talking to his diplomatic contact and then to Kathmandu, talking to Joe again. Joe and her father, sorting it all out together. As soon as everything was arranged she went to bed exhausted and lay curled up, thinking about Joe on the plane flying through the night until she went to sleep.

Chapter 19
On the Run

Alex stared absently past his reflection in the dusty window of the bus into the darkness outside. Could he be sure no one had seen him leaving Varanasi? He'd left it until the last minute to get on the bus to cut down the risk of anyone getting on behind him. And how would anyone already on the bus have known which bus he would be getting on? Unless they'd bought off all the drivers. Which was quite possible, from what he'd seen of these guys.

He had managed to get a seat towards the back and he was moulded into the corner, head down, trying not to attract attention, moving as little as possible. With much of his face hidden behind the keffiyeh, he started to check out the other passengers. Across the aisle from him a young Western couple were already sleeping, hair bleached to the same colour by the sun, heads tucked together. Oh, if only life could be that simple. But they certainly didn't look too threatening. An Indian man of indeterminate age with a shaved, pitted head and both arms wrapped tightly round his rucksack. He looks more suspicious than I do, Alex thought. A teenager showing off his school report cards to an American tourist. In happier circumstances, this would probably have made him smile.

Further up front he could make out the lumpy shapes of other passengers in various slumped sleeping positions, stirring as they went over the worst bumps in the road. Exactly the sort of assorted collection of travellers you would expect. Nothing too unusual. A night-time quietude, peaceful apart from the odd snore, settled in for a long journey. No obvious babassus.

He felt his body relaxing a little more with every hour that passed, leaving Varanasi further behind. It had been a long day. He had been extraordinarily lucky with the woman at the temple—there had been a strange aura about the whole thing. For some reason he didn't entirely understand, he had been given protection. But the urge to bolt had still been strong. That and the white-knuckle fear had kept his adrenalin levels far too high to sleep or even doze in the temple and he had ended up going round the same thoughts over and over again.

"If they find me here, I'll be dead in seconds. Wouldn't it be better to run?"

"No, you've got to keep calm. Wait until tonight. They're not going to find you here. Just hold on. By tomorrow morning, you can be across the border and out of India for good."

He wondered where they were now, those babassus out hunting for him. Thank God he had spotted them in time back at the Guest House—they must have been really pissed off. That had been a close shave. He wondered how long it would take them to catch up with him again. It'd been a few days before they had found him in Varanasi, but now they would have all their contacts, whoever they were, out looking for him. They wouldn't be far behind him.

None of the passengers looked remotely dangerous as far as he could tell. But what about the driver? Maybe this gang had some way to alert all bus drivers travelling out of Varanasi to look out for him. They didn't even need to buy the drivers off, all they needed was access to their radio system. Did they have a radio system? He couldn't hear one. But that wasn't to say they weren't all in contact with each other. They could have covered the trains that way too, via the guards. Everyone seemed to be in league with everyone else here.

Why bother to spend the day scouring Varanasi for him when they had a stranglehold on all the exit points instead? That's why they hadn't found him—they hadn't been looking for him. He looked at the dark shape of the driver's back in the distance through the half-light, his suspicions gaining strength. Maybe he was being paranoid, but based on the evidence so far, maybe not. He tugged at his scarf until it covered most of his face. There was too much at stake not to suspect everybody.

He could feel the panic coming back again as he realised he could be trapped on this bus, waiting for the driver to deliver him straight into the hands of the babassus. He really would be much safer on some sort of transport he could control, under his own steam. A motorbike, for example. As it was he was totally stuck until the bus stopped, and it wasn't going to stop in the middle of the night.

He spent the next few hours uneasily twisting in his seat, trying to get some sleep, wondering whether he would ever be able to get off and if so whether he would be able to maybe hire a bike and keep moving, hoping so because he didn't have any other plan, his hopes fading as the bus passed through smaller and smaller villages where the fastest mode of transport seemed to be an oxcart.

And what on earth must Nicky and Anna think of him? He kept picturing them coming down to breakfast and wondering where he was, why he had disappeared without even leaving them a note. Talking to reception, checking his room and finding his things still there and being more and more confused as the day went on and he did not reappear. Or perhaps they would just shrug their shoulders and think how they had misjudged him. Quite right, too.

Why should they care about a travelling companion they hardly knew? But if his room had been turned upside down, like in Kanpur, would they go to the police? Or report it to the hotel management, who were bound to be under the babassus' control by now? That could put them in real danger. In fact, they were probably in danger anyway. If the gang had tracked him to the hotel, they would know about the girls too. Would the babassus assume that he had told them what he knew? He really should have warned them. Or perhaps it was too late. Perhaps, like Scott, they were already dead.

After an anxious night during which he got little sleep, the darkness began to lift and the sunrise that followed revived his fighting spirit. Soon after dawn they drove into the scruffy little town of Gorakhpur, which he guessed from the general air of anticipation and rearranging of luggage on board was going to be a stopping point.

At last—a chance to get off. He had no luggage himself and as the doors opened he slipped in amongst some of the other passengers as they shuffled like zombies down the steps and out into the open air. He heard the doors close and braced himself for a tackle from behind, but it never came. Pulling his keffiyeh over his head he shrank into an alleyway just behind the bus station, melted into a doorway and held his breath. Nothing. Quiet. Perhaps by some miracle he'd actually got away with it.

It was still only about 7am and too early for many people to be about. He could see a row of makeshift kiosks with corrugated iron roofs opposite, their proprietors lurking in the half-light behind the usual shopfront of children's clothes and stale crisps strung onto a washing line at head height. Cows, of course, and rib-thin dogs. A few buildings which as usual were crumbling and neglected. The stench of urine.

Sadly, no gleaming showroom full of brand new motorbikes and a uniformed receptionist with a clipboard standing by the door to welcome you in. "Nearly new motorbike for you to escape from murderous gang over the Nepalese border, drive off-road, trash and never return, sir? Certainly, sir. No paperwork required. Please, help yourself!"

That was hardly what he'd expected, of course, but some sort of miracle would have been nice after all he'd been through. There were a few motorbikes about, sure, but people were riding them, two or three up, and they weren't at all gleaming. Not that that mattered very much. Still, there must be some way to get hold of one, surely.

He spent the next hour making slow progress across the town, sticking to the side streets, covering and recovering his tracks just in case. Once he was satisfied no one was following him he strolled into a café not far from the market square, trying to look as confident as anyone could after 24 hours on the run. He badly needed something to eat and drink and if he was ever going to find a motorbike in this place he was going to need local knowledge.

The café, if you could call it that, was grey with dirt and only loosely connected to the municipal electricity supply with visibly sagging cables. Its main feature was a sad row of bottles of Coke in a Coca Cola fridge but he firmly ordered coffee, bread and jam instead, which was accepted without protest and produced almost immediately.

He sat down at a formica table so old it was almost back in fashion. Substandard coffee, bread and jam had never tasted so good. He ate the whole lot and then looked up and caught the eye of the greasy teenager behind the counter, who nodded and came over to him.

"Do you know where I can find a motorbike to rent?"

The waiter looked sullenly back at him, picked up the selection of rupee notes Alex had left on the table and then disappeared through the kitchen door. There was no indication he had even heard Alex's question. *Damn*, thought Alex. If everyone in Gorakhpur was like that, he wasn't going to get very far.

He got up to leave but before he reached the door a second man, older than the first, emerged from the kitchen with a proprietorial air. Alarmed, Alex grabbed the door handle but the man walked towards him, shouting "Eh. You." Reluctantly, Alex turned to face him.

"You got money?" he said in a low voice, not looking at Alex but out into the street.

Alex nodded, wondering how foolish it was of him to admit this, even non-committally. Lucky he had had his wallet and passport with him yesterday morning in Varanasi. But then on the other hand, after a day hiding up in

Varanasi followed by a night on a bus, tired out, with crumpled clothes and the beginnings of a beard, perhaps he no longer looked in a position to hire a bike.

The man finally looked Alex in the eye.

"You wait here."

Seeing Alex about to ask a question, he nodded firmly.

"You wait."

A boy in a grey T-shirt with New York College written on the front—an optimistic claim, even if there was such a thing, which he doubted—appeared from nowhere and after an excitable exchange in Hindi he disappeared at a run. The manager nodded at Alex again.

"Please, sit."

Alex had absolutely no idea was going on. The sullen waiter had disappeared and this other man could easily be some sort of local hood for all he knew. He hadn't understood a word of the exchange with the boy in the T shirt. What were they waiting for? He didn't like it. But the minute he got up to go there was more nodding.

"Please, please to come. Come, come, come, this way please."

The boy had returned and was leading them out through the back of the café into a tiny alleyway. This was insane. Presumably he was about to be offered up to some hit man. How had they known? But they couldn't have, so perhaps they really were fixing him up with a motorbike. He had been pretty clear that was what he was after. And he didn't have many other ideas.

Bracing himself against imminent attack he followed them through a web of dark passageways that ran between the walls of houses, sometimes only a few feet wide, through people's backyards, past rotting piles of garbage, watched from the shadows by the dark, staring eyes of women and children who would never normally see tourists come this way, even scruffy ones. This was real poverty, worse than anything he'd seen, even in Varanasi.

Then without warning they turned into a doorway which led straight into a dark, bare room. As his eyes adjusted Alex picked out a skinny old man in a floor-length brown kurta standing behind what had once been an office desk complete with legs but now needed various bits of flotsam and jetsam to keep it on the level. Another excitable exchange in Hindi took place.

"Please to sit." Alex's hopes rose slightly as he sat on the velveteen seat of an imitation mahogany carver, flanked by his escort from the café, opposite his host who was now sitting in an executive swivel chair which had been extensively repaired with parcel tape. Could this man actually have a motorbike to rent? It seemed unlikely, but stranger things had happened. At least he hadn't been beaten up so far.

"You have licence?"

"Yes," Alex nodded. "But do you have motorbike? I need to see motorbike."

After that, things got easier. Amazingly there really was a motorbike which was produced and coaxed into life. An Enfield Silver Bullet, to be precise, once beautiful, now rather rusty, not quite the gleaming model Alex had pictured but a lot, lot better than nothing and it had the advantage of looking exactly like the thousands and thousands of other aging Bullets on the road. Alex realised he was going to have to buy this piece of scrap metal and that the amount he was going to end up paying for it would probably buy at least three clapped out old bikes under normal circumstances. Well, at least those doe-eyed children would eat for a few days.

It turned out that they were sitting in what served as the local business centre and there was even some paperwork being prepared—title and insurance documents—of dubious provenance, probably, but hopefully enough to get by if he was stopped by the police. An ink pad was produced and there was a lot of authoritative rubber-stamping. In the end, they even threw in a small backpack and a bottle of water, after which they all parted on excellent terms. It seemed his luck had turned.

* * *

Alex started to relax and even to enjoy himself as he got used to the Royal Enfield. It didn't exactly go like a bullet but on the upside he felt like he was in a 1950s movie. How ironic that India had adopted such a very British machine and absorbed it so totally into its own culture. And here he was, a Brit, on a battered old Enfield which he had bought from an Indian. There was a symmetry to it somehow.

He had done the right thing getting off that bus. He'd been bloody lucky to find a bike so quickly, lucky to have gone into that café, lucky to have taken the risk on the manager and not bunked out. It looked as though he had managed to leave Gorakhpur without being followed. The bike was comfortable to ride as long as he didn't push it too hard and he felt a lot better now that he was in control. And he had always loved riding bikes—the speed, the wind rushing past your face, the sense of freedom and adventure. The more miles of open road he covered, the more his mood lifted.

They had told him that to cross the border into Nepal he had to head for Sunauli, 70 kilometres to the north. Gradually, the terrain changed from plains to hills and the air cooled as he gained altitude. There was a lot of traffic on the road, one of the main routes into Nepal, and it swept him along, forcing him to concentrate and pushing everything else from his mind. When he saw the Indian border checkpoint in the distance, he pumped his fist in the air, shouting "Yes!"

At the border itself, his papers were accepted without difficulty and then he was gone, out of India, out of reach, gliding along beautiful smooth Nepalese roads towards the mountains, clear streams and dark, rich greenery. He would never, ever go back. On to Kathmandu!

* * *

Compared to Varanasi and Gorakhpur the Kathmandu Guest House was magnificently normal. It was designed to cater for western travellers, of which there were many, and English was the official language—the only language, in fact. It wasn't what Alex had expected at all. Kathmandu had always sounded so magical, so third world—about as far away as you could get, in every sense. But here people drank orange juice for breakfast out of Pyrex mugs, ordered Nescafé and caught up with the BBC News.

Travellers picked up their mail and stored their surplus luggage here, wrote their diaries, met up with each other, made plans—some of them even seemed to have made a life here, demonstrating their credibility by doing business over their coffee. That afternoon, as Alex sat with his Gorkha beer watching them, he noticed that the spiritual intensity of India and the gentleness of its people had gone and he missed it.

Right outside the Guest House gates was Thamel Market, a congested mix of yak wool knitwear, ironmongery, jewellery, pashminas—and climbing gear. Alex had never seen so much North Face clothing in one place before. There were azure blue and white photographs of Everest and Annapurna everywhere, just in case you were in any doubt what the point of it all was.

He could feel the excitement in the air, of expeditions preparing to leave for the Himalayas, busily stocking up on kit and provisions. Such a long way from home and yet they were all so terribly British, as if the only way to climb Everest was to insist on having everything exactly the same as you were used to, to make the point that it was the geography you came for, not the culture. The stores were full of English tea, English biscuits, English chocolate, English cereal. He was sure they would even be able to produce Marmite if you asked for it.

That suited Alex. His immersion in Indian culture had hardly been an unqualified success and it was a relief to see something familiar, even if it was only coffee and biscuits. He was on his way home now anyway. He had briefly considered going on to Malaysia or Thailand, but the truth was he was more excited about going home to be an artist than he was about more travelling. Now that his life had become clear to him there seemed little point in delaying it any further.

He established that he wouldn't be able to fly home without a transfer somewhere, but there was absolutely no way he was going to go back to Delhi, even for a few hours—he was determined never to step on Indian soil again. He managed to get a seat on a cheap flight via Doha and then set off to buy some essentials for the next two days and tidy himself up a bit before he flew home to surprise Joe and Emma. He couldn't wait to see them.

* * *

Alex was pleased to find as he explored the city the next day that there was another Kathmandu, a more native one—and it was full of temples. In this tiny country squashed between India and China, the religions of both seemed to have got hopelessly tangled up and wildly proliferated.

He wandered through the main square, past Indian saddhus and Buddhist monks and temples with layered roofs like Chinese pagodas decorated inside with wooden Hindu carvings. Low tables crammed with flickering butter lamps, offerings of sweets and coloured paste. Buddhist prayer flags strung from every possible vantage point fluttering above rivers of blood from Hindu animal sacrifices flowing down the streets.

Freak Street was more interesting for its memories of the 60s and 70s than its souvenir shops of today. He sat on the steps where Mick Jagger, Jimi Hendrix and Bob Marley sat and smoked 30 years before, politely declining the offers of hashish whispered in his ear. In the evening, he went to Sam's bar and studied the walls covered with graffiti from exultant climbing trips completed long ago, whose climbers were probably back at home working in a bank by now; and then to Rum Doodles, where if you have managed to climb Everest you get to eat for free, which presumably makes all that altitude sickness worthwhile.

He was on his way in through the huge black and gold gates of the Guest House after a trawl round the market the next day, trying to find a really good present for Emma, when he heard a commotion in the guardhouse. As one of the guards picked up the phone and started shouting into it, the other burst out straight into Alex's path.

"What's going on?" he asked, his relaxed mood evaporating.

"Nothing for you to worry about, sir. We're just a little concerned about a bunch of Indian thugs who've been hanging around here asking a few too many questions. It happens sometimes. The situation's under control—we've called in the police, but it's just a precaution. You're quite safe here, sir."

"Questions about what?" Alex said, trying to sound normal.

"They were looking for someone, I think."

* * *

That was when he had fled Kathmandu, knowing that he had no time to lose. He had checked out, got on his bike and headed straight out of town. He wanted to try and reach Tibet—perhaps he could find some sort of sanctuary there for a while, a monastery perhaps, some compassionate monks, surely you could trust them, especially up in the mountains, and then if he could make it to Lhasa he could head for Beijing and then fly home.

He had been so close but it seemed about as likely now as flying to the moon. Still, first things first. Pokhara was the first place he needed to get to, a seven hour trip by road, and then up towards the Tibetan border. It was his only option.

They must be in league with the border guards and the Kathmandu police too, he thought bitterly. There were Indians everywhere in Kathmandu, you could even use Indian rupees here. It might as well be the same country. How in God's name was he supposed to stay ahead of a set-up on this sort of scale?

He had ridden the Royal Enfield up the long straight road to Pokhara as fast as he dared, stopping only to eat and drink and occasionally to wash his face in a mountain stream, trying to get the grit out of his eyes. Pokhara had a beautiful mountain lake, he remembered, with little coloured boats and mountains reflected in the water, surrounded by vivid green tropical vegetation.

He had passed fields of rice, thick, glossy-leaved trees, red earth, startlingly bright flowers. The light became clearer as he gained altitude and above them tier after tier of mountains were spread right across the skyline, the colours dimming as they receded into the distance. In Pokhara, he had stopped only briefly, bought some warm clothes from a stall at the side of the road, filled up with petrol and then set off again towards the mountains.

Up and up the winding roads, gaining height, past little smallholdings clustered with their patches of rice, coffee and bananas by the side of the road, sometimes dodging past a cockerel or a goat, sometimes a group of children on a long trek to school. On up above the tree line, the road narrower, cut out of the rock, through some low cloud, the mountains getting closer. And then things got hazy—he couldn't remember—but looking down at his hospital bed he knew he never made it to Tibet.

Something must have gone wrong. So where was he and how on earth did he get here? No wonder he felt frightened. They must be here, now, somewhere. How long had he been here and why hadn't they killed him already?

Chapter 20
Kathmandu

As the Air India flight started its descent into Kathmandu through a thin layer of cloud, Joe could see snow-covered mountains in the distance and flashes of fertile green terraces below. They flew over deep rifts and chasms in the earth and then the first scattering of buildings came into view followed by the town itself, looking surprisingly big and surprisingly normal. Joe was expecting something a lot more remote, more primitive, more—mythical. He certainly hadn't thought of Kathmandu as the important capital city it obviously was.

The plane taxied towards the airport terminal, a properly built, substantial modern building rather than the aircraft hangar he had been expecting, and Joe started to think about what lay ahead of him. Up until now his plans hadn't got much further than his arrival in Nepal, but in just a few minutes he would be walking out of the other side of that airport terminal.

Where on earth was he going to start looking for his brother in a city this size? It was all very well for Alex, taking off with all his usual free-spirited nonsense, but he never thought about who was going to have to come chasing after him when it all went wrong. As if Joe didn't have anything better to do.

He shuffled through the aircraft door and down the steps behind a plane-weary stream of fellow travellers. He squinted as his eyes adjusted to the light, then came to a standstill as he took in the breath-taking backdrop of snow-capped mountains and breathed in the clear air. The Himalayas. Quite something.

In the arrivals hall, he had no trouble getting an entry visa as Richard had predicted, although he was unnerved by the presence of armed police looking like urban soldiers in their camouflage uniforms. Not very Heathrow. Then he was out through the exit into Nepal and he couldn't help feeling a little thrill of importance when for once amongst the gaggle of drivers holding their handwritten signs out towards the new arrivals there was one with his own name on: Mr Joe Russell.

They drove straight to the Embassy where, as the driver explained, he was due to meet with the First Secretary, Jeremy Dalton. The Ambassador himself had sent his apologies but was up in Pokhara for a few days and was unable to meet him personally. Joe sat back in the diplomatic car feeling like royalty. This was all down to Richard—pretty impressive. One day he would like to have that sort of influence himself.

They bounced over the bumpy streets, making slow progress through the heavy traffic past block after block of apparently derelict buildings which nevertheless had tribes of people living in them. He certainly hadn't been prepared for this degree of chaos on the roads, the noise, the dust and the adrenalin of vehicles moving in all directions at once. His eyes gradually got used to the dark faces, the sherpers with huge loads and the old men in their interchangeable tapestry hats. As they drove past a putty-coloured square building with cracked stone balconies and a row of bikes outside he noticed a sign above the door that read 'Bir Hospital Emergency'. You wouldn't want to be in need of a hospital in a place like this, he thought.

The Embassy itself, however, was an island of Britishness. The colonial-style main building was set in mature, well-clipped gardens awash with flowers that even he recognised, like fuchsias, geraniums, marigolds and nasturtiums. He was shown into a comfortable meeting room and seated at a reproduction antique dining table with a pot of tea and a plate of shortbread biscuits, for all the world as if he was in Godalming. The smell of furniture polish reminded him of home.

Jeremy Dalton did not keep him waiting for long. Smartly dressed in an expensive-looking grey suit and radiating smooth self-confidence he swept in with a couple of junior staff in his wake, introduced himself and took charge. Clearly a fast-track diplomat, Joe thought, destined for greater things. Probably went to the right school. Joe jumped up and they shook hands, both keen to show their credentials as down to earth men of the world. Jeremy introduced his juniors at high speed and then motioned for everyone to sit down.

"It's early days but we've put some feelers out. The first thing to establish is whether your brother is still in Nepal—we're checking with the border authorities to see if there's any record of him leaving the country. I gather we do know he was in Kathmandu less than a month ago from his credit card records."

He looked up for confirmation from Joe before going on.

"Then we can check round the tour operators to see whether he's booked himself on a trip of some sort. We'll ask round the normal backpacking hostels to see if anyone remembers seeing him. And, of course, we'll check in with the police, although at this stage there's no reason to believe they would be involved. Please rest assured, Mr Russell, we will do absolutely everything we can to find him."

Joe sat back in his reproduction chair, mentally checking for anything they might have missed. Jeremy Dalton clearly knew what he was doing even if the charm was a bit overpowering at times. Then he pulled out his wallet and handed over the photos of Alex he had brought.

"Ah yes, very useful, very useful, Joe. May I call you Joe? And please do call me Jeremy—much easier. Well done, excellent. Doesn't look much like you, does he?"

* * *

In the Bir Hospital, Alex opened his eyes and looked slowly around him. The sounds and smells that had become so familiar at last began to take on visual form.

He looked down at his body lying on the primitive iron bed. His legs were hidden under a thin blanket but even so he could see that they were heavily dressed or possibly even in plaster. His whole body hurt—his ribs, his back and his head, which seemed to be wrapped in bandages too. He looked at his hands lying on the sheet and saw a catheter feeding fluid into his veins from a bag suspended on a stand beside him.

He was relieved to find that he could at least move his hands freely. His mouth felt dry and his tongue didn't seem to fit properly, and his head felt too strange at the moment for him to risk moving it more than a little from side to side. How long had he been here? He closed his eyes again, tired already.

The next time he opened his eyes he already knew there would be a nurse standing beside him because he had learned to sense her presence. She had her back to him and he watched her checking the drip and then the dressing on his leg. He could see she had dark skin, a slim body, black shiny hair and a clean blue uniform pulled in at the waist with an elastic belt. She turned and saw him looking at her.

"Ah! You 'wake! You come back to us!"

Alex tried to smile and nod, not entirely successfully. Then he started to speak but nothing much happened.

He looked directly into her eyes, willing her to understand. "Doctor?" he croaked. "Doctor here?"

"Yes! Doctor! Dr Sharma, yes, yes!"

She turned and scuttled out of sight.

* * *

Once the meeting at the Embassy was over Jeremy allocated one of his minions to take Joe over to his hotel, a dull red Lego block less than a mile up the road. He resisted the hotel porter's attempts to part him from his luggage as he checked in, determined to avoid the awkwardness of having to tip him later, but he still had to put up with an enthusiastic demonstration of the tea and coffee making facilities, minibar, safe, television and even the hair dryer. As soon as he had closed the door behind the wretched man he turned off the air conditioning, drew back several layers of curtains and flung open the window.

Although the Embassy had promised to ring if there were any developments, Joe hadn't come all this way just to sit on his hands in a hotel room. Down in reception again he worked his way through all the tourist information on offer and quickly established that Thamel, with its 'mix of eastern and western shops and bars', would be as good a place as any to start.

He decided to head over there and ask around, half expecting that he would just bump into Alex in the street. But first he needed some sleep. After a tepid shower back in his room, which was like a furnace now despite the open window, he threw himself onto the bed face up, damp towel still round his waist and one long leg trailing over the edge, and passed out.

* * *

Alex was tentatively testing out his legs to see which bits of them still moved when he heard a familiar voice in the distance. He was surprised when he saw a small, neat Indian man in a doctor's coat coming towards him—somehow he had imagined someone bigger, more imposing. But it was the doctor all right and he was beaming at Alex.

"Young man! May I be the first to welcome you to Kathmandu's fine Bir Hospital! What a pleasure it is to meet you at last! I am hoping perhaps you speak English? Oh, please excuse me. I am Dr Sharma. I have been looking after you."

Alex automatically lifted his right hand to shake the doctor's and then realised it was the one that was cathetered up to a drip.

"Careful, please!" The doctor moved swiftly round to the other side of the bed and patted the drip back into place. "We have a lot to talk about, young man. But first things first. How are you feeling? How is the pain?"

Alex tried to smile and instead shrugged his shoulders awkwardly.

"What happened?" he croaked.

Dr Sharma pulled up the plastic chair by the bed and sat down. "We are not absolutely sure. You were brought here to the Bir Hospital two weeks ago. You had a motor bike crash near Pokhara." The doctor paused to adopt a more gentle bedside manner. "I am sorry to tell you that you have some bad injuries, very bad. The legs, the ribs, the head also. But I am also very happy to say that you are now making a good recovery."

"Who? Who brought me here? They want me dead. If they find me here, they will kill me." Alex looked nervously towards the end of the ward and then back at the doctor. "Are you sure it's safe here?"

"Yes, of course it's safe here. You are in hospital. We are in the business of making our patients well here, not killing them—"

"I was trying to escape. They followed me from India, that's why I was on the motorbike."

Dr Sharma nodded sympathetically.

"I see, yes, yes."

He poured a glass of water from the stand beside the bed and held it while Alex took a few sips.

"You are English then? What is your name? Where do you come from? Why were you on that mountain road?"

"Alex. Alex Russell. Yes, I'm English."

Alex nodded, suddenly exhausted. The doctor probably thought he was still off his head but he was too tired to explain it all at the moment. He closed his eyes and when he opened them again the doctor had gone.

* * *

Dr Sharma had returned to his office and was staring intently at the telephone. He had promised to inform the police as soon as the boy came round and he had some basic information for them at last—his name and nationality. Not much more, but that should be enough to identify him and contact his relatives, at least. But he was puzzled by the terror the boy seemed to be experiencing. Could it be some sort of paranoia caused by the brain injury he had sustained? Or perhaps he really had got himself into some sort of trouble. Either way, he clearly needed some help.

"Hello? Yes, Dr Sharma here. I have some news for you on our young motor cycle accident! British, yes—speaks English, of course, yes. He's still very weak—Russell. Alex Russell."

Dr Sharma put down the phone and thought for a moment. Then he made two more calls—one to the hospital psychiatrist, the other to the head of security. If he was delusional, some extra protection would put his mind at rest. And if he wasn't—well, they might all need protecting.

* * *

Joe had no idea which part of town he was in, let alone how to get from there to Thamel, but he hopped into one of the aging taxis outside the hotel and hoped for the best. At the mention of Thamel, the driver had nodded his agreement and swerved out into the traffic, giving Joe confidence in his local knowledge if not his driving skills. He sat back on the threadbare upholstery of the back seat, watched the rupee counter shoot up at an astonishing rate and hoped there was only one Thamel and that it was not too far away.

Soon they were off the main roads and into narrow streets so crammed with people, bikes and rickshaws that it was scarcely possible to get through in a car. This must be it—the streets were lined with shops, although some of them were little more than market stalls and the whole place was plastered with shop signs and advertising hoardings.

"Here is Thamel. Where you want?" The taxi driver, defeated, had taken his hands off the horn for a moment and was waving them accusingly at Joe.

"OK, yes! Here is good." Joe leaned forward with a handful of rupee notes, which felt like an absolute fortune but was probably about £1.50, and got out.

How odd, he thought, to have come all this way and yet for it to be so familiar, in some respects anyway. Amongst the mandala galleries, singing bowls and incense there were money exchange counters, cashmere jumpers, scarves and silver earrings. He could hear plenty of English voices amongst the crowds and familiar Western music pumping out of an English bar. It was almost like Kensington Market. Then there were shops full of climbing gear and supermarkets with all kinds of familiar-looking groceries. He could just imagine Alex here. This was why he couldn't leave it totally up to the Embassy to find him. They didn't know Alex like he did.

He spent an hour or so walking the streets, scanning every white face he passed, drifting in and out of the shops. *Where would Alex have gone? A bar, surely*, he thought, as he followed the arrows up some steps to a bar called Jimmy's. Yes, that's exactly what Alex would have done. Headed for a bar. Maybe even this one. He sat down at a table, looked briefly at the menu and ordered a local beer.

As his eyes got used to the semi-darkness he looked around him. On every available surface—walls, plant pots, even the floor—people had written their little bons mots. The whole place was covered in graffiti. *If life gives you lemons, make lemonade. If you're not on the edge, you're taking up too much space.* He wondered what sort of experiences lay behind these travellers' pearls of wisdom. Were they enlightened or just trite?

They were, however, almost all in English and the bar seemed to be populated exclusively by English people. Or English speaking, anyway. He reached for the photograph he'd put in his wallet and started showing it to one little group of customers after another. They all peered at it and then reluctantly shook their heads, saying how much they wished they could help.

"Tell you what you could do, mate." Joe turned towards a friendly Australian voice. "You could ask over at the Kathmandu Guest House across the road. You get a lot of Brits staying there. Worth a try, anyways." The Australian grinned and shrugged.

Bingo. Excited, Joe quickly downed his bottle of Everest and turned to go.

"Good luck!" a blonde girl in the group called out and Joe waved his thanks. Salt of the earth, Aussies. They always seemed to know what was going on. But could it really be that easy? Was Alex really going to be sitting in the Kathmandu Guest House right across the road, minding his own business? Perhaps they would just be able to make their apologies to everybody and go home. Perhaps it would all turn out to be a massive waste of time. If so, he'd definitely kill Alex. But at least Emma would be happy.

The reception at the Kathmandu Guest House was chaos. Joe settled into an ancient leather armchair amongst a crowd of travellers and their heaps of rucksacks and carrier bags and spent half an hour sussing things out. People came and went, checked their luggage in and out of the hotel's cavernous storage room or met up for tea or a beer in the huge open air courtyard outside. They were all travellers, just like Alex.

When he finally got the attention of the reception staff with his photo they were unhelpful at first, but he persuaded them to check their guest records. Yes, they reported with no surprise, it seemed that Alex had indeed stayed here. No, he had left just over two weeks ago. No, they had no information on where he had gone. No, they did not know whether he would be back.

Pleased with himself for making such good progress, Joe sat down again, imagining Alex sitting in this very chair next to him. He'd better check in with the Embassy, he thought as he got up again to head back to his hotel. He didn't want to be too cocky but he doubted whether they would have anything to report yet. On his way out through the big wrought iron gates of the Guest House, he stopped to ask the security guards whether they had seen Alex.

"Oh yes, I remember him," one of them nodded, studying the photo. "I remember him because he was on a motorbike. He left in a hurry."

As soon as Joe got back he called the Embassy and was immediately put through to one of Jeremy's team. Covering up his excitement he started to report on what he had discovered, but the aide quickly cut him short.

"We've been trying to get hold of you, sir. It looks like we've found your brother. We have just been notified by the police that he is in the Bir Hospital right here in Kathmandu. If you could wait in the hotel reception downstairs, please—the First Secretary is on his way over now to pick you up."

* * *

Alex opened his eyes at the sound of approaching footsteps. He was looking forward to talking again with Dr Sharma, the one reassuring presence during his time in the hospital. But it wasn't Dr Sharma coming, it was another doctor or at least someone disguised as a doctor. He scanned the ward, hoping to see a nurse or anyone he could call out to, but everyone had evaporated. Or had been evaporated. As soon as Alex heard the doctor's unfamiliar voice he knew he was in real trouble.

"Hello, Alex. It is Alex, isn't it? You've certainly kept us guessing. But you're not going to give us the slip this time—oh yes, this is where it ends, stupid English boy."

The doctor's menacing tone left Alex in no doubt. He was holding something which Alex couldn't quite make out—he was keeping it hidden. A knife, it must be some sort of a knife. Had he been stabbed already then? He couldn't detect any pain that wasn't there before. Then the doctor slowly and deliberately lifted his arm up and moved it towards him. Alex closed his eyes as the knife pushed downwards through the air towards his chest. If it hit him he knew there was no way he could possibly survive the impact. He gritted his teeth and with every last ounce of strength in him he rolled over onto his side, away from the doctor, and crashed heavily onto the lino floor.

* * *

Outside the entrance to the Bir Hospital there was a hell of a commotion going on. The doorway had been sealed off by blue-camouflaged policemen who were trying to calm an emotional crowd on the point of boiling over. As Joe and Jeremy Dalton stepped out of the diplomatic car onto the pavement the crowd parted and they found themselves face to face with the police officer in charge.

"I'm sorry, sir. We can't let you enter the hospital without security clearance. We have a heightened security situation here."

Jeremy's diplomatic pass made short work of that and they both strode into the hospital. Joe followed Jeremy down the brightly lit corridors past medical departments half-familiar from human biology lessons at school—pathology, renal unit, urology, haematology—until they reached intensive care, where they were intercepted by a pint-sized Nepalese doctor who introduced himself as Dr Sharma and ushered them firmly into his office.

"You must be Alex's brother—Joe? And Mr Dalton—how nice to meet you, sir."

"I'd like to see Alex now, please." Joe was not prepared to believe that Alex was actually here until he had seen him with his own eyes and he was not going to be prevented from doing that by some jumped up Nepalese medic.

"Of course, of course. We will go and see him very shortly. But there are some things I need to explain to you first. I'm afraid he is not conscious at the moment."

Jeremy turned to Joe.

"Best let him brief us first, old boy."

Dr Sharma explained how Alex had been found half way up a mountain, the injuries he had sustained and the operation he had carried out to relieve the pressure on his brain.

"I will be honest with you. His injuries are serious. He is still in intensive care and he regained consciousness for the first time only yesterday. Up until then we had not been able to identify him. I can't promise at this stage that he will make a full recovery, although we're doing everything we can."

Dr Sharma paused, then looked up again.

"There's something else. When I spoke to him yesterday, he seemed convinced that he was being pursued by a gang of men who were trying to kill him. You may have noticed the additional security we have put in place downstairs, purely as a precaution."

Jeremy and Joe exchanged sardonic glances.

"When our hospital psychiatrist visited him a short while ago with a sedative he became very distressed. It seems he believed the doctor's syringe was a knife and that he was about to be stabbed. He managed to throw himself onto the floor, not a good idea in the circumstances. We are checking him over at the moment to make sure he has not sustained any further injuries.

"I am hopeful he will not have suffered any complications but the incident does confirm my suspicions about his mental state. I'm afraid he is severely delusional, Mr Russell, and experiencing fantasies which he genuinely believes are real. This may be the result of his brain injury but I strongly suspect it predates his accident. Indeed, it may well have been the cause of it."

* * *

Dr Sharma stood up and led the way out of his office. Joe followed, more subdued now and with a great deal more respect for the doctor, while Jeremy brought up the rear. Joe tried to prepare himself for what Alex might look like, mentally erasing the holiday snaps he had brought with him from his mind and bracing himself for a shock. It looked like his brother really had gone and done the job properly this time.

On the ward, he looked around for a Western figure amongst the prostrate dark-skinned Nepalese patients who somehow managed to make the hospital

214

beds look enormous. Yes, there he was—white skin, blondish hair, straggly beard. Could that really be him?

Joe took in Alex's heavily bandaged legs, the dressings round his head and the drip by the bed. He looked into the little bit of his face that wasn't bandaged or bearded. Alex's eyes were closed but his breathing was steady. Dr Sharma pointed to the plastic chair by the bed and Joe sat down and picked up Alex's hand from where it lay on the sheet.

"I've come to take you home, Alex."

Alex's eyes flickered and then opened, confused. Then he recognised Joe and managed a limp smile before drifting back into unconsciousness.

Chapter 21
Bir Hospital

Joe was striding up and down the narrow channel between the end of the bed and the huge TV in his hotel room. At least he had found Alex, as he had never doubted he would. But in his mind the story had ended with him flying home triumphant and handing his brother over to a grateful Emma, after which they would all live happily ever after.

The reality had turned out to be rather different. The hospital had insisted on sedating Alex again and monitoring him closely while they carried out more tests. Joe had not even been able to talk to him yet and had very little idea what to expect when he did. And although Dr Sharma had earned his respect, the Bir Hospital itself did not inspire much confidence.

He wanted to get Alex back home to an English hospital, especially with the mental problems he seemed to have developed, but it looked as though it might be some time before he would be well enough to travel. The journey was tough enough for a normal person let alone someone with broken bones, a head injury and some sort of psychosis. Alex could hardly have chosen anywhere less convenient to fall apart.

Jeremy Dalton had been excellent, he thought. Just what you imagined British Embassies abroad to be like. He and his team were in regular contact with the medical team at the hospital to make sure Alex got the best possible care and were also liaising with the police, who were still trying to piece together what had happened. Then there was endless paperwork to be done, apparently, reports to be written, repatriation agreements to be reached and a new passport to be issued.

So Jeremy was holding all the strings and although the last thing Joe wanted to do was hang around in his hotel room, he didn't seem to have much choice. Until Alex regained consciousness there really wasn't anything he could do. He couldn't bear to be out of contact for long so sightseeing was out of the question—not that he could have really concentrated on it anyway. But he did need to call Emma with the good news so he picked up the phone and braced himself for a tussle with the international telephone network.

"Emma? Can you hear me?"

"Joe! You're a bit faint but yes! What's happening?"

Hearing Emma's voice desperate for news Joe realised how difficult it must be for her, stuck at home, wondering what was going on. Thank goodness, the news he had was mostly good.

"We found him, Em! He's here in Kathmandu! We've got him!"

"Oh, that's wonderful! What a relief, Joe! That's amazing! Is everything all right? When are you coming home?"

"Well—he's actually in hospital at the moment. He had a motorbike crash. He's fine but he's a bit beaten up."

"Oh, my God! I knew it! I told you something was wrong! What happened? Is he OK?"

"We don't know everything yet, but don't worry, he's all right. He's going to be fine. He's sedated at the moment and his legs are a bit bashed up and he's got a head injury—"

"WHAT?"

Joe realised then that he couldn't tell Emma anything about Alex's delusional state over the phone. That wasn't going to help anybody. He'd have to let the first instalment sink in first.

"Yes, he's been in hospital here for a couple of weeks. He was brought here from Pokhara—that's where he had the crash, apparently, up in the hills."

He heard his words echoing down the line across whole continents.

"Hello? Are you still there, Em?"

"Yes. That sounds awful."

"Well, it's not great, but he's OK. He had to have surgery to relieve the pressure on his brain. He was in a coma until yesterday, they had no idea who he was or they would have tried to get in contact with us sooner. When they found him he had nothing on him at all, no papers or anything. They reckon everything had been nicked before they got there."

"I just knew something was wrong! That's so weird, because that Tarot woman said he was in hospital—"

"What Tarot woman?"

"Joe, I told you! Oh, never mind—Do you really think he's going to be all right?"

"Well, they've been carrying out some more tests and I'm just waiting to hear how they went. But yes, I'm *sure* he's going to be all right. Of course he is!"

"How does he seem?"

"He's still sedated so I haven't been able to talk to him yet. From what I can see he's got quite a beard and he's lost weight—that's about all I can tell you so far." In fact, he had been shocked at Alex's appearance and the obvious extent of his injuries, but there was no point in upsetting Emma any more than necessary. He had enough to cope with here without worrying about her as well.

"How are you, Em? How are things in London?"

"Fine." The line crackled.

"But I don't understand, Joe. If he's been in hospital for two weeks why are they doing more tests now? If he's had brain surgery and been in a coma, do they think he might have brain damage or something? How on earth did all this happen? And when are you coming home?"

"Look, Emma, I don't have all the answers yet. The important thing for the moment is that we've found him. There's a man at the Embassy, Jeremy Dalton, who's helping with everything, thanks to your father. He's pretty good, actually. He seems to think it's all going OK. I'll bring Alex home as soon as I can but he may not be able to travel straight away and we have to get him a new passport and so on."

"Well, at least you found him. So it turned out I was right then."

"Yes, OK. You were right."

"I wish I hadn't been."

"Well, I'm sorry I haven't got more to tell you, Em. I thought it was pretty good news. And I'm doing everything I can."

I really am, Joe thought, so why am I apologising? I've come half way round the world, I'm tackling embassies, hospitals and armed police forces. I'd like to know what more I could have done.

"Yes, it is—it's wonderful news. You're doing brilliantly, Joe."

Somewhat mollified by being called brilliant, Joe did his best to reassure her.

"Please try not to worry, Em. There's no reason. He's here and he's going to be fine. I'll bring him home as soon as I can. If I hear anything more, I'll let you

218

know straight away, I promise. Why don't you give Richard a ring and let him know what's happening? And can you ring Dad for me as well?"

"OK, I will. Thank you, Joe. I love you."

"I love you too, Em. I'd better go now. Bye—"

* * *

At her desk at Withers, Emma put down the phone carefully and stared at the stack of papers in front of her. She looked round to see if any of her colleagues had been listening in to her conversation—you weren't supposed to have a private life at Withers or at least you weren't supposed to admit to one—but they were all absorbed in their work or away from their desks. As casually as she could she got up and headed for the Ladies where she splashed some cold water on her face and looked intently at her reflection in the mirror.

She should be pleased that Joe had found Alex. She *was* pleased. But it was so hard to tell from Joe's voice over the telephone long distance what was really going on. Brain surgery! She had a feeling he hadn't told her everything. And the tightness in the pit of her stomach she'd had for ages hadn't gone away.

Once her head had cleared a little she wiped the smudges of mascara from under her eyes, brushed her hair off her face and walked out, determined to show a bit of backbone. She found an empty office with a telephone and soon she was perched on the wrong side of the desk with her feet up on the chair, dialling her father's office number and being efficiently intercepted by Caroline.

"He's not here, I'm afraid. He's really busy today. He's behind with all his calls and he won't be back here for a couple of hours at least. Can I tell him you called?"

"No, it's all right—" Emma couldn't hide her frustration. Having a successful father was all very well except that he was never there when you needed him. "I'll see him at home later. He hasn't got a dinner or anything, has he?"

"No, not tonight. Tell you what—I'll try and get him home nice and early this evening. I can tell you need him more than the office does today."

"Thank you, Caroline."

Emma put down the phone and thought for a moment, then picked it up and dialled again, half hoping there would be no answer.

"James, it's Emma!" She tried not to sound too nervous, although she couldn't remember ever having had a proper face-to-face conversation with him before, let alone a telephone conversation.

She had known him for almost as long as she'd known Joe and Alex but he'd always been in the background, somehow never a person in his own right. Lately he had been such a lost soul that she had shied away from making any real contact with him so she'd hidden behind Joe and left it to him. Now she saw how much more she could have done, how little real interest she had shown in him. Perhaps it was about time she started to treat him like a real person instead of just Joe and Alex's dad. They were all adults now and after all he might even end up being her father in law.

"Hello there, Emma! How are you?" His voice was friendly and he seemed genuinely pleased to hear from her, much to Emma's relief. If he had noticed her lack of effort, he clearly didn't hold it against her.

She passed on Joe's news to him in as much detail as she could.

James listened carefully and then thanked her very much for her kindness in calling him.

"Actually, Emma, I've had some news too. I would like to have told Alex myself, but perhaps Joe can pass it on to him. It might cheer him up, you never know."

"It's about his family, his birth family. You know he's adopted, don't you? Well, I had a phone call today. Apparently Alex has a half-sister who wants to contact him. After all these years! Extraordinary, isn't it?"

* * *

Joe was on his way to the Bir Hospital. Although he was gradually getting used to being in Kathmandu, he had decided that frankly it was a bit of a dump. The roads were in a dreadful state and the pavements were absolutely lethal, inset with ugly lumps of concrete and bits of bent piping. The vast majority of the buildings were falling down, no doubt contributing to the dirt and dust that coated everything, and abject poverty was the normal state of affairs for their inhabitants. Then there were the cows grazing on the rubbish that lay everywhere and leaving a trail of steaming faeces behind them. He really couldn't see the attraction—in fact, he couldn't wait to get out of the place.

Jeremy had been in touch to say that Alex was now conscious and asking to see him. Joe didn't need any encouragement to get out of his hotel room and do something. And anyway, he needed to know that Alex, his brother Alex, was still in there somewhere under all those bandages and drips.

The hospital was calmer today now that the extra security had been stood down. As he headed upstairs he noticed that the floors were clean, it had the right hospital smell and he even saw a nurse or two clipping along the corridors with a reassuring air of professionalism. Perhaps it wasn't so bad after all. Better than it looked from the outside, definitely.

Another nurse showed him to Alex's bedside.

"Alex, there's someone here to see you."

"Joe!" They beamed at each other. Joe supposed that he ought to be giving his brother a hug but he was terrified of hurting him. And anyway he knew Alex wouldn't expect that—it had never been their style. Instead he pulled up the plastic chair by the bed and the nurse melted away.

"Alex, what on earth happened?"

Alex tried to sit himself up in bed and Joe jumped up to prop him into position. He looked down at Alex and tried to remember what he had looked like before. He was so much thinner and more ragged now, he had been through so much that Joe didn't know about, it was almost like looking down at a stranger. He wondered whether they would ever catch up.

Alex began to talk with an effort. "It's a long story."

"Are you all right? Does it hurt?"

"Not really. I think they're giving me morphine or something." Alex lifted his cathetered hand off the bed.

"I'm going to get you out of here as soon as we can move you."

Joe wondered where on earth to start. What did Alex think had happened and what had actually happened? How much had the hospital told him about the psychosis? He decided to start with something recent.

"Why did you think that doctor was attacking you yesterday, Alex? Why did you dive onto the floor like that?"

Alex closed his eyes for a moment, then took a deep breath.

"Some people sent by the ashram were after me. That's how I crashed the motorbike. These people, they want me dead. I knew they would turn up here sooner or later."

"Who are these people, Alex?"

"I found out something by accident. They killed Scott and I knew they were going to kill me so I ran. But they just kept on coming after me. They're probably out there now, somewhere. They've tried to kill me twice already, next time I expect they'll manage it."

Joe was sitting very still, staring at his brother. "Are you *sure*?"

But Alex lay back on the pillows, exhausted.

"Alex, the doctor you thought was trying to kill you the other day was a psychiatrist. He wasn't trying to kill you at all, he was about to give you an injection."

"Yes, they told me that."

"And do you believe them?"

"No."

* * *

On his way out, Joe called in to see Dr Sharma. He was overwhelmed by his brother's condition. The physical injuries seemed a lot worse than he remembered but at least he had some hope of understanding them. The paranoia was something else.

The doctor went through it again. As well as the head injury Alex had broken a few ribs, which were healing but causing him a lot of pain, and he had had a metal pin inserted in one of his legs which had been badly broken.

"But, of course, his mental state is also a cause for concern. Our psychiatrist is starting to talk to him about what he remembers from before the crash, but he is not making much progress yet. Alex's response is much as you experienced yourself. He has been prescribed antipsychotic drugs which will certainly help when they start to take effect. You should know that once the delusions fall away he may well be frightened and confused. He will need to work through his memories as they come back to him and try to understand what really happened. The more you can help him with this the better."

Joe nodded.

"I can do that. When can I take him home?"

"I am sure you will understand that is impossible at the moment. I could not permit a long flight, indeed any flight at all, for at least a week, possibly more.

"However I have had a number of conversations with the British Embassy today. If his condition stabilises over the next 24 hours, I would be prepared to consider discharging him into their care."

* * *

Emma walked back to her desk in a trance as her conversation with James gradually sank in. Alex had a half-sister, she had a half-brother. Alex, Asha. It made sense. Could it just be a coincidence? But the timing, too—and their age— and Exford—everything fitted. She sat down and stared at the papers in front of her. What a day for all this to happen. She was stressed out enough already about this afternoon's meeting, which she'd been dreading all week. It was with her biggest client and they were in the middle of a takeover bid. The company's bankers, brokers and lawyers would all be there, trying to prove their immense value and justify their fees.

Beneath the bonhomie the atmosphere would be tense, with everybody trying to win brownie points and show everybody else up in front of the client's Chief Executive. Although she would probably be the most junior person in the room, it was her job to make sure her team had all the briefing papers they needed to keep them out of trouble. She'd already been through everything with a fine toothcomb but she still needed the rest of the morning to go over it one last time. She was going to have to be totally professional and put the whole business with Alex out of her mind till later. And anyway, it wasn't definite yet.

Richard was already back when she got in, going through some papers at his desk—Caroline had been as good as her word and delivered him home early for once.

"How did it go, darling?" he called out from his office and started to get up, his eyes still on the document he had been reading.

"It was all right actually. Well, nothing went wrong, at least. I didn't have to say anything and I don't suppose anyone noticed I was there. We're making good progress though, I think." Now that it was over, she was proud of the part she had played, but they both knew she couldn't discuss any of the details.

"Great news from Kathmandu, Dad! Have you heard? I spoke to Joe this morning and they've found Alex! He's in hospital but Joe says he's going to be fine."

"That's wonderful news! In hospital? What on earth happened—what's the matter with him?"

"I'm not really sure. Joe said he'd been in a motorbike crash. He said something about a head injury and being in a coma—but he said he didn't know exactly, that they were waiting for some more tests or something. It doesn't sound too good actually." Emma sat down in her coat and put her head in her hands.

"Darling, I'm sure he'll be fine. Things can sound much worse from a distance, you know. It's a good thing Joe's out there. Is there anything I can do?"

"I don't think so—apparently the chap at the Embassy has been great."

Richard smiled modestly.

"There's something else, Dad."

Richard sat down beside her, gently took her coat off and put an arm round her, making her feel like a child again. He always seemed to know, somehow.

"You know I went to see the Vicar in Exford and he said that he would get in touch with Asha, you know, my half-brother, to see if he wanted to get in touch with me?"

"Yes—" Emma knew her father didn't want to talk about this. He had been relieved to hear that Frances really had died all those years ago and he'd been right all along. He could have swept the finer details under the carpet if it hadn't been for Asha, whose existence made it all a lot messier. And in any case, as he had pointed out, this child could have ended up anywhere—he had had an itinerant hippy father and then been adopted under the radar. What chance was there that he and Emma would have anything in common?

But Emma needed to tell him and anyway there was no way she was going to have another black hole in the family after all those years of not talking about her mother. This time, things were going to be different.

"I spoke to James this morning after I heard from Joe. To let him know about Alex. He said that he had a message for Alex. It turns out he's got a half-sister who wants to make contact with him."

Richard looked confused.

"Doesn't that seem an extraordinary coincidence to you? That I should find out I have a half-brother and try to contact him at the exact same time that Alex finds out he has a half-sister? Elizabeth Duncan said his name was Asha, but maybe they gave him a new name. After all, Asha *was* a bit of a weird name. And Alex would be about the right age—and he lives just up the road."

But Richard wasn't listening anymore. Now he was the one with his head in his hands.

* * *

Joe was sitting beside Alex's bed in a bungalow in the British Embassy compound. Now that he was ensconced in Irish linen and being fed regular, wholesome meals, which he was hoovering up in huge quantities, physically he was making a remarkable recovery. As soon as Dr Sharma had authorised the removal of the drip and everyone had agreed not to blame the hospital if there were any medical repercussions he had been eased into the back of a van and bumped painfully over the potholed streets to the leafy sanctuary of the Embassy.

His immediate fears about being killed in his bed were subsiding, but as Dr Sharma had predicted, confusion was taking their place. Joe had spent hours encouraging him to talk about what had happened to him since he left home and although Alex's explanations were fragmented at times, Joe now had a good picture of his travels across Turkey, central Asia, Pakistan and India. Clearly Alex had been in a considerably worse state than he and Emma had realised when they said goodbye to him and Joe was beginning to realise that they should never have let him go off like that. But that part of the story was not something he and his brother could easily discuss.

Instead Joe set about persuading Alex that he had imagined much of what had happened after he found the suitcases.

"How did you know Scott had been killed, Alex?"

"It's obvious. He must have been, he just vanished off the face of the earth. And they knew that he knew what we'd found."

"But what exactly *had* you found?"

"I told you. We saw them delivering a whole load of suitcases in the middle of the night."

"OK—but they were locked, weren't they? You didn't know what was in them, Alex, you just guessed."

"I heard them talking about a delivery and a contract. And why bother to deliver them in the middle of the night if it was all perfectly legit? Those guys weren't messing around, I can tell you."

"Well, it does sound as if they were up to something. But money laundering? Drug dealing? What made you think it was that rather than, say, fake designer clothing? Think back, Alex. What was it that made you think it was something so dangerous?"

"I don't know."

"Did they have guns, weapons?"

"No, I don't think so."

"So it could have been something perfectly harmless?"

"Maybe."

"OK. Let's go back to Scott. Tell me again—why did you think he had been killed?"

Alex sighed. "Because he knew about the suitcases."

"Is it possible he could have just packed up and left of his own accord? You didn't know each other *that* well. Had you been getting on OK? Had you had a row or anything?"

Alex thought for a few minutes.

"I couldn't convince Scott how dangerous the situation was. He didn't believe me. He kept telling me I'd got it all wrong and to leave things alone. I suppose I might have lost my temper with him."

"But Alex, maybe you *had* got it wrong. Maybe he just decided he'd had enough. Perhaps *you* frightened him, Alex. Do you think that might be possible?"

"Maybe."

Chapter 22
Coming Home

"Ah! I'm glad I've caught you both. I've just had an update from the police."

Jeremy's polished black lace-up shoes had preceded him into Alex's room, followed by the citrus smell of Eau Sauvage which accompanied him wherever he went. Joe had been helping his brother with a trial run across the room on crutches but it was slow progress and he sank into a chair without any protest to hear what Jeremy had to say.

"They've been in touch with the Indian Police, asked them to check out Ramana Ashram. Seems they've been keeping an eye on it for quite a while, apparently—some sort of illegal export business, they think. But they've got bigger fish to fry on their patch—this is low-level stuff. Definitely not drugs or money laundering."

Joe glanced across at Alex but his brother was nodding.

"Yes, I understand that now."

"Would it help if we could find Scott, Alex? Would that help put your mind at rest?"

Alex nodded.

"If it's possible."

"We could try and track his father down in Toronto—from what you've told us it should be possible I think, yes. At the very least, he can tell us when he last heard from Scott."

Jeremy perched on the narrow window sill and leaned forward. "That just leaves the break-in to your hostel room at Kanpur to be explained. Perhaps not such an unusual event in itself. Could have happened to any tourist, don't you think?"

Alex shrugged. "I don't know what happened anymore. Maybe I imagined the whole thing. Maybe I never left home. Maybe I'm at home now."

Joe and Jeremy exchanged glances.

"Come on, old boy, let's get you back into bed. Up you come."

Joe struggled to manhandle Alex up onto his feet and together they shuffled back across the room. Jeremy discreetly took his leave while Joe helped his brother back into bed.

"Try not to worry too much, Alex. Everything's going to be fine."

Once Alex had closed his eyes, apparently exhausted, Joe caught up with the First Secretary, who as he expected was waiting for him outside.

"I'm pretty concerned about him, Jeremy. I'd like to take him home as soon as possible."

"Yes, I think that would be best in the circumstances. We could probably look at a flight in a couple of days' time. By that time, we will have sorted out what we need to do here. Alex seems to be making reasonably good progress, although of course we'll need to check in with the hospital. The police are satisfied that there was no foul play involved.

"I'd say the sooner he starts treatment at home, the better."

* * *

At Kathmandu airport, Joe and Alex were given something of a royal send-off. Several of the Embassy staff, headed by Jeremy, came to see them off. Joe was surprised at how difficult it was to say goodbye to these people who he hardly knew and would almost certainly never see again—but it had been an emotional week and he had been moved by their kindness. He didn't know quite what he would have done without them.

"Do send our regards to Richard, won't you, Joe!"

Of course—wheels within wheels. Well, fair enough—Jeremy had done a great job and deserved the credit for it, even if the extent of his ambition had been rather nakedly exposed. Somewhere down the line he would no doubt get his payback.

"Of course. And thanks again for everything!"

Then they were off, Joe steering Alex's wheelchair with their passports tucked under his thumb, Alex's brand new one on top. He could tell that Alex was nervous and not just because of his atrocious wheelchair driving. Hobbling backwards and forwards across your bedroom on crutches was one thing, but setting off on a plane journey half way round the world was quite another.

Physically there was still the chance that Alex would have a permanent limp and even a degree of brain damage. Mentally, his brother clearly needed professional help. He was nervously looking around in all directions and was almost completely concealed in a hoodie and scarf.

* * *

Joe heard Alex breathe a sigh of relief as they took off and they both looked out of the window to catch one last glimpse of the Himalayas.

"You know, I imagined this so many times. I thought I'd made it and then I had to get back on that wretched bike again—"

Alex had told him that he was trying to cross over from Nepal to Tibet and then into China when he had the accident. That was why he had been on a mountain road, heading towards what he had hoped was a pass. Except that there was no pass there and no way through. The Himalayas were more effective than any border control. His journey had been destined to end in failure, one way or the other.

"Do you think you'll ever come back?" Joe joked, trying to lighten the mood. He knew that Alex was still haunted by what he had been through and couldn't help even now looking round every few minutes to check whether anyone was following him.

"Yeah, maybe, one day. But right now I just want to go home. Some of the places I went to were incredible, I'll never forget them. In some ways, it was really good. Travelling makes you think, being away from home makes you face up to who you really are. I didn't know who I was, you see."

"And now you do?"

"I've got a better idea. I only knew who I wasn't—I wasn't like you or Mum or Dad. Why would I be?" Alex shrugged and then smiled, to Joe's relief. He had never given much thought to who he was, it had always been obvious.

* * *

Joe had rung Emma with the details of their flight so she could pick them up from the airport. James came up on the train from Tiverton Parkway the afternoon before and stayed in Joe's flat; he had insisted on coming to the airport with her, saying rather gallantly that she couldn't possibly go on her own. Emma suspected that, like her, he had needed to feel he was doing something to help. And anyway he would want to see Alex as soon as possible, which she quite understood, and she accepted his company gracefully.

"How's Alex doing, do you think?" James asked as Emma drove her VW Golf down the inside lane of the M4 at a steady 60 miles an hour. Having someone strange in the passenger seat always made her feel as if she was in the middle of her driving test.

"Joe said he's much better. He's walking on crutches apparently and looking forward to coming home."

"Good! Good!" James had never been much good at small talk and most of the journey passed in silence. Emma hardly noticed, she was so busy thinking about seeing Alex again and wondering what he would say about having a half-sister.

Emma was shocked when she saw Alex coming through Arrivals. She hadn't expected the wheelchair, but it wasn't only that; Alex seemed to have shrunk into the chair, something strange had happened to his hair and he kept looking round him as if he was about to be attacked. This wasn't the confident Alex she used to know—he'd come back broken, an invalid, a stranger.

Emma was relieved to see Joe behind the wheelchair, the same Joe, grinning and waving triumphantly as if to say—look, I did it! I brought him home! Emma found herself jumping up and down with excitement and completely forgetting James for a moment she ducked under the tape barrier and ran towards them, straight into Joe's outstretched arms. Then Alex was struggling to stand up and hug Emma too, while James beamed as if he had personally given birth to all three of them.

The next thing was to get Alex into the car, which kept everyone busy for a while. What with the wheelchair and the crutches he seemed to have an awful lot of stuff. Joe and his father managed between them to manoeuvre him into the front seat beside her, slid as far back as it would go, one plastered leg pressed awkwardly up against the glove compartment.

With all the fuss, it wasn't until they were out of the car park and on their way home that Emma was really able to take stock of him. James and Joe were by this time squashed side by side into the back, knees up against their chests, working their way through the merits of alternative airline routes from Kathmandu to Heathrow.

"How are you, Alex?" Emma asked. "I've been so worried about you."

"Yup, I'm all right. Well, I will be all right. Bit smashed up, actually. I can't tell you how good it is to be home." As he turned and grinned at her she was relieved to see the old Alex just about visible underneath.

"We're going to take you back to Joe's flat. We thought you could stay there for a bit until you're completely better and you've decided what to do next. Joe and I can look after you—James is there at the moment too but when he's gone home I'll come and stay so I can keep an eye on you. Is that going to be all right? We'll all be able to manage together, won't we? It'll be fine, Alex, I promise."

* * *

Alex nodded, utterly exhausted. He was past caring and the journey had completely worn him out. He didn't know what he thought about anything and he certainly couldn't cope with difficult questions like that. Jeremy and Joe had made all the decisions for him out in Kathmandu and now Emma needed to realise that she was going have to do the same. He wasn't sure whether he would ever be able to cope on his own—in fact, he couldn't even remember how you did it.

His brain could only absorb the simplest things, one at a time. The warmth of a rug round his shoulders. The taste of a cup of tea. Emma might as well be driving a spaceship rather than a car, it seemed so far beyond his capabilities. Even sitting in the front seat he felt like putting a blanket over his head so he wouldn't be able to see so many things moving in different directions. God only knew what was going to become of him. But at least he was home, really home at last, with the people he loved most. He was happy to settle for that.

* * *

Richard was on the telephone. All Emma could see of him was his back as he peered out of the window, alternately pushing his spare hand through his hair and waving it expansively in the air. He had made it quite clear that he expected Emma to be at Regent Mansions to report back to HQ by the time he got home from work. And there he was, suit jacket and tie off, sleeves rolled up, swinging into action. Emma shuddered for anyone who found themselves on the opposing side to him.

At least she had been able to stay long enough to get Alex settled in. He had refused to get into bed—"For God's sake. I'm not ill!"—but she and Joe had managed to get him onto the sofa with plenty of pillows and rugs and he seemed reasonably comfortable.

Of course, there was nothing edible in the flat, only a mouldy old loaf of sliced white bread and a greenish packet of bacon, both of which had gone straight in the bin. She'd had to go to the corner shop for something to tide them over (plus some rubber gloves to muck out the fridge with). Then, leaving strict instructions with James for care of patient and boyfriend she had reluctantly left them to get on with it and gone home to debrief her father.

"I'm glad I got hold of you at last, Jeremy. I wanted to tell you myself how grateful we are. Good job. Can't say I understand it all yet. Well, I'll wait to hear—although what he was doing up there, God only knows—Joe? Oh, yes, Joe's a completely different kettle of fish. Glad you liked him. Yes, let me know—yes or my office—thanks again. Bye for now."

"It must be 2 o'clock in the morning in Kathmandu by now, Dad! The poor man's probably trying to get some sleep."

"I know, I know." He was holding his hand up in the air now as if to prevent a physical barrage of criticism. "But I had to speak to Jeremy direct. Been trying to get hold of him. It's important, you know—there are still things to sort out. Can't let them leave the job half done."

Emma couldn't help but be impressed and wondered for the millionth time whether she would ever develop her father's superhuman stomach for a fight on behalf of a client—in this case, Alex, which had meant setting aside his personal feelings completely. How did you decide when the job was done? And how did you adopt a cause with such passion that you would fight for it until the bitter end?

But Richard had now turned back into a normal human being again, thank goodness, and was thundering towards the drinks tray to pour them both a gin and tonic. When she heard him rattling the ice into the glasses out in the kitchen, she realised how hungry she was and hoped Jessie had left them something to eat.

"There's a rather interesting looking shepherd's pie out here, Em! Shall we put it out of its misery? I'll bung it in the oven."

There was more rattling and crashing from the kitchen and then Richard reappeared with the drinks.

"OK, Miss. Let's hear it."

"Alex looked absolutely dreadful, Dad. Honestly, you'd hardly recognise him. He was in a wheelchair—and Joe says he might always walk with a limp—but he looked so thin and sort of—haunted. Not like Alex at all."

"Hmmm. Well, he's had a tough time, by the sound of it. But he's basically a fit and healthy chap, you know. He'll get over it. He just needs a bit of time, that's all."

"I hope so. But he seemed awfully confused. They reckon he must have had some sort of breakdown when he was travelling and he started imagining things. That's how he had the accident—he thought he was being chased by a gang of Indian thugs. Which he wasn't, of course."

"I see."

"He's on medication, which is probably making him seem worse than he is—for the pain and for the mental stuff. But it's quite hard to understand what's going on."

"You know I really can't believe this was all because of you and Joe. He must have been pretty unstable in the first place to end up like this."

"I know how you feel about Alex, Dad. You've made that pretty clear. No. That's what started it, but then it turned into him never having got to grips with being adopted, deep down I mean because he was fine about it on the surface. And he'd never really thought about it all before, just gone along with everything and then it all just—boiled over. We didn't realise that's what was going on. If we had, we would never have let him go off like that."

"Maybe. But I don't want you and Joe thinking you're responsible. That's nonsense."

"I don't think you can blame him for what happened either, Dad."

"Perhaps not."

"Poor Alex. He's really been through a lot."

"Yes, it sounds like it. He wants to get himself checked out properly, you know. God knows what they did to him in that hospital out there. And it sounds as though he needs a good psychiatrist, too. The sooner, the better."

"I don't think James or Joe would know where to start with all that."

"I'm not sure I would either—but Caroline can sort him out with the best people. She's marvellous at that sort of thing—right up her street."

"Thanks, Dad, that would be great. And you don't blame Alex, do you?"

"Well, I suppose not, no. Let me know if he needs anything, won't you. I'm not that much of an ogre. I'll do what I can."

* * *

Alex quickly became fed up with being an invalid. Once he'd got the hang of his crutches the walls of the flat started to close in on him. He had exhausted Joe's modest video library, consisting of a shelf of pretty suspect titles—Bambi? Brewster's Millions? He was sleeping a lot and there were endless visits to various specialists which took up a huge amount of time. Then there was the therapy.

His therapist, Julia, seemed nice enough, although sometimes he wondered whether they were really getting anywhere. He remembered he'd started to see things a lot more clearly when he was on the ashram with Scott, but trying to explain it to her was like wading through treacle. They always asked you loads of questions but they never told you whether you had given the right answers.

He had told Joe and Emma about learning to meditate but back here in London it had all sounded a bit alternative—they clearly thought so, anyway. He couldn't explain why sitting on the floor and emptying your mind of thoughts was worth the effort or even why it was so difficult. So he decided not to talk about it, even though he suspected he had stumbled on something important. He had plenty of time to meditate every day and it did seem to be helping, he wasn't sure how exactly.

Things that had mattered so much before didn't seem to bother him anymore. He was beginning to find it an enjoyable experience that he looked forward to, which made it easier to keep going. Sometimes he was able to come to rest on some sort of inner stillness where he felt undisturbed by the world, totally at peace.

He realised how lucky he had been to have the chance to get started the way he did. If you tried starting from scratch in London, you'd never make it. But it felt like he was doing OK. People said that the right teacher would somehow appear at the point when you needed them, so perhaps he didn't need one at the moment.

James had gone back to Somerset, apparently satisfied that the 'young' could look after themselves perfectly well without any further help from him. He had visibly brightened up when Alex promised to visit him soon. Emma was coming over as much as she could, although Richard had put his foot down over her actually staying in the flat. As well as enjoying her company Alex was definitely enjoying her cooking—he couldn't remember ever feeling so hungry in his life.

He was putting on some of the weight he had lost and now he had had a decent haircut and a shave or two he was starting to recognise his reflection again. He had even got used to being with Emma and Joe together. To his relief it wasn't a problem at all—it was almost like the old days, the three of them. He couldn't think why he had ever made such a fuss about it.

But just as he was beginning to think that his life was becoming a bit more manageable, Joe and Emma dropped the bombshell.

"Alex, there's something we need to talk to you about." Joe looked so serious that Alex assumed he'd put his foot in it somehow and got ready to apologise.

Joe looked pointedly across at Emma, who carried on.

"We didn't want to tell you until you were feeling a bit better, otherwise James would have told you while he was here. The thing is, he's been contacted by someone about your birth family. Well, about your half-sister, in fact. Apparently, you've got a half-sister and she wants to meet you."

"No, I don't have a half-sister. It must be a mistake. I don't know anything about my birth family, never have. So how could she possibly know I'm her half-brother?"

"I don't know, Alex. You would have to ask her that. But you need to think about whether you want to meet her."

Alex shook his head.

"I don't see the point really. After all this time. I can't believe she really is my half-sister anyway. It'd turn out to be a mix-up, I bet. I'd rather not go there."

"Well, think about it? You don't have to decide straight away."

Emma switched on the television and they started watching Blackadder. Joe and Emma debated whether it was funnier or less funny than the previous one with the Prince Regent in it. As always the issue had to be resolved, another piece in the giant jigsaw that was becoming their synchronised view of the world.

Alex hardly noticed. Of course he wanted to meet his half-sister! But there was no way he was going to show his excitement in front of the others in case it came to nothing. To think he might actually have a biological relative who he could actually meet! He had just about accepted that he would never have a blood relative, no genetic link to anyone he was ever likely to meet, so this seemed nothing short of a miracle. She might even know something about his mother and why she had abandoned him.

He managed to look as though he wasn't bothered, throwing in just enough chat to not look too thoughtful but not enough to give himself away. As soon as he could reasonably get away with it he feigned tiredness and went to bed, although he knew he would never be able to sleep.

What would she be like? Would she be pretty? Older or younger? Would they get on? Yes, of course they would. What would Joe and Emma think of her? What about his father? Would it seem very ungrateful? And what on earth would Lorna have thought? Perhaps it was just as well she would never know.

He heard Emma leave and then Joe go to bed, crashing around clumsily as if his limbs were too big for him as usual. Then silence. He wondered how alike they would be, this new sister and him. Would she be artistic, like him? Where would they meet? Where did she live? Where would they begin? Perhaps it would be awkward to start with. She might even live right here in London. But what if it all came to nothing? Would he be able to cope with that?

At about two in the morning he fell asleep, only to wake up again as soon as it started getting light. He sat up in bed and read his book, although he knew he wouldn't remember any of it. At last, he heard Joe stirring in the bedroom next door, getting up for his Saturday morning football on the common. He got out of bed then and pottered round the kitchen, laying out breakfast for both of them and pressing cups of coffee on his bemused brother with almost manic politeness.

For the love of God, would he never leave? Alex hobbled back and forth, clearing dirty plates, picking up socks and even plumping up the cushions while Joe spent an age in the bathroom. The effort to look casual as Joe finally left nearly killed him and the minute he heard the front door click shut Alex picked up the telephone and dialled his father's number.

Chapter 23
Brothers and Sisters

Emma was in despair about the lack of progress and was beginning to wish she had never found out about having a half brother in the first place. Could it really be Alex? It seemed more and more fanciful. It really was unbearable not to know. She had heard nothing from the Vicar and she couldn't understand it. A few days, he'd said. He must have known exactly where Asha was. How long could it take to make that phone call, for goodness sake? Vicars couldn't be that busy. No, he must have made the phone call and Asha either didn't want to meet her or hadn't decided. Perhaps there would never be an answer.

That would be awful—even a rejection would be better than this silence, this not knowing. Or maybe it was a good sign he hadn't called—perhaps there was still hope. Although if Alex's reaction was anything to go by it would be foolish to hope for anything. She couldn't understand that at all. Perhaps it was a boy thing. Not to want to meet a blood relative when you had no other blood relatives? And if Asha *was* Alex—but that was a dangerous route to go down. She may never know the answer. Either way it was beginning to look as though her search for Asha had reached a dead end.

So when she got home a few days later and found a message on the answering machine from the Vicar she was ecstatic. She played it five times, trying to decipher whether he had good news or bad news for her from the tone of his voice. She picked up the phone, put it down again. If this was to be her last moment of hope, she might as well enjoy it for a while. So she took off her coat, poured herself a glass of wine, went through the motions of tidying her room— but it was no good, she just had to know.

So, she sat down in front of the telephone and composed herself. After all, this might be a moment she would remember all her life. Or it might not.

"Ah, Emma! Thank you for calling back—How are you, my dear?"

Emma replied as briefly as she could and then fell silent, not wanting to encourage any more small talk. The pressure mounted.

"Well, you want to know how I've got on, of course. I've managed to get in touch with your half-brother at last. It's taken a while, I must say! You young people can certainly be hard to pin down."

"Yes, I suppose we can," said Emma politely, trying to hide her impatience. No one would find it hard to pin *her* down—she'd been living in the same place for her entire living memory.

"I haven't actually spoken to him myself, only to his father, but I do have good news for you! Apparently, he would like to meet up with you."

"Oh! That's wonderful!" And it *was* wonderful—except that it meant he couldn't be Alex.

"Yes, isn't it? He's happy for me to give you his contact details and then you can get in touch with him. I don't think you don't really need me to get involved—his name is not Asha now, it was changed when he was adopted. His name is Alex. Alex Russell. And his telephone number—"

"Oh, my God! Oh, sorry! Oh, gosh, I mean! I thought you were going to say that—at least I didn't know—but I've known Alex since we were children. And I thought it might be him because he's just found out he's got a half-sister, but I didn't want to hope too much in case it wasn't. It's funny because there's always been a close connection between us. No wonder! Oh! I can't believe it!"

"Good heavens. Well, that makes things rather easier! Remarkable. Synchronicity at work, I suppose—but still. Remarkable. Well, it seems that my job is done here. I wish you both well, of course. These things can be difficult sometimes. But then I suppose you hardly need to get to know each other, do you? Perhaps you would both like to come and see me together one day. That would make me very happy."

How extraordinary, Emma thought as she put down the phone. Alex must have changed his mind. He kept that one quiet—obviously a bit more on the ball than she thought. How typical of Alex. Her brother. And she burst into tears.

* * *

Richard sat at the head of the dining table at Regent Mansions and looked around with satisfaction. Several weeks had passed since Alex had come back from Kathmandu and he had thought it was time for a proper celebration. With

Emma spending most of her time at Joe's flat with the boys, he felt rather left out of all the excitement. He had always known that she would grow up and away from him one day but he was damned if it was going to happen just yet.

He watched her sitting next to her uncle Robert, deep in conversation.

"So how did you actually tell him that you were his half-sister? There you are, about to drop this bombshell, which after all you'd had plenty of time to get your head round. But he had absolutely no idea. What on earth did you say?"

"I know. It was weird. When it came to it, I could hardly get the words out. And Alex thought I was joking to start with. He didn't believe me. There he was, expecting some gorgeous blonde to arrive in his life, and he gets the girl up the road! I was a bit worried he would be disappointed, actually. But he's stuck with me now."

Alex chipped in from across the table.

"Em, that's rubbish! I'm really pleased about it, you know that. Of course I am. But I couldn't see how you could have known. Or how anyone could have known because no one knew anything about my birth family. And I knew perfectly well Em didn't have a brother either. Because at that point you hadn't told me about your mother and all that other stuff, Em!"

"I know, I'm sorry. I just thought you had enough to think about—you see, Robert, Alex was away when I first found the letter my mother had left Dad. That's what started it all off. Then after I read the letter I decided to talk to Jackie about her. Goodness knows why it took me so long, she said she'd been waiting for me to ask for years."

"She told me a lot about my mother. Then she put me in touch with Elizabeth Duncan, this woman in Bath who had known her at the commune she went to in Exeter. It was Elizabeth who told me I had a half-brother. For a while, I thought my mother might still be alive but of course she wasn't. She'd committed suicide years before when Alex was a baby."

Robert looked sympathetic.

"I know. Well, I'd always thought she was dead, but for a while I didn't. It would have been so wonderful to meet her. But anyway, that left Alex an orphan because his father had long since walked out and they didn't know what to do with him because he didn't officially exist. He'd been born at the commune and his birth was never registered."

"They couldn't just hand him over to the authorities, even if they'd wanted to. So they took him to the Vicar at Exford. The Vicar asked James and Lorna if they would be prepared to adopt him, and they agreed."

"Well I got hold of the Vicar, which wasn't difficult because by some miracle he was still in Exford, so I went to see him. He's quite old now."

"Aren't we all—" Robert murmured to himself.

"He said he would help and then I didn't hear from him for ages. And in the meantime James heard that Alex had a half-sister who wanted to get in touch with him! It was such an extraordinary coincidence, but I still didn't dare think it might be me. Then Alex came back from Nepal in such a bad way that we couldn't tell him about it straight away. And I still hadn't heard back from the Vicar. It nearly killed me and all the time I was wondering whether it was going to be him or not. THEN he pretended he wasn't interested—!"

Alex laughed. He still thought back to that conversation with Emma often, even though it was several weeks ago now. He really had thought she'd been joking at first. He'd had enough trouble getting his head round the idea that he might have a half-sister at all, let alone that it would turn out to be her. It was just extraordinary.

She'd had to talk him through the whole story several times before he'd really got it. But looking back it seemed as if they had always known. They had always felt like brother and sister although they'd never realised it. Over the last few weeks they had talked for hours every day, rewriting their history, going over all the times they had spent together and reliving them as brother and sister. Joe had been very good about it, really. But then he was already connected to both of them so he could hardly complain.

Having Emma as a sister was absolutely brilliant. But so was knowing who his mother had been and his father too, sort of. At last, he had a few clues as to what family traits he might have. He and Emma had been back to see Elizabeth Duncan, who had done her best to tell them everything she could remember about Frances. They must have driven her mad with their questions. Of course, Richard was the one who had known her the best. Emma hadn't wanted to push him too hard just at the moment but they were both hoping to persuade him to tell them more about her.

Alex was pretty sure he was like his mother. That was obviously where he got his artistic talent from. Her manic depression—if that was what it was—was a bit alarming. Hopefully he hadn't inherited that too. But it meant a lot to him to know that she hadn't abandoned him after all—she had kept him with her right up until she died. He and Emma had visited her grave together and had arranged a headstone with all three of their names on it. It had made them both feel closer to her.

Alex had been worried about what his father's reaction would be, but he had seemed genuinely pleased for Alex. In fact, it had been his father who had finally persuaded him to go ahead. Odd really, when he seemed so out of his depth with his own life. But that was another story.

Across the table, Robert was frowning at Emma.

"But wasn't that an extraordinary coincidence? Of all the places you could have ended up, the two of you growing up side by side in exactly the same village?"

"I know. But it's not such a coincidence in fact. You see when Mum and Dad were at Exeter they used to go to Exford a lot. It was a special place for them. That was the reason that Dad bought a cottage there and that was also the reason that Elizabeth took Alex—Asha as he was then—there when Frances died. She knew it was special to her and she says it seemed the right thing to do.

"Actually, Alex, I've got a good mind to call you Asha from now on! You might at least have the decency to adopt it as your middle name. If I've got Emerald Venus it's the least you could do, frankly."

On the other side of the table, Jackie was quizzing Joe.

"How's Emma doing really, do you think?" she asked, watching her joking with Alex.

"Well, I know she looks all right, but it's been a lot for her to deal with. Alex is the easy part for her—it's all good. But finding out that her mother deliberately walked out on her all those years ago, that's more difficult. I think it's probably just as well she didn't know that when she was younger. Alex has been helping her because he knows just how it feels—it's what he always thought had happened to him. But it's still hard for her to accept.

"She needs to know what her mother was really like, warts and all. You and Richard need to tell her as much as you can. Then she'll understand that she was a real person, not some sort of maternal goddess—that's how she always imagined her, you see. If she can understand what Frances went through and why she did what she did it might make it easier. She needs to see it from Frances' point of view, even though she's not here to tell her herself."

"Poor little darling. How clever of you. She's lucky to have you, Joe. It's been a lot for you to cope with, too." Jackie looked approvingly at him.

"I know you've always been very important to her, Jackie."

"Well, I've tried to fill the gap as best I could. And I don't think she's turned out so badly, do you? I'm glad it's all out in the open now. I got rather caught in the middle, wanting to be honest with her but not wanting to drop Richard in it. He's been a good father to her, you know. I think this will bring them closer together."

At the head of the table, Richard looked around at his growing brood. He'd done roast beef on the bone with plenty of Yorkshire pudding, roast potatoes, roast parsnips, Brussels sprouts, carrots, horseradish sauce, gravy—and just as well, too. He'd forgotten how much boys in their early twenties could put away and Alex still looked distinctly scrawny, poor boy. But Joe was coming on very well. He was beginning to think he couldn't have chosen a better boyfriend for Emma if he'd done it himself.

Beside him was a new visitor to Regent Mansions, Joanna. They'd been friends for years but lately they had become close. Surprisingly, she had never married, although she had never been short of admirers—taller than most women, with expertly highlighted blonde hair, a figure honed by daily games of tennis at the Harbour Club and a wicked sense of humour. But she was also intelligent, well-connected and good at keeping him up to the mark. He was rather enjoying having her around and he hoped this family onslaught wasn't going to put her off too much.

He had thought she and Jackie might have something in common and so it had proved—the two of them had quickly struck up a rapport. He hadn't been so sure how Emma would react but she'd been marvellous and given Joanna a genuinely warm welcome. Perhaps if he had been braver about bringing his previous girlfriends into the family things might have turned out differently. But they were where they were and he couldn't be happier. Putting his hand on Joanna's arm, he asked her whether she had had the chance to meet everyone properly before lunch and she nodded and smiled as she caught his eye.

With Joe and Emma engrossed in a private conversation of their own, Jackie turned her attention to Richard.

"I gather Alex is planning to be a full-time artist?" she said, looking across at Joanna to bring her into the conversation.

"I believe that's the plan eventually, yes. He's got a way to go yet before he's really well enough—he needs another operation on his leg and he's still seeing a therapist every week. He managed to do himself a lot of damage out there. But he'll get there eventually—we'll just have to see how it goes."

"I should think painting would be good therapy for him. How exciting though, Richard! We'll have an artist in the family again!"

Richard noticed how naturally Jackie had referred to Alex as being part of the family. Frances' son. Extraordinary, really. Over the past few weeks he had had to face up to some home truths that he had been avoiding for years. He had loved Frances very much, and for all her faults she had been a remarkable person in many ways. But he had shut her memory out of his life for so long that it was almost as if she had never existed.

Now, he saw her all the time in Alex. Maybe that was why the boy had always made him feel uneasy. It would certainly be interesting to see how much of her creative talent he had inherited. Poor Frances. He hadn't really understood about her illness at the time. But then, they had been so young.

Alex was deep in conversation with Robert.

"Actually, Robert, there's something I wanted to ask you."

"Fire away."

"I wanted to ask your help. I'm hoping to set up a charity for doctors in Nepal. They need good doctors there so badly and the training in Nepal isn't the best—they need to come and train here, in the UK. The doctor who looked after me at the hospital in Kathmandu, Dr Sharma—he saved my life. He used to come and talk to me—although I was unconscious, somehow I could still hear him. He told me about how difficult it is to train as a doctor in Nepal. It was his dream to come to England. His son wants to be a doctor too. I'm hoping he'll help with the charity at the Nepal end."

Alex had ground to a halt and he stopped for a few moments to collect his thoughts. The truth was, now he had been persuaded that much of the disastrous journey that had landed him at the Bir Hospital was down to his own inner turmoil rather than a gang of Indian mafiosa he was deeply embarrassed about having put everyone to so much trouble.

Emma had been out of her mind with worry about him; Joe had had to come chasing half way round the world; Richard had pulled a lot of strings for him. Not to mention James, although quite honestly, most of the drama seemed to have passed him by. And Dr Sharma too, who had gone way beyond the call of duty to bring him back from the brink. He was keen to redress the balance in whatever way he could, to give something back, and setting up a charity for Nepalese doctors was his way of doing that.

"I wouldn't be able to put much money in to begin with, but as soon as I start selling some paintings I'll be able to do a bit more. I'm working on a whole series of paintings based on my travels in India and I thought I could have an exhibition of them to launch the charity. I've started doing some preliminary sketches already. It's such a wonderful place to paint, you know. Really inspiring—I'm hoping to go back at some point. I've got lots of other plans for fundraising too. It's all the financial stuff I don't know how to do—getting it all set up and everything. And I wondered if you would consider being a Trustee."

"I'd be delighted, Alex! Tell you what. When you're a bit more settled, why don't we have a proper chat about it? I'll give you my number and I'll leave it to you to get in touch when you're ready. Where do you think you'll be based?"

"I'm going to have to stay in London for the next few months to have some more treatment on my leg, amongst other things, so Joe's going to have to put up with me for a bit longer. But once all that's out of the way I'm going to go home and live with Dad and paint there. He's got loads of room and he's rattling around down there. We're a bit worried about him, actually. We'll be able to keep an eye on each other."

"That sounds like a very good idea."

"Yes, I think it'll be good. Dad gets lonely on his own. I can look after him a bit. And quite honestly, I'm not sure whether I'll ever be up to living by myself in London—a quiet life in Somerset will probably work much better for me. Joe and Emma will jolly well have to come and see us lots."

Hearing his name mentioned, Joe looked across at Alex.

"No more secret love trysts for Dad then—the game's up! As for you—no doubt you'll have Somerset's finest in hot pursuit in no time. I feel sorry for them already."

Joe had already been busy trying to trace Alex's two girls—the ones from Varanasi, Nicky and Anna—although there was not much to go on. Alex's therapist had suggested that if they could be found it would be helpful for Alex to meet up with them. Rebuilding his memories of his time in India on the basis of fact rather than delusion would help him to put the episode behind him. The same went for Scott, although arranging a reunion with him was obviously going

244

to be harder, especially as his father had not heard from him for several months now and had asked the Canadian authorities if they could help to locate him.

Alex was apprehensive about these meetings, unsure what sort of reception he would get. After all, it looked like he had parted on bad terms with Scott and he had certainly bailed out on the girls. Joe could understand his worries but he'd managed to persuade him to see it as an opportunity to show them what he was really like.

Richard had quietly suggested to Joe that they meet up for lunch in the City soon to get to know each other better. Joe had walked about six inches taller for days after that. Not only had he apparently been accepted into the family but Richard had treated him as an equal too. It felt almost as good as the day he had passed his financial exams.

* * *

Everybody looked up as Richard pushed back his chair and tapped his knife against his wine glass.

"I know this is an informal—indeed a family—occasion. But there are one or two things I would like to say."

Six faces around the table composed themselves into warm, expectant expressions.

"I wanted us all to get together to celebrate Alex's safe return from Nepal. Alex, you showed great courage in the face of adversity and you continue to do so. We all hope that you make a full recovery. I couldn't be happier to welcome you into our family as Emma's half-brother."

Emma and Alex exchanged sheepish grins.

"I am also very happy to welcome Joanna to Regent Mansions. I must admit I wasn't sure whether it was really fair to subject her to you all like this and I was quite expecting her to tell me I was insane. But she seemed surprisingly keen to meet the rest of the family and so far, she seems to have survived."

Richard gave her his most winning smile.

"And lastly, I'd like to propose a toast to my dear Frances, mother to Emma and Alex. Frances was a very special person, much loved by all who knew her. She had a troubled life and suffered a great deal. I only wish I could have done more to help her. And I should have guessed that she would still be with us all so profoundly more than twenty years after her death."

"To Frances."

***

A few days later, Joe was browsing through the Sunday Times at Regent Mansions over a cup of coffee with Emma, a much more civilised way to spend a Sunday morning than at his now rather overcrowded flat. They were discussing whether it would really be a good idea for Alex to go back to India as he intended when a small piece in the news section stopped him in his tracks.

"Two English girls who died in a hostel fire in Calcutta have now been named as Anna Chatsworth and Nicky Granger. Police have not been able to establish the cause of the fire, which remains under investigation."